THE MAGICIAN OF LHASA

Other titles by David Michie

Fiction

Conflict of Interest

Expiry Date

Pure Deception

Non-fiction

Buddhism for Busy People

Hurry Up and Meditate

The Magician of Lhasa

A novice monk. A quantum scientist.
An ancient secret.

David Michie

Trapdoor Books · Lyons, Colorado

Trapdoor Books is an imprint of Trapdoor Publishing.
First Edition

Discovered by Rowan Matney
Edited by Beverly Friebel
Book design by Sue Campbell
Flap copy by Mitchell Duvall

Cataloging in Publication Data available.

ISBN: 0-9842070-0-7 (hc)
ISBN-13: 978-0-9842070-0-8 (hc)
ISBN: 0-9842070-1-5 (pbk)
ISBN-13: 978-0-9842070-1-5 (pbk)

Post Office Box 1989
Lyons, CO 80540-1989
www.trapdoorbooks.com

Printed in United States of America

The path of Tibetan Buddhism is both extraordinary and profound—but it is not an easy one. Those who choose to follow the Dharma often devote tens of thousands of hours to the practice of meditation. As a consequence of this internal journey, an advanced practitioner will sometimes develop psychic abilities including clairvoyance. Such a person is called a siddha *or magician.*

Prologue

Tenzin Dorje

(pronounced Ten-zin Door-jay)

Zheng-po Monastery—Tibet
March 1959

I AM ALONE IN THE SACRED STILLNESS OF THE TEMPLE, LIGHTING BUTter lamps at the Buddha's feet, when I first realize that something is very wrong.

"Tenzin Dorje!" Startled, I turn to glimpse the spare frame of my teacher, silhouetted briefly at the far door. "My room. Immediately!"

For a moment I am faced with a dilemma. Making offerings to the Buddha is considered a special privilege, and as a sixteen-year-old novice monk I take this duty seriously. Not only is there a particular order in which the candles must be lit, each new flame should be visualized as representing a precious gift—such as incense, music and flowers—to be offered for the sake of all living beings.

I know that nothing should prevent me from completing this important rite, but is obedience to my kind and holy teacher not more important? Besides, I can't remember the last time that Lama Tsering used the word "immediately." Nor can I remember a time when anyone shouted an order in the temple. Especially not Zheng-po's highest-ranking lama.

Even though I am only half-way through lighting the candles, I quickly snuff out the taper. Bowing briefly to the Buddha, I hurry outside.

In the twilight, disruption is spreading through Zheng-po monastery like ripples from a stone thrown into a tranquil lake. Monks are knocking loudly on each other's doors. People are rushing across the courtyard with unusual haste. Villagers have gathered outside the abbot's office and are talking in alarmed voices and gesturing down the valley.

Slipping into my sandals, I gather my robe above my knees and, abandoning the usual monastic code, break into a run.

Lama Tsering's room is at the furthermost end, across the courtyard and past almost all the monks' rooms, in the very last building. Even though his status would accord him a spacious and comfortable room directly overlooking the courtyard, he insists on living next to his novices in a small cell on the edge of Zheng-po.

When I get to the room, his door is thrown open and his floor, usually swept clean, is scattered with ropes and packages I've never seen. His lamp is turned to full flame, making him look even taller and more disproportionate than ever as his shadow leaps about the walls and ceiling with unfamiliar urgency.

I've no sooner got there than I turn to find Paldon Wangmo hurrying towards me. The pair of us are Lama Tsering's two novices but we have an even stronger karmic connection: Paldon Wangmo is my brother, two years older than I.

We knock on our teacher's door.

Lama Tsering beckons us inside, telling us to close the door behind us. Although the whole of Zheng-po is in turmoil, his face shows no sign of panic. But there is no disguising the gravity of his expression.

"This is the day we have feared ever since the Year of the Metal Tiger," he looks from one to the other of us with a seriousness we only usually see before an important examination. "Messengers have just arrived at the village with news that the Red Army has marched on Lhasa. His Holiness, the Dalai Lama, has been forced into exile. A division of the Red Army is traveling here, to Jangtang province. At this moment they are only half a day's travel from Zheng-po."

Paldon Wangmo and I can't resist exchanging glances. In just a few sentences, Lama Tsering has told us that everything about our world has been turned upside down. If His Holiness has been forced to flee from the Potala Palace, what hope is there for the rest of Tibet?

"We must assume that the Red Army is coming directly towards Zheng-po," Lama Tsering continues quickly. From outside we hear one of the women villagers wailing. "If they travel through the night, they could arrive by tomorrow morning. *Definitely,* they could get here within a day. In other parts of our country, the army is destroying monasteries, looting their treasures, burning their sacred texts, torturing and murdering the monks. There's little doubt they have the same intentions for Zheng-po. For this reason, the abbot is asking us to evacuate."

"Evacuate?" I can't contain myself. "Why don't we stay and resist?"

"Tenzin Dorje, I have shown you the map of our neighbor China," he explains. "For every soldier they have sent to Tibet, there are ten thousand more soldiers ready to take their place. Even if we wanted to, this is not a struggle we can win."

"But—"

Paldon Wangmo reaches out, putting his hand over my mouth.

"Fortunately, our abbot and the senior lamas have been preparing for this possibility. Each of the monks has a choice. You can return to your village and continue to practice the Dharma in secret. Or you can join the senior lamas in exile."

He holds up his hand, gesturing we shouldn't yet reply. "Before you say you want to join us in exile, you must realize this is not some great adventure. Traveling to the border will be dangerous—the Red Army will shoot dead any monks trying to leave. Then we must try to cross the mountains on foot. For three weeks we will have to travel very long distances, living only off the food we can carry. We will have to endure much hardship and pain. Even if we finally arrive in India, we don't know if the government will allow us to stay, or send us back over the border."

"But if we return to our villages and continue to wear our robes," interjects Paldon Wangmo, "the Chinese will find us anyway, and punish our families for keeping us."

Lama Tsering nods briefly.

"If we disrobe, we would be breaking our vows." Paldon Wangmo has always been a sharp debater. "Either way, we would lose you as our teacher."

"What you say is true," Lama Tsering agrees. "This is a difficult decision even for a lama, and you are novice monks. But it is important that you choose, and do so quickly. Whatever decision you make," he regards each of us in turn, "you will have my blessing."

From outside comes the pounding of feet as people hurry past. There can be no doubting the crisis we're facing.

"I am getting older," Lama Tsering tells us, kneeling down to continue packing a leather bag, which is lying on the floor. "If I had only myself to think about, I might go into hiding and take my chances with the Chinese—"

"No, Lama!" I exclaim.

Next to me, Paldon Wangmo looks sheepish. He has always been embarrassed by my impetuousness.

"But the abbot has asked me to play an important part in the evacuation."

"I want to come with you!" I can't hold back any longer, no matter what Paldon Wangmo thinks.

"Perhaps you like me as a teacher," Lama Tsering is cautioning. "But as a fellow traveler it will be very different. You are young and strong, but I may become a liability. What happens if I fall and hurt myself?"

"Then we will carry you across the mountains," I declare.

Beside me Paldon Wangmo is nodding.

Lama Tsering looks up at us, an intensity in his dark eyes I have seen only on rare occasions.

"Very well," he tells us finally. "You can come. But there is one very important condition I have to tell you about."

MOMENTS LATER WE ARE LEAVING HIS ROOM FOR OUR OWN, HAVING promised to return very quickly. As I make my way through the turmoil in the corridor outside I can hardly believe the condition that Lama Tsering has just related. This is, without question, the worst day in the existence of Zheng-po, but paradoxically for me it is the day I have found my true purpose. My vocation. The reason I have been drawn to the Dharma.

Opening my door, I look around the small room that has been my world for the past ten years: the wooden meditation box, three feet square; the straw mattress on the baked-earth floor; my change of robes and toiletry bag, the two belongings monks are allowed at Zheng-po.

It is hard to believe that I will never again sit in this meditation box, never again sleep on this bed. It is even more incredible that I, Tenzin

Dorje, a humble novice monk from the village of Ling, have been accorded one of the rarest privileges of Zheng-po and of our entire lineage. For together with Paldon Wangmo, and under the guidance of my kind and holy teacher, we are to undertake the highest and most sacred mission of the evacuation. It means that our flight from Tibet will be much more critical, and more dangerous.

But for the first time ever, at sixteen years of age, I feel in my heart that I have a special part to play.

My time has come.

Chapter One

Matt Lester

Imperial Science Institute—London
April 2007

I'M SITTING IN THE CRAMPED CUBBY-HOLE THAT PASSES FOR MY OFFICE, late on an overcast Friday afternoon, when my whole world changes.

"Harry wants to see you in his office," Pauline Drake, tall, angular and not-to-be-messed with, appears around the door frame two feet away. She looks pointedly at the telephone, which I've taken off its cradle, before meeting my eyes with a look of droll disapproval. "Right away."

I glance over the paperwork strewn across my desk. It's the last Friday of the month, which means that all timesheets have to be in by five. As research manager for Nanobot, it's my job to collate team activities, and I take pride in the fact that I've never missed a deadline.

But it's unusual for Harry to dispatch his formidable secretary down from the third floor. Something must be up.

A short while later I'm getting out from behind my desk. It's not a straightforward maneuver. You have to rise from the chair at forty-five degrees to avoid hitting the shelves directly above, before squeezing, one leg at a time, through the narrow gap between desk and filing cabinet. Then there's the walk through a rabbit's warren of corridors and up four flights of a narrow, wooden staircase with its unyielding aroma of industrial disinfectant and wet dog hair.

As I make my way across the open plan section of the third floor, I'm aware of people staring and talking under their breath. When I make eye contact with a couple of the HR people they glance away, embarrassed.

Something's definitely up.

To get to the corner office, I first have to pass through the anteroom where Pauline has returned to work noiselessly at her computer. She nods towards Harry's door. Unusually, it is closed. Even more unusually, an unfamiliar hush has descended on his office, instead of the usual orchestral blast.

When I arrive, it's to find Harry standing, staring out the window at his less-than-impressive view over the tangled gray sprawl of railway lines converging on King's Cross station. Arms folded and strangely withdrawn, I get the impression he's been waiting especially for me.

As I appear he gestures, silently, to a chair across from his desk.

Harry Saddler is the very model of the mad professor, with a few non-standard eccentricities thrown in for good measure. Mid-fifties, bespectacled, with a shock of spiky, gray hair, in his time he's been an award-winning researcher. More recent circumstances have also forced him to become an expert in the area of public-private partnerships. It was he who saved the centuries-old institute, and all our jobs, by completing a deal with Acellerate, a Los Angeles-based biotech incubator, just over a year ago.

"A short while ago I had a call from L.A. with the news I've been half-expecting for the past twelve months," he tells me, his expression unusually serious. "Acellerate has finished their review of our research projects. They like Nanobot," he brushes fallen cigarette ash off his lapel. "They *really* like Nanobot. So much that they want to move the whole kit and caboodle to California. And as the program originator and research manager, they want you there, too."

The news takes me completely by surprise. Sure, there've been visitors from the States during the past year and earnest talk of information exchange, but I never expected the deal with Acellerate to have such direct, personal impact. Or to be so sudden.

"They're moving very quickly on this," continues Harry. "They want you there in six weeks ideally. Definitely eight. Blakely is taking a personal interest in the program."

"Eight weeks?" I'm finding this overwhelming. "Why do I have to move to California at all? Can't they invest in what we're doing over here?"

Harry shakes his head in weary resignation. "You've seen the new shareholder structure," he says. "As much as Acellerate talks about respecting our independence, the reality is that they hold a controlling interest. They call the shots. They can strip what they like out of the institute and there's really not a lot we can do to stop them."

I'm not thinking about Acellerate. I'm thinking about my fiancée, Isabella.

Harry mistakes the cause of my concern. "If you look at what's happened to the other research programs Acellerate has taken to L.A.," he reassures me, "they've gone stratospheric." Pausing, he regards me more closely for a long while before querying in a low voice, "Isabella?"

"Exactly."

"She'll go with you!"

"It's not that simple. She's only just been promoted. And you know how close she is to her family." I glance away from him to the where a commuter train is chugging slowly into the station.

Harry and I go way back and he knows a lot about Isabella and me—he's been there since the beginning. But the main problem with Isabella leaving London is something that's only happened very recently. Something I haven't told him about. The truth is, Isabella and I are still getting to grips with the enormity of the news ourselves.

"A girl like her," Harry has met her at institute functions over the years, "she'll get a job like that in Los Angeles," he snaps his fingers. "And you'll be giving her family a good excuse to visit Disneyland."

As always, Harry is trying to focus on the positive. I understand, and I'm all the more appreciative because I know how hard this must be for him. Nanobot has always been one of his favorites. It was Harry who brought me into the institute when he discovered the subject of my master's thesis. Harry nurtured the program through its early stages. He and I enjoy a close relationship—more than my boss, he's also my mentor and confidant. Now, just as the program's starting to get interesting, he's having it taken off him. What's more, who's to say it will end with Nanobot? It seems that Acellerate can cherry-pick whatever they like from the institute and leave Harry with all the leftovers. Small wonder he's in no mood for the Three Tenors.

"Try to see this as the opportunity that it is," he tells me. "With Acellerate behind you, you can ramp up the program way beyond what we can afford here. You could get to prototype stage in two to three years instead of seven or eight. The sky really is the limit."

I'm watching the fingers of his right hand rapping the desk.

"You'll be working at the heart of nanotech development for one of the best-funded scientific institutes on earth. Plus you can catch a suntan."

I look up, eyebrows raised. Tanning is not a subject in which I've ever had an interest. As Harry well knows.

"Think of it as a great adventure!"

His phone rings, and we hear Pauline answering it outside. Evidently Harry has told her we aren't to be disturbed—something he's never done before.

There's another pause before I finally say, "I guess whatever way you package it, I don't have much choice do I? I mean, Acellerate isn't going to leave the program in London just because of Isabella and me."

Harry regards me significantly, "Of all the programs we're running, yours is the most likely to make the most revolutionary impact. You're the first cab off the rank, Matt. It's flattering that Acellerate is so keen to take you off us."

"It's a bit sudden, that's all," I'm nodding. "I mean, ten minutes ago, my main concern was getting the time sheets in."

Harry regards me with a look of benevolent expectation.

"I'll have to get used to the idea."

"Good."

"*And* speak to Isabella."

"Of course." Harry reaches into a desk drawer, takes out a large white envelope which he hands me across the desk.

"Before you make up your mind, you might like to study the terms and conditions," he says.

A short while later I'm heading back to my office in a daze. Not only is Harry's announcement life-changing, the conditions of my appointment are way beyond anything I could have imagined. Almost too much to believe.

As I return through HR, I'm so preoccupied I don't notice anyone. Even the reek of the stairs passes me by. I'm trying to get my head around the paradox that this is terrible news for the Imperial Science Institute, but an amazing opportunity for me. It's even more confounding that Isabella is about to be upset by what is an opportunity for me beyond my wildest dreams.

I have to speak to Isabella.

BACK IN OUR FLAT OVERLOOKING CLAPHAM COMMON, I HEAR ISABELLA before I see her. There's the thud of the front door being shut. The brisk staccato of her heels on the staircase.

"Isabella," I kiss her as she arrives in the lounge.

"Babe," she hugs me, before stepping back. "I looked for you in the pub on the way home. Not in the mood?"

Isabella is tall and svelte with the dusky skin of a Sicilian. Her eyes are gleaming amber flecked with green. Dressed for business, the jet-black formality of her jacket and skirt shows off her sculpted figure, but also draws attention to her face: The high, leonine cheekbones and strong chin. The dark, shoulder-length hair, brushed in loose, flowing curls and framing her full, sensual lips.

As she stands, poised and confident, I glance from the sparkling welcome in her eyes to the silk, crimson scarf at her neck.

"There's something we need to discuss," I tell her. "Actually, something I need you to read."

She raises her eyebrows. "Now?"

"If you don't mind. I'll pour you a wine."

"The Semillon we opened last night would be nice," she kicks off her patent leather stilettos and massages her heels as she looks up at me expectantly.

I hand her the Acellerate work contract before going into the kitchen. I can't bear to watch her go through it. What I'm still finding hard to believe is that Nanobot is to become one of Acellerate's three *lead* programs. A flagship for one of the world's foremost technology incubators. Funding is to be increased to twenty million dollars over the next two years to fast-track its progress. Ten full time staff will be deployed to work out of Acellerate's headquarters.

On matters more personal, I'm to be promoted to director level. My salary is to be one hundred fifty thousand dollars—three times what I'm getting at the institute, plus a fully-fuelled executive car, generous performance bonus schedule, and a share-option package.

The money is beyond all my expectations, as is the promotion. But while that side of things is exciting, I am very much more excited by the fact that the research project which I conceived, and has been my obsession for the past seven years, is about to get the funding it deserves. Since I began working in nanotechnology as a post-graduate student, I've believed that it represents the next big technological leap that its consequences will be like the industrial revolution— but bigger. Creating highly functional robots of microscopic size—nanobots—will transform every aspect of life on earth.

In medicine, for example, tumors will be destroyed not by invasive surgery or toxic chemicals, but by robotic devices a fraction of the size of a human hair, dismantling unwanted growths, cell by cell. In food production, instead of having to rely on good weather and farming methods, nanobots will rapidly assemble grains of wheat or apples—minus the cores—entirely from their chemical constituents. Never will it have been easier or cheaper to transform the physical world around us. Current agriculture and manufacturing techniques will quickly disappear. All forms of waste will be completely recycled. Hardly surprising that so much money is being pumped into nanotechnology research. Or that nanotech has become such an all-consuming part of my life.

In the past decade I've been to all the major conferences, received all the industry journals, and kept a very close eye on what my fellow researchers are up to. I eat, sleep and breathe Nanobot, and Isabella often teases me that she takes second place to it. She knows how much it means to me, how developing Nanobot is my dream, and it touches me how much she's taken it all to heart and made it her dream, too. Which makes Acellerate's offer all the more bittersweet.

When I return, Isabella looks up at me, wide-eyed. "This is amazing, Matt! Fantastic! For you *and* Nanobot. It doesn't say when—"

"That's the thing. They want me over there right away. They're talking six weeks, maybe eight."

"For how long?"

She hasn't registered yet. "I mean, if the program's being transferred where does that—"

"It's permanent."

Her face clouds in bewilderment.

"It's not something I asked for. It's just come out of the blue. Bill Blakely has taken a sudden interest."

She raises a hand to her face, covering her eyes with her immaculately manicured fingers.

I know exactly what she's thinking.

"I told Harry it was difficult." I murmur. Then after a pause, "I reminded him how close you are to the family."

That's as far as I want to go, because what we'd just heard was still so new, so raw, we haven't even talked about it ourselves.

"And what did Harry say?" her voice is weary.

"That we should see this as a once in a lifetime opportunity. And that you'd get a job in L.A.," I snap my fingers, "just like that."

Isabella shakes her head. "Bertollini's right in the middle of planning next year's pan-European campaign," she looks up, eyes flashing. "If I went now I'd really be leaving them in the lurch. Not," she looks up pointedly, "that that's even the start of it."

I hand her the glass of wine. She puts it on a side table without a sip. "What about staying here? Can't they keep the program in London and fast-track it?"

"That's the first thing I suggested. But they want to relocate it."

"Even if you don't play ball?" she's incredulous. The Nanobot program evolved out of my master's thesis, and with the exception of part-time assistants, I've run it pretty much single-handedly from the beginning.

"If I don't play ball," I reply, "I guess they'll just carry on without me."

"But you *are* Nanobot."

For a long time I hold her gaze—a turmoil of agitation and anxiety. Then I tell her, "I started the program, for sure. But the intellectual property belongs to the institute, at least ninety-five percent of it does. No one's indispensable."

She looks back at the contract, scanning the paragraphs, shaking her head in amazement. "Twenty million dollars in funding," she reads from one of the paragraphs. "Ten dedicated staff."

"There's no point getting too excited," I tell her. "It doesn't matter how wonderful the offer is, I'm not going without you."

She looks up at me with an expression of anguish. "But you have to. Nanobot is you," she makes a definitive gesture. "It's who you are."

I meet her mercurial gaze evenly.

Isabella and I have this decision game we sometimes play. A way of helping us make choices. If there's two people on the first floor of a burning house, or two options of some other kind, and we have a ladder and the capacity to rescue only one of them, which one do we save? No thinking. No weighing up of alternatives. What is our immediate instinct?

"If it was you and Nanobot in a burning house," I tell her now, "I'd always go for you. Ten times out of ten."

"Yeah," she tosses her head away, gold earrings glittering in the evening light. "Only it's just not that simple, is it?"

WE'D MET AT A NEW YEAR'S EVE PARTY AT A NEARBY RESTAURANT. Le Bouchon, a French brasserie on Battersea Rise, had put on its traditional, five course feast, and by nine o'clock the whole exuberant, jam-packed diner was already in full swing.

I'd been immediately attracted to the dark-eyed friend-of-a-friend opposite. I remember thinking how vivacious she was—and how exotic. I loved the way her scarlet, off-the-shoulder party dress revealed her lithe shoulders, the way her sleek, bronzed skin molded over her collar bones, how she laughed from the belly, her whole body shaking. I was fascinated that those amber eyes seemed to burn to green as she became spirited, and the expressive hand gestures that sent the multiple bracelets on her arms chiming. That night she'd been wearing a gold, chain necklace that danced and glittered all the way down to her cleavage. She'd been irresistible.

The evening had roared on to an alcohol-fuelled climax. At midnight we found ourselves kissing. Skin to skin I caught my first breath of her perfume, musky and potent. *Parfum d'Isabella.* Some time afterwards, we were outside exchanging phone numbers as she climbed into a friend's car. Within days we had confirmed all we intuitively felt about each other on our first date.

The January that followed was one of the wettest on record. Bleak clouds and interminable rain rolled unceasingly across Clapham Common, but in my bedroom it was our best January ever. We were thrilled by the romantic intensity and voracious passion we shared. Once unleashed, there had seemed no end to our craving for each other. Suddenly, the words of a hundred love songs seemed to have been written just for us, and there wasn't a single detail about each other we didn't want to know. Lost to each other, we spent every waking moment we could in the warm glow of my flat. Sometimes we'd emerge to go out for a meal, or huddle together for a walk across the common, looking up at where empty branches of the trees formed fragile silhouettes against a bruised, gray sky. Winter had never seemed so beautiful.

I'd had girlfriends before, of course. There'd been attractions since university days, some with girls so awkwardly self-conscious there could never be any real fulfillment for either of us, and others so matter-of-fact, so pedestrian in their nakedness that there was never going to be any magic.

Isabella had been different from the start. That same energy that made her sparkle in company was transmuted to a different form when we were alone together. I'd never been with anyone else who seemed such a perfect fit. She was so responsive, so uninhibited, and seemed to want whatever I wanted. In bed, her vivacity became a force of passion, vocal and unrestrained, and her eyes would lock to mine, savoring the exultant intensity of our passion when we truly became one.

But it was not just the great sex. We seemed to complement each other in all kinds of other, different ways. I needed her fire as much as she needed my equanimity. I lived in the world of thoughts and ideas, while she lived in the here and now of touch and taste. Together, we found a perfect balance between sensual and cerebral. For the first time in my life I knew what yin and yang meant as a living reality, not just an intellectual abstraction.

"You're so good for me," she'd said to me one morning during those first months, leaning over to kiss me where I was sitting at the kitchen table in my jeans and T-shirt, reading the paper. I'd reached up to trace her cheek. "You have this calmness I need. This peacefulness."

In the morning light her eyes were warm amber. "Long as calm doesn't get boring."

She shook her head. Just out of bed, her hair formed a loose, dark mane about her shoulders. "You don't know what I mean. Most of the guys I know, like the guys at work, they're so blokey. They're such lads. It's all about beating the competition and the bottom line and the one-upmanship and going out to get hammered. *That's* boring. But you . . . you *know* so much."

"Not everyone thinks nanotechnology is that important."

"I'm not talking about nanotech. I mean, just look at the books," she pointed to a pile on the corner of the table: *The Mozart Effect, Eastern Body, Western Mind, Leonardo: The First Scientist.*

"That's why I need you," I reply. "I live in my head too much. Always thinking, thinking, thinking."

"You say that like it's a bad thing."

"It is when you're so busy thinking you don't notice anything else. Anyone else."

"Oh, someone else can always get noticed if she wants," the intensity in her eyes had given way to a suggestive expression.

"My point exactly."

Then as she pushed aside the thick terry bathrobe to reveal a naked thigh, I continued in mock protest, "Here I was planning to spend the next twenty minutes reading up about Franco-German relations in the EU."

"What about relations right here?" she raised her eyebrows.

"On the kitchen table?" I murmured as I stood, slipping my hands inside her robe, savoring the nakedness of her breasts.

"Good a place as any."

Her lips met mine and our mouths parted, our appetite quickly awakening. She slid her legs open as I drew her to me, our voracity as urgent as if we hadn't found fulfillment in each other for weeks, instead of only hours. And when I pulled apart from her, tugging the robe from her shoulders to reveal her taut arousal, she looked at me, eyes bright with a desire as demanding as my own unslaked passion.

⁂

She had moved in a few months later; there seemed little point in her paying rent for a bedroom when we spent so much time in mine. And as well as the sexual intensity of our first months together, we also lived through the highs and lows of each other's careers. I knew very little about marketing before meeting her, but quickly became aware of the relentless demands of budgeting, branding, packaging, and new product launches. As a born communicator, marketing was as logical for her as nanotech was to someone like me. But while I'd been able to find an area of research in which I was fully engaged, selling soft drinks and vodka had never been a subject Isabella could get passionate about. Though it was only one step removed.

Since the age of twelve, when her parents had first allowed her a glass of wine with the evening meal, Isabella had been fascinated by the art of wine making. Much of this was her father's influence. A proud Italian, who would have liked to have been a sommelier, Julio had passed on his own enthusiasm and reverence for wine making to his daughter. In her late teens, Isabella had joined tours to wine-growing regions in France and Italy. She'd been on wine tasting courses and, as I quickly discovered, would spend ages in small, independent wine shops seeking out a particular varietal or estate or vintage.

As far as I was concerned, wine was just wine—some I liked and some I didn't. But for Isabella, wine was a passion she loved to share. She relished blind taste tests, discerning the difference between a Chenin and a Semillon, a Shiraz and a Merlot. I'd always been skeptical about so-called experts who claimed to detect tones of blackberry or passion fruit in a bottle of wine. But Isabella showed me differently.

She also loved matching the flavors of wine and food, and over the months I began to realize there were principles behind this. Why did a sweet white wine so perfectly complement a strong blue cheese? What was it about burgundy that made a simple stew taste like a gourmet delicacy?

Eating out with her was always an adventure. And the trips we had away held an enchantment I would have never imagined. Whether just a pub-stay in England, or a weekend break in Paris or Prague, Isabella made me see and savor things that, too absorbed in thinking, I would have never even noticed.

We also had other, less romantic discoveries to make about each other. Like the time I bought us a week's holiday in the Caribbean over Christmas. Leaving our itinerary in a red envelope with a bottle of champagne for Isabella to discover on her return from weekend shopping, instead of the thrilled response I was expecting, Isabella had been distraught about my lack of consultation. She'd spent every Christmas of her life with her family and it would devastate her mother if she were to change now.

I'd never forget the dark look she gave me as I'd opened the door, the stormy display of Italian brio that followed. It was as though I'd fallen over a tripwire I hadn't seen because I'd assumed that Isabella's family was pretty much like mine and that a Christmas apart would be no big deal. I'd made the more fundamental error of believing that an exotic festive season with me would trump any calls her family had on her.

As it turned out, we never went to the Caribbean. After a blazing row, followed by a week of tension, I'd phoned the travel agent and cancelled the trip. I'd lost my deposit, but kept my girlfriend and learned an expensive lesson: I should never underestimate Isabella's closeness to her family.

Even though we had our own life together which, for me, was all I needed, Isabella was bound by blood ties much stronger than I'd ever experienced. My father, who had always seemed to be away on business when I was growing up, had died when I was still an undergraduate. Mum, who ran her own landscape gardening business, found her own fulfillment in the beautiful gardens she created. We enjoyed a warm relationship, my mum, older brother and I, but it was one in which we gave each other plenty of space. We were always there for each other, just a phone call away. But there were no expectations about how much time we needed to spend together. And nothing like the tug of Isabella's family who lived in nearby Dulwich and exerted a constant, gravitational pull.

The sobering news we'd received only ten days before would make that tug all the more powerful. Which is why I'm not making any assumptions about California. And why, the night I come home with the Acellerate offer, I tell her we have the rest of the weekend to think about it. It's the end of the week and we're both tired and hungry. I suggest curry at our favorite Indian place on Northcote Road.

BUT IT'S HARD TO PRETEND THAT EVERYTHING'S NORMAL AFTER AN offer like Acellerate's. Despite our efforts that evening and the following day to find distractions, for the first time there's something in our relationship that neither of us knows how to handle. Something we've never experienced before threatens to set us apart.

Isabella's reaction to the Caribbean Christmas holiday, while a shock at the time, had never posed any real danger to the two of us. It had been a bump in the road, an obstacle we could navigate. All it took was for me to acknowledge my mistake, swallow my pride, and let go.

But the Acellerate offer is a lot different. Isabella's family loyalties are more complicated than ever, and now that we're engaged, I too, have become a part of the difficult network of emotions affecting her whole family. Then there is her job at Bertollini and the hard-won work promotion also making it difficult for her to leave. Would I be a fool for love if I stayed in London, giving up the project I'd been working on for the past seven years? And what is Isabella thinking? All through that long Saturday of contrived activity and unnecessary errands I wonder constantly what is going on in her head—and her heart. Is it really a case of torn loyalties, or is the decision already an inevitable conclusion but she just doesn't know how to break it to me?

⁓

SOMETIME AROUND THREE O'CLOCK ON SUNDAY MORNING I WAKE TO find the bed empty. Getting up, I step through to the lounge to where she's leaning against the bay window in her Tintin nightshirt, fiddling with her engagement ring, cheeks flecked with silver.

I can't bear to see her so upset and, walking over, take her in my arms. I hold her for the longest time, feeling her body against mine as she sobs silently.

Finally, she pulls away, covering her face with her hands, "I just don't want to hold you back," she says, embarrassed by her own tearfulness. "You'll hate me if I'm like an anchor, weighing you down."

It's a while before I reply. It melts me to see her so miserable and to know I am the cause. "And I don't want you to hate me for making you give up your job."

I mention her job deliberately, because it seems to me if that's going to be a problem, there's no point even talking about her family.

"But that's all it is—" she reaches over to a box of tissues and pulls out several, before wiping her face, "a job. It's not like what you've got. It's not a personal discovery, or something really important. Nanobot will change people's lives. Who cares if people in Slovakia drink more Bertollini vodka than somebody else's—does it really matter?"

"It matters to you."

"Only because of where I'm working. Before I was promoted, you know what it was like, I was getting bored. Really bored. I was ready to take the next step up but I had to wait. And in eighteen months, two years, I know I'll be on top of this job. It'll be the same thing all over again, I'll be looking for something different . . ."

I'm not sure where she's heading with this, and can't account for the ambivalence in her voice.

"I'd look after you in L.A."

"I've got savings," she says, needing to assert her independence even in her unhappiness. "I wouldn't have to live off you."

"It's not like that! I want to take care of you."

"Harry's probably right," she shrugs, "I probably could get a job over there quite quickly."

"No probably about it!"

"Not that I could compete with you," her tone is rueful.

"Our relationship is about more than job titles, isn't it?" She looks away at Clapham Common, lit with a string of glowing yellow lanterns, unfamiliarly deserted.

"So you'd be okay about leaving Bertollini?"

"That thing you said about no one being indispensable," her eyes meet mine. "If they can run the Nanobot program without you, and you invented it, then I guess Bertollini can get themselves another group product manager from all the bright young things snapping at my heels."

I step over to hug her. I know how much she's put into her work. All the early morning flights out of Heathrow and Gatwick on rush trips to European cities. The weekends spent revising budgets and forecasting figures. The sheer energy she's invested in launching new products and running campaigns. And she's prepared to walk away from all that just for me.

"Not that it's really about the job" she murmurs at my chest, in an acknowledgement of the subject we haven't mentioned all weekend.

Isabella is the third of three children, the only daughter, and the object of her parents' and maternal grandparents' constant attentions. Pretty little Isabella, the daughter so long in coming, in who they've invested such high hopes and expectations. Isabella, the attentive daughter who has never let them down. She is the only one in the family with a university degree, the only one with a high-flying career. She is the family organizer, the convener of Mother's Day lunches, the one who arranges joint birthday gifts and Easter family gatherings.

In fact the only impediment in an otherwise perfect picture is me. Not personally, though her parents would probably have preferred a nice, Italian boy—but more the facts of our living arrangements. For weeks after handing back the key to her old flat, Isabella's parents would only ever call on her mobile. Isabella had been vague and furtive about this until confessing, one night before a weekend visit to see them that she hadn't told her parents she'd moved in with me. She hadn't been ready because she knew how disappointed they'd be.

She'd had to tell them in the end, and they had been disappointed. Her mother had treated me to a lecture on the sanctity of marriage, while her father was studiously distant. It hadn't been an easy start to family relations, until some months later we went away to Florence on a weekend break, and there, in a jewelry shop on the Ponte Vecchio Isabella saw the most beautiful diamond ring.

"Shall we get engaged?" I'd responded to her excitement, "Then you'll have a *very* good reason to wear it."

We'd already talked about getting married and had agreed it was what we wanted, though from my side there hadn't been a rush. Few of the other couples we knew in our age group were married. But there on the Ponte Vecchio, outside a jewelry shop, we had agreed. And getting back to London with my new fiancée, not only was Isabella able to proudly display her star-shaped diamond ring, her family became a lot more accepting. A genuine warmth had developed over the past couple of years, in particular a mutual respect between Julio and me. It helped that both of us were mad keen Chelsea supporters, and we'd spent many a Saturday afternoon watching our side play home games at Stamford Bridge, or glued in front of the Giladucci's TV.

But the news which had overshadowed all of this came ten days ago, after Julio had been to the doctor suffering from what he thought was stress. Even though he'd officially retired from running his electrician's business some years ago, at seventy-two, he still did all the accounts, and things had been getting on top of him. Instead of sending him home with a prescription, however, the family doctor had scheduled him to have blood tests, a CT scan and finally an MRI of his brain. After which came a diagnosis that had shaken us all: Julio had Alzheimer's.

No one in the family knew what to make of this and it had taken weeks for the news to sink in. Julio himself had withdrawn, spending hours in his workshop smoking his favorite Havanas, contemplating his inexorable journey to oblivion.

NOW IN THE DARKNESS OF OUR FLAT OVERLOOKING THE DESERTED Common, Isabella hardly needs to say, "With Dad's situation, the timing of this whole thing is really terrible."

Holding her close to me, there's no need for a reply. Julio's condition, and what it would mean to Isabella, had been my own first thoughts when Harry had broken the news.

"Even before the diagnosis, my folks were so reliant on me . . ."

"Of course. If it was anything less than a spectacular opportunity that was being offered, I wouldn't be giving it a second thought. But if Julio keeps up with the medication and lifestyle changes, you know what the doctors are saying. He's been diagnosed early. His situation could be exactly the same in two years."

On our most recent visit to the family, Julio had emerged from his self-imposed isolation, adopting a more stoical attitude to his illness.

"And in two years time," Isabella follows my line of thinking doubtfully, "you will have built your Nanobot prototype at Acellerate?"

"Yes."

"And if Dad takes a really bad turn, you'd be happy to walk away from the program at just that moment?"

"It wouldn't be easy. But given the choice, I'd rather do that than walk away from it now." I look down at her questioning expression. "With two years of Acellerate under my belt, all sorts of doors would open. I could take my research in a new direction. There's no telling what opportunities might come up."

"It just seems that if I have to give up Bertollini now, and you have to give up Nanobot in two years time, we're both losing."

"You can't say that until you know what'll replace them. It could be something even better. Plus we get to stay together."

That, at least, was something we can both agree on without reservation.

Or can we?

"Even putting to one side what's happened to Dad, the idea of me taking off for America would still be devastating for them," Isabella says breaking away from me. "It's so completely unexpected. I haven't prepared them for it."

I'd noticed in the past the way she was careful to negotiate changes with her family. Even something as small as shifting a family gathering from lunch to breakfast was something which had to be first hinted at as a possibility, before being revisited in a later conversation, then discussed at length before finally being agreed to. I don't pretend to understand why. Is it a daughter thing, an Italian thing, or just something you have to do with aging parents?

"I guess, trying to get them used to the idea—" I begin.

"In six weeks?!"

I have to tread carefully. While Isabella often rails against her family's ways, the slightest criticism from me immediately puts her on the defensive.

"Even in six months they wouldn't understand."

"I'm sure your Dad would." But to my surprise, Isabella is shaking her head, "It's a great opportunity for *you*," she meets my eyes, with a look of anguish.

"Surely what's good for me—?"

"I'd be walking away from my job, that's how they'd see it. Giving up everything to be with you—"

"And we're not even married," I realize, finishing for her.

She doesn't say anything. She doesn't have to. I can almost hear the conversation around the dinner table if we went to L.A., about how young Matt may be a nice bloke, but he's taking advantage of Isabella. How his head could be turned by some pretty girl in California and, pfff, just like that, Isabella would lose everything.

What I say next is something I've been thinking about constantly since Friday night. "If you wanted me to make that commitment—"

"No!" she holds up a hand, her eyes meet mine with an intensity that blazes through the semi-darkness. "I'd never want to go there because you're in a corner. I'd want it to be for the right reasons."

She speaks in such a determined tone that I know not to push. We stand, eyes locked for what seems an eternity before I finally confess, "I don't want to lose you, Isabella. I really am willing to try anything to make it work."

Chapter Two

Tenzin Dorje

Jangtang Province—Tibet

Even though Lama Tsering has warned us that our journey from Tibet won't be a grand adventure, that's just how it feels, in the beginning. Within an hour of the dire news reaching Zheng-po, Lama Tsering's patron, a wealthy man from the nearby village, has commandeered a small bus. It's an ancient government vehicle, only supposed to seat twelve, but twenty-one monks are crammed in, and we set off immediately. The bus driver is local and knows all the roads in Jangtang, which is just as well. We are leaving at eight o'clock, there are no streetlights in rural Tibet, and we need to travel as far as possible before dawn.

On the bus Lama Tsering tells us more about the Zheng-po evacuation plan. For the past ten years, longer than I've been a novice monk, the abbot and high lamas have made preparations for what is happening tonight. While I have always revered them as elders on the spiritual path, I'd never have guessed they could develop such elaborate preparations to close down the monastery. But their evacuation plans are meticulous.

After using whatever government or private vehicles are available to move all the monks southeast through the province of Jangtang, all sixty of us are to divide into groups of three. We will then make our way to the mountains which mark the border with India.

"We have studied guerrilla warfare," Lama Tsering tells us to our surprise. "We realized that moving large groups of people through rural areas would be too much risk. We need to avoid roadblocks and all the main towns. This is much easier if we travel in small groups."

Every group of three has been provided with rucksacks containing maps, canned food and water bottles—all of these materializing from a storage room at Zheng-po. We have also been given a small amount of money to help pay for transport and other essentials.

The preparations haven't ended with our departure from Zheng-po. Lama Tsering tells us that local villagers will remove all wall-hangings, butter lamps and ritual ornaments from the temple and keep these stored in their homes, for one day in the future when we may return to Zheng-po. Under the abbot's direction, sand and wood-ash will be scattered through the carefully-swept rooms and temple, the old library building will be burned out, rocks will be thrown into the courtyard. Every effort will be made so give Zheng-po a look of abandonment.

"If the Red Army thinks Zheng-po is a derelict monastery," explains Lama Tsering, "they will not come looking for us monks. Perhaps," his face hardens, "they will not be tempted to raze it to the ground."

But the most critical part of the evacuation plan has been put in place years earlier. It is the part Lama Tsering explained to us back in his room, when he told us about the one condition he has placed on our making the journey into exile with him. The condition has given me a sense of destiny like no other.

"The purpose of this mission is not about saving our lives." Light from the flickering butter lamp had revealed the gravity of his expression. "If you decide to make the journey, it must be for a higher purpose than self-preservation."

Out the corner of my eye I could see that Paldon Wangmo is following our teacher as intently as I am.

"As both of you know, one of the reasons the Dharma is so precious is because it is a living tradition. The Buddha's wisdom has been passed down from teachers to students, through oral transmission, since the time of Shakyamuni Buddha. We don't follow our practice because we believe certain things. We do so because teachers can show us how they work and we can check up on them for ourselves. But all of this—" he wagged a finger, "relies on correct teaching. And to keep the lineage pure, to make sure the teachings are in accord with the meaning of our spiritual masters, what must we rely on?"

"The holy scriptures," Paldon Wangmo responds in an instant.

"Correct," Lama Tsering nods firmly. "Without the scriptures to guide us, perhaps teachers will have different explanations of the practice. Or they may have faulty memories. Students will only receive some teachings but not others. If we rely on oral transmission alone, in a short period the peerless teachings of the Buddha and other masters will become degenerate and corrupted. This is why," he lowers his voice, so we have to lean forward even closer to hear him, "the real purpose of our journey is to take our most precious and sacred texts out of the country, to freedom."

Instantly my imagination is alight! The library of Zheng-po monastery is one of the most revered in Tibetan Buddhism. Although only a small monastery of sixty monks, it is also one of the oldest in the Gelug lineage and our library is the repository of some of the most ancient and precious texts. Several times a year visitors arrive from other monasteries to study the original scriptures or make copies. Even visitors from universities in America and Europe. Sometimes they would stay for only a few days. Usually, however, they would pore over the scriptures for weeks or even months.

As a novice monk, I have only ever been allowed access to copies of the main texts. The more advanced teachings are strictly off-limits, made available only to those who have the required initiations.

The thought that I, Tenzin Dorje, would help ensure these texts survived the Red Army invasion, is an overwhelming prospect. Suddenly, from nowhere, I have a chance to do something meaningful—even historic!

"Our library is so big," Paldon Wangmo, with his incisive mind, was always thinking ahead, "how can we take it all?"

"You may have noticed many visitors over the past few years," Lama Tsering looked up from the neatly tied-up bundles on his floor. "They have made copies of many of the texts and, leaving the copies, have taken the originals into India already."

"It's a long way to take them," commented Paldon Wangmo, as yet more feet thundered outside Lama Tsering's room towards the monastery gates, "all the way from here to India."

"What I am about to tell you is to be kept only between the three of us," Lama Tsering sounds severe. "The texts which we are to take have already been removed from the monastery. Some years ago, soon after 1951, when the threat of invasion became real, we moved them to a secret cave in the Himalayas. They are already close to the border. Our mission is to retrieve them from where they are being stored. We didn't want them to leave Tibet unless it became absolutely necessary. That moment has come."

The more I hear, the more astonished I am. All of this, it seemed, had been planned for years, and yet none of us had even suspected what was going on.

"Will we be taking out the sacred *vajrayana* texts?" I ask.

"No, Tenzin Dorje—we have been assigned an even more important task. We will be retrieving a small number of scriptures whose very existence has been kept secret for over a thousand years."

By now, both Paldon Wangmo and I gaped at our teacher.

"There are original poems, written by Milarepa—," I could hardly breathe: the twelfth century Milarepa was an icon, a legend to all the people of Tibet. "Transmissions received directly by the great yogi Naropa in the eleventh century. Even some very fragile, but quite legible fragments of writings by Padmasambhava."

Padmasambhava! He was the historic figure who re-introduced Buddhism to Tibet in the eighth century, and who was revered throughout the land as a saint.

"As you know, Padmasambhava not only founded the first Buddhist monastery in Tibet, he was also a highly realized master who made many prophecies. One of these you may remember: "When the iron bird flies—"

"And horses run on wheels," we chanted in unison with him, as we always did when reciting the scriptures, "the Tibetan people will be scattered like ants and the Dharma will come to the land of the red people."

"In taking these most precious manuscripts out of Tibet to the land of the red people, the land of the Westerners," said Lama Tsering, "the three of us will not only be fulfilling Padmasambhava's famous prophecy. We will be carrying his very words on our backs, including the words you have just spoken."

THAT FIRST NIGHT, AS WE DRIVE AWAY FROM ZHENG-PO, DESPITE THE comfortable rhythm of the bus on the narrow road, I am far too excited to sleep. I keep imagining how Lama Tsering will show us to the secret cave in the foothills of the Himalayas. How the three of us will outsmart the Chinese army, and make our way through the mountain passes with our precious cargo. How we will arrive as heroes in Northern India and all the high lamas, maybe even His Holiness the Dalai Lama himself, will know that the most sacred texts in Tibetan Buddhism had been rescued by Lama Tsering and his two novices.

I also remember Paldon Wangmo's earnest probing about why Padmasambhava called westerners "red people" or "red-faced people" as some versions put it.

"I'm not sure the reason for this," Lama Tsering had said. "Perhaps it's because, unlike us, their faces burn red in the sun?"

SEVERAL TIMES DURING THE NIGHT, THE BUS HAS TO STOP AT A RURAL outpost to refuel. On each occasion a villager has to be awakened to unlock a diesel pump. Those of us who are awake get out to stretch our legs; inevitably we talk to the villager and his wife or anyone else who is awake. There is only one subject of conversation.

His Holiness has already arrived in Northern India says one villager. He has heard it on the radio, so it must be true. But at another stop the news is very different. The Red Army has burned down the Potala Palace, according to a messenger from Lhasa, and the Dalai Lama has been seized as a prisoner of war. When we ask Lama Tsering what to believe, he tells us to ignore everything we hear unless it is first hand information from a reliable source. Of one thing, however, we are in no doubt: the Red Army is marching through Tibet and its main purpose seems to be the destruction of every monastery and eradication of every monk.

"Why do they hate us so much," I ask Lama Tsering in the early hours of the morning, "when all we want is to free all beings from suffering—the Chinese included?"

I expect him to say how deluded they are, especially their leader, Chairman Mao. But, as often happens, I am surprised by his answer,

"We should feel sorry for all the soldiers in the Red Army, Tenzin Dorje. The suffering they inflict on us can last only one lifetime. But the suffering they are inflicting on themselves will last countless lifetimes."

"Even more important, we should not forget that what is happening to us arises from our own karma. The Red Army soldiers are merely instruments delivering the effects of causes which we ourselves have created. To feel angry at them is like feeling angry at a whip, instead of the person wielding it."

I wonder what cause I have created in the past, which has produced the effect of finding myself on an ancient bus in the middle of the night, a novice monk fleeing from soldiers. Even though Lama has often explained that karmic causes may have been created lifetimes ago, I wonder if it is something I have done in this lifetime.

There is one action, in particular, for which I have always felt regret. Since arriving in Zheng-po, not a day has gone by when I haven't thought about it with an aching heart, and wondered if perhaps I'm too bad to become a fully ordained monk.

In my home village of Ling near Purang, in the West of Tibet, many families followed the Tibetan tradition of sending a son to a nearby monastery to be trained in the Dharma. There were many reasons for doing this. Offering a son to uphold the Dharma was considered a great service to the tradition. Monasteries provided the best education in Tibet. Some of the reasons were not so noble; a family finding itself with too many mouths to feed, or a son who had grown unruly, might also entreat a monastery for support.

In the case of my own family, there had never been any doubt that Paldon Wangmo, the first born, was well suited to a monastic life. Throughout her first pregnancy, my mother had vivid dreams of *dakinis*, or female sky-walkers, in white robes, dancing in celebration at the birth of her son. And when a high lama happened to pass through Ling, on seeing my pregnant mother he prophesied that she would give birth to a son, who would bring many, many people to the Dharma.

After Paldon Wangmo was born there were more auspicious signs. Like most people in the village, my parents were peasant farmers, growing barley and raising yaks. My father was also a skilled carpenter who, for many years, had been working at his craft earning extra money making furniture. Shortly after Paldon Wangmo's birth, he was commissioned by a nearby monastery to fit out its gompa with shelves from floor to ceiling, and to make meditation boxes for all the monks. Not only were the family fortunes suddenly improved, my father's meticulous designs were so admired by monks from other monasteries, that he was soon being commissioned to make furniture for them, too.

Meanwhile, Paldon Wangmo was growing up to be a very unusual little boy. From the age of three he would often be found sitting in a quiet place, legs crossed in meditation position, chanting mantras. He began to read at the age of four, and seemed able to memorize holy texts with little difficulty. It was, my mother used to say, because he only needed to be reminded of them. Whenever he caught sight of a monk in saffron and maroon robes, he would rush over to greet them.

Rather than entrust the education of their precious son to a local teacher, my parents had set about finding the monastery which was both small enough to provide personal tutoring, as well as being of equal prestige and standing as the major monasteries like Sera-je and Drepung. They found this at Zheng-po, a monastery three days from Ling, which was where my father took Paldon Wangmo, at the age of eight, to begin his new life.

In the meanwhile, my mother had given birth to my sister and me. There were no auspicious signs around our births. But my sister, Dechen, was considered a great beauty, and from a young age we all knew she would be sought-after as a wife. And as the baby of the family, I had a special bond with my mother. We were a close-knit family, and as my father spent increasing amounts of time away from home on his commissions, the burden of farming and housekeeping fell on the three of us.

For my own part, I showed none of Paldon Wangmo's contemplative leanings or intellectual curiosity: in fact, I was a slow learner when it came to reading and reciting texts by rote. But from the start I had a heartfelt sense of connection to other beings, especially animals.

Walking around our village, I couldn't bear to see animals suffering or in pain. Even the sight of other boys jumping on ants would make me upset. As a seven-year-old I happened to be walking past the village butcher who had been ordered to slaughter five yaks that day. He had already killed four of them by the time I walked past the alley to his shop. I was horrified to see their severed heads tossed aside in a jumbled pile. Their eyes, glazed open in pure terror. The fur of their faces matted with blood.

Worse still was the single remaining yak, which was tethered tightly between two posts. Foaming at the mouth, it was panting, great sobbing breaths of air, the whites of its eyes showing as they rolled in panic. Beside it stood the butcher, drenched in blood. Sharpening his knife.

Without thinking I'd rushed over to him and thrown myself around his legs. Clutching them tightly, I screamed out for him not to kill the remaining yak. Blood was smeared all over my face and clothes. At first he tried to push me away. But that only made me more insistent. Feeling the animal's dread, I knew I mustn't give up. How could he kill the poor, innocent yak?

This man had been the village butcher for as long as I could remember. Killing yaks was what he did for a living. But something changed that day as I clung whimpering at his legs. Was it my impassioned plea to remember that the yak had been his mother in a previous lifetime? Or had he become simply tired of the horror his livelihood entailed?

Whatever the reason, on that particular occasion he put down his knife. He released the yak to the pastures outside the village. Some weeks later, we were told he had given up butchery altogether.

Every year, after an intensive retreat, Paldon Wangmo would come home to spend part of the summer with our family. These visits were always a great highlight for me. For days before, I'd climb up the mountain in which our village nestled, surveying the road to Zheng-po for a sign of the bus that would bring Paldon Wangmo home. As I sat there, I'd take out the cords of rope I often carried in my pocket, and while away the hours in my favorite hobby of tying and untying intricate knots.

For days after Paldon Wangmo arrived back I'd be plying him with questions about life at the monastery. Did they have to work hard? How did the food compare to our mother's cooking? Were the monks friendly or stern?

Inevitably, Paldon Wangmo would talk about the Dharma, too. Sometimes in the summer, especially after the day's labors, we'd go up onto the mountain to enjoy the long, warm evening, and Paldon Wangmo would tell us about the teachings he'd received.

I am not sure when I first realized one of the most important teachings in the Dharma—that while scholarship is valued, having an open heart is valued even more. Gradually I began to think that maybe I should become a novice monk, too. I might not be academically clever, like Paldon Wangmo, but I felt compassion for living beings. I also had an inexplicable feeling that, if I were to join a monastery, I would also find a special purpose in life.

The first time I tried to explain this to my mother, she laughed. Life in a monastery would be too harsh, too demanding for me, she said. I didn't have the temperament for it.

"But you don't have to be so clever to be a monk!" I protested. "Paldon Wangmo even said so."

"Oh yes?" my mother was wry. "Then what sort of monk do you wish to be?"

"A yogi." I had already worked it out. While many monks spent their time engaged in rituals and study of the scriptures, there were a smaller number who dedicated themselves to spiritual development through meditation. Known as yogis or siddhas, they often developed special powers such as clairvoyance, as side-effects of their progress. The siddhas had always fascinated me.

"You want to become a magician?" teased my mother.

"Why not?"

"Next you'll be telling me you want to go to Lhasa to live in the Potala Palace."

"So?" I failed to share her humor.

"The magician of Lhasa!" she laughed.

But she no longer laughed when I persisted with the idea, several days later. With my father traveling away so much, she told me, the family needed me at home to help with the yaks and the barley.

What about Dechen? I demanded. She also helped with the work and had shown no interest in becoming a nun. Besides, my father frequently told us that there wasn't any need for the family to keep on farming. His rising status as a craftsman placed him increasingly in demand, and his earnings had made us comfortable.

But my mother's views would not be changed and, being cast from the same mold as her, nor would mine. Forced to keep my feelings to myself, the more I dwelled on them, the more they intensified.

The next time Paldon Wangmo came home, I questioned him more intently than ever about Lama Tsering. It was clear he had a special bond with his teacher who, quite apart from being one of the most important monks at Zheng-po, was also kind and gentle with his students. I didn't reveal my plans to Paldon Wangmo, but I thought perhaps if I could persuade Lama Tsering I should become a novice monk that he could intercede with my parents.

Which was how I came to run away to Zheng-po, leaving Ling very early one morning, walking far along the road that led to the town of Purang, and eventually getting a ride with a government worker. My mind was in turmoil throughout the journey. I knew that back at home, my mother would soon find the short note I'd left, saying I was going to Zheng-po. I felt it was my duty, at least, to do that. But would she try to come after me? Would she get news to my father, and would he try to stop me? For three days I felt like a criminal as I begged for both food and rides, half expecting someone in authority to apprehend me at a moment's notice.

But to my amazement, as much as Paldon Wangmo's, I found myself walking through the gates of Zheng-po late in the afternoon of the third day. As it happened, the monks were emerging from the gompa just as I arrived. Seeing me standing with my small bag at my feet, Paldon Wangmo hurried across the courtyard, his face filled with concern. He thought I must be bringing bad news. When I told him of my plan, he was sure of it!

Nevertheless, he couldn't hide me, and I was soon ushered into the presence of my teacher for the first time. Stumbling to explain my predicament to Lama Tsering, far from getting angry, as I'd half feared, he burst out laughing at the idea that I'd run away from home to join a monastery. Despite my relief at his reception, and the instant liking I felt for him, Lama Tsering said he could not go against my parents' wishes. So, after giving me two days at Zheng-po to recover from my journey, he sent me back home—bearing a letter for my parents. A family conference was duly held, my mother's expression strongly disapproving, my father showing his concern. On the table, the letter from Lama Tsering, offering to take me on as a novice, if my parents wished.

While my adventure to Zheng-po hadn't achieved all that I'd wanted, it had shown my parents how determined I was. And in the end they decided it would be wrong to hold me back from growing in my wisdom of the Dharma, if that was what I so energetically wished to do.

The second time I left home for Zheng-po, the official time, both my parents and Dechen were there to say goodbye, as well as our neighbors and some other villagers. Even the ex-butcher came along to the bus stop.

In the days before my departure however, a change had come over my mother. Instead of the stony censure she'd maintained up until that time, she showed another emotion which struck me like a blow to my heart. My mother was grief-stricken!

Always a reserved person, who concealed her emotions behind an appearance of good manners and self-control, on the afternoon before my departure I came across her dabbing her eyes in the woodshed behind our house.

I didn't need to ask why she was crying. Instead, I felt as though something was exploding inside me. My mother's disapproval had been much easier to bear than her unhappiness. It had made me think that perhaps the close bond we'd always shared had changed, become more distant. Now I realized that wasn't so.

Putting my arms around her, I felt her whole body shuddering.

"Don't you want me to join a monastery?" I asked, after her tears had subsided. It was an appeal to her pride—the thought of having two sons who were monks.

"That's not it," she pulled away. "It's just that when you leave here, I'll be losing you for the rest of your life."

"That's not true!" I was adamant. "I'll be coming back all the time, just like Paldon Wangmo."

But my mother shook her head inconsolably. "It will never be the same," she said.

ON THE BUS NOW, I WONDER IF THE EMOTIONAL PAIN I INFLICTED ON my mother is the karmic cause for me having to flee from Zheng-po, like a thief in the night. Should I have remained at home, the loyal son, tending the yaks and growing the barley? But if I'd done that, I would never have met Lama Tsering. I couldn't have grown in the Dharma. Most importantly of all, I wouldn't be taking part in this mission—one of the most important in the history of Tibetan Buddhism for over a thousand years.

There's another experience I would have missed out on if I'd remained at home. An experience which has made me eager to go to India and which, to my sense of shame, I have been thinking about from the moment Lama Tsering told us about the journey across the Himalayas.

During the summer of the Year of the Fire Rooster, three monks from Lhasa came to visit Zheng-po. While there was nothing unusual about receiving such visitors, what made this especially memorable was what the visitors brought with them. One night the abbot announced that instead of the evening meditation session, we were going to watch a movie. In Lhasa, His Holiness the Dalai Lama had long had a great interest in movies—in fact, the projector and film the three monks had brought with them had been used by His Holiness himself.

A buzz of curiosity had followed this announcement. No one at Zheng-po had seen a movie before and we wondered about the practicalities. How would we see the movie if we were to watch it in darkness? How could all forty of us get to view it at the same time, no matter how much we tried to cram together?

All our questions were answered when we went outdoors to the courtyard after nightfall, as directed by the abbot, taking our meditation cushions with us, and sitting facing the gompa wall. Suddenly, a large square of light appeared on the wall and the next thing we knew, the most incredible fantasy of color and music.

The movie was called *Rock Around the Clock* starring Bill Haley and His Comets and I sat through the entire performance entranced. It didn't matter that the characters were all American and that I couldn't understand a word they said. I was utterly engrossed by the beautiful women, the gleaming cars, the palatial houses and especially by the music. From the moment I heard the title song, I was filled with energy—my foot tapped against the meditation cushion as though it had a life of its own.

Not all the monks were quite so impressed. After half an hour or so, some had had enough, and went off to their rooms to meditate. Many left later on. But I stayed until the very end, and afterwards I went up to the monk who had been operating the projector. He showed me a record sleeve of *Rock Around the Clock* with a picture of Bill Haley and His Comets and told me how Bill Haley had invented a kind of music called rock and roll. When I gazed wistfully at the record cover, the monk told me that, while it was the property of the Potala Palace, before he left Zheng-po he would write down all the words of the song for me to keep.

In the following weeks I made it my purpose to learn all the words in English, by heart, with the same determination as an important prayer. For months afterwards, whenever I was doing repetitive chores at Zheng-po, like sweeping floors or polishing windows, instead of reciting mantras as I knew a good monk should do, I would find myself humming:

When the clock strikes two, three and four,
If the band slows down we'll yell for more,
We're gonna rock around the clock tonight,
We're gonna rock, rock, rock, 'til broad daylight

I had no idea what the words actually meant, beyond the general idea that they were about dancing all night. But I also had the feeling that it didn't really matter. It was the power of the melody which was so catchy, and which would arise in my thoughts, especially in certain situations.

Such as now on the bus, with the ancient engine grinding beneath us, and most of the monks, asleep in their seats, rocking like sacks of barley. In my mind I am sitting on my meditation cushion back in the courtyard of Zheng-po, Bill Haley and His Comets have appeared on the gompa wall, and I hear the irresistible refrain:

One, two, three o'clock, four o'clock, rock,
Five, six, seven o'clock, eight o'clock, rock

Some time during the early hours I must have fallen asleep, because the next thing I know, it is getting light outside, and the bus is slowing. I am aware of agitation, and as I blink open my sleepy eyes, the first thing I see is Lama Tsering in the seat in front, shaking Paldon Wangmo awake and pointing out the side of the bus.

We are in an unfamiliar part of the province, on a road hugging a sheer cliff around the side of a great mountain. The narrowness of the road, and the size of the rocks strewn across it would be scary enough, but this is not what is causing concern on the bus.

At first, I can't see the cause of the consternation. But rubbing my eyes, through the pre-dawn gray, it comes into focus. Two forty-gallon drums stand across the center of the road. Between the two of them is a great log.

By now I am wide awake. I know the roadblock is a favorite technique of the Red Army. It is how they control traffic in occupied territory; how they have found monks—even those who have hidden in lorries among livestock or behind bales of straw—monks who are summarily executed.

The agitation on the bus is followed by a long and eerie silence. Even though we hurried from Zheng-po eight hours ago, it seems we have left our escape too late.

Chapter Three

Matt Lester

Imperial Science Institute—London
April 2007

HARRY HAD ASKED ME FOR A RESPONSE TO THE ACELLERATE OFFER first thing this week, and Monday morning finds me heading into the office with powerfully-mixed feelings. This past weekend has been the most traumatic since the start of my relationship with Isabella. It's hard to avoid the paradox that the most spectacular career opportunity of my life has become the cause of our greatest heartache, and to recognize that fault lines have been exposed in our relationship—profound, unspoken differences which I'd never really known were there.

It's one of those London spring mornings when the sky, a cloudless and promising blue, is accompanied by a wind so cold it chills to the bone, It couldn't reflect my mood better, I think, hurrying along Euston Street from the tube station to work.

Harry always gets in early to avoid the worst of the commuter rush, and by seven forty-five I'm making my way up the stairs, crossing the open plan section of the third floor, observing the scrutinizing glances as I make my way past the HR department. Harry's door is open and his sound system is silent. As I approach he looks up from behind his desk, eyeballing me closely. I can tell he hasn't had a good weekend either. No doubt he has also been preoccupied by the Acellerate offer. Not only in his formal capacity as boss of the Imperial Science Institute, but also as the guiding spirit behind the Nanobot program.

Harry was a strong influence in my life even before I started working at the institute. It was Harry who'd been the first one outside the university establishment, to take an interest in my area of nanotechnology. And it was Harry who'd taken me out for a beer when I'd still been in the early days of my master's. Right from the start, the two of us had seemed to share the same excitement about the possibilities of the Nanobot program. Possibilities, it seems, destined never to be realized at the Imperial Science Institute.

"It's been difficult," I tell him, unnecessarily, in the stark Monday morning light of his office.

Harry's face is drawn with fatigue. "I resisted the temptation to phone over the weekend—"

"Just as well," I confirm, sitting opposite.

"She's so vivacious, Matt. She'd take them by storm in L.A.—"

"Her job's an issue, but not *the* issue. There's also her family, and the traditional ideas they have about marriage."

Harry knows about the subterfuge after Isabella moved in with me. It had all seemed very amusing when I'd told him about it over a beer at our local pub, but since then the implications have become anything but funny.

Harry is following me closely, a wariness in his eyes as he suspects there's more to come.

In confirmation I finally tell him, "And I haven't told you about Julio."

"The father?"

I nod. "Diagnosed with Alzheimer's. Only a few weeks ago—nobody except the immediate family knows."

Harry raises a hand to his face. After a long pause he murmurs, "That's got to be tough."

"Especially for a dutiful daughter," I agree. "It *is* late onset, and they seem to have diagnosed it early. He's doing all the right things to manage it and, who knows, there might not be any change over the next few years."

Harry regards me somberly across his desk. "So where does that leave you?"

In the dark hours before dawn the morning before, Isabella and I had sat in the bay window of our flat, facing each other across the divide that had opened up between us. We talked about Julio's chances of remaining mentally stable and active for the next several years. We'd discussed

Isabella's hypothetical job prospects in Los Angeles, with or without the help of contacts she'd made at Bertollini. There were so many considerations and important choices, but in the end Isabella believed none of them mattered if she couldn't convince her family she had a strong enough reason to follow me to America.

We found ourselves discussing the family occasion when Julio had announced his plans to fight against his illness. How he'd spoken about his regret at not passing on more of his culture.

"What do you think he meant by that?" I'd asked Isabella. "When you know so much about wine?"

"I'm an enthusiast," she replied. "An amateur. I don't know nearly as much as Dad, and neither of us are any match for the professionals."

"You think that's what he would like for you?"

She nods. "A proper job in the industry, or formal training. Something to show he's passed the torch onto the next generation."

It's a long while before I ask, "Isn't America's wine industry based in southern California?"

Neither of us had put it together until that moment. We'd immediately got online to find out more. While we already knew that the Napa Valley, just outside San Francisco, was the epicenter of industry activity, there also seemed to be a buzz around L.A. Given the city's size, surely it had to be a major market? With all the wine and related companies operating in L.A., we felt sure there must be one that could use Isabella's talents and experience.

Our mood changing from despair to hope, we were quickly surfing websites and working it all out. There were major Californian wine companies who marketed their ranges into UK and Europe—the very markets Isabella knew so well. Business would have her coming back to London frequently, when she could keep in touch with her parents. Yes, she'd be moving away in the short term, but this would be balanced by important compensations.

"The way we're explaining it to her family is not so much my own offer, but more the opportunity for her. This is also her big chance to move into the industry she's always wanted to. And where she'll be fulfilling Julio's dream."

"An elegant solution." I can see the relief in his expression.

I smile. "For a while there I couldn't see any way forward for us. But we realized we can make it work for both of us."

"So when I call Acellerate in fifteen minutes, it's a yes?" Harry tilts forward in his chair, gesturing his phone.

I nod.

"Well done!" he's leaning over the desk and shaking my hand, a twinkle returning to his eye. "And well done to Isabella! I'm sure you've made the right choice. You're both on your way."

From the moment I give the official yes events move swiftly into overdrive. Within hours, a smiley-voiced HR lady from Acellerate has interrupted her L.A. weekend to talk to me about a relocation allowance, vehicle choices, health insurance and Medicare. She tells me about another Acellerate employee who is vacating a house on Rosewood Avenue, West Hollywood, less than twenty minutes drive-time from the office. Would I be interested in seeing some digital photos of the rental property?

As the news of my imminent departure spreads, I start getting calls from people I haven't spoken to for ages—in some cases, years. Some just want to confirm if the story they've heard is true, and there are some pretty wild stories out there. Like the one that I've been poached to work for the US military; or that I'm to be involved in some nanotech project run out of NASA; or that I've been made vice president of Acellerate.

Bill Blakely is a hot topic. Some regard him as the patron saint of nanotechnology, and want me to talk to him about funding their research program. Others think differently: do I know about Bill Blakely's track record as a rapacious asset-stripper? Do I realize how many talented researchers he's eaten up and spat out?

It's these calls that worry me the most. I know very little about Bill Blakely apart from the well-known fact that he's a charismatic entrepreneur who made his first fortune in the dot-com boom, before returning as a biotech buccaneer. Since then, he's set up Acellerate, attracted large sums of East coast venture capital, and is said to be gearing up Acellerate for a NASDAQ listing.

Later in the week I go upstairs to discuss things with Harry. Amid the crisp, string chords of a Baroque divertimento—he's obviously feeling better about things. He tells me to ignore everything I hear about Blakely unless it's first hand information. Before signing the partnership deal with Acellerate the year before, he appointed auditors to undertake due diligence, and they didn't turn up a thing on Blakely or Acellerate.

Harry's shrewdness as a deal-maker comes as a complete surprise. It's Harry who has negotiated the key conditions of my offer from Acellerate. It is he who has insisted my new position should be at director-level and that my pay should be consistent with that of other directors.

"What about IP?" I ask. As a researcher with the Imperial Science Institute, five percent of the value of all intellectual property I develop, remains mine. While currently this is an entirely theoretical value, when Nanobot is commercialized it could amount to a multi-million dollar fortune.

"All researchers' IP agreements are transferred to Acellerate," he confirms. "That was part of the deal we did with them last year."

When he puts a thick document in front of me to sign—the formal offer from Acellerate—he tells me that, officially, he is required to suggest I have the contract looked over by a lawyer.

"Officially?" I raise my eyebrows. We know each other far too well for that.

"I negotiated the document," he tells me, rapping his nicotine-stained fingers over the document. "It's water-tight."

"Good enough for me," I confirm, signing. "Though I'll take a copy away for the record."

——

ON THE HOME FRONT, AFTER ALL THE AGONIES OF THE WEEKEND, things have taken a turn for the better. The reaction of Isabella's father to our news is not as negative as we had feared. Julio said he was thrilled to hear Isabella's plans, believing that after she'd started on a career in the wine industry, there'd be no stopping her. Because he was so determined to remain positive about his own future, as well as hers, the fact that she'd be living in California for the next two years seems to be less of a worry than we had imagined.

Not that it was all smooth sailing. Isabella's mother had had different concerns.

"Do the two of you have a date?" she'd phoned back a short while later, when Julio was out of earshot. Isabella had her on speakerphone.

"Just as soon as we can wrap up our jobs—"

"Not a leaving date. A wedding date."

Isabella's face had darkened. "That's not something we've thought about."

"Well, if you want your father to walk you down the aisle, you *should* think about it."

Isabella had glared at the telephone.

"How are you going to arrange a wedding from thousands of miles away?" her mother's voice rose. "Don't you owe it to your father to be the wedding host while he still has all his faculties?"

Snatching the receiver off the base set, Isabella had stormed out the room and finished the conversation from our bedroom. She emerged a very short time later wearing a troubled expression I knew not to question.

The work situation also proves to be a challenge for Isabella. There's angst and outrage about her handing in her resignation so unexpectedly, and having invested so much energy in her job in recent years, she hates leaving the company under a cloud. In the weeks leading up to our departure she works even longer hours, taking on more responsibilities, trying her best to make everything right. Although she wants to spend more time online finding out all she can about the wine industry in California, there's not much left between work and weekends, which are more intensely family-focused than ever.

But she's managed to identify the grand dame of recruitment to the wine industry. San Francisco-based Marcia Schwartz has been at the heart of things for thirty years and maintains a high-profile presence. Isabella keeps coming across her name on different sites and trade journals. She puts a lot of effort into preparing an updated resume, making it as wine-friendly as possible, and sending it with a carefully written cover letter to the eminent Marcia.

Touching down at L.A. airport we are met by a limousine service, whisked out of the airport and onto a sixteen lane freeway, our first taste of the big, brash, auto-filled sprawl that is Los Angeles. Having decided to take the Rosewood Avenue house in West Hollywood, we watch the suburbs pass by with a sense of nervous anticipation. We're relieved when the limo pulls off La Cienega Boulevard into Rosewood, and we find ourselves in a street lined with tall, shady trees, trim-cut lawns, and neat, detached homes. Our place is a pretty, Spanish-style hacienda, with white plaster, wooden window shutters and a small front porch. As we arrive, lugging our overweight suitcases up the steps, we discover a paper plate, covered in a kitchen towel on the porch table. We lift the towel and find a bunch of glistening red grapes together with a scrap of white paper saying, "Welcome from neighbor."

"This is the very last thing I'd expected coming to L.A.," I shake my head, as I fish in my pocket for the front door key that had been mailed to me.

"Someone's got you pegged," Isabella smiles.

Red grapes are a big favorite of mine and the gift is not only a surprise but bizarrely well chosen. However in the flurry of our arrival, I don't have time to think about it.

We arrive late morning, and midway through that afternoon I have my first appointment at Acellerate with none other than the great Bill Blakely himself.

It's impossible not to contrast Acellerate headquarters with the Imperial Science Institute back in King's Cross, London. Instead of a grime-smudged Victorian building in utilitarian brickwork, Acellerate occupies a towering thirty floor cube of gleaming blue glass. The atrium's soaring roof and cascading water feature couldn't be more different from the low ceiling and battered wooden desk of the institute reception. I can't help smiling at the difference as my heels click across a highly-polished floor, inlaid with the Acellerate logo, before finally reaching a marble desk, and two immaculately made-up receptionists.

Within moments Bill Blakely's executive assistant, a power-dressed young woman in her late twenties who introduces herself as Casey Barrend, is ushering me through an impressive security system, comprising glass cubicles which can be exited only via palm-print recognition or a remote-controlled surveillance camera. Prompted for a code to access the penthouse floor, I notice that the number comprises four digits followed by the date.

After an ear-popping swift rise, we arrive in the penthouse quarters of the Acellerate boss. It's like stepping onto a private viewing platform with floor to ceiling windows providing a panoramic sweep across L.A., and a vast acreage of deep-pile carpet sprinkled with expensive, minimalist furniture. I notice two antique urns displayed on plinths—to my untrained eye they look as if they're ancient Chinese. And on one wall, glass-fronted cases display yellowing scrolls written in strangely alluring oriental script. Is Bill Blakely a collector of eastern antiquities? There's a further walk to a spiral staircase, which we ascend into his private eyrie—a glass-walled dome that crowns the Acellerate tower, and provides a three hundred sixty degree vantage of the city.

Blakely himself is working at his desk as we appear. But as soon as he sees us, he rises, and strides forward.

While I've seen media photos of Bill Blakely, none of these have prepared me for the face-to-face encounter. Tall, dark haired and glowing with good health, he is a more forceful presence in person than in his publicity shots. Everything about him just seems perfect, from the immaculate sweep of his dark hair, to the heavy-weave cotton shirt with its razor-pressed lines. In fact, he's almost too perfect, like a Hollywood actor playing the part of the heavy-hitting CEO.

Within moments I am sitting on a sofa opposite him, while he is congratulating me on Nanobot.

"We saw it as standout science from day one," he fixes me with penetratingly ice blue eyes. "Nanobot was one of the main reasons we wanted to form a partnership with ISI. But it needed funding."

I'm nodding vigorously.

"Harry's told you where we want to take Nanobot in the next two years?" he asks. But before I reply, he's already into rapid-fire delivery, "We've already assembled a fully-resourced team of specialists. Next step is for you to download every program metric, current and planned: every objective and challenge, every milestone of the development plan. We want to know every last detail going on in your head." He speaks in a way that makes me feel like a living treasure.

"We'll fast-forward the development program. Hit key milestones. Aim for a prototype in twelve months. I'm throwing the full weight of Acellerate's resources behind Nanobot. Why? Because it's one of the most exciting technologies on the planet."

Harry has told me much the same, but when Bill Blakely says it, it seems to carry more weight. Perhaps that has to do with the glass dome on top of the thirty floor tower, or the bronzed skin, clear-eyed conviction, and the knowledge that this man is already a billionaire several times over. In this moment it's easy to believe that Nanobot is poised to become a research program as significant as I've fantasized; that the program will be celebrated in the global research community and written up in Scientific American; that I'm set to achieve a whole new level of recognition as a research scientist.

"I read your master's thesis," leaning forward, elbows on his knees, he rapidly switches subject.

"Really?" I'm not only astonished and finding it hard to keep up with his mental gyrations, I'm also wondering if it's Bill or Mr. Blakely.

"Identifying kinetic drivers will be the most significant breakthrough for nanotechnology," he quotes, and I'm even more flattered. "You're quite right of course. But unlike most researchers who just talk about it, you've actually made progress."

"Thanks . . . Bill." I'm unused to this intensity of admiration.

"Tell me, there's something I've wanted to ask you in person ever since I came across your work," he fixes me with a look of intense personal interest. "What put you onto Nanobot?"

It's not the first time I've been asked the question, and the truth is that I stumbled into the area. But meeting Blakely's enthusiastic scrutiny, I don't want to let him down with a dull reply. "I've been interested in quantum science since I was a teenager," I tell him. "I found it exciting the way that quantum physics turns our whole idea of reality on its head. Then I heard about nanotechnology and I loved the paradox."

"What paradox?"

"That it's only now that we have the technological sophistication to be able to copy nature, and create things from the bottom up, rather than top down."

"What we're engaged in—" it's as though what I've said has propelled him to his feet with excitement, "is the most important purpose of our time. Knowledge is power, no doubting it, and the more revolutionary the knowledge, the greater the power."

Poised, mid-dome, against the backdrop of Beverly Hills, with the iconic Hollywood sign, faint and white in the distance, Bill Blakely has an intuitive sense of drama.

"Hiroshima not only ended World War II, it also confirmed the United States as a world superpower. And why?" he demands, "Because Hitler exported knowledge in the form of a small group of persecuted Jewish quantum scientists who knew how to unlock the power of the atom. Just imagine if he hadn't persecuted them, and Germany had developed the bomb. What very different lives we'd all be living!

"The point is, Matt, that wisdom is precious. Those who develop it, those who carry it forward and transmit it—*they* are the true heroes, not the leaders on whose watch their ideas are used."

From his look of approval, I have no doubt that I am among those he admires.

"My vision is for Acellerate to be the repository of the most significant knowledge in the world today. To develop the most transformational technologies. Most of all, to be the home of pioneers who are fulfilling a purpose that goes way beyond their own personal journeys, whose work will touch the lives of millions."

⁓

Bill Blakely has a way with words, no doubting it, and I arrive back on Rosewood Avenue on an all-time high to find that Isabella has her own cause for excitement. Having already hooked up her laptop to the phone system, she's found an e-mail in her in-box from Marcia Schwartz. Marcia says she finds Isabella's resume intriguing, and asks her to call the following morning to discuss her options.

"That's fantastic news!" I hug her. When she's on a high, Isabella feels things with a passion I find utterly compelling—I have never felt so emotionally bound to another person.

"The door-opener herself!" I congratulate Isabella.

"I know. I can't believe I got right through to her—"

"It was your résumé," I tell her. "All your hard work—"

"Don't know about that," Isabella is always quick to brush off compliments. "I think I just got lucky."

"You mean, she meant to e-mail someone else, but put your name in the address bar by mistake?" I pull a droll expression.

"Come," she takes my hand, leading me through the house.

In the hours I've been at Acellerate, Isabella has also visited the nearby Beverly Center and bought a whole lot of stuff to make the rental house our own. There's a richly-patterned throw and crimson scatter-cushions to brighten up otherwise plain-looking sofas in the lounge. She's got our iPod and docking station set up on a corner shelf and a vase with some flowers from the garden on the mantelpiece. One of the bedrooms has been converted to a study with laptop and phone lines all operational. And for the master bedroom she's bought a new duvet and pillow set in pleated burgundy and gold diamonds. "Very opulent" I say, glancing around the room. "I can't believe you've done all this in just a couple of hours."

"The bedding in the cupboard was pretty grungy. We had to get our own stuff," she says, though I can tell from her smile she's pleased with the result. "And I thought we should start as we mean to continue."

I catch the meaningful expression in her eye. Walking across to where the bedroom window overlooks a small, paved garden and shared swimming pool at the back, I draw down the wooden blinds, adjusting them so the late-afternoon sunlight falls in softly slatted shadows onto the bed.

Then both of us are stripping off our clothes, dumping them on the floor in our hurry to undress. There's simple lust, of course, the physical compulsion that's like the glue binding us together. But there's more to it. There's also the need to mark this moment—the novelty of our new home, our new life, our very adult bedroom in Los Angeles.

And there's also excitement. From the moment I came home with the Acellerate offer, we've been living with the trauma it caused for Isabella's family and work. But now, in this moment, it feels like all the negativity has lifted, and whole new worlds have opened up.

Isabella strips out of her underwear and kneels at the bottom of the bed, a celebratory glint in her eye. We search one another's bodies, mouths hungry for each other, craving a different kind of relief. To me, the taste of her at moments like these is the taste of sex. Hot. Briny. Insatiable. Until I climb on the bed next to her and her kisses descend my body, and she takes me in her mouth with uninhibited relish. I love her look of complete abandonment when she does this. It thrills me how she draws back the long, dark curtain of her hair especially so I can watch her every movement.

When she looks up into my eyes, mischievous and provocative, I can bear it no more. I tug her off me and throw her back on the bed.

"You know I can only take that so long until . . ."

"Until?" she taunts, legs sliding open as I kneel over her.

"I must have you."

Much later, in the middle of that first night, jet lag wakes me at three o'clock, and I decide to get up for a walk. I've done this sometimes back in London, walking round Clapham Common in the early hours when I've had too much on my mind to sleep. From what I've seen, West Hollywood seems a safe kind of neighborhood. Leaving Isabella sound asleep, after a celebratory dinner at a local restaurant, I slip on pants and a sweater and venture out.

I decide to make a circuit of just a few blocks, up to Melrose and back, and it's on the last part of the walk that I have the most unusual encounter. Attracted by the scent of a frangipani tree growing in a neighbor's garden, my footsteps come to a halt. I pause to study the flowers—delicate, five-petal stars—which grow in perfumed profusion, casting ribbons of ethereal fragrance in the darkness.

"They smell sweetest at night," says a voice from somewhere very close.

I'm startled to find I'm not alone and look through the monochrome shadows to see a face that's both foreign as well as oddly familiar. He is an older man, oriental, with a round, shaven head and open features. His smile is serene as the moon.

"Also having trouble sleeping?" I ask.

He steps towards me and it's only then I notice that he's wearing robes and sandals. In the moonlight his habit seems almost pitch black, except for the glow of saffron about his neck. I realize he is a Buddhist monk, and feel absurd having asked such a question.

But if he takes offense, he isn't showing it. "I usually get up at this time," he replies. "First meditation of the day in Tibetan monasteries."

I glance at my watch. "You have to get out of bed at three thirty?"

"It's optional," his eyes are mischievous. "You can start earlier if you like."

Then as I smile he says, "I began when I was very young. By my age," he shrugs, "it is just habit."

Studying him more closely, I wonder how old he is. His skin is clear and unlined, making it hard to guess, and his eyes convey a timeless luminosity. I have no idea why I sense a strange, intangible connection to him, but at the same time, for some unaccountable reason, find myself resisting it, as though I'm aware, at some level, that he knows everything about me. Or at least, everything that counts.

"So, you are having trouble sleeping?" he asks.

"Jet lag," I tell him. "Though I probably think too much about work."

He's nodding. "What kind of work?"

"I'm a scientist," I say. "Nanotechnology." I always add the qualifier when I want to avoid the subject. It's amazing what a conversation-stopper those six syllables can be.

But next to the frangipani tree, they have the opposite effect. "Nanotech. Excellent choice! I once went to a lecture by Richard Feynman."

I am astounded. I wouldn't have thought anyone outside quantum mechanics would have heard of Feynman. Especially not a monk.

"You came here from England, yes?" he asks, picking up on my accent.

"I was made an offer I couldn't refuse." It's the phrase I've routinely used to explain the move to friends and family back in England. But instead of the usual flush of pride, for the first time the words sound strangely self-centered. No doubt the monk's motivations for being here are very different.

"And you're here from—?"

"Tibet," he says. "Many of us went into exile in 1959."

It is more than my whole lifetime ago. "Why Los Angeles?" I ask.

The lightness that's never far from his features becomes a glowing smile, "To be here for you."

Disconcerted, I step back. For a moment I take his comment personally, before telling myself I have misunderstood. This isn't all about me. The only reason we're even talking is because, by coincidence, we live on the same street and it's the middle of the night and I've been stopped by the siren scent of the tropics.

"I help with the Dharma Center," he continues, gesturing behind him.

Suddenly I make the connection. "Was it you who gave us the grapes?"

He smiles, "That was Mrs. Min, the housekeeper."

"Please tell her thank you."

"Perhaps you can come to say hello? Mrs. Min would like to see you."

"Sure," I nod, bemused, wondering why an Asian housekeeper would want to meet me.

As I turn to head back home I ask, "Do you have any advice for the sleepless?"

The monk pauses for a while, considering this carefully before he says, "One thing can always be relied upon," he nods significantly, "change. In time, the causes for everything must alter or disappear. Even jet lag."

At the end of a first day in Los Angeles that has felt surreal, meeting a Tibetan Buddhist monk at three in the morning might have been the final, bizarre twist, but it doesn't feel that way. Instead there's been something profoundly reassuring about the encounter.

I think of his reply to my request for advice. He is right about the jet lag, of course. I'll acclimatize and within a few days I'll be well and truly on L.A. time. But what he'd said about change seems to have been phrased deliberately to apply to more than jet lag, and I wonder what else he intended by it. Was he intuitively responding to something else that was going on in my life?

Our lives?

After walking on a short distance I halt, turning round. But the monk has vanished, and the only movement in the garden is the white, fragile stars of frangipani trembling in a midnight breeze.

Chapter Four

THE VERY NEXT EVENING I RETURN HOME TO FIND ISABELLA DIS-traught. Her phone call to Marcia Schwartz, far from opening new horizons, has left her red-eyed and anguished.

"I thought she was intrigued by your résumé?" I ask, shaken by her distress.

"She was intrigued. She liked my London experience. The pan-European campaigns. But she thought I wanted a job in San Francisco."

"Surely someone like her must be just as well connected in the L.A. wine industry?"

"That's just it," Isabella turns to face me tearfully. "There isn't an L.A. wine industry."

Putting down a folder of overnight reading, I feel suddenly hollow. "But surely—"

"Not according to Marcia Schwartz. And she should know." Isabella twists her engagement ring. "I feel like such a fool for not finding out all this before I came. I mean, that was supposed to be my job. Understanding foreign markets. Marcia says the best I could hope for in L.A. is some kind of sales rep job. . ."

I step over to hold her. Along with the shock, an unexpected burden of responsibility descends, with a sudden, dead weight. But Isabella doesn't respond and stands stiffly resistant to my embrace.

After a few moments I back away. "Marcia Schwartz may be one of the best agents, maybe even the best," I tell her. "But there'll be other agents with different points of view."

"What Marcia told me isn't a matter of opinion, Matt." Isabella only ever uses my name when she's upset. "It's not like the whole industry will relocate to Los Angeles just because I speak to someone else."

"That's not—"

"Besides, I already have spoken to other people today. Over ten of them. And they all say the same thing. Our great idea about me realizing Papa's dream, trying to convince him about his legacy—it's all just a crock!" Her tearful expression is so intense it seems to burn. "That plan for me to gallivant off to Europe four times a year—that's all bullshit, too. Marcia says that if wine company execs get to London once a year they're doing well."

I know she's just venting, but it's hard to avoid taking this personally.

"Resigning from Bertollini to come here has been the biggest mistake of my career!" she blazes. "A total wild goose chase!"

"You can't say that at the end of one day."

"After the day I've had I bloody well can say that! It's just been wishful thinking. An uninformed decision. I've thrown everything away for nothing but a pipe dream!"

THINGS ARE SO TENSE THAT WE HARDLY SPEAK FOR THE REST OF THAT evening. And next morning when I get up to go to work, Isabella stays in bed. The days that follow are increasingly pressured for me at Acellerate, where I discover there is no honeymoon period for settling in—only long hours, relentless meetings, and huge volumes of material to absorb at the end of each working day.

Returning home in the evenings feeling exhausted, it's to find Isabella distracted, regretful and remote. She has always been ultra-organized, and I know she leaves no stone unturned in her efforts to find a solution to the painful reality that, for her purposes at least, we're living in the wrong city. And all the time is the unspoken knowledge that she would never have given up her high-flying job, or left the side of a much-loved and ailing father, if it hadn't been for me.

Things come to a head at the end of that first week. I can tell from the moment I step through the door of the spare room Isabella uses as an office that we're in for a stormy night. She's sitting at her desk in a tracksuit, face drawn and hair pulled back in a pony tail. She doesn't look up, but announces,

"I just can't make it work here."

"We've been here in L.A. less than a full week. We didn't know anyone when we arrived—"

"But I've spoken to enough people," she's shaking her head and refusing to meet my eyes. "Same feedback. I'm in the wrong place for the wine industry. I hate this place!"

"You can't say that!"

What I should do is let go of this one, let her have her say. But I'm wound-up with everything that's going on at Acellerate. It's been a punishing week of late nights and intensive meetings which nothing in my previous experience has prepared me for. "We don't even know L.A.!" I yank the tie away from my neck, and tug open the top button. "There could be all kinds of opportunities—"

It shocks me to see that her desk, usually covered in carefully-ordered paperwork, is now empty. Isabella has never been a quitter.

"It's nothing like I expected. There's nothing here for you unless you're some showbiz wannabe or high-tech propeller head."

"What about the soft drinks industry. Or vodka."

"What about it?" she shoots back. She's still not looking at me.

"Maybe you could get into a Bertollini-style job until—"

"I didn't come here to continue what I was doing in London."

"I know you didn't—"

"I came to broaden my horizons."

I walk over to the window, staring out into the darkness for a long while. As always, I find it hard to see beyond the fact that it's only because of me that she's in this situation. Finally I say, "Maybe we need to do some lateral thinking."

"Yes," she agrees, bleakly.

I turn to meet her eyes, but she only glances at me briefly before turning back to face the wall. It seems we concur on something, but I have an uneasy feeling that our interpretations of "lateral thinking" may turn out to be very different. Responding to the certainty in her voice I say, "You have something in mind?"

She nods. "Doesn't pay anything, but combined with my marketing experience it could lead somewhere. It's a wine training program run by the Californian wine industry."

"Sounds good." It's taking me a moment to process, but if it's something definite and she wants to do it. "In fact, sounds fantastic!"

Even now she won't face me. "Thing is, like everything else, the wine program is up in Napa Valley."

"What?"

"I first heard about it on Wednesday. When I phoned, they told me it was booked out months ago—they only have these intensive programs once a year. I insisted they take my name anyway. Then this morning I got a call saying there'd been a last minute cancellation and I should get my paperwork in by lunchtime. I did. And I'm in."

"Tight deadline?"

"That's just it. The program starts on Sunday."

"On Sunday you're . . . leaving?"

"It is residential," she's still looking determinedly away.

So this is what it's all about. "For how long?"

"Six months. They concentrate what normally takes two years into a six month intensive."

"I thought the whole point of coming here was . . ."

In the heat of the moment I'm finding it hard to separate reasons from justifications. In the long pause that follows she has to look at me, and when she does she sees my shock.

"This is one of the premier wine making courses, and not just in America," she's insistent. "People fly in from all over the world. It's something I could never have done in London."

I should, of course, accept the inevitable. Get over my shock and come to terms with the change of plan. But along with the shock and the stress, an unexpected resentment wells up inside me. Nothing I'm proud of. Nothing I won't look back at later and wish, with all my heart, that I could change. But the anger is suddenly there. "Sounds to me like a *fait accompli.*"

"I did try calling you this morning, but you were in meetings."

I'd been in sessions all day, that much was true.

"I had to get the forms in by lunchtime."

Turning, about to go through to the kitchen, I say. "Seems like you've already made your decision."

"I hoped you'd be happy for me!" The words come out highly charged.

But happiness isn't something I'm feeling right now. "Just seems there's one rule for you and another for me."

"What do you mean?!"

She knows exactly what I mean, but I don't hesitate to remind her. "You were mighty pissed off when I bought that holiday in the Bahamas without talking to you. And that was just a ten day holiday."

"I *did* call this morning," she's defensive.

"Anyway, how do you know there aren't other courses? Other opportunities?"

"Like what?"

"For all you know, there's a whole bunch of other courses right here. Have you tried calling universities in L.A.?"

"If there are, I haven't heard of them," she's defiant. "I've been in touch with all the agents I can find, and none of them mentioned any. But they all rate the Napa program."

There's a pause before I shrug. "Well, that's just great," I say, before starting towards the kitchen.

"Don't walk away before we've had a chance to discuss things." There's softness in her tone, an as yet unspoken regret to which I know I should respond.

But I don't. "Sounds like there's nothing to discuss. You've already made up your mind. You just want me to say it's alright to go."

"Well, isn't it?" her voice hardens.

"We're supposed to make the big decisions together, right?" Going through to the kitchen, I open the fridge and pull out a Corona. "That's how relationships work."

"I thought relationships were about compromise," she storms after me. "Like giving up your job, and leaving your family when they need you most, and moving to another country because your partner gets a career break."

I twist the screw cap off the beer and flick it in the dustbin, "At least we talked about it first."

"Yeah, right," she's standing, hands on hips. "Like you'd have turned them down because of me."

"I didn't ask you to give up everything." It's a lame argument, and I know it.

"But I did," her eyes are green with rage. "For you. Now all I'm asking by way of return is a few months out."

"Go on the bloody course, then!" I yell. "Just don't expect me to jump up and down about it."

"And don't you expect me to jump up and down about staying engaged to you, when you can't commit!" Pulling the engagement ring off her finger, she slams it on the kitchen counter.

"What the hell are you talking about?" her theatrics infuriate me. "I offered to marry you when we talked about all this."

"And real romantic that was, too. Just like when you got down on bended knee and proposed to me."

"I don't have the energy for this crap!" storming past her, I flop down in the lounge and flick on the TV.

Not only do I handle Friday night badly. I don't patch things up with her the next day either. Both of us are determined we're right. Stubborn. Dumb. The two of us hardly speak to each other until Sunday morning, when a cab arrives to take her to the airport, and suddenly she's wheeling her suitcase out of the house. There's so many things that should have been said which haven't been. The engagement ring still sits on the kitchen counter, exactly where she left it.

By then it's too late. And in the early hours of the following morning I find myself helplessly out of control. Face down on a cold, hard surface, I'm struggling to get onto my knees, desperate to halt my slide towards an unknown but terrifying fate. My heart pounds as I scramble, arms and legs flailing for a foothold. Searching for something, *anything* to cling to.

But I'm powerless to avoid the unseen forces acting on me. I just can't stop sliding, further and further. Frantic though I am to clamber up, it's all I can do to lift my head from the slippery surface. To glance around me, trying to make sense of what's happening.

But all that I become aware of is the pitch darkness that envelopes me. And the howling. Low and malevolent. An unnerving portent which, from the moment I become aware of it, makes my skin crawl.

Now I'm jolting even further. I know I'm about to cross beyond the point of no return. My survival depends on halting right here. Right now. But I've been sliding for too long and it's much, much too late. Thrashing about me, panic stricken, I feel myself sliding over some unknown threshold. Tumbling into darkness. Freefalling into oblivion. I have never been so afraid.

I wake up, sweating, the sheets twisted about me. Getting up I go to the kitchen, turn on the light and swig orange juice out of a carton from the fridge. I try to reassure myself it's only a dream. But where does it come from and what does it signify? Most especially—why now?

MEANTIME, THE SCHEDULE AT ACELLERATE CONTINUES AT ITS INTENSIVE pace. Week two continues in much the same way as the first week—wall-to-wall sessions in which I brief the ten, youthful and high-powered members of the Nanobot team on each aspect of the program. With specialists in microbiology, nano-engineering, kinetic science, you name it, the team members are among the brightest and best of their generation. And Acellerate is paying every one of them top dollar to work on Nanobot. It's the kind of situation I would have fantasized about, back in London. But now that it's actually happening, I'm discovering the downside: Nanobot is no longer my own baby.

Be careful what you set your heart on, runs the old cliché, and it's starting to feel that way with Nanobot. Instead of knowing every aspect of the program inside out, there are soon whole modules of research from which I'm marginalized. As though to underline the point, my office—impressive, glass-walled and elegantly appointed as it is—is two floors removed from the rest of the Nanobot team.

Then there's Dan Stenner. Hyper-bright, bursting with energy and so full of respect for my work it's sometimes embarrassing. Of all the Nanobot team he's the one whose job I understand least. "Project overseer" was how Bill Blakely had pitched him to me on my first day. "Your right hand man," is how Dan himself describes his role. He's shadowed me to every meeting, works two floors below with the rest of the team, and has already produced more updates, timelines and milestone calendars than I ever knew existed. It feels like control of my own project is slipping away from me.

BY THE FRIDAY NIGHT AT THE END OF MY FIRST WEEK WITHOUT Isabella, I find myself reflecting how very swiftly and dramatically my life has changed. Returning to the emptiness of the house on Rosewood, I'm struck by the recognition, as though for the first time, that there can be no going back—not to the way things were with Nanobot, nor with Isabella. The London chapter of our lives is over. Like my neighborly monk said, the only thing you can be sure of is change.

Feeling weary from a week of disrupted sleep, recurring nightmares and the threat of oblivion which has spilled over into my waking hours, I go to the fridge to collect a beer. As I open the door, I remember our heated exchange in this same room two weeks before. Since then, and Isabella's trip to Napa, we've exchanged a few e-mails and spoken by phone twice. The first time she'd called to give me her contact details. Neither of us, still too stubborn and proud, had apologized for our behavior, but the knot of tension I'd felt in my stomach, from the moment she'd announced her plans to go away, began to relax. At least we were talking.

Isabella had told me she was sharing a small, cheap flat on the outskirts of Napa with a French student, Collette. Work pressure would be intense, and they'd been told to expect many late nights at the study center. She'd been assigned to a study group led by an Italian called Paolo. I'd asked her where she was studying, how far she'd be traveling, what she'd be doing on her course. After the break in communication, the first in our three-year relationship which had lasted any length of time, it was a relief to know we were in contact again. The communication breakdown had been a jolting reminder of just how much she meant to me, and how closely enmeshed her life was with mine. I never wanted to go through that again.

At the end of the call I'd told her that I loved her. After a moment's hesitation, she'd said the same thing to me. Some of the familiar warmth had returned to her voice, which made me feel better. I knew it would take more than a long-distance phone call and a few endearments to repair the damage. But at least we seemed to be on the right track. Maybe, when she came back to L.A., she'd put the engagement ring back on. Maybe we could even set a date.

The mood of the second call had been quite different. I'd phoned Isabella last night at about nine. She'd only just ended a disturbing conversation with her mother. Although Julio had embraced his healthy new lifestyle with confidence, believing he could keep his disease at bay, two nights earlier the family had gone out to their local Thai restaurant, ordering all their usual dishes, when Julio had been unable to remember the wine he always ordered.

"What would you like to drink?" he'd apparently asked Isabella's mother.

"Just the usual," Tina had replied.

No one who'd ever dined with Julio at that particular restaurant was in any doubt about the varietals he believed were the best complement to spicy food. And for years, in that particular restaurant, he'd always faithfully ordered the Brookwood Sauvignon Semillon Blanc, an Australian wine. But two nights ago he'd studied the wine list as though for the first time before turning to Tina and asking, with evident rising panic, "What *is* the usual?"

He'd been peculiarly quiet for the rest of the evening, and in a state of depression ever since. And as if all this wasn't enough, Tina had opened a recipe book that evening, to prepare the family meal, when she'd discovered a pile of utility bills jammed in the front. Julio had always been responsible for paying the bills, and had been meticulous in doing so. Keeping all the paperwork in his home office, the discovery of the invoices, some of which were overdue, came as another shock. It also left Tina in a dilemma. She didn't want to mention the bills to Julio and only make him feel worse. But if she quietly took over paying the utilities, would she be risking a more harmful confrontation with him later?

"I'm really worried for Mum," Isabella had told me the night before, her voice strained. "If Dad continues to unravel like this, their lives are going to change drastically. I don't know how she's going to cope."

"But the doctors said it would be like this," I tried to reassure. "They said he sometimes might forget the most obvious things, but that didn't mean there'd be a permanent change."

At the other end of the phone, Isabella didn't sound convinced. What we were talking about, although we weren't acknowledging it, had direct implications for us. When we left London we'd agreed that if Julio's condition deteriorated suddenly, Isabella may have to return home. Julio's optimism and our own hopes had meant we'd pushed these fears to one side. But there could be no escaping the implications.

Now I sit alone on the front porch, watching the Friday night traffic cruise down Rosewood Avenue. I've tried watching TV, channel-hopping from a grim documentary on climate change, through a news special on suicide bombers, the raucous laugh track of a sitcom, then onto a business interview on instability in global markets. Overwhelmed by what's on offer, I can't watch any of it. Instead, on my own at the end of the week, I'm struck by a sudden sense of loneliness, as unexpected as it is deeply familiar. I'm taken back to the time, before I met Isabella and was still new to London, when I would return home to my Clapham flat at the end of the week, and watch the traffic crawling round Clapham Common. It feels now, as it felt then, that everyone else had homes to return to, lovers to make love to, parties and dinners and weekend pleasures to look forward to. Those were the things that made all the hard work worthwhile. Lovers, friends, family—didn't they give life its true purpose?

Once again I find myself like the small boy with his face pressed to the sweet shop window, looking inside at everyone else enjoying the good things. Only this time it feels worse because, unlike my early days in London, I know what it's like to love someone with every part of my being, and to feel completely loved in return. To share an intimacy so close that there are no thoughts, no secrets we haven't shared.

To make love with such abandon I don't like to recall even moments of it now, because it's just too painful to remember what I'm missing.

And, it seems from our latest conversation, I'm now at risk of losing it all permanently. Because if things continue to get worse for Julio, I know that nothing will keep Isabella from returning to London when her course finishes. Even if I decide to sacrifice my work with Acellerate to go back with her, it'll be to a different relationship than the one we had before. One that comes with no guarantees.

As the night gets cooler and I finish a second, then a third bottle of beer, I'm no closer to finding an answer. Exhausted before I even sat down on the porch, after three beers I surrender to fatigue.

——

Next morning, Saturday, there's laundry to be taken care of. Normally, it's something I would have left to Isabella, but without her I've had to come up with my own plan of action. Norbert's Launderette is located just a few blocks away and, according to the jauntily-written window notice, it provides a same-day wash, dry and iron service. What could be easier?

I decide to take a ride down there in my favorite perk of the Acellerate job—the sleek, silver, Mercedes 230 SLK which still makes me smile when I look at it with the pride of ownership. There's not only a basket load to get out to the car, there are also several bin liners full. Placing these carefully behind the driver and passenger seats, as I stand back to close the car door, out the corner of my eye I see a hand waving. I'm being beckoned from the porch next door. Quickly remembering my conversation with the monk, I realize I'm being summoned to meet Mrs. Min.

It was Mrs. Min who had arranged the "Welcome from neighbor" grapes, for which I have yet to thank her. During the past five weeks, when I've left for work in the mornings, I've noticed the constant presence on the front porch of the elderly Asian lady who sits in a crimson shawl, back as straight as a dowager empress. I haven't been actively trying to avoid her, but neither have I felt any great inclination to make contact. She's an elderly Asian lady—what is there to say?

Nevertheless, I decide to do the neighborly thing. I walk round to see her, telling myself this will only take a few minutes.

I am greeted at the steps by another middle-aged Asian lady, all smiles and laughter, who ushers me with some ceremony over towards the end of the porch. Mrs. Min is sitting in a sturdy cane chair and two things make an immediate impression. The first is the upright posture I have noticed when driving past, lending her an aura of almost regal dignity. The second is the curiously penetrating quality of her dark eyes, which I feel fixed on me from the moment I step onto the porch.

As I approach her, I notice that her face is very lined, her silver hair pinned in a neat bun. She is collecting up a tartan blanket from her knees which she passes to the other woman.

"Please don't get up," I gesture. But she ignores this and steps towards me.

Extending my hand to her, instead of shaking it, she holds it to her heart with both of hers. She studies me with an intensity I find surprising, before breaking into a smile. Then turning to the other woman she speaks in rapid Tibetan.

"Mrs. Min says how tall you are," the translator tells me with a giggle.

I've never thought of myself as especially tall, but it's true that I tower over her diminutive figure.

Mrs. Min is reluctant to let go of my hand and gestures that I should sit beside her. This is not what I've had in mind, but I suppose Norbert's Launderette will still be there in five minutes.

"Thank you very much for the grapes," I say, waiting for it to be translated.

There's a searching intimacy in Mrs. Min's eyes which I find uncomfortable.

"Mrs. Min wants to know if your parents live in the town or the country?"

"In a small village in Hampshire, England." I reply, somewhat surprised by the question. "My father died, but Mum's still in Hampshire. I moved to London when I was eighteen."

"What year was that?"

"1990."

No sooner is this relayed than Mrs. Min has another enquiry, "What kind of food do you like?"

Food, I wonder, taken aback. Strange question to be asked by someone from a different culture, a different age, whom you've only just met. Though as I answer, I smile, "All kinds. But especially red grapes."

This is translated for Mrs. Min whose expression remains unreadable. Then she reaches over and touches my shirt. It's a sweatshirt I have worn during the week and picked up off the floor to wear to the launderette.

"Mrs. Min," explains the translator, "says we will do your washing."

They must have seen me ferry the basket and bin liners to the car, I think. While I am surprised by the offer, I am also pleased by it. What could be more convenient than having someone next door to do my laundry?

"You bring your washing here this morning," continues the translator, "we have finished by tomorrow morning."

"Do you do this . . . washing service for other people?" I ask.

The translator creases with laughter, replying without saying anything to Mrs. Min. "No, no! This is a present from Mrs. Min."

"I must pay you."

"Oh no!" There is more laughter and an exchange between the two women. "Mrs. Min says payment is not necessary."

I have no plans to become a charity case, and intend finding out the going rate. But all the same I can't help wondering about Mrs. Min's motivations. Why would she make the offer?

A short while later, I am transferring the laundry basket and bin-liners from car to the neighbors, taking them through the house to the kitchen.

It's a modest house, wooden floorboards worn but polished, and in the hallway, a neat row of shoes. Following the translator's lead, I add mine to the row before venturing further, walking through a small dining room and kitchen to a laundry area, which is clean and tidy, if austere. I wonder where the monk has his bedroom and if the translator lady lives here, too.

On our return outside, we find Mrs. Min standing in the porch, neat as a petite, porcelain antique. Ordering the translator back inside on an errand, she gestures me to stand beside her, taking my hand in hers again and nodding with a smile.

While we stand there, I feel a brushing against my legs and look down to see an exotic-looking cat, with long, cream-colored fur, a charcoal face, and two startlingly sapphire-blue eyes, staring up at me.

"Tashi," Mrs. Min tells me.

"Tashi," I repeat, bending down to stroke her. I'm not generally a cat person, but Tashi is particularly beautiful, and friendlier than most.

Moments later, the translator has reappeared carrying a shoe box.

"Mrs. Min would like you to have a small gift," she says, taking off the lid and holding it towards me. "You choose."

Again, I'm taken aback by the unexpected generosity. But I don't want to cause offense. Perhaps this is some sort of cultural exchange carried out between new neighbors back home in Tibet. I peer into the box and find an odd assortment of items. A small bell with a brass handle. A bar of chocolate. A necklace of wooden beads.

Tempted though I am by the chocolate, which happens to be a favorite brand, I opt for the necklace, lifting it from the box and holding it up to the light. It's not the kind of necklace Isabella usually wears—she's more gold and diamonds than ethnic Asian. But there's something about the beads that I like, and perhaps she'll be drawn to them too, and the quirky way I was given them.

"Can I have this one?" I ask Mrs. Min.

She and the translator are both nodding, laughing. Distracted by a movement behind them, I turn to see the monk standing at the door. Just like the first time we met, I feel a sense of immediate warmth the moment I see him, coupled with a curious hesitation about engaging with him.

"Mrs. Min has offered you a gift?" he has a lively expression.

"Yes. A necklace. My . . . fiancée might like to wear it."

"Not for wearing," he corrects me. "This is a mala. For counting mantras."

"A rosary?" I run the beads through my hands, surprised. I don't know any mantras and certainly don't plan on counting any. But the wood beads have a pleasantly soothing effect.

As a new group of visitors open the gate and make their way up the pathway, Mrs. Min bows in farewell, before returning with her translator friend to the other end of the porch.

I step back. "Well, I'll be on my way," I tell the monk.

"Where to?"

I'm surprised by the question and think quickly. In reality, I'd been planning just to go home, but now I say "Urth Caffé," before continuing after a pause, "Would you like to come?"

It's a calculated offer, because I don't think he'll say yes. Monks aren't supposed to be into worldly pleasures, are they? He probably has a few thousand mantras to chant himself before lunch time.

But to my surprise, he nods. "That would be very nice! But only if you can afford to. Monks don't have their own money."

"That's okay." I stand, uncertain for a moment, before he makes a gesture, implying we should leave.

"I don't know your name?" he says, as he comes to where I'm stepping onto the sidewalk.

"I'm Matt. And what should I—"

"Students call me Geshe-la," he says.

We set off down Rosewood Avenue in the dappled sunlight. It's a clear, blue morning and I feel self-conscious walking next to a Tibetan Buddhist monk in full get-up.

"How's the jet lag?" asks Geshe-la.

"Over," I nod. I wonder what to talk about. What do you say to a Buddhist monk? Most of the usual topics of conversation aren't going to work. In a way I feel there's no place to go except to the essentials. Which may be why a part of me wants to hold back.

Some while on I finally tell him, "I've been thinking about how you said the causes for everything must change or disappear. Bit depressing though, isn't it?"

"Oh," A smile twitches about the corners of his lips. "Why is that?"

"Because no matter how hard you try to be happy, to get a great job, or hold together a good relationship, something will come along to change things."

"Of course!" Geshe-la is chuckling. "This is our experience of life. But it doesn't have to be depressing."

"How could it not be?" I'm slightly irked that he's not taking me seriously.

"Because those things you just mentioned—jobs, relationships—they are not true causes of happiness."

"Of course they are!" My voice rises in indignation as I remember Isabella and how we were that last time together. Making love with the evening sunlight filtering through the wooden blinds. Her urgent cries as we'd both reached the point of no return. Probably Geshe-la has never felt the rapture of passion, but he can't tell me it doesn't exist.

But his conversation takes an unexpected turn. "When you apply heat to water," he says, "this is a true cause of steam. Agreed?"

I shrug, wondering what this has to do with anything.

"It doesn't matter who applies the heat to the water, or how often the heat is applied, or whether the heat is applied in Los Angeles or London. Heat applied to water will always produce steam; this is a true cause."

"Okay."

"Tell me, do you know any object that will always give happiness no matter who has it, where they have it, when they have it, or how many of them they already have?"

As my mind races to respond, he continues, "When it comes to relationships, do you know any person who always, unfailingly, gives only happiness and bliss?"

I remember Isabella's announcement about Napa. Slamming her engagement ring on the counter. The way we'd hardly spoken all weekend. How, two weeks later, our relationship has moved into a different key.

The way Geshe-la puts it, there's no way on earth I can say that Isabella is a true cause of happiness. As we reach the traffic lights at Melrose I look over at him, startled by how swiftly and calmly he has demolished my argument.

Much more than that, how he has exposed so many of the assumptions by which I live.

——

A SHORT WHILE LATER WE ARE SITTING AT A TABLE INSIDE URTH CAFFÉ. It's a hip and happening kaleidoscope of New Age types and nouveau riche, of tourists and locals. And like so many places in this part of town, it's the kind of place where people are always looking over their shoulder, half expecting someone famous or semi-famous to show up wanting a latté.

As we sit down with our mugs of Rainforest organic coffee, I am impatient to continue.

"If what you're saying is true—" it's hard finding the right words, "why does everyone chase after the same stuff? I mean, *why isn't* a great job or a girlfriend a true cause of happiness?"

"And money," jokes Geshe-la. "You left out Westerners' route number one to happiness." Across the table his eyes twinkle indulgently. "You're the quantum scientist."

I frown. What has quantum physics got to do with it?

"Tell me . . . Matt," as he uses my name for the first time there is a mischievous glint in his eye, "you have studied quantum science from a young age, yes?"

I nod. As a kid I'd had an aptitude for science and a particular fascination for quantum physics. So great was my enthusiasm that late at night, after lights out, I'd stay awake reading books on quantum theory under the sheets with the aid of a flashlight. For hour after hour I'd memorize this definition, that theory, the teachings of all the great teachers from Einstein to Richard Feynman.

"And what would you say is the essence of quantum theory?" Geshe-la asks now.

"I suppose," I say, unsettled by his conversational ambushes, "that the idea of substantial reality is an illusion."

"Very good!"

"Quantum scientists have shown that atoms are only energy that briefly condense into a particle, before dissolving back again into energy."

"So," he wants to confirm. "No object has any real substance?"

"That's right."

"Everything around us has the possibility of forming in a particular way, or maybe not?"

"Correct. Like a field of possibilities instead of solid things."

"So nothing has intrinsic qualities of its own?"

"Not at all." I am surprised he gets this so quickly. I have given the same explanation to family and friends, and most of them need to hear it four or five times before they even begin to make sense of it.

Geshe-la pauses before saying, "That's astonishing, isn't it? Everything we see and touch—"

"Is like an illusion," I finish for him. Then remembering a student textbook, "As Niels Bohr said, 'Those who are not shocked when they first come across quantum theory cannot possibly have understood it.'"

It is only as I say the words, that I realize why Geshe-la wanted me to explain quantum physics. And for the first time I begin to realize that his mind goes way beyond anything I might have imagined when I'd first met him. The simple robes and benign smile have had me fooled. The reason why neither Isabella, nor anyone—or anything—else, can be a true cause of happiness, is because they have no intrinsic qualities.

"Buddhism says exactly the same thing," says Geshe-la. "Nothing in this world has any inherent existence."

"What you're saying," I want to get this straight, "is that my girlfriend, Isabella, isn't a true cause of happiness because she has no happiness-causing characteristics?"

"You are a very good student!" beams Geshe-la.

"But sometimes she makes me happy."

"Where does that happiness come from?"

"That's what I'm asking you!"

"There's only one place it can come from." He leans over the table, all his attention focused on me so that it feels like his knowledge is being transmitted by more than words alone. "If nothing around us has any genuine substance, then all the happiness or unhappiness we feel comes from our mind. All qualities, attractive and unattractive, are a product of mind alone."

Even while discussing a serious subject there is a lightness, a pliancy about Geshe-la, that makes everything seem somehow simple.

"You and I can experience the same thing, listen to the same music, watch the same movie, but we react in different ways."

These are amazing ideas, I think, with life-changing implications.

"It's not what's going on out there that makes us happy or unhappy," he says. "It's what's going on in here," he touches his head. *"It's not what happens to you that matters, but the way you interpret things."*

"I like to tease my students about how superstitious Westerners are," it's as though he's admitting me into his confidence. "They all believe there's a direct connection between what's going on around them and the way that they feel. We all need to free ourselves of this superstition. We need to discover for ourselves that happiness and unhappiness are a projection over which we can take control."

When Geshe-la talks, everything he says seems to make perfect sense. But I know there's a lot to think about. In particular, I'm amazed by the way that everything he says parallels with quantum science. As though the mysticism of Tibet and contemporary physics, the essential truths carried by the two, persecuted groups of German Jews and Tibetan Buddhists are converging in the same place.

And in a strange, intuitive way I can't account for, I feel as though I've been particularly positioned to make this connection.

— —

The full convergence between Geshe-la's insights and the work that I do is one that has yet to occur; though it is about to receive a dramatic push forward. The very next week I'm behind my elegant ash desk at Acellerate when an e-mail arrives from the svelte and soigné Casey Barrend, Bill Blakely's executive assistant. There's an important presentation to Acellerate's venture capital investors next week, she tells me, at which a review of the company's main research platforms is to be presented. She's attached a copy of the PowerPoint slides and asks me to review slides 28–35, which deal with Nanobot.

It's the first I've heard of the presentation, and I'm disconcerted that material on my own research program has been drafted without me. Working my way through the seven Nanobot slides, however, I am impressed. The main commercial outcomes of the program have been presented with precision and impact. Milestones are well-summarized, and progress is reported in a balanced but upbeat style, along with glowing endorsements of the program that I didn't even know existed.

Flicking through slides for some of the other programs I see the same high level of professionalism is maintained. The Bill Blakely touch, no doubt. I can see him keeping a roomful of investors spell-bound with his smoothly delivered lines and dramatic timing.

It occurs to me, however, that the presentation is too long for a single person to present. And it's when I click back to the start of the presentation, that I'm dazed and bewildered. The second slide, after the title, lists four presenters. Bill Blakely plus the leaders of each of Acellerate's flagship research programs. The head of Nanobot is listed as Dan Stenner.

It's a mistake, of course. And in moments I'm working out what's going on. Dan probably sent Casey Barrend material on Nanobot for the presentation. She's assumed he runs the program, and has listed him at the front instead of me.

But it's unsettling to discover I'm supposed to be delivering an investor's presentation in a few days' time. Public speaking, especially with such an important audience, is something I like to be well prepared for.

Picking up the phone, I dial Blakely's Executive Assistant.

"The slides on Nanobot look great," I tell her. "But I've spotted an error on page two."

"Uh-huh?" she registers skepticism along with surprise.

"Head of Nanobot is named as Dan Stenner."

"That's his job title, isn't it?"

I'm surprised by the cool return. Surely she knows what I'm doing here? "I don't know what his official title is," I explain. "But I'm the director. He's a project coordinator."

"I'll check with Bill and get back to you," she tells me, hanging up.

Getting up from my desk, I walk across the office staring, unseeing, across Beverly Hills. It's ridiculous to be unnerved by a twenty-something girl who knows little about the program. But the assurance with which she demanded "That's his job title, isn't it?" makes me question myself. Not for the first time I find myself wondering about the day to day activities of Dan Stenner, two levels below me. And what the hell his job title really is. Am I naïve not to have questioned it earlier?

Stepping back to my desk, I check the internal telephone directory, but there's no job title listed there. Clicking onto the Acellerate website, the only mention of him is as one of the Nanobot team. My own profile identifies me as a director.

But then a new thought registers. An idea which makes sudden, awful sense.

What if Bill Blakely is just using me? What if he's brought me over, taken my program off me, and put his own, blue-eyed boy in charge? What if this whole thing has been a ploy to take over Nanobot in such a way that by the time I've realized what's happening, it's already too late?

Moments later my e-mail in-box is registering a delivery from Casey Barrend. It's just half a line long. "Bill has confirmed Dan Stenner job title," it says.

I stare at the screen, scarcely able to believe what I'm seeing. No room for ambiguity now. I remember how Blakely had introduced Dan Stenner as Nanobot's "co-ordinator"; how Stenner has sat in on every meeting I've attended, every project download I've given. Meantime the high-sounding title and office that have been lavished on me are meaningless. All part of the same, perverse plan.

But if Blakely thinks I'm just going to roll over, he's very much mistaken. Whatever else's happened, I still own five percent of Nanobot's IP. My name is on the international patents. And he can forget cherry-picking any more ideas from the Imperial Science Institute.

Temper rising, I stride from my office to the elevators, step inside the first one and hit the penthouse button. I'm immediately prompted for a code. Recalling the four digit number used by Casey Barrend on my very first day, I follow it with today's date. In moments I'm heading swiftly upwards.

Blakely's PA looks up from behind her desk in surprise as the elevator doors slide open.

"Got to see Bill," I tell her, heading towards the spiral staircase.

She jumps to her feet. "You can't just go up!" she calls after me, her tone a mix of consternation and anger.

"Watch me!"

I don't care how big a name Bill Blakely is. How many billions he's worth. What he's doing right now. If he thinks he's pulling a stunt like this on me, he's seriously mistaken.

Though as I glance out the penthouse floor windows, instead of the eagle's eye sweep across L.A. I saw the first time here, I feel stabbed at the heart by a very different sensation. The sheer, vertiginous sides of the office tower take me to the threshold of my recurring nightmare. The point beyond which I find myself tumbling into the sudden, dark maw of oblivion.

What if the dream hasn't been a reaction to what's gone before in my relationship with Isabella? What if, instead, it is a horrific premonition of an event yet to come?

Chapter Five

Tenzin Dorje

Jangtang Province—Tibet

THE BUS GRINDS SLOWER AND SLOWER AS WE APPROACH THE ROAD-block. By now, all of the twenty monks inside are wide awake and watchful. Braced for the sound of gunfire. The shatter of glass. In the cold, gray light of a threatening morning, fear is palpable.

Sitting next to Paldon Wangmo, the two of us try to take our lead from Lama Tsering in the seat in front of us, looking ahead calmly, a *mala* running through his fingers as he recites mantras in his mind.

But as much as I'd like to calm my mind, my imagination is running wild. We have all heard the stories about what Red Army soldiers do to "Counter Revolutionaries." They have inflicted unimaginable torture on hundreds of monks. They have driven thousands from their cloisters, because of misguided ideas about what we supposedly "believe." In reality, they are the true believers. They believe in the ideology of Chairman Mao, while we monks are the ones who are trying to free ourselves of all superstitions about the nature of reality. But that's an intellectual debate of no interest to soldiers. They will continue to destroy out of ignorance and hatred, and simple boredom.

Just in front of us Mr. Keng, the driver, is looking about him, eyes wide with terror. Perhaps he is regretting his brave offer to drive us monks to freedom. I notice the sleeves of his faded, brown shirt, and how they are trembling. His hands are clenched tightly to the steering wheel as he brings the bus to a final halt.

The waiting continues, interminably. Where are they, these soldiers? What are they planning for us? Is it too much to hope they have abandoned their post? Or is this some trick to lure us out of the bus—perhaps onto landmines?

We are whispering these thoughts to each other. Murmuring under breath so we don't miss any sound from outside. And as we watch, and listen, and think the tension becomes even greater.

Until a figure appears in the road in front of the bus.

A shabby, thin man in rags. Two others emerge behind him. Are they connected to the roadblock? Are they beggars who just happen to be on the road coming towards us?

They are joined by another man carrying a rifle which looks old-fashioned even to a novice monk like me.

Then we realize. This *is* a military roadblock—but set up by a small group from the Tibetan army.

Relief passes through the bus. There is laughter and raised voices. Even Lama Tsering turns to us with a broad smile. "It seems we are not about to go through the *bardo* states, after all," he says.

Mr. Keng has got out from behind his seat, climbed across the front, and opened the bus door, where the Tibetan soldiers are gathered. He quickly relays the obvious. The soldiers are starving, having not eaten for days. Can we help?

Within moments, barley is being offered in small sacks, together with a container of yak butter. A precious leg of cold, roast meat is also offered.

Several of the senior monks, including our teacher, get out to remove the roadblock. The starving soldiers are too intent on eating, hacking chunks of meat with knives and stuffing them hungrily into their mouths.

As the empty drums are pushed aside, the monks exchange a few words with the soldiers, before getting back on board the bus.

With little ceremony, we are on our way again.

After all the tension, being able to move forward freely again comes as a great reprieve. But there is also something strangely anticlimactic as we drive past the small huddle of threadbare soldiers, ravenously tearing at the meat. Looking down from the bus window as we pass, I see weariness etched on their faces.

"They intended rolling a boulder onto the Chinese," Lama Tsering tells a group of us at the front of the bus. Of course we can't see up the sheer cliff, but can well imagine a great rock poised high above us.

"They have only two rifles and limited ammunition. But there has been little traffic and no sign of the Red Army."

With this news, we begin to feel more relaxed, thinking how with every mile that we drive, we are putting greater distance between the invaders and ourselves.

But any idea I have about looking out the window at the passing countryside soon ends when Lama Tsering turns to tell us that, just because we're on a bus, doesn't mean we can stop our Dharma practice. Single-pointed concentration might be difficult in this environment, but we can at least conduct some analytical meditation.

"I want you to reflect on the Four Immeasurables," he tells us. "Practice the visualizations you already know, while mentally reciting the verses."

The Four Immeasurables—love, compassion, joy and equanimity—are foundation values in our tradition, and each day in the monastery begins by reciting the verse for each of the immeasurables:

May all beings have happiness and the causes of happiness,
May all beings be free from suffering and the causes of suffering,
May all beings never be parted from the happiness that is without suffering—great nirvana liberation,
May all beings abide in peace and equanimity, their minds free from attachment, aversion and free from indifference.

They are called "immeasurables" because when we recite the verses, we remember the immeasurable living beings to which they apply. The visualizations Lama Tsering means are of friends and family, strangers and those we don't like. Even Chairman Mao and his soldiers only wish for happiness and to avoid suffering. So, while Paldon Wangmo and I sit on a bus fleeing from the Red Army, in our minds we are visualizing how wonderful it would be if the Chinese soldiers were bright with happiness and free of all delusions. If only this were so, I think, they would not be chasing us! But even though this isn't so, the *real* reason for this practice is to develop our own capacity for love and compassion—the true causes of happiness.

From time to time I open my eyes and see the mountains drawing closer. Up until now, the soaring Himalayas have always been a source of awe and wonder. But now as I look up at the successive mountain ranges, each higher and icier than the one before, I am filled with apprehension. How can we possibly make our way over them on foot? We are only three people, and none of us mountaineers.

Then I remember I'm supposed to be meditating, and return my concentration to the Four Immeasurables.

Concentration becomes especially difficult, however, as we come to the place where the track to Ling meets the main road. Having often walked here from our village when I was a young boy, almost always to wait for others to depart or arrive on the weekly bus, it is the only section of the main road I know. More recently, this is the place where Paldon Wangmo and I have exited from the bus when returning home for holidays.

As the bus curves slowly out from behind a mountain, we are suddenly in a familiar landscape. I recognize a cluster of whitewashed smallholdings huddled together, dwarfed by the monumental scale of the ice-capped peaks behind them. There's the wind-stunted juniper trees at the roadside; I've stood beneath them in the middle of summer, and also sought protection beneath them from the rain. A host of memories come flooding back, all of them involving my family, especially my parents and sister I now know I won't be seeing for . . . who can say how long?

I remember my mother's emotional reaction when I was leaving home for Zheng-po: "When you leave here," she'd said, "I'll be losing you for the rest of your life."

I hadn't believed her at the time. And in subsequent years, when we returned from Zheng-po to help our parents on the small-holding, I had felt only more certain that this was the pattern we would always follow. We'd be there for our parents as they grew into their old age. We'd see Dechen take a husband and have children and make her own life. We'd always be connected to our family, and to the village, and to and the rugged landscape of our childhood. This was where we belonged.

But mother's intuition has turned out to be true.

I recollect the last time I saw her. Strangely, on our last visit she and my father had walked all the way with us along the track to the main road. Even though, after a six week stay at home, we didn't have anything of importance to say to each other, she'd remained with us until the arrival of the bus which would take us towards Zheng-po. My father was always matter-of-fact in his welcomes and goodbyes, and my mother, too. Although this time, as the bus loomed into view, she'd hugged each of us with more feeling than usual.

"Paldon Wangmo and Tenzin Dorje, I am very proud of you both," she'd told us. It was the first time she'd ever said that, and now I wonder if she knew. It had also been the first time she'd ever called us by the names we'd been given when initiated as novice monks. It is traditional in Tibetan Buddhism for monks to replace family names and former identities with Dharma names which have a particular meaning. In my own case, Tenzin, the name I share with the Dalai Lama, means "holder of Buddha's doctrine."

As we pass through familiar fields towards the bus stop, I remember how Lama Tsering, always respectful of our family, had made no effort to persuade us to join him on this journey. How he'd been careful to emphasize he would not judge us if we decided to return home, or even disrobe. In particular, he hadn't used the secret scrolls to persuade us that we had a historic purpose, only revealing the true reason for our journey once we'd already made up our minds to go with him.

Even now as we come to the track that leads, in time, to our village, he turns to Paldon Wangmo and me.

"It's not too late," he says. "You are free to go home with my blessing."

But Paldon Wangmo shakes his head. "Thank you, Lama. I want to stay."

Remembering the last time my family was in this place, and my mother saying "I'm proud of you both," and her previous heartbreak about losing me for the rest of my life, I can't trust myself to speak. Instead, I just nod my head in agreement.

Lama Tsering turns to face the front and, seeing my expression, Paldon Wangmo leans across putting his arm around my shoulders, giving me a reassuring hug.

Our efforts at meditation become more difficult when, from the side of the road, four monks appear and wave down the bus. They are from another monastery much further east and closer to Lhasa. They fled a week before we did, but for the past two days have had to move forward slowly on foot. They beg to be allowed to travel with us.

The conditions are already over-crowded and allowing the new visitors on will make things even more uncomfortable. But of course we gesture them to join us as soon as possible. It is a privilege to be able to help fellow monks in their time of need. Bright smiles and respectful head-bows greet the new arrivals.

No sooner have we adjusted to the extra passengers, however, than we are stopped again, this time by an elderly woman with her grandson—barely more than a toddler. The little boy is sick, and the nearest clinic is in the next village we will come to. Will we save them a long, uphill walk?

The bus is now crammed to twice its capacity. There is now no possibility of study or meditation. Confined as all of the monks are, there are no complaints. We consider ourselves to be the lucky ones.

The monks who join us tell of how they'd heard the Dalai Lama was arrested in the Potala and has been taken in chains to Beijing. But the aged grandmother says she heard a broadcast that morning on her transistor radio, and that His Holiness is already in India and has been welcomed by members of the government there.

As talk of the Dalai Lama and Chinese invasion continues all about us, Lama Tsering turns to the two of us and murmurs, "Yapping dogs." He doesn't need to say any more. He has already taught us that engaging in idle speculation is a pointless exercise of benefit to no one just like the sound of barking dogs. Better to turn our minds to more positive, happiness-creating purposes.

We reach the village where the clinic is located and drop off the grandmother and her child. We also need to refuel again; we have now been traveling for twelve hours. All of us get out for a comfort break and to stretch our legs. The senior lamas check with Mr. Keng that he is not feeling too tired to drive. But Mr. Keng says he is used to this—it is a journey he makes every month and besides, there will be plenty of time to sleep later. It will not be much longer, he says, before the road comes to an end.

It is at this stop that we are confronted by a horrific reminder of the risks we face. From a small house, barely a hut, at the edge of the village emerges an elderly Nyingma monk—the oldest order in Tibetan Buddhism. Bent in pain and barely able to walk, his robes are torn and filthy. His face puffed and dark with bruising, a great, black welt covers his left cheek. As he moves his torn lips we can see that whatever teeth remain have been brutally smashed, so that only a few stumps remain.

With the greatest difficulty he manages to explain that he escaped the Red Army five days earlier near Lhasa. He urges us to hurry from Tibet as quickly as we can. Because he is so frail, he himself has no choice now but to remain in hiding and hope for the best.

Lama Tsering offers him a fresh set of robes, which he gladly accepts. Turning away to go back inside the small house, I will never forget the sight of his back where his robes have torn away. A great, suppurating wound stretches right across his back, revealing the white of his spine; this old man in his seventies has been whipped to the bone.

Continuing our journey after several more hours of grinding, uphill travel, the bus so slow at times we could have walked faster, we finally get to the point where the narrow, rock-strewn road fades away completely. Tracks lead to half a dozen small villages in the mountains. Looking out the bus window, while I am relieved to be getting out after the long journey, I also know that when the bus drives away, so too will our link to civilization.

I am struck by the recognition, as though for the first time, that there can be no going back—neither to Zheng-po, nor home.

I feel sure many others on the bus are thinking this, too. After we have all disembarked from the bus, taking care to collect our few belongings, we watch Mr. Keng laboriously turn around in a confined strip of land, and head back towards the last roadside village.

It is mid afternoon and the twenty four of us are now standing in completely unfamiliar territory, like the survivors of some disaster. In a plain which stretches to the foothills of the Himalayas, as we look out across the province of Jangtang, it is as though we are surveying a past to which we will never retrace our steps. Turning to face the future, we are met by the most bleak and forbidding mountains in the world. But across those mountains, the thought suddenly arises in my mind, is another world of movies, records—and Bill Haley and His Comets.

For a moment I wonder if I'll ever get to the land of the red people. Will I ever see, with my own eyes, their palatial houses and glamorous women and shining Cadillacs? Will I ever go to a rock 'n' roll concert where they play Bill Haley music? For a reason I can't explain, I feel as though I'd experience some amazing revelation by going to one.

We begin our goodbyes, for at this point we must split up into groups of three. We also remove the sandals we wear most of the year, and replace these with shoes suitable for climbing. Because of the great secrecy of our missions, none of us knows the immediate destinations of the others. We hope to meet again, before too long, in Northern India. But the Zheng-po chapter of our lives is now over.

Some of the monks are unusually quiet, while others put on a show of bravado, as we hitch rucksacks onto our backs. However, even the noisiest among us is silenced by the sound of a low drone growing louder and louder. Looking up at the sky we see the cause is a low-flying aircraft. As it gets closer we see it is painted in military gray, and emblazoned with the red star of China.

"Do you think they've seen us?" asks someone nervously.

"Twenty five monks in maroon, standing in the middle of nowhere," comes the reply. "What do you think?"

Fearful, we wonder what this could mean for the rest of our journey.

I am relieved when Lama Tsering beckons Paldon Wangmo and me to follow him down a path away from everyone else.

"The cave is a day's walk from here," he tells us after we have left the other monks well behind. Already he has set a brisk pace. "We can't afford to waste a moment."

He has made this trip several times during the past few years, securing the sacred texts in a cave where they will never be found. I try to imagine Lama Tsering walking through the Tibetan countryside, carrying the prophecies of Padmasambhava, the poems of Milarepa, and other unimaginable treasures on his back. Nobody would have believed such a thing possible. Which, I suppose, is part of the brilliance of this plan.

Thinking about some of the other senior monks from Zheng-po, who are leading other teams of three, I am especially relieved to be making this journey with Lama Tsering. Not only because he has made this trip before—at least, as far as the hidden cave, but as we walk together and I keep looking up at the mountains ahead, dark, and impossibly high, Lama Tsering is the one person in the world I can count on more than any other.

It was his letter which originally persuaded my parents to let me become a novice at Zheng-po, even though they had different ideas for my life. Since then he had become not only my teacher, but my mother and father, too.

The title "Lama" comes from the two Tibetan words "la" meaning "unsurpassable" and "ma" meaning "mother." Like a mother whose love and compassion makes her want to nurture her child through to maturity, so too a Lama is moved by an unsurpassable love and compassion to lead his students to full enlightenment, Buddha-hood.

Especially in the early days at Zheng-po, it required all Lama Tsering's patience, as well as all the determination I possessed, for me to get through my studies. Not possessing a sharp intellect like Paldon Wangmo, I couldn't remember pages of scriptures from just reading through them a few times. But knowing how much it grieved my mother for me to be away from home, I decided to work to the very limits of my capabilities in my study of the Dharma.

Late at night, after most of the other monks had gone to bed, I would stay awake in my meditation box, reading the holy texts by the glow of an incense stick. For hour after hour I'd memorize this scripture, that definition, the teachings of Tsong Khapa, Nagajuna and Asanga and all the great sages through to our present day Dalai Lama. I knew I could never come close to the effortless brilliance of some of the other novices. But I did the best I could.

At some point, a few months after arriving, I had foolishly told one of the monks about the conversation with my mother when she'd teasingly referred to me as "the magician of Lhasa." The monk thought this very funny and soon repeated it to others. And so it became my nickname, used by many in Zheng-po as a term of wry affection.

But Lama Tsering didn't laugh at the phrase, and once he even said to me "Perhaps you will turn your wish into reality." He also never rebuked me for my intellectual failings during the many times when our examination results were announced, and mine were only average. Instead of chastising me as he did some of his other students who scored poorly out of laziness, he'd tell me instead, "Tenzin Dorje you must never forget that you have a great purpose in life. One day you will find out what that purpose is—perhaps sooner than you think."

Before our evacuation from Zheng-po I had always known that when Lama Tsering said something, he was drawing on a special wisdom, a precognition to which other people didn't have access. I had discovered this, many times, in small ways. Now as I quite literally follow in his footsteps, I realize that I am fulfilling the great purpose he has always promised me. My faith in him grows even deeper.

WE HAVE BEEN WALKING HARD FOR ABOUT AN HOUR WHEN HE PAUSES for a rest. I am relieved when he does. Even though I am used to much longer walks, today I am tiring quickly, perhaps because last night, on the bus I had hardly any sleep at all.

We turn, looking back in the direction from which we've come. As we scan across the broad panorama of the countryside, in the long, slanting rays of afternoon sun, there's no sign of distinctive maroon. All twenty four of us seem to have melted away, and the road along which Mr. Keng brought us is only a faint outline in the distance. But as we turn back in the direction in which we're heading, it feels as though we've made hardly any progress at all. The mountains seem no closer.

"It continues like this for a short distance," Lama tells us. "Then it becomes a harder walk, more of a climb. There's a small village of only about six or seven houses. If we make good progress we can get close to it by nightfall."

"Close?"

Lama Tsering nods, "Where we'll camp the night."

"Aren't we staying in the village?" I ask, not even trying to hide my disappointment. It's a well established tradition in Tibet for traveling monks to ask for accommodation. And such visits, especially in far-flung rural villages, are often a cause for some celebration with delicious food prepared and news exchanged. In my mind I'm already inside one of the houses, safe and snug.

But Lama Tsering regards me carefully, "If the Red Army has soldiers in the area, the first place they'll try will be the villages. It isn't safe to stop." Then regarding my weary expression he continues, "Perhaps in the morning we can ask for food."

Turning, he starts again along the path, once again setting a steady pace.

A short distance behind him, Paldon Wangmo asks, "How likely do you think it is that there are Red Army soldiers in the area?"

"You saw the airplane," replies our teacher. "For all we know they could be on the ground already."

We carry on walking for several more minutes, before Paldon Wangmo persists, "But why should they bother with outlying areas?"

"Why should they bother with Tibet at all?"

It is the kind of challenge which Paldon Wangmo can't resist, as Lama Tsering well knows. Perhaps he thinks a debate will be a good distraction from our tiring limbs.

"The Chinese resent that we possess the great treasury of the Dharma," declares Paldon Wangmo.

"But they say the Dharma is just primitive nonsense," retorts Lama Tsering.

Paldon Wangmo needs time to reflect on this before he says, "They may say it is just nonsense, but they know that the West sees the Dharma as a source of inspiration. And Tibet as the mystical kingdom of Shangri-la.

They may not value what we have for themselves, but they want to destroy it so the West cannot have it."

"A well-observed point," Lama Tsering praises him. "And you will note the great paradox."

We walk for a long while before Paldon Wangmo has to admit, "I don't, Lama."

"Tenzin Dorje, what about you?" he asks.

"Is it," I ask, in a moment of rare inspiration, "that by invading Tibet, the Chinese are forcing us to take the Dharma to the West?"

"Congratulations!" His voice is warm with approval. "In future times, maybe only fifty or a hundred years from now," he half turns to us as he walks, "people in the West, the lands of the red faces, will say 'thank you' to China, because by invading Tibet they have bestowed on them the greatest gift they have ever been given."

By the time we approach the small village, two hours later, all three of us are growing weary. The bracing speed set by Lama Tsering when he started out has been reduced to much slower progress as we pick our way along the narrow, rock-strewn path towards the mountains.

We know we have walked a long way from any settlement because of the few signs of religious devotion, such as brightly colored prayer flats which Tibetans love to hang by the hundred from the branches of juniper trees. Nevertheless, from time to time we come to a curve in the path and, at the side, a row of stones carved with the most famous mantra in Tibet: *Om mani padme hum*, "Praise to the Jewel in the Lotus!" Whatever we are thinking of at the time, the *mani* stones are a useful reminder to return our minds to the Dharma.

The village Lama has told us about is no more than a collection of a few houses at the intersection of two paths. The path on which we're walking heads south west, directly into the mountains. The other, which intersects it, runs along the foothills of the Himalayas from west to east.

Twilight is already falling as the houses come into view. There's nobody visible outside, though smoke curls out of the top of several chimneys, and in my mind's eye I can picture the warm glow of a fire in a kitchen, the inviting softness of blankets and a straw mattress. It's been a very long time since I felt this tired—I know I will sleep well tonight, mattress or not. Glancing at the faces of Lama Tsering and Paldon Wangmo, I can tell it is the same with them, too. Although Lama Tsering has always been fit for his age, I am sure he is making an effort to hide his fatigue.

We become especially careful as we get closer to the village. Lama doesn't want anyone to know we have been in the area, at least until tomorrow. I know why he's being careful, even though I think perhaps he's being over-cautious. After all, there has been no sign of Red Army soldiers on the main road. And although we saw the airplane, we don't know who was in it, or whether they saw us. Even if they did, they have no idea where we might be now. Besides, didn't they have more important things to do than to chase after a few monks?

Nevertheless, following Lama Tsering's example, we move off the path to the east, away from the houses. As it happens, we find ourselves downwind of the settlement. Gusts of *tsampa* and *thukpa*—roasted barley flour and noodle soup—blow in our direction. The staple of Tibetan cooking, everyone's tsampa smells and tastes slightly different. As we walk past the village I think how much the mouth-watering smell reminds me of my mother's tsampa.

The other two must be able to smell the warm food too, but they are more stoical than me because they're not showing it. I think about the cans of food we're carrying on our back. No doubt canned meat will be good for us, but right at this moment, the prospect of tsampa and a bowl of butter tea in front of the fire is much more appealing.

As we stumble and scrape through a rocky outcrop, I try to dismiss these images from my mind. But instead, they only crowd in, all the more vivid. I can already taste the tsampa, just like my mother's. I am cupping the bowl of *cha* so that it's warming my hands.

Some distance away from the houses, and well out of sight, Lama Tsering pauses to look about. "We need to find a good place to sleep," he tells us, glancing across the barren hillside. "We can have something to eat. Then early tomorrow, if it's safe, we'll go into the village and ask for some food before setting off."

Regarding my despondent expression he says, "It's better this way. In other places the Red Army have ambushed villages in the early evening or at night. If we go in the daytime, we can keep a close watch on all the paths to make sure no one is approaching. It'll be much safer."

I nod in agreement. "They make good tsampa," I say. The way I meant it was that I looked forward until tomorrow morning. But the words betrayed the images that had been playing in my mind.

And Paldon Wangmo's mind too judging by what he says next, "If we were to ask for food tonight, and keep some for tomorrow," he suggests, "we'd preserve the food we're carrying."

It is a good argument. Giving us our rucksacks at Zheng-po, Lama had emphasized the importance of conserving our food as much as possible. No one could tell how long it would have to last us.

In the semi-darkness Lama Tsering looks from one to the other of us. At that moment, as though to reinforce what he'd said, Paldon Wangmo's tummy rumbles loudly.

"I know one of the householders, and she's very kind," Lama Tsering says at last, and I know we have a breakthrough. "If we were to go to see her we could ask for food, but we must not stay." He regards me sternly, as though he has already seen the image in my mind of the blankets and the soft straw mattress.

"No Lama," we shake our heads in unison.

"Don't forget our true purpose. If we lose our lives, it is not only a matter of individual importance. We have pledged to undertake this mission for the benefit of all beings."

A short while later we are walking towards one of the houses. Lama Tsering has stayed here before on his way to and from the secret cave. Even before we have approached the door, it is opened by a woman with a broad smile. She has no teeth, and her face is very flat, but as she opens the door I can smell the tsampa coming from her kitchen. Lama introduces her to us as Mrs. Gyatsal.

Across a small paddock, other neighbors are waving to Lama Tsering as well. He is evidently quite popular here. Within moments the woman has told us her husband and sons are in the mountains, herding yaks, but that we are welcome to come in for tsampa. Lama Tsering explains that we can't stay overnight—it wouldn't be safe for us and he doesn't want to put her in danger either. She tells us that no one in these parts has seen any sign of Red Army soldiers. Reassured, we go into her house.

It is warm and cozy inside and, after the wind blowing across the mountains, it is also suddenly quiet and peaceful, with only the soothing crackling of the fire in the kitchen hearth. The woman prepares more tsampa and in the meanwhile pours us each out a bowl of cha—thick, butter tea made from yak's milk. After our long walk, it is the best cha I have tasted for years.

We exchange what news we have about the situation across the country. It now seems certain that His Holiness has succeeded in reaching India, and that thought encourages us when we consider our own journey. The woman also tells us she has seen far more people on the mountain paths in recent days, all of them taking the path we were on which leads through the mountains.

Talk continues in this way for a while. Then it is Paldon Wangmo who notices the strange noise first. A buzzing sound. "D'you hear that?" he asks.

"What?"

Lama Tsering and Mrs. Gyatsal are speaking.

"That!" he says, louder, as they stop.

Now we can all hear it. A mechanical noise but not the same as an airplane. It's more shrill and varying in pitch. And it's getting closer.

Lama Tsering runs outside. We quickly follow. We can see the cause of the noise immediately. Headlights of motorbikes are coming along the foothills path. They are already close, just a few hundred yards away. As few locals could afford such transport, we immediately guess who is riding them.

"The woodshed!" Mrs. Gyatsal orders us. She points to a small stone building near her house.

We hurry towards it. I am about to go inside when Lama Tsering tugs my arm.

"Behind the shed!" his voice is urgent. "We mustn't be trapped!"

We only just make it to the other side of the shed when the motorbikes arrive. Their headlights swing across the shed, and the yard and flood the woman's house in a blinding, white glare.

There are two motorbikes and three soldiers. The first Red Army soldiers I have ever seen. I am surprised how short they are—they are no taller than I. But as they swing off their motorbikes and swagger towards the house, they make up in aggression for their size. They wear dark uniforms, and their eyes are as watchful and aggressive as wild dogs. One is holding a rifle which looks sleek and deadly.

Walking, uninvited, directly into the house, almost immediately there is shouting. "Who are you cooking for?!" followed by the clang of a pot on the floor.

The three of us exchange glances with each other. My heart is pounding heavily in my chest. This is the most shocking thing I've ever seen. I notice Mrs. Gyatsal's neighbors from across the paddock are watching, too.

"I have visitors coming!" we hear her protest.

"You pour out cha before they've even arrived?"

Though the open door we can see bowls being thrown to the floor where they shatter.

Mrs. Gyatsal is crying.

"Who is this tsampa for?" the accusation is repeated.

"Friends coming for supper."

"You are feeding monks?!"

"No!"

We can hear doors being pushed and furniture moved as they look for us. I wonder if we should run away, but it's impossible. The mountainside is barren and empty. There's nowhere we can run to where we wouldn't be seen.

"If you're feeding monks—" one of the soldiers is shoving the woman outside with the butt of his rifle, "we'll kill you for lying."

He cracks her over the shoulder so she falls to the ground.

Looking over at Lama Tsering, the pain on his face is as though he himself has been struck.

Paldon Wangmo gestures, "Should we give ourselves up?"

But Lama Tsering frowns. "Wisdom!" He mouths.

The other two are coming out of the house. "Nothing," they tell the soldier guarding Mrs. Gyatsal.

"Over there," he orders, pointing directly to the woodshed.

The two unbuckle their holsters as they approach the shed, drawing out pistols. One of them marches to the door of the shed. We hear him draw open the bolt before kicking it open. He is only a few feet away from where we are hiding. Through a crack I can see him prowling, like a beast of prey. Pausing to sniff the air as though trying to catch the scent of us.

Slowly he turns and looks at the wall, on the other side of which we're hiding.

"Behind!" he gestures to his comrade.

Chapter Six

Matt Lester

Acellerate Headquarters—Wilshire Boulevard, Los Angeles

"Matt!" Looking up from his desk as I emerge from the staircase, it's as though Bill Blakely has been expecting me. Bronzed and relaxed in an open neck shirt, he walks over to greet me with a genial handshake. "Very good to see you!" he gestures towards a pair of sofas. "To what do I owe the pleasure?"

"Casey just e-mailed me a copy of the investor presentation to check." I have recovered from my vertigo, but still feel somehow surreal in Bill Blakely's dome.

"Good." Perching on the sofa opposite he fixes me with a solicitous expression. "We're keen to have your input on that. Do you think Dan's done a good job?"

Is he crazy? Does he think I'm going to give Stenner my endorsement? "That's not what concerns me," I shoot from the hip. "I want to know why you've put Dan in as head of Nanobot?"

Blakely shrugs, as though surprised this is of any consequence. "Would you prefer us to call him something else?"

"Until a couple of weeks ago, I was in charge of the program," I tell him firmly. "I didn't think my job description had changed."

Blakely's forehead furrows. "Nor did I. What did your job in London entail?"

It's my turn for surprise. What is this—some kind of head game? "I worked across the whole Nanobot program. I carried out all the scientific enquiries, led all the research—"

"As you do here, except you've got help."

We seem to be talking at cross purposes. "So if I'm in charge," I demand directly, "why is Dan Stenner being called head of Nanobot?"

"Tell me, are the heads of either of our other two programs director-level?"

I hadn't thought about it that way, but I do now, and shake my head.

"Your job, as director of research is to lead the company's high-level thinking. Sure, you'll have a special emphasis on Nanobot. But you mustn't be constrained by that. We're looking for new science, Matt. Fresh thinking. Head of program is essentially a management job. Running a team of ten people is a very different proposition from managing two part-time staff," he refers pointedly to my position at the institute. "It's our experience that great scientists," he gestures towards me, "are very rarely great managers. Do you really want to spend your day dealing with HR issues? Revising budget forecasts?" He pauses long enough for the rhetorical questions to be answered. "Dan's there to look after all that stuff for you, leaving you free to do what you're best at—pure science."

It sounds good, no doubting it. But isn't that what Bill Blakely's all about—arranging the facts to suit himself? "What worries me is the impression given to the outside world," I persist.

"Outside world," he delivers a dry smile. "We're careful to avoid job titles on the Acellerate website. As for the presentation, that'll be delivered to a group of less than ten investors. Not exactly the world."

In just a few minutes, Blakely has taken the wind out of my sails, not only countering all my objections, but turning the tables so effectively that now I'm sitting opposite him, made to feel like a status-obsessed prima donna.

"I think you'll be happy with Dan as your program head," Blakely pushes the point home. "You can come to a presentation run-through if you like. He's an excellent presenter. Before joining us he was with a corporate consulting firm and led road shows to New York and Europe several times a year."

Driving home later, as I replay every moment of that afternoon, from the arrival of Casey Barrend's e-mail, to my descent down the spiral staircase after seeing Blakely. I can hardly believe the turn of events, or even that it's me, Matt Lester, who is going through this. Until only a few months ago, Bill Blakely was a legendary figure I only ever read about in newspapers or heard spoken about at conventions, and I was an ordinary researcher at the Imperial Science Institute. I never imagined coming into contact with someone of his status—let alone bursting, uninvited into his office with all guns blazing.

How quickly things change.

As for his reassurance about my position, I'm still wondering what to make of it. I know very well from very personal experience that most scientists don't make good managers and not having to look after any of the admin has come as a relief while I've been at Acellerate. But I'm also apprehensive about what I'm supposed to be doing; I'm having to shift my own ideas. If my position really is to come up with new science, it could be a lot more of a challenge than I'd bargained on. Back at the institute it had been easy to think of myself as the ground-breaking researcher, working hard to make my innovative Nanobot concepts work. What's clear to me now, even if it wasn't before, is that the idea I had of myself, as a creative scientist, has been based on the most protected circumstances. Running my own program back in London, no one expected me to keep on coming up with new ideas, new Nanobots. But at Acellerate, it seems, that's exactly what I'm being paid to do. It's a daunting development.

Soon after getting home from work, I see cars pulling up in the street outside, and groups of people making their way to the Dharma Center. I remember Geshe-la telling me about their evening classes and inviting me to come along to one. At the time he made the suggestion, I hadn't given it a second thought. A casual chat about Buddhism was one thing, though I wasn't so interested that I wanted to spend a whole evening on it.

But with everything that's going on with Isabella and at work, I'm feeling differently. For a reason I can't put into words, I'd like to experience that glow of good feeling I feel in Geshe-la's company. I guess it's the reassurance I get in his presence, the inexplicable sensation he seems to emanate that everything, right now, is exactly as it should be. I'd like to experience some of his peace, which couldn't be in more marked contrast to the way I'm feeling. There's an uneasiness about evenings on my own on Rosewood Avenue where I've begun to dread going to bed and experiencing the nightmare that so often follows. I'd also like to shake off the weariness that has accumulated from nights of broken sleep.

Which is why a short while later I'm stepping onto his porch and through to the hallway, where people are taking off their shoes. I remember this ritual from my last visit here with Mrs. Min. Copying the others, I carefully line up my Docksiders on a shoe rack, before following the other students down a corridor to the right.

It's a lengthy passage, the wooden floorboards covered by a deep, red runner, and the only lighting coming from two candelabra on the walls. There's a subdued hush, a sense of leaving the outside world behind, as we make our way along the carpet, in our socks.

I don't know what to expect of the meditation room, but as I step inside, I pause in surprise. The atmosphere is unlike any I've ever encountered—there's an unexpected but quite palpable sense of enchantment.

A ten-foot high brass statue of the Buddha, his face painted in gold leaf, and blue eyes serene in meditation, dominates the large chamber. Four vases of massed, pink and white oriental lilies are arranged about his base, a vase at each corner. A hundred flickering candles in brass butter lamps stretch across the front of the room, lighting both the Buddha and the lilies.

Inhaling the air steeped with ambrosial incense and the scent of flowers, I glance around the walls, taking in the vivid wall-hangings in their brocade frames, the shelves to either side of the Buddha, laden with sacred books, the ornate cornice carvings of what I later discover to be the eight auspicious symbols, lending the room an aura of mystery and magic.

There are no chairs, but instead, rows and rows of maroon cushions placed on square, maroon mats. At the front is a raised platform to the left of the Buddha. Most of the cushions are already taken, but I'm glad to see there are still a couple free. Not wanting to draw attention to myself,

I find one in the very back row and, copying the other class members, sit down cross-legged.

It's strange to be here. Me, the research scientist, the skeptic, sitting on a meditation cushion. There's something so overtly mystical about this room with its brass Buddha and candles and incense. Yet, nothing that Geshe-la has told me goes against my scientific experience. On the contrary, he seems to talk about the same essential truths but from a different perspective.

What's more, despite the unfamiliarity of this astonishing place, I am curiously relaxed about being in here. It feels as if I've left the outside world and my usual concerns in a different time and place. Isabella and work seem to fade into the background. The preoccupations that fill the media and too often my head—conflict, terrorism, all the worries, known and unknown, that threaten our lives—feel somehow less imminent. In a curious way I feel as though I'm coming home.

A minute before seven thirty, those who have been talking, end their conversations. Silent anticipation precedes the arrival of Geshe-la. An attractive young woman is making her way up the side of class, holding a brocade-wrapped clutch of books in one hand, and a bottle of Evian in the other. Barefoot, she walks with the easy grace I've observed in yoga practitioners, her blonde hair falling in tousled, shoulder length locks to a light blue cotton dress. She carries herself in a way that suggests she is completely oblivious to her own feminine allure, even indifferent to it.

I'm surprised when, instead of sitting on a cushion a few rows ahead of me, she keeps going until she reaches the front of the class. There, she prostrates to the Buddha statue, before sitting in meditation posture on the teaching platform.

No one in the room seems the least surprised as she takes her place, looking down as she undoes the ornate fabric in which her books are wrapped. I realize I've made an assumption in thinking that Geshe-la would be teaching tonight. Watching this other teacher closely, I take in the broad forehead and the high cheekbones of her down-turned face, the svelte ease with which she sits on the cushion.

It's when she looks up to greet the class that I'm startled by the vivid blueness of her eyes; they're a bright, sky blue and seem to light the whole room with energy. As she smiles, she meets us with an expression of such enthusiasm, such anticipation, it's as though she's been looking forward to this session all day. As though she firmly expects that in the next hour something wonderful will happen. All this seems to be communicated as she regards us with a thousand kilowatt smile.

She instructs us to straighten our backs and close our eyes before leading us in what she terms a relaxation meditation, where we have to focus our minds on just the sensation of our breathing. This, she explains in a gentle voice, is useful in helping settle the mind and cultivating inner peace.

Not that my mind is very settled or that I'm feeling very peaceful. This is the first time I've ever sat in a room with a whole bunch of people with their eyes shut. The first time I've been in a Buddhist meditation room. The first teaching I've ever attended. None of it is turning out the way I expected. My mind jumps from one subject to the next with a level of restlessness I've never really noticed before. But it's important to think, isn't it?—I tell myself. Wasn't Descartes' famous declaration "I think therefore I am?"

No sooner have I thought this than our teacher is drawing the distinction between considered analysis and disjointed, uncontrolled chatter. We need to allow this agitation to settle, she says, if we are to see things clearly. Develop a state of relaxed concentration to get the most out of tonight's teachings. The greatest obstacle to our own happiness, she tells us, is too much thinking.

Alice, as she introduces herself to us some time later, starts by saying that this evening's class is about karma. I sit up and pay attention. "Karma" is one of those words in constant use, but almost never by people who know anything about it. I'm looking forward to hearing an expert on the subject.

"The law of karma is also known as the law of cause and effect," says Alice. "When you think about it, we take this for granted every time we turn the ignition key in our car, switch on a television, throw a ball in the air," she says.

"Everything in the material world acts in accordance with this law. Nothing happens by chance. So too," she pauses significantly, "with our minds."

I sit listening to her speak, mesmerized by her poise, her fluency, the same relaxed ease I've noticed in Geshe-la. Despite being the same sort of age as me, there's a timeless wisdom about her which intrigues me. Is this a Buddhist thing, I wonder?

"Every thought we have, every word we say, every action we take, creates a cause. Over time these causes ripen to become effects. Or in the words of Shakyamuni Buddha:

The thought manifests as the word;
The word manifests as the deed;
The deed develops into habit;
And habit hardens into character;
So watch the thought and its ways with care,
And let it spring from love born out of concern for all beings . . .
As the shadow follows the body,
As we think, so we become."

This is a very different understanding of karma from what I'd always thought. This has nothing to do with Fate or pre-destiny—it's the exact opposite.

"The Dharma talks about a mindstream, rather than mind, because of the way we experience our minds" says Alice, "not as fixed matter, but as a constant flow of consciousness. Into this flow we introduce actions which condition us to experience future events in a positive or negative way. Moment by moment," she tells us, bright with energy, "we are creating our karmic destiny. *We* are the ones creating our own future experience of reality. Whether we have pleasant or unpleasant experiences is up to us."

Of course, I'm thinking about Isabella and me. By Alice's definition, all our problems are entirely self-inflicted—an idea that doesn't exactly thrill me. Is she really saying it's all my own fault that Isabella couldn't find any work in L.A. and decided to head off to Napa? That I'm to blame for what's happened to Julio and all the pressures it's brought to bear on us?

"We don't all experience reality the same way," she continues. "There are twenty of us sitting together in this same room, going through the same thing, and yet we're having twenty different experiences. Ditto work or personal relationships. I'm sure you can all think of situations where one person feels one way about something, but someone else feels very differently. If the person or thing had any inherent qualities, surely we'd all agree what they were?"

"Think of the music you enjoyed as a teenager," she smiles. "And your parents' reaction to it. The same sound waves are striking identical receptors," she tugs her ear, "so what explains the different reactions? Obviously the music isn't the happiness or unhappiness from its own side. Rather, it's our own minds that project pleasant or unpleasant on it, depending on our karma, or our conditioning. And it's the same with everything else, too."

I see how karma ties in with the conversation Geshe-la and I had, and with quantum science which shows that nothing has any inherent characteristics. What gives them characteristics, Alice seems to be saying, is our own thoughts projected by karma. They are two sides of the same equation.

Which is all very well from an intellectual point of view. But exactly what causes have I created to be feeling so unhappy about Isabella? So unsettled about my job?

Our current moment of consciousness, says Alice, is part of a far greater mental continuum. In the same way, our current life is part of a much bigger picture. And because our mindstream continues from one lifetime to another, a karmic cause that may have been created a lifetime ago, may ripen in this one.

"If we want to know what our life will be like in the future, maybe even our next lifetime," she tells us, "look at the causes we are creating right now. How can positive results arise from a negative cause? But if we want to be treated with love and compassion in the future, it's up to us to give others happiness, and help them avoid suffering as much as we're able."

As Alice talks more about karma, I listen, but I'm not taking much in. From what she's told us, my mind is already buzzing. I'm startled by how directly relevant Buddhist teachings are to my situation right now. Struck by how methodical, almost mathematical, the concept of karma is. But when it comes to the idea of a mindstream, and therefore karma, continuing from one lifetime to the next, I'm less convinced. If we've all lived before, for countless lifetimes, why can't we remember a single one of them? Who really knows for sure what happens when we die?

Class comes to a close, and the others have their eyes closed and are repeating dedication verses which they know by heart. At the end there are a few moments silence. I suppose I should be experiencing deep tranquility, that the timeless chanting, the incense and the candles should all have a calming effect. But this is all so new, and the idea of karma so confronting, my mind won't sit still.

All too soon, people are getting up from their meditation cushions and stretching their legs. They're returning down the corridor to the hallway and finding their shoes.

I follow, looking about me, hoping to catch a glimpse of Geshe-la, but he's nowhere to be seen.

As I slip back into my shoes in the hallway I ask a group of the others, "Does Alice teach here every week?"

"Tuesday night classes," a middle aged man replies.

"She and her Josh are an institution here," says a woman.

"Aren't they just!" chimes another in the flow of good feeling towards Alice and the guy I take to be her partner.

Outside, as I make my way home, I find myself thinking how new this all is. How, after living a settled existence in London for so many years, here I am returning home from a Dharma class instead of the pub, walking along a street with manicured verges instead of strewn garbage. Relying for transport not on the overcrowded Tube, but on my sleek, silver SLK.

Hearing the sound of a car door unlocking in the quiet of night, I look across. It's Alice.

"Thanks for the class," I say, trying not to seem too eager, but hoping she might say something. There's no sign of Josh.

She pauses by the open car door, hugging her books to her. Her silver jewelry gleams in the lamplight including, I notice, the ring finger of her left hand. "Nice accent," she smiles. The Smile. "Have I seen you here before?"

"No. First time."

"Your first Dharma class." she takes a step closer.

In the semi-darkness, the blueness of her eyes gave them a penetrating clarity. And they're focused on me. I feel self-conscious just being looked at by her. In that moment I'm also aware of the delicate scent of frangipani, ethereal in the night. A scent which takes me back to a different encounter.

"Is it what you were expecting?" she asks.

"I didn't know what to expect. It was really interesting."

"Good!"

"I guess I was also expecting Geshe-la to be there."

"Geshe-la?" she's surprised. "He only teaches the *vajrayana* students."

I have no idea who they are, but from the sounds of things they're quite exotic. I must be looking confused, because Alice goes on to explain that Geshe-la lives mostly in seclusion in his own room across a courtyard at the back of the house.

"He comes out to teach the more experienced students, but most of the time he lives in semi-retreat."

"Really? So, I mean, you don't just drop in to see him?" I ask.

"People have tried," she laughs, "But he has this lady who looks after him, Mrs. Min. She's very strict and won't let anyone near him."

I think about my visit only two days before: Mrs. Min's warm welcome; her box of gifts and offer to do my laundry; how Geshe-la had made an appearance without my having to ask. I've never had the impression Geshe-la lives like a recluse; he has always initiated the contact with me.

"Even to talk about Dharma things?" I persist. "Can't you take him out for coffee and a chat?"

"How wonderful that would be! Believe me, most of the students here would give a month's pay just to sweep his room."

"I had no idea," I wonder what to make of this.

Alice is regarding me with a playful smile. It's hard to break away from that oceanic gaze—there's something strangely intimate about being the focus of such immense blueness.

"Do you know much about Geshe-la?" she asks.

"I just know he fled from Tibet in 1959," I say, hoping she's going to tell me more. That she'll stay here talking to me.

"Geshe-la is what we call him at the center," she says. "It's like a respectful nickname because he's a *Geshe*—that's like a PhD. Quite a few high-ranking lamas are called Geshe-la for the same reason."

"I just assumed he was an ordinary monk."

"Oh, he's very special," there is warm respect in her voice. "After his Geshe degree, the highest in his class at Serajey Monastery, he got a master's in comparative religion at Oxford. For a long while he was the abbot of one of the two big tantric colleges in India."

Everything she says is making me more and more surprised about the way Geshe-la has been treating me. And embarrassed by the way I've just assumed he was a humble monk. "What's he doing in L.A.?" I wonder out loud.

"That's a very good question," she replies. "He says he's here for a particular purpose, but no one's been able to figure out what." Her eyes meet mine, and I try to return the gaze unwavering. "The point about Geshe-la is that he's regarded as highly for his . . . special insights as he is for his job titles."

"You mean he's a kind of yogi?" I ask. "A clairvoyant?"

"Let's just say," she turns to her car, opening the door and placing her books carefully on the back seat, "he has qualities way beyond most ordinary people."

I sense my reference to clairvoyance has made her back off. She's reluctant to talk about such things.

"Is teaching . . . what *you* do?" I ask, as she firmly closes the back door of her car.

"Goodness, no! I love teaching, but my day job is in scientific research."

"Me too!"

A flash of recognition passes between us, though I can't match her luminosity.

"What area?" she wants to know.

"Nanotechnology," I say, for once hoping that mention of it won't be a conversation stopper.

And, for the second time in recent weeks, it doesn't. If possible, Alice seems to be even more enthusiastic. "Quantum physics is a great area for someone interested in the Dharma," she says. "So many parallels!"

"So I'm discovering. What's your research area?"

"I'm at the Mind-Body lab. UCLA. My program studies the effects of meditation."

To my embarrassment, I have to stifle a sudden yawn. "I'm so sorry!" I tell her. "That's the reaction I usually get to nanotechnology! It's nothing to do with your research—"

"I noticed you yawning in class." Her sympathetic expression embarrasses me only more.

"Not sleeping well," I admit. Before getting the conversation back on track,

"You got into that line of work because—" I gesture the center.

She shakes her head. "Other way round. I came to the Dharma because of meditation. A lot of people do. You know it's only in recent years we've had the technology to prove the benefits that Buddhism has always taught."

"Sounds interesting."

"Oh it is!" her eyes fix mine with that clear radiance. "We've been doing scans on different people meditating using fMRI equipment. We can watch, real time, how different kinds of thinking affect the brain."

I'm shaking my head, "I wish my own work was so . . . tangible."

"Come up to the lab," she offers, reaching into the driver's seat, picking up her purse, and handing me a business card. "I'll show you around. Get you to meet Josh."

——

A SHORT WHILE LATER I'M BACK AT HOME, LOOKING AT THE PHONE. It's my turn to call Isabella, a prospect that fills me with strongly mixed feelings. The tension between us over her move to Napa is still far from resolved, and has shifted the tone of our relationship. Things between us remain unspoken. For the first time we're not sharing our real feelings.

And even though the six month duration of her course feels like a life sentence, with everything that's happening in London I realize that things could turn even worse. Every time I step into our kitchen, I'm visibly reminded of that.

Isabella had phoned at the weekend and we'd had a stilted conversation. She'd been under obvious pressure from having to learn pages and pages of information about varietals off by heart. "I haven't had to memorize anything like this for years," she'd told me. "Not since university. I'm finding it really hard."

"But sounds like you're learning a lot."

"I'm realizing now how little I knew to begin with," she refuses to be cheered.

"It's always like that when you really get into a subject. When you start out you don't know what you don't know. But," I remind her, "you'll be making Julio proud."

There'd been a pause while we both thought about her father. How all the while that Isabella's knowledge is growing in richness, his own experience of the world is degrading. As her own understanding becomes a more vivid, multi-layered tapestry, all the color of his own wisdom is fading inexorably away.

She'd told me how her mother, still in a quandary about what to do with the overdue bills, had phoned each utility in turn to find that all, but one, had already been paid. The single outstanding bill, for London Electricity, was only due the following day, and she'd settled it, relieved that while her husband had mislaid the invoices, at least most of them were paid.

The very next day, however, she'd had an awkward confrontation, when Julio burst into the sitting room waving a copy of the electricity bill. He'd phoned to settle the account, as he always did on the very last day, to find it had already been paid. Did she know anything about it?

Tina had to confess, which led to a blazing row and continental theatrics. No matter how much she pleaded she'd been trying to help, he repeated that she obviously didn't trust him. She must think he was already gaga. "Just because I forgot the name Brookwood Autumn Harvest doesn't mean I've lost my mind!" he'd shouted, storming out of the house.

I never would have imagined that the minutiae of paying a London Electricity bill in Dulwich could have such significance for two of us in California. But it does. And any optimism about Julio's condition is harder to sustain after Tina reported that he'd launched into a tirade of abuse when one of his longest-standing customers reminded him about an appointment. Julio had accused him of treating him like a child, furiously demanding to know if he thought he was losing his marbles. His customer had been reduced to a state of shock.

Where all of this leaves Isabella and me is a subject I don't want to think about and most of the time I'm too busy anyhow. But I can't avoid picking up the phone any longer. Looking at my watch I see its just after nine o'clock. She may still be at the study center I guess. But it's worth a try.

I'm not surprised when my call goes to her answering service. Nor am I surprised at nine thirty, or even nine forty-five. But when I still don't get an answer at

ten fifteen, I wonder what's going on. Isabella and I have never been late night people. We've always been in bed by eleven, sometimes earlier.

Getting up from the sofa, where I've been channel surfing, I go through to the kitchen and get a beer from the fridge. I'm starting to get tense about a conversation I know I should be having in a relaxed state of mind. I find myself wondering what Isabella might say, and how I would respond and again I'm going over the imagined conversations I've had with her before.

There's nothing at ten twenty. Or five minutes later.

Finally, at ten thirty, the phone is answered after just two rings. A French accent I take to be Colette. When I tell her it's Isabella's fiancé calling from L.A. she sounds surprised. But there's something else in her voice. Judgment? Admonition? Or am I being hyper-sensitive?

"Is she there?"

"No. I've just got in myself."

"Could she still be at the study center?"

"Closes at ten." There's a pause before she adds, "I was there all evening and didn't see her."

"Oh." As I'm digesting the information she suggests, "Have you tried Paolo's?"

"No." There's a casualness about the suggestion I find disturbing. "I don't have his number."

She's rattling off digits she either knows by heart, or which must be written down by the phone. Seizing a pen from the kitchen top, I scribble the number on the back of an envelope.

"Is there a message?" she asks, about to hang up.

"Um—" caught by surprise, I can't think of anything. "If you could just let her know I called . . ."

Moments later I'm cracking open another beer and thinking about Paolo. Who is this guy? Okay, so he runs the study group, but what is she doing at his place at ten thirty? It's a subject I really don't want to think about. Which, I guess, is why I can't stop.

I look down at the envelope. Paolo's number. Do I call now, after ten thirty at night? What if there is a study group session going on? Interrupting them would be another black mark against my name. I could leave it for half an hour, I guess. But what if they'd long since finished, and I disturb Paolo in his slumbers? That wouldn't exactly be giving happiness to Isabella either.

I should have asked Colette what time study group sessions ended. But she'd seemed in a hurry to get me off the phone and I don't want to call back again. Nor do I want to call Paolo.

Taking another gulp of beer, I think what an anti-climax my happiness-giving attempt has been. After one and a half hours all I have to show for my efforts are three empty beer bottles and a whole bunch of unanswered questions. Questions to which I will only find the answer tomorrow; first thing, I resolve, I will call Isabella at her apartment.

Going to bed a short while later, I climb under the duvet, check the alarm, and am about to turn out the light when I see the mala from Mrs.

Min lying on the bedside table. I put it there the day she gave it to me, puzzled by it. Without thinking, I pick up the mala, letting the beads slip through my fingers, feeling that same, curious reassurance I'd felt the first time I touched them, before putting the mala under my pillow and switching off the lamp.

~~

The Dream: Tonight it's as vividly disturbing as ever. I'm slipping across the cold, wet surface, clawing for something to hold onto, knowing I have to save myself. And suddenly I realize—I'm sliding down a sheet of ice. It's tilted against me, not a steep, insuperable incline, but one that's even worse because salvation feels possible.

At first it seems my new discovery will change things, somehow staving off my slide into oblivion. But as I scramble to get upright I find my new knowledge changes nothing. I am still quite helplessly out of control. Desperate for a foothold. Trying to clamber onto all fours but succeeding only in raising my head into the darkness, and becoming aware of that evil howling.

Shuddering down the icy surface, once again I'm aware that I'm crossing the point of no return. I also know that if I save myself tonight, I'll never have to go through this again. But it's no use. Flailing against the ice, blood thundering through my ears, there's just no stopping the slide. Further and further. Then across the threshold.

I plunge into darkness.

For a few moments I'm in freefall, seized with pure terror. But miraculously, my feet gain purchase. I find a minute toehold, and hold there uncertainly. My footing is unstable and could give way at any moment. The volume of that malevolent howling grows even louder.

I know this is only temporary respite. I have a precarious footing, but only for so long. And amid that appalling blackness, I become urgently aware that there's something I have to do. But what? And how? And why is this happening to me?

~~

At seven o'clock, the earliest I dare call, I'm dialing the phone number of Isabella's apartment again. Colette answers, sounding half asleep.

"It's me again. Matt," I tell her. "Can I speak to Isabella?"

"Just see if she's here."

I try to visualize her apartment. It feels terrible not being able to picture her room. Not knowing where she works . . . where she sleeps. I try to imagine a bedroom in an apartment in a town I've never visited. Colette tapping at a door. Isabella, sitting up in a bed I've never shared.

"Non," Colette abruptly interrupts my imagined version of events. "Did you try Paolo's?"

"I didn't want to interrupt the study group."

"Group assignment one is finished," I can almost hear the Gallic shrug at the other end. "Try now. She might still be there."

I pause, trying to get my head around this. "How d'you mean *still*?"

There's a click at the other end.

I sit, staring at the receiver. I try to convince myself there could be an innocent explanation. But if group assignment one has finished, why else was she at Paolo's all night?

Can this really be happening?

Chapter Seven

Tenzin Dorje

Jangtang Province—Tibet

FROM ACROSS THE SMALL PADDOCK A WOMAN CRIES OUT, "WE'RE here! Mrs. Gyatsal! Sorry we are late!" She's opening the wooden gate between her property and Mrs. Gyatsal's. Her husband and son follow. The three of them have been watching everything from inside their house.

Their arrival catches the soldiers by surprise. The one in charge, guarding Mrs. Gyatsal, points his pistol at them. But despite the darkness, he can see they're harmless peasants. The woman is holding a plate covered with a piece of cloth. Both of the two men behind her have arms full of firewood.

With a grunt the soldier shoves Mrs. Gyatsal to the ground, where she cowers, clutching the shoulder he struck. "We're watching you," he barks at her. "All of you," sweeping his pistol he includes her neighbors in the threat. "We can come at any moment. Anyone guilty of feeding monks will be executed."

Thrusting his pistol back into its holster, he jerks his head at his two comrades, gesturing them away from the woodshed.

We hardly dare breathe, as we watch the other soldiers turn from the shed and walk back towards the motorbikes.

Not that they're ready to go. Not just yet. One of them, whose black leather head and armbands make him look demonic, walks over to the neighbor. He flicks the cloth from her plate.

Without a sound, he picks up a dumpling and bites into it, before spitting it onto the ground.

"Tibetan shit!" he snarls, striking the plate from the woman's hands so hard that it flies through the dark, landing on the stony ground with a clatter. I bristle. The woman, just like my mother, has devoted hours to preparing the evening meal. It was courageous of her and her family to pretend to be visiting their neighbor. Now all her hard work is destroyed. And she's being insulted by this evil soldier!

At the same instant the anger rises inside me, I feel Lama Tsering's hand squeeze my shoulder. I know what it means: wisdom.

While the woman stands frozen, her face filled with shock and dismay, the other soldiers are sniggering at their comrade. Then they swagger back to the motorbikes, roaring the engines to life. Like devils from the hell realms, all noise and smoke, they pull away down the track that leads along the foothills of the mountains.

For a while everyone remains motionless. We need to be sure that the soldiers aren't coming back. As the threat of capture recedes with the fading drone of the motorbikes, we can hardly believe we have escaped capture. For my own part, I am numb with shock.

Mrs. Gyatsal is the first to move. From the ground, she rises to her knees, then struggles to stand. Still clutching the shoulder where the soldier struck her she is in obvious pain.

Her neighbor hurries over, helping Mrs. Gyatsal to her feet with consoling murmurs. Lama Tsering tells us to wait, before moving around the side of the shed.

I wonder what will happen next. I realize we can't possibly stay, and that the neighbors will have to take care of Mrs. Gyatsal. But I also think about all the food scattered across the ground. Perhaps, my stomach says, if we gather up some of the food, the neighbors will let us take them with us.

But seeing Mrs. Gyatsal's face as Lama Tsering appears from behind the woodshed, I know we have already asked too much. Instead of the unaffected warmth and friendliness with which she received us only a short while ago, her expression now conveys a very different emotion. It is powerful and undisguised. And watching it, I feel a stab of pain. Mrs. Gyatsal is staring at Lama Tsering with dread.

"I am so sorry." Standing half way between the shed and where Mrs. Gyatsal is being supported by her neighbors, it is as if Lama Tsering has been stopped in his tracks. "Can we help you?"

Mrs. Gyatsal shakes her head. The woman who had her food destroyed looks away from Lama, as though embarrassed. The two men are staring at the ground.

"Then we will leave immediately."

"Thank you."

Their collective relief is instantly apparent. Clasping hands together at their hearts, they all bow briefly to Lama, who returns their farewell. Turning, he comes back to collect us.

We follow Lama Tsering along the path that leads directly into the mountains. There is no need for words as we continue our journey along the narrow trail, with only the pale light of the moon to guide us.

What we have just experienced is the most dramatic thing that has ever happened to me. I have no doubt that if we'd been captured, the Red Army soldiers would have shot us dead, or at the very least, beaten us severely. I remember the wrecked figure of the Nyingma monk we met on our bus journey. The seeping wound on his back revealing his spinal column. The bruised jaw and shattered teeth. I think how being shot dead would be better than slowly wasting away after horrific torture.

As we climb, further up the stony pathway, I replay in my mind every moment of that evening, from when Paldon Wangmo first heard the motorbikes, to the expression on Mrs. Gyatsal's face on seeing Lama Tsering emerge from behind the shed.

And as I recollect it, I cannot believe this is happening to me—that it is I, Tenzin Dorje, who has come so close to capture by Chinese soldiers, and who is now fleeing into the Himalayas at night. Only three days ago I was a novice monk, leading a life of study, meditation, and work in the grounds of Zheng-po monastery. In such a place it was easy to imagine that I was working steadily to attain an attitude of serenity, and that whatever turmoil and pain might rain down on me, because of all my meditation and mental training it would be like water off yak hide.

But within just a day of leaving Zheng-po, here I am caught up in a turmoil of agitation, fear and anger over what has just occurred. Remorse for the suffering we've caused Mrs. Gyatsal and her neighbors. And most of all, profound regret for the way Paldon Wangmo and I persuaded Lama Tsering to stop at the village against his better judgment.

It is clear to me now that the idea I have had of my spiritual progress has been based on contrived circumstances. The moment I've been removed from those circumstances, I find I am behaving just like anyone else.

I also find myself wondering about karma. If it was Mrs. Gyatsal's karma to be beaten on the shoulder, would that still have happened even if we hadn't been there? Would the Chinese troops still have arrived? Would they have found some fault with her and struck her so harshly?

And perhaps the neighbor would have burnt her dinner anyway on the stove that night if we hadn't made an appearance—it would have amounted to the same thing.

But I can't think that way for long before catching myself out. My mind is up to its old tricks trying to justify, rationalize, and make me feel better. I remember sitting in the courtyard of Zheng-po early one summer morning, with Lama Tsering holding some black sesame seeds in his hand.

"You see these?" he reached forward so we could see the tiny, black specks in his hand. "They are like black karma. If I do not plant them in soil, will they ever grow?"

"No, Lama."

"And if I plant them in soil, but give them no water, will they grow?"

"No, Lama."

"And what if I plant them in soil, and give them water, but never allow light to fall on the ground. Will they grow?"

"No, Lama."

"Karma is the same—whether black or white. It requires conditions in order to grow. Without such conditions, it can never flourish. This is why we must always be sure to avoid creating conditions for negative karma to ripen, and instead create conditions only for good karma to grow."

So you see, I tell myself, accusingly. We created the conditions for all the negative karma to occur. If we hadn't begged Lama Tsering to stop, but rather obeyed our guru as it says in the scriptures, we wouldn't be battling up a mountain in the darkness.

For hours we continue climbing. The adrenalin in my system has long since burned out and all I can think of is food. Even before stopping at the village we had all been very hungry. After several hours of relentless toil I am so starved, I feel my arms begin to tremble.

I try to think of other things. Recollecting the longest prayer we recite in the monastery, I set myself the challenge of completing it from start to finish. But it isn't long before I am smelling the tsampa in Mrs. Gyatsal's kitchen, or thinking about the dumplings scattered in the darkness. Instead I try to repeat mantras, unwinding the mala from around my wrist and repeating a mantra which invokes good conditions.

When even that is in vain, I try to pass the time by remembering all the lyrics of "Rock Around the Clock." However, all my thoughts come back to food. The feasts my mother used to prepare for visiting monks and novices such as ourselves. The times at Zheng-po when we prepared special meals for high-ranking lamas visiting us from monasteries like Drepung and Sera-je.

Although Paldon Wangmo, ahead of me, is saying nothing, I can tell from the way he's moving that he too is hungry and tired. But after what happened earlier, we would both rather collapse from exhaustion than plead with Lama Tsering to change his plans.

From the position of the moon I judge it to be about eleven o'clock when our teacher finally pauses. We have reached a place on the path protected on three sides by rock face, and slightly elevated.

"This may be a good place to eat," he says. From his tone of voice it's as if we have just been for a gentle twenty minute stroll, but just hearing him speak makes me feel reassured and warm inside.

We quickly settle on the rock ledge. Paldon Wangmo and I need no prompting to eat. In moments we have our rucksacks unstrapped and are pulling out packets of chickpeas. Stuffing our mouths we give each other side-long glances as we chew. Normally we wouldn't dream of bolting down such food. Instead we would prepare a stew flavored with tomato and relish. But tonight we do not care. Unflavored chickpeas, with no seasoning at all, taste better than the most delicious meal I can remember. I can hardly wait to swallow one mouthful before pushing more in my face. Gulping from our water bottles as we chew, Paldon Wangmo and I eat like ravenous beasts.

Sitting opposite, in the light of the half moon, Lama Tsering makes no pretense of his hunger, although he isn't in quite such a hurry to shove food in his mouth. As he carefully mixes dried chickpeas with smoked fish, before chewing mindfully, I think how, despite being nearly four times my age, he has more physical stamina than I do. I know the reason, of course. It is the power of his mind. He has such control, such strength, that unlike us he can withstand the harshest adversity and still maintain his equanimity. Cramming my mouth with more chickpeas, I hope that one day I will be like him.

It is only after the worst of our hunger has been sated that we're able to think about anything apart from food. Wiping his mouth with the back of his hand, Paldon Wangmo looks up at Lama Tsering and says,

"I'm sorry I asked you to stop at the village."

Before Lama Tsering has the chance to reply I blurt out my own apology, "Yes, I'm also sorry Lama."

With grease running down the inside of my arm, and a mouth half full of smoked fish I mean no disrespect, though I know, like Paldon Wangmo, I should have swallowed my food before apologizing.

"It was also my decision to stop," Lama regards both of us with a wry expression.

"I have been worrying that I left Zheng-po only yesterday—" continues Paldon Wangmo, "and already I have caused trouble. Poor Mrs. Gyatsal—"

"Yes and I've been thinking about karma and conditions," I interrupt him, the words tumbling out of my mouth, "and how—"

"We have created so much bad karma," finishes Paldon Wangmo. This is not a thought I'd been having, but as soon as he says it, I realize it is also true.

"But surely—"

"Boys!" Lama Tsering stops us, looking from one to the other of us with a familiar droll expression. "You know what your problem is?"

Both of us regard him solemnly, chewing our food, before shaking our heads.

"Too much thinking!"

It isn't the first time he has told us this. In fact, scarcely a week goes by that he doesn't remind us of the fact.

"There is a story of two novice monks who left the monastery on a journey, just like you."

Lama Tsering has always known how to get our attention—by telling us stories.

"They come to a river. At the side is a young woman. Like them, she wants to cross over, but she is too frail. One of the young novices tells her to climb on his back, before giving her a lift across. When they get to the other side, he puts the woman down before he and the other novice continue on their way."

Lama leans forward regarding Paldon Wangmo and me closely. "After a few hours of walking in silence, the other novice turns to him and says, "You know, you shouldn't have picked that woman up. One of our vows is not to have any physical contact with a woman." But the other monk says to him, simply, "I put the woman down four hours ago."

He gives us time to work out the meaning ourselves, before emphasizing, "thinking about the past, especially going over bad things that have happened in our minds again and again, serves no purpose. It is completely useless mental activity! In fact, it is worse than useless, because it can only harm our happiness."

I know Lama Tsering is talking about much more than the story he has just told us, or even what happened earlier that night down at the village. It is by no means the first time he has given us this instruction—but how easily we forget!

"Surely Lama," Paldon Wangmo can't resist debating, "we have to think about what happens to us. Otherwise, how do we ever learn?"

"Of course. Analytical meditation is a good thing. It is the uncontrolled mind that I'm talking about. The mind which gets up caught up in fruitless fantasy and projection, even if it likes to clothe itself with higher purpose."

Paldon Wangmo looks away, abashed. As usual, Lama has cut through a clever rationalization with a self-evident truth.

"But Lama—" I know my own argument is much weaker than Paldon Wangmo's, yet it comes from the heart, "Isn't it better to contemplate karma and conditions than to focus on my hunger and tiredness?"

Lama Tsering chuckles. "There are better ways to bring your practice of the Dharma to the present moment. Recollecting your motivation is a good start. What is your purpose in life?"

"For the sake of all sentient beings," Paldon Wangmo and I chant together, "to attain enlightenment."

"And do you think that saving the most precious texts in Tibetan Buddhism from destruction will be of benefit to sentient beings?"

"Yes Lama," we reply without hesitation.

"Will the lineage you are helping protect benefit numberless beings in the future."

"Yes Lama."

"Very good! Then every time you feel your limbs ache you should think, "Whatever suffering I am undergoing is for the benefit of innumerable living beings." If you feel hunger pains in the stomach, consider, "This is part of a precious opportunity I have to take the Dharma to the land of the red-faced people." Whenever you want to stop from exhaustion, steel yourself by deciding, "I *must* fulfill this mission, because so many people in the future depend on me bringing them these peerless teachings."

⸻

There is ample opportunity to put Lama's instructions into practice during the long hours that follow. After we have eaten, we rest only briefly before our teacher tells us we must continue. Our aim is to reach the cave where the sacred texts are stored. Once there, we can rest in safety. However there is still some distance to cover and we must complete this part of the journey tonight.

We haven't been hiking long before I feel as if we had never stopped. The familiar aching returns in the calves of my legs and my thighs, and my exhaustion is even greater since we had supper. Inevitably I find myself thinking how if I had decided to return to our home in Ling, I would now be soundly asleep in bed. I would remain there until morning, and when I awoke my mother would prepare the whole family yak tea and dumplings for breakfast.

But instead of continuing my thoughts along those lines I try to put Lama Tsering's teachings into practice. If I had chosen to return home, I tell myself, I would have missed an opportunity afforded to very few monks through many generations. Exhausting though my journey is right now, it gives my life a purpose beyond any I could have imagined at that very first moment when I told my mother that I wanted to become a monk. Apart from anything else, choosing to go home would have meant separating from my guru—and that alone was reason to stay the course.

As I follow Lama Tsering's footsteps, which never hesitate in their progress along the path, it's a while before I realize that I've been so absorbed in thoughts about my motivation that I haven't thought about my fatigue.

We carry on through the night, our journey all the more arduous as the sky clouds over and it becomes difficult to see even a short way ahead. At times the path seems to fade away altogether, and as we clamber across rock shelves and over gigantic boulders I have lost all sense of direction. Without Lama as a guide, Paldon Wangmo and I would never find our way even through the foothills of these forbidding mountains. But it is a path that our teacher seems to know well.

Inevitably, my thoughts turn to that other reason I want to cross the Himalayas. The words of "Rock Around the Clock" return, unbidden, to my mind. They go round and round in my head even when I want them to stop. And I find myself wondering, as I often have in the past, what one of the lines means. It's something I've puzzled over in silence since the day I first received the lyrics from the Lhasa monk. I haven't asked Lama about them because I know I should be thinking about the Dharma, not about rock and roll.

But tonight, perhaps because I am so tired, and the music in my head is so insistent, I just have to find out.

"Lama—" I ask, as we near the crest of an isolated mountain, surrounded by the soaring, ice-capped peaks of the Himalayas, "what does the English phrase 'glad rags' mean?"

"Hah! I wondered when you were going to ask," he replies, and I know he is aware how much the song has been going through my mind. "And I'm afraid, Tenzin Dorje, I don't have the answer."

"But you are an expert at English!" I protest.

"Just because I know more than some of the other monks doesn't make me an expert," he replies, though I can tell he is amused by my conviction. After a while he murmurs, "I think 'glad rags' is not strict English. It's colloquial English, which I've never learned. Glad means to be happy. Rags are strips of cloth, like you might use to clean a window. Remind me of the context?"

"*Put your glad rags on and join me, hon,*
We'll have some fun when the clock strikes one,"

I feel almost relieved to be saying the words out loud, as though getting them out of my system.

For a long while we continue climbing. Happy rags? The words seem to make no sense. Then I remember an Indian dancer who once passed through the village of Ling and I suggest to Lama, "Do you think 'glad rags' are like silk scarves the women use for dancing?"

"Could be," says Lama.

Then a while later, "I hope that when we get to India I'll meet someone who can tell me what the whole song means, and maybe I can even see the movie again." This is the first time I have confessed my secret longing to Lama Tsering.

While my confession probably comes as no great revelation to him, his answer certainly surprises me: "Tenzin Dorje, I promise you that after you leave Tibet you will have as much of Bill Haley and His Comets as you like."

"That's wonderful!"

"No. Not wonderful. It's only your karma. How many monks were watching the Bill Haley movie that night?"

"About forty."

"And how many sing 'Rock Around the Clock' to themselves every time they sweep the courtyard?"

So he knows about that! After a pause I offer, "Just one."

"What does that tell you?"

Before I can answer, Paldon Wangmo replies for me, "That there is nothing inherently attractive about 'Rock Around the Clock,' but that Tenzin Dorje has the karma to think it's attractive."

"Correct, Paldon Wangmo."

It's a physically strenuous night, despite my best efforts to let go of Bill Haley and to continue my Dharma practice. Having hardly slept on the bus the night before, I am well past the point of exhaustion. From comments Lama has made during brief rest stops, I have resigned myself to having to walk through the night. So I am surprised when, several hours before dawn, our teacher turns to us and points to a crevice in a rock face a short distance to the side of the path. "That's our destination," he says.

From the position of the moon, I judge it to be about three o'clock. As we climb away from the path, edging along the base of the great, stone face, I murmur, "I thought we would be walking until sunrise."

"Too dangerous," replies Lama. "Dusk and dawn are the times when the enemy is most likely to attack." He is probably referring to his study of the tactics used in guerrilla warfare, I think.

The crevice in the rocks seems no different from the many other cracks between boulders in the mountains through which we're traveling. There is certainly nothing about the area to draw special attention. Just beside the crack grows a straggly birch tree, partially obscuring the depth of the gap between two large boulders, which stretches back for several yards. As Lama's footsteps come to a halt at the base of the crevice, he reaches into his robe, hands me a box of matches, and tells me to make my way up between the two boulders, using the tree trunk for support. A short distance up the boulders, he says, there is a small rock shelf on the left hand side. When I have climbed onto it, I should tell him.

Even though my arms and feet are aching, and all I want to do is to sit, I obey my teacher. I imagine him doing this same thing, and the thought of it takes my mind off my own weariness for a few moments. Lama Tsering, the highest Lama at Zheng-Po except for the abbot, climbing up between boulders like a monkey!

"Like a monkey!" Lama teases me from below, gently chiding me that I should be thinking such thoughts, and reminding me of his own telepathic powers.

"Sorry Lama," I grunt, heaving myself upwards, my back pressed to one boulder, feet on the opposite side of the crevice, and hauling myself up using the tree trunk.

It is some way up—at least six to eight feet, before I see the gash in the rock opposite. Because of the darkness, I can't see how deep it goes and I am a little scared. But trusting Lama's instructions, I swing my legs into it, and wriggle my way onto the shelf, finally letting go of the tree trunk.

"I am here."

"Very good," he murmurs below. "Now, on your stomach, move away from us towards the back of the shelf. You can light a match to make sure the way is clear."

I do this, and everything around me is suddenly illuminated in the amber glow, I find myself in a kind of tunnel. Where I am lying, on my stomach, the tunnel is quite high, easily high enough for me to move forward on my knees. But ahead of me it narrows like the end of a cone, to about half that height, and only a few feet wide. There are no snakes or bats that I can see, but nor is there very much space in here. Is this where the three of us are to rest?

"The way is clear, Lama."

"Move along to the end of the shelf, where it gets very narrow."

A short while later I am able to report that I have reached this point. Behind me, I can hear Paldon Wangmo clambering up between the boulders.

"When you are so close that you can easily touch the rock at the end, reach out to the top, and right. Run your hand over the stone until you find a strip of leather sticking out."

As soon as Lama mentions the strip, I can guess where this is leading. And, once again, he has astonished me. In my home town of Ling it is quite common for villagers to use pieces of yak hide to serve as door handles. On small, wooden entrances the leather is nailed to the outside. For heavier doors, the leather runs behind the door and is used as a flexible lever. As I feel around in the darkness with my fingertips, I think that perhaps this rock shelf is not the end of tonight's journey after all.

It takes a while to find the leather because the stone has so many bumps and ridges. When I first locate it, it feels hard and dry, like a piece of bark that has somehow stuck to the rock. Had I not been directed specifically to it, I could never have possibly found it, so well is it hidden and disguised.

"I have found the leather," I tell my teacher.

There is a pause before he murmurs, "I'm sure you know what to do. Just be careful as you pull the stone. It is very heavy."

Holding on with both hands and summoning all my strength, I pull the leather strap. There is no movement at all to begin with. Then, a sudden lurch, and to my amazement the stone is rolling smoothly as a wheel as I guide it towards me, Paldon Wangmo reaches from behind to help settle it to one side, so we can crawl past.

Immediately I feel a gust of warm air strike my face. In the darkness, it's hard to make out anything about the newly-revealed entrance, except that this is some form of tunnel continuing into the distance.

Hearing Lama climbing after us up the boulders, I continue on cautiously, reaching out into the darkness with my hand first, making my way forward, inch by inch, on my stomach. The entrance itself is very narrow, but once we are through it, we don't have far to go before I realize I can get up on my hands and knees and progress much more easily.

I sense that Paldon Wangmo is through the entrance behind me, and then Lama. Pausing, uncertain what to do next, I hear a noise to my left, like a wooden box being opened. Then Lama has lit a candle and is standing beside where the two of us are still crouched on all fours. In the light of the single flame we discover we are in a large vault of a cave.

We stand in astonishment, taking in the scale of the secret cavern, which is easily as big as the meditation hall at Zheng-po. At one end, chests are neatly stacked. Were each of them carried in here individually,

I wonder? Closer to us, a small shelf has been carved out of the rock on which rests a brass statue of Shakyamuni Buddha.

Beside us, Lama Tsering looks at our expressions of surprise with amusement before saying, "There will be plenty of time to explore the cave tomorrow. Now, it is time to rest."

A short while later, after we have secured the stone at the entrance with a steel bar, and pulled out straw mattresses and blankets—such luxury!—from one of the trunks, we lie down.

"It's been a long journey—" I hear Lama say, as I rest my head on the mattress. "You have both done very well."

Within moments I have fallen asleep.

Chapter Eight

I awake to the delicious aroma of cha and legs so stiff that at first I can hardly move them. After a while I open my eyes, and focus on where Lama Tsering is sitting next to a small, paraffin burner a short distance away from me.

I remember where we are.

It is unusually bright for a cave, I observe, lying motionless on my side, watching my teacher as I slowly wake up. Having boiled water and added cha from a small leather pouch he has strapped at his waist, next he opens a can of condensed milk. This is in place of the yak milk we'd usually have—all of us are carrying tins of condensed milk in our rucksacks. Three enamel mugs and three wooden bowls rest on a stone beside Lama. I look across the cave—the air in here seems to sparkle—to where the white enamel gleams in the light. After a short while, Lama takes the pot off the flame, and carefully pours the cha into each of the three mugs. Not for the first time I think how lucky I am to have a teacher like Lama Tsering. Most of the other lamas at Zheng-po are much more strict, and would insist it was the job of their novices to make them cha, not the other way around. But Lama has told us he is as concerned about our physical well-being as he is about our spiritual progress: balance in all things is the key to accomplishment. And part of physical well-being is good food.

"Time for breakfast, Tenzin Dorje," he looks directly over at me, sensing that I'm awake.

"Lama," I yawn, stretching out under the blanket until my arms and legs tremble. Slowly I roll over and get to my feet. As I walk over towards him, I look up at a wide gap in the boulders above us. Staring up at it I see that, high above, someone has secured a wide, metal grille. Closer to us, just a few feet away, is a long, narrow strip of plastic.

"So that's why it's so light," I murmur, sleepily settling close to Lama and raising the cup of cha to my lips.

"And dry," says Lama. I haven't thought about it until then, but I realize this is so. It is as dry in here as in the best-constructed home in Tibet, and surprisingly warm, too.

Paldon Wangmo comes over from where he has been sitting on his mattress. "Ideal for storing texts," he says.

Lama hands Paldon Wangmo his cha before looking from one to the other of us. "Do you want to know how long you've been asleep?" he asks. Even though my sight is still blurry with sleep, I can tell from his expression it has been a long time. I smile.

"Twelve hours," he confirms. Then looking at Paldon Wangmo, "And you, one hour less."

I glance over at Paldon Wangmo sheepishly. We both know that Lama has probably been up for hours. At Zheng-po he is known as the monk who never sleeps. Through the ten years he has been my teacher I have seen him asleep only once, on the only occasion he was sick. Every other time I've knocked on his door, no matter when, it has been to find him studying texts or sitting in meditation, his mattress propped behind his door. Once, when I asked him if he ever slept he just laughed and told me that both mind and body benefit from meditation more than sleep.

Lama pours a little cha into each of the three bowls and opens a screw-top container of barley flour. Tsampa is made by adding flour to the butter tea, kneading the mixture into a dough and then breaking off small pieces to eat. Very soon all three of us are enjoying the cha and tsampa, made all the more delicious because it is the first cha of the day after an arduous journey the night before.

"Where did you find the water, Lama?" asks Paldon Wangmo as we eat.

Lama gestures a passageway behind him. "If you follow that tunnel, it leads to a spring outside. It is one of the extraordinary features of this cave." Then gesturing towards the many chests stacked at the end of the chamber he says, "There is sufficient food here to keep many monks fed for several months."

As I look around at the cave, blinking away my sleepiness, I notice the ornate wall-hangings, or *thankas,* with images of different Buddhas woven from very high quality brocade. Under the Buddha statue I'd noticed the night before, Lama has lit a row of seven butter lamps, which flicker in the semi-darkness. The way the Buddha is positioned in the wall, he looks as though he is floating in mid air, an ethereal presence with gold face and serene blue gaze. Many of the walls are heavily ornamented with calligraphy—the precious texts and the magical symbols of Highest Yoga Tantra. There are gilt-framed photographs of His Holiness the Fourteenth Dalai Lama, as well as his previous incarnations, the Thirteenth and Twelfth. Swags of bejeweled cloth drape across an altar in a grotto to one side of the main cavern.

But quite apart from the man-made treasures in the cave, I am struck by something else about this place. An energy. This cave, I am beginning to realize, is more than a useful storage facility even for the most precious texts. There is something very sacred about the place.

"A few of us have known about this cave for many years," Lama answers my question before I utter it.

"A few lamas from Zheng-po?"

"Zheng-po," he nods, sipping his tea. "And Lhasa."

My eyes widen. By "Lhasa" he means the highest levels of our tradition—monks who work at the Potala Palace. Maybe even the Dalai Lama himself.

"It has been a secret," confides our Lama, "guarded by a handful of us in the Kagyu and Gelug traditions for many centuries. We have always been mindful of Padmasambhava's famous prophecy—how one day the Dharma would leave the land of Tibet and be taken to the land of the red-face people. In fulfilling the prophecy this cave," he nods seriously, "is of the highest strategic value. It is the last, secret sanctuary before the border. When we leave here, it is a few hours walk to the trading village of Tang and then, very soon, we leave Tibet."

"Is that a painting of Padmasambhava?" my brother asks, gesturing to one wall.

Lama Tsering nods. "Well observed, Paldon Wangmo. In these main caverns, and in the tunnels and caverns that surround them, you will see many images of Padmasambhava. This cave is strongly linked to him. It is said he completed an eight-year retreat here, which is why the whole mountain is thought to be pervaded with a special energy."

I am looking around with even greater wonderment.

"Some of the paintings on the wall are said to be his work. And there are holy relics which the legends say belonged to him."

"What sort of relics?" I ask eagerly.

"A conch shell, one of the eight auspicious gifts. A prayer wheel of great antiquity. You will find them on the altar."

My gaze shifts to the altar and, somewhat awestruck I try to imagine the great and glorious Padmasambhava sitting in meditation right here, where I'm sitting. Meantime, Paldon Wangmo is typically questioning, "Lama, have you checked up?" he asks. Lama is always exhorting us not to believe anything we are told until we have checked up on its authenticity. Blind faith is not a quality to be encouraged.

"In what way?"

"Checked up if the legend is true? If Padmasambhava did ever undertake a retreat here? If the conch shell really did belong to him?"

Before Lama can answer, I find myself replying "How can you check up on something that happened a thousand years ago?"

Paldon Wangmo's skeptical nature has always irked me.

But Lama Tsering regards me with a frown of concern. "It is a good question, Tenzin Dorje. Your brother is right to want proof. We mustn't just believe things because we like the sound of them."

Then glancing over to Paldon Wangmo. "A thousand years is a very long time ago to check up. In fact, it's twelve hundred years since Padmasambhava brought the Dharma to Tibet. I can't give you absolute proof, but . . ." he looks down at his cha for the longest time before looking up at us both with a meaningful expression, "there is something of direct relevance I need to tell you both."

He has the same seriousness about him as that last night at Zheng-po when he called us both to his cell. There is the same sense of significance that once he has said what he about to say, there can be no going back.

Paldon Wangmo and I draw closer.

"You will remember I told you that it is our responsibility to courier the original works of Milarepa, of Naropa and several of Padmasambhava's famous prophecies to safety?"

Paldon Wangmo and I nod in unison. How could we possibly forget?

"While these are some of the most treasured and sacred texts in our tradition, there are two other scrolls which may come to eclipse them. They may be regarded as even more treasured and sacred in the future."

Regarding our puzzled expressions he continues.

"We all know that Padmasambhava was a great teacher and seer. How was he to know, twelve hundred years ago, that one day there would be such inventions as motor cars and airplanes? Yet his most famous prophecy about iron birds and horses than run on wheels clearly speaks of these things.

"Even despite our great respect for him, it seems we may have underestimated his importance to our tradition. Not only did he help establish the Dharma in Tibet, he may also have an important part to play in establishing it in the land of the red people."

Both of us are following Lama so closely we can barely breathe. But he seems to be speaking in riddles. Where is he leading us?

"Paldon Wangmo, you asked for proof of the great yogi's presence in this cave. Well, here is some food for thought. Last time I brought a precious cargo of texts here was during the summer of the Year of the Earth Dog. You may remember, I let you and Tenzin Dorje return to your village for two months?"

I remembered it well. It had been at the end of that visit that my mother had walked with us both all the way from our home village of Ling to the bus stop, something she'd never done before. The time she'd told us how proud she was of us both.

"After securing the scriptures here in the cave, I made a visit to Tang, the trading village. I thought it might be important, when our time came, to have carried out this reconnaissance trip.

"On my way back from Tang to the cave, I encountered an old peasant woman. It was on the mountain path and I had no idea where she was coming from or going to. There are no farms in the area as the land is too barren. It is as though she appeared from nowhere."

"We stopped for a conversation, though to begin with I tried hard not to show my reaction, because she was, without question, the most hideous creature I'd ever encountered. She was bent forward like an old tree stunted by the wind. Her hair was matted with filth, and every visible inch of her skin was begrimed and covered in sores. The stench of her was so pungent I had to fight to control my stomach. The bag on her back was stained and putrid. When she turned to look at me, I saw that half her face had rotted away, leaving exposed gums and eyeball."

Paldon Wangmo pulls a disgusted expression. Always the more squeamish of the two, I shudder.

"When I asked where she was going, she ignored me. Instead she demanded a drink of water."

"What did you do?" I ask.

Lama shrugs. "What could I do? I am a Buddhist monk. It is my duty to give protection and help to all sentient beings. I had a bottle of water so I gave it to her, knowing I wouldn't be able to drink from the bottle again."

"She barely sipped from it before throwing it to the ground and demanding food. As it happened, in Tang I had been given four delicious strips of cured meat which I was looking forward to eating for lunch. Carefully taking out two of them, I handed them to her. She set upon them like a ravenous dog, before demanding more." Lama shrugged, "I had to give her the remaining strips."

"Then she wanted money. As it happened, the abbot had given me a small amount with the strict instruction it was to be used only in an emergency. I decided that this woman had more need of it than I, so I gave her all the money I was carrying."

Having drunk the water, eaten the food and taken the money I was of no further use to her. But before she went, she turned and, for no apparent reason, quoted me a verse of text which mentions Tang. It is an obscure verse, and not one I had thought about for years even though I had just been in the village:

From Tang in the West, one thousand,
Beneath the tail of the unequal snow lion,

Paldon Wangmo joined in the recitation. I was only half surprised. We all knew what an exceptional memory he had.

My two most precious, bound for the land of the red-faced,

Paldon Wangmo continues alone,

Await the Dharma warriors.

Lama nods, approvingly. "A strange verse is it not?"

"Especially coming from an old woman in the mountains," observes Paldon Wangmo.

"Exactly," nods our Lama. "On my way back to the cave, the verse occupied my thoughts. You do know who wrote it, don't you?"

We both shake our heads.

"It is attributed to Padmasambhava himself."

"It is twilight language," I say.

"Of course."

Many of the most sacred texts in our tradition are written in a form of coded verses, called twilight language, rendering them meaningless to those who don't know what they refer to. A form of memory aid, or mnemonic, the purpose of twilight language is both to help students remember key instructions and to protect those same instructions from the uninitiated.

From Tang in the West, one thousand,
Beneath the tail of the unequal snow lion,
My two most precious, bound for the lands of the red-faced,
Await the Dharma warriors.

Lama repeats the whole verse so we can ponder its meaning. Before he continues, "I had learned the verse in my youth, but I had never received any teachings on it. Nor had I ever paid it any special attention, until my unforgettable encounter with the old woman.

"Having been reminded of it while on my mission to secure our most precious texts, I began to realize its exceptional significance. "The lands of the red-faced" was clearly the same allusion as in Padmasambhava's most famous prophecy—the West. So what was 'My two most precious' which was bound for them? 'From Tang in the West' was also self-evident. There are a number of places called Tang, and of them all, *this* Tang is the most Westerly. But what did 'one thousand' refer to? Could these be some kind of direction?"

"One thousand miles?" prompts Paldon Wangmo.

"In Padmasambhava's day, they didn't measure distance in miles. But you are along the right path."

"Hours?" I offer, with a shrug.

"Steps," suggests Paldon Wangmo, before hesitating. "Though one thousand steps isn't far."

"I also wondered about 'one thousand steps'" replied Lama, "but then there was the question of 'the tail of the unequal snow lion.' Where could that be?"

Many places have been named after the snow lion, a mythical creature and heraldic symbol in Tibet. In sacred art, snow lions are often seen supporting the thrones of enlightened ones, and in the countryside there are references to snow lion mountains, rivers and passes.

"I wondered if any of the mountains around Tang were known by this name. I also thought of this very cave, where Padmasambhava was said to have lived. But when I returned here, and studied all of the detailed maps I'd brought with me, I could find no reference to a snow lion in these parts."

There is another long pause as he sips his cha.

"For the next few days I spent all my available time thinking about the verse. When I wasn't meditating, I was poring over maps, trying to work out distances: one thousand steps, one thousand hours, one thousand days. What if the village of Tang had moved during the past twelve hundred years? Had there been another Tang in the West?"

Shaking his head he tells us, "All the time I was trying to work out a solution, I was making a mistake."

Raising his eyebrows, he invites us to suggest what his mistake might be. But neither of us wants to suggest a flaw in our teacher. Eventually he tells us, with a chuckle, "Too much thinking!"

For a while we share his amusement.

"On the fifth day, I realize my mistake. "Today there will be no more thinking about Padmasambhava's verse or the village of Tang" I decide. "I will just be mindful. When I eat tsampa, I will be mindful of tsampa. As long as I remain in this cave, I will be mindful of the cave."

"I was sitting where the two of you are, now," he says, "facing that wall, to the right. Within a few minutes of practicing mindfulness I had realized the answer."

We look at him, startled. It is unusual for Lama Tsering, the most modest of monks, to make such a claim.

"Padmasambhava's code was so simple it had escaped me. I was trying to make it all too complicated. Once the two of you have finished your breakfast and performed your ablutions, I want you to try practicing mindfulness, and see."

HALF AN HOUR LATER, WE ARE FED AND WASHED AND READY TO MEDITATE, though I want to protest that I am only a novice monk and Lama Tsering is the highest Lama at Zheng-po; that high realizations are beyond my capabilities; that after a night like last night, I should be given time to rest and relax my mind.

In response to my turbulent thoughts, Lama Tsering looks at me, "For a short time only, Tenzin Dorje. Just be mindful."

Paldon Wangmo and I sit in meditation posture, facing the wall indicated by our teacher. Initially my mind is crowded with images of the hideous old woman, and thoughts of the strange verse by Padmasambhava. I also have to ignore memories of the frighteningly close encounter with Red Army soldiers the evening before. But with the practice of many years of mind training, I am able to let go of my thoughts and, for a few minutes, simply experience the quietude of the cave.

Lama has always taught the importance of precision in giving and following instructions. In the Dharma, he frequently reminds us, there is no place for woolly thinking—*everything* has a clear definition and purpose. As we sit, I remind myself of what he has instructed, "Try practicing mindfulness, and see."

I focus on the wall of the cave ahead of me. While no direct sunshine penetrates the deep cleft in the rock as far as the cave, a shaft reflected off a stone face above us gives the light in this cavern its hazy, ethereal quality. As I sit, I hear the wind breathing through the hidden channels and secret passageways like the bass notes of a wooden flute. The currents of air I'd first noticed the night before are warm and subtle on the skin. It is as if this cave has its own life.

The wall I am facing falls in a sheer, vertical drop until a point around chest level, where it curves away into a darkened crevice stretching, who knows how far, into the distance. Like many of the walls of this cave, at some time in the past the flat surface has been painted with the image of a Buddha. Despite the patina of very many years, some of the colors are still vivid, especially those using malachite for green pigments and cinnabar for red. They could be centuries old, I reflect, perhaps even more than a thousand years. Then I check myself. I am not supposed to be engaging in thought and speculation. I am only to be mindful, to observe.

After a while my breathing becomes slower. My mind calmer. I become present only to each moment as it arises. It is a peaceful feeling, one to which I know I can always return through meditation. But because I am not yet a highly accomplished meditator, my mind has still to be purified. I enjoy only a few minutes of tranquility at a time and then a thought appears as if from nowhere, like a bubble rising to the surface of consciousness, "Try practicing mindfulness—" Lama had instructed us "and see."

Was it mindfulness of sight we are supposed to be practicing? If I study the wall in front of me will I find the same clue, unlocking Padmasambhava's code, which Lama Tsering had discovered when he sat in this same place?

I scrutinize the rock wall with renewed focus. I wonder if, among its many grooves and cracks there is hidden access to a secret chamber. Perhaps this wall, like the mountain itself, conceals some treasure?

If it does, I cannot see where. All I notice is the painting of the Buddha, mildewed with age and scarred by the weather, only the red and green colors still clear. But perhaps my inspection is too intense, I think. Mindfulness is not the same as active engagement. It is instead a state of relaxed awareness. Looking—yes—but without urgency or attachment. In this state, Lama has taught us, we become aware of those things we cannot see if we try too hard. Paradoxically, by letting go of expectation we are more likely to find that which we seek.

Relaxing my concentration, I try to look at the wall with calm equanimity. More time passes in the serene stillness of the cave as I regard the ancient Buddha. Perhaps, if I had continued in this way I would have had the same realization my brother did. Because I was coming to see that there was something unbalanced about the image of the Buddha, something that went beyond the damage of the elements. But Paldon Wangmo gets there first.

"Lama, the snow lion?!"

It is extremely unusual to speak during meditation. I can remember such an interruption happening only once before at Zheng-po when one of the monks noticed that a building had caught fire. But there is no disguising the excitement in Paldon Wangmo's voice.

Focusing on the snow lions supporting the throne on which the Buddha sits, I see that instead of a pair supporting each corner of the throne, only the pair on the right stand in place. On the left there is only a single lion.

"Is that the unequal snow lion?" Paldon Wangmo persists.

Unequal? I am wondering. And then the sudden recognition. Yes, there is a fourth snow lion, only it has eluded me because the outline is so faint and the lion is so large that its paw is as large as its partner.

From behind I hear out teacher say, "Why don't you find out for yourself?"

Immediately, Paldon Wangmo is on his feet. I soon follow. As we make our way to the wall, Padmasambhava's verse thunders through my mind:

From Tang in the West, one thousand,
Beneath the tail of the unequal snow lion,
My two most precious, bound for the lands of the red-faced,
Await the Dharma warriors.

So, we are in Padmasambhava's sanctuary, one thousand steps from Tang! Here, right in front of our eyes is the unequal snow lion! Like all verses written in twilight language, once the meaning has been deciphered it becomes so obvious, so direct.

Gathering robes up to our waists, we crouch down to bend into the place where the wall curves away. It is dark, and the crevice becomes rapidly narrower, so that we're soon on our hands and knees. Ahead of me, Paldon Wangmo is running his hand along the rock face as he ventures further and further.

When he pauses, calling "There's something here," I reach up and feel where his hand is. A break in the surface has created a lip. We feel behind the protruding stone. I think what a perfect hiding place this would be.

"What have you found?" Lama asks.

"A place something could be hidden," I reply, "but there's nothing here."

On our hands and knees I wonder if we will have to get down onto our stomachs.

"Well done!" comes the reply. "The reason you find nothing is because I have already removed it. Let me show you."

We make a scrambled about-turn and are heading back towards the main cavern. We realize our teacher has been leading us to this moment of revelation. Instead of simply telling us everything, he has been guiding us to discover for ourselves the meaning of Padmasambhava's directions.

There are some moments when Lama Tsering seems like a conjuror, seems able to arrange events or situations in a particular way for maximum effect. As we crawl from the crevice, first on hands and knees, then bent forward, we find the light in the cavern has changed. While that soft, astral light continues to pervade the main cave, now a shaft of sunlight falls directly into the cave, just in front of where Lama Tsering is sitting. It illuminates two slim canisters of a kind I have never seen.

Lama watches us closely as we step back to join him, kneeling on the ground to inspect the metal tubes. His eyes convey a powerful energy, and in his voice is an excitement I rarely hear,

My two most precious, bound for the lands of the red-faced,
Await the Dharma warriors.

"These two sealed scrolls are the object of Padmasambhava's verses. His most precious teachings. Not only did he predict that the Dharma would one day leave Tibet, he prepared for it. Over a thousand years ago he wrote teachings of special value for the red-faced ones, for Westerners. He stored them here in this secret place, safe from fire and rain and theft. And he left specific directions."

I am still staring at the cylinders. They are about two inches in diameter and eight inches long. The smooth metal has long since crusted over with oxidation. Two thirds of the way along each canister is a wax seal around the circumference. Both seals are intact.

"They are not opened," I observe.

"Because it was the great and glorious Padmasambhava who sealed these sacred teachings, the Abbot and I believe they should be opened only by the leader of our tradition, His Holiness the Dalai Lama."

As I continue to study the cylinders, mesmerized by their significance, Paldon Wangmo asks, "Do you think they could be rusted through?"

"It's possible, but unlikely," says Lama. "Fifty years ago, during building work at the Potala Palace, similar scrolls were found, and in similar condition. I know this because the Abbot was present when His Holiness had them opened. The teachings inside were in perfect condition because the metal is very thick."

Lama offers one canister to each of us. As I take it from him, I am surprised by its weight. I hold it, awestruck, knowing it's the most valuable treasure I have ever touched.

"Do you think the Buddhas sent that smelly old woman?" I ask, not daring to look in Paldon Wangmo's direction.

"I don't know, Tenzin Dorje," says Lama, "but I have learned always to pay attention to coincidence. Because everything arises from mind propelled by karma, when several different actions converge at the same point, we should take special note."

The spotlight of sunshine illuminating the place where the two canisters had stood, quickly clouds over. In the silvery semi-light, the words that Lama speaks next seem to hold greater consequence:

"That old woman reminded me of a verse at a precise time and place which was exactly right. For over one thousand two hundred years, that verse has been memorized throughout the monasteries of our tradition to keep alive a set of directions. Monasteries from across the whole of Tibet and even large parts of China, immense stretches of land from mountainous regions to vast plains, from big cities to tiny villages. And from throughout that vast area, the directions led to just one specific place, this very cave in which we are now sitting."

"Through a stretch of twelve centuries since they were written, the verses were kept alive to be used on just one day. Today. The day of our departure from Tibet."

By now the hairs on the back of my neck are standing upright. Even Paldon Wangmo, I notice, is struck by the significance.

"As for the recipients of the message, out of every lama including the very highest lamas, out of all fourteen Dalai Lamas, out of every abbot, yogi and yogini who has lived throughout the ages, out of every teacher, superior *bodhisattva*, and *arhat*, the instructions were written specifically for who? For the three of us."

Meeting Lama Tsering's eyes, I can't help an involuntary shiver.

"*We* are the Dharma warriors of whom Padmasambhava spoke," Lama tells us, his voice filled with portent. "Whatever awaits us, when we climb across the Himalayas, we must never forget our sacred and historic duty."

WE SPEND THE REMAINDER OF THE AFTERNOON MEDITATING, RESTING, and exploring some of the wider passageways leading off the main cavern. Lama goes about his preparations, carefully wrapping the sacred texts we are to take. He also packs additional food from stores kept in the cave, using every available space in our rucksacks.

At Zheng-po, as at all other monasteries, the main meal has always been eaten in the middle of the day. But today we prepare our main meal in the late afternoon. Apart from tsampa, it is all out of cans, but we eat it with relish, treasuring these last minutes in the haven of Padmasambhava's cave, knowing that we have a long night's journey ahead.

When we return to the path that leads through the mountains it's with a very different feeling than when we left it. Not only are we rested and fed. We also have the energy which comes from knowing our special purpose, from realizing that this journey the three of us are making has been directly ordained by no less than the great and glorious Padmasambhava himself.

We haven't been walking long when we approach the village of Tang, which consists of a dozen or so houses. It is now two hours after nightfall, and the villagers are mostly indoors. We keep our distance from the settlement, traveling on a path that winds above the village. The familiar scent of wood smoke and cooking carries through the air. Through partly open doors and a few small windows we catch glimpses of warm domesticity; people gathered about their fires, preparing their evening meals. The sound of laughter as they share a joke. In a field close by, a young woman is carrying a bundle of firewood on her shoulder. Even though she is some distance away, I can tell she has beautiful, refined features. Despite her burden she carries herself with a poise, a gentleness which suddenly reminds me of my sister Dechen.

Once again, my thoughts return to my own family in Ling. Yes, I will miss them in India, I think. But whatever longing I have to be with them is more than equaled by the sense of destiny that I am one of only three monks entrusted with a historic mission.

Leaving Tang far behind, for the next few hours we continue climbing. We have passed the furthest point to which Lama Tsering has ever traveled, and are now venturing into the unknown. A short distance outside Tang, the path becomes suddenly less visible. Much of the terrain is barren rock, and while we know the overall direction in which we should be traveling, and are guided by a small compass and maps which Lama has studied in detail, it is still sometimes confusing which way we should go.

Here it is so remote there are not even the occasional row of mani stones to give us comfort that a fellow Tibetan has trod this path before. It would be difficult enough to make the journey by day, but with only the light of the moon and stars to guide us, our task is even more difficult.

Still, I reassure myself as we return from an unnecessary diversion around several huge boulders, whatever challenges we might face, surely we have the protection of all the Buddhas to ensure that we complete our journey safely? If not, what would be the point of keeping a set of directions for over twelve hundred years?

I imagine how it will be when we finally arrive in Northern India. As soon as our presence is known, there seems little doubt that we will soon be ushered into the presence of His Holiness the Dalai Lama. I have heard many stories about the effect this living Buddha has on people when they meet him. How some people find tears spontaneously welling up in their eyes. How others can't stop smiling because of the bliss they feel in his presence. I wonder what effect he will have on me? I can imagine his joy at knowing we have brought these most precious of texts to safety.

The scene plays out in my mind of his greeting each of us warmly. How Lama Tsering tells him about the realization of Padmasambhava's prophecy, and the secret cave one thousand steps from Tang. How we offer the metal canisters to him, and how one of his attendants carefully opens them. No doubt other Lamas will be there to witness this historic moment. I wonder if they will be wearing their ceremonial gold hats, as they look at the three of us from Zheng-po with warm regard. Perhaps they will insist that Paldon Wangmo and I immediately become fully ordained monks because of our service to the tradition? Perhaps we will each be assigned our own room in quarters nearby and receive teachings directly from the most high-ranking Lamas?

It is these precise thoughts which are going through my mind when we curve around a bend, and the way ahead becomes broad and flat, and there's movement from the shadows on the left hand side.

"Halt!" The order freezes us in our tracks.

I see the glow of a cigarette before I make out the Chinese soldier smoking it. Lounging against a rock, he slowly rises to his feet, drawing his rifle to his chest. He's pointing it directly at Lama Tsering.

There is something surreal about all this. It *can't* be happening! It's all too ordinary, too matter of fact. I'm so shocked I'm not even scared.

Perhaps the soldier is surprised also. For a few moments he just stands there, studying us. He draws on the cigarette, so that the circle at the end crackles from red through to bright orange.

In the darkness, to the side, I make out two other soldiers. Asleep. Despite everything I've heard about Red Army soldiers, despite seeing the Nyingma monk, despite what we went through last night, I wonder: might this soldier let us go? Perhaps he is kind. Perhaps if it is just up to him he will wave us on. Even if he is not kind, if he's lazy that's good enough. What's to be gained from arresting three harmless monks on a mountainside? Why bother?

Exhaling noisily, the solder flicks his cigarette butt to the ground. He kicks his sleeping comrades with his foot. They clamber to their feet, cursing at us for having broken their sleep. The first soldier orders us to the ground.

The path here is wet and muddy. Because we have been taught to take good care of our robes and respect what they stand for, at first I sit before reluctantly lying back, hoping the rucksack will not get too dirty.

Both Lama and Paldon Wangmo are face down. The soldier, seeing me on my back, snorts, shoving me over roughly with his boot so now I'm covered in mud, front and back.

As we lie with our cheeks, foreheads, and noses in the sludge, the soldiers exchanging their strange, harsh language, the truth of our situation begins to sink in. And the foolishness of my fantasy that we could be set free. All the same, I think how ordinary this capture has been. No drama. No tension. One moment we are walking through the mountains; me with my head full of pride and thoughts of self-importance. The next moment we are lying with our faces in the mud, under arrest.

As one of the soldiers roughly seizes my wrists and trusses them in a knot, I feel like a beast for the slaughter. I wonder what will become of us. Are they going to shoot us dead, right now? If so, why tie us? Are they preparing us for some barbaric torture? The image of the Nyingma monk comes into my mind—but I chase it out.

In the midst of these thoughts I suddenly remember Lama Tsering's words: *"If you decide to come with me, it must also be for a higher purpose than saving your lives, precious though they may be."*

Here I am, worrying about my own well-being, while in my rucksack are the most precious scriptures in our tradition. Texts so rare, they haven't yet been opened, let alone copied and transmitted to others. And it is I, Tenzin Dorje, who has been entrusted to protect them.

To remind us of just how powerless we have become, and how much contempt he has for us, the first soldier is standing at our heads. He laughs harshly to his comrades as he undoes his fly. Moments later we feel his urine spraying on our hair and faces, stinging our eyes so we have to shut them. Urine runs across my cheek and up into my nose so I have to swallow it.

With an aching heart I think of my beloved guru, the highest Lama of Zheng-po and one of the most revered teachers in our tradition, lying in the mud and soaked in the urine of a common Chinese soldier.

Our humiliation is complete.

~~

Six hours later we approach the village of Tang.

Utterly exhausted, we have walked through the night, our exertions made all the more difficult by the rope that binds the three of us together—Lama in front, me in the middle, Paldon Wangmo behind.

Even when the soldiers had stopped for a rest they wouldn't let us sit. When Paldon Wangmo had said he needed to go to the toilet, one of the soldiers told him, sneering, to soil his robes.

Feet aching and faint with fatigue, my wrists chafed raw, I am well over the shock of what has happened. As I watch my teacher grow weaker and weaker in front of me, stumbling as he slips on the rocks, I think how foolish we were not to overpower that first Red Army soldier, when his colleagues were both asleep. How our surprise, and obedience has made fools of us. How much all three of us stink of urine.

I also wonder why we are being taken to Tang. Is it only a stopping off point towards a further destination in some remote jail? Or are we being taken there for a specific, and horrifying purpose? Most of all, what will happen to our priceless cargo?

I get my answer soon enough. Although it's soon after dawn, as we stumble down the path towards the settlement, the sky is dark and the air thick with smoke. I wonder where it's coming from—in this part of the mountains, there is not enough vegetation to create such an acrid pall. But as we get closer I realize, with horror, what has happened.

Tang has been ransacked. Most of the houses are smoldering ruins. Some are still ablaze, flames leaping from their smashed windows. The small village we passed earlier in the night, that seemed such a haven of rural contentment, has been torched and vandalized.

A single, Red Army soldier is guarding a group of disheveled villagers, most still in night dress, huddled in front of one of the few buildings that hasn't been destroyed. Around them are strewn smashed crockery, stray pieces of furniture, a smashed transistor radio—the few possessions from their humble dwellings. Terror is etched deep on their faces.

Two more soldiers appear through the smoke. Between them is the girl I noticed the night before draped in nothing but a torn, bloodied sheet, her hair matted and head hanging listlessly. There is no doubt what she has been subjected to. For all my tiredness, anger burns in my stomach like molten lava—it's as though my own sister, Dechen, has been raped.

Is it really possible that just three soldiers can do so much damage in such a short space of time, I wonder? Three evil beings with guns have ripped the heart out of a village which has been here since Padmasambhava's time.

The soldiers are about to throw the girl to her fellow villagers when we appear. Instead, they hold onto her, yelling boastfully towards our own three captors. Despite the arduous journey, our soldiers are quick to approach, grabbing the girl and dragging her into the darkness and to further violation.

The other soldiers are forcing us before the villagers a few yards away. One of them, walking behind us, has slashed the straps of our rucksacks, which fall to the ground with a thud. He kicks them in front of us before forcing Lama Tsering to the ground, ordering him to open them.

In halting Tibetan he shouts at the villagers, through the swirl of acrid smoke, denouncing us as traitors. He claims we have been arrested for trying to smuggle things from Tibet. Whatever he finds in our rucksacks will prove his point. It is just a game to him.

As Lama Tsering produces the first, carefully wrapped text, the soldier demands he unfold the cloth in which it is wrapped, laying bare a precious text of inestimable value and antiquity.

"You see!" demands the soldier, stabbing through the pages with his bayonet, and raising the scriptures above him. "These criminals are stealing from the people of Tibet!"

I look up at the holy text impaled on the end of a bloodied bayonet. Fury rises inside me, about to erupt. We have been humiliated enough by these gun-wielding devils. I can't allow them to destroy the whole purpose of our mission. The time has come to act.

Chapter Nine

Matt Lester

Eventually I get to speak to Isabella. It's a brief conversation on her cell phone five minutes before she's due to go into a lecture. She's sounding flustered and is quick to say how the pace of her study work hasn't let up.

I tell her that I'd tried calling her at home, only to find that she'd spent the night at Paolo's.

"Oh, that was a one-off," she dismisses my discovery casually. "A couple of us from group assignment got together for a tasting. I had too much to drink and didn't feel like walking home."

Saying she's about to step into a lecture theatre and has to end the call, there's not a lot I can say. Now is not the time to tell her that until very recently I'd taken it for granted that the two of us were a couple, held together in intimacy and trust. That I'd never had a moment's doubt she felt the same way. But since she'd gone to Napa it was as though the connection between the two of us had become suddenly open to question. As though what had bound us together had been cut loose and I am falling out of reach.

After the conversation, I wonder what that tone of voice meant when she'd used the term "one-off." In my gut it means something I don't want to believe. That she's trying to disguise "one night stand" as "one-off," to conceal the truth of what had happened behind a story of student camaraderie and too much wine.

In London when we met friends for a drink or went out to a party, it had always been Isabella at the center of a group, attractive and vivacious. Whatever pangs of jealousy I felt when she flirted with other men didn't trouble me much—I knew I was taking her home. Having her desirability affirmed by a circle of adoring men only added piquancy to the knowledge that I was the one who would be with her later in bed.

But this was different. Knowing nothing about Paolo left me with my worst imaginings. She'd mentioned he was from Italy—was that something that drew her to him, some kind of tribal instinct triggered by her father's failing health? Was this Paolo one of those strutting Latin types, all fire and libido?

Ever since Colette had uttered the fateful words "she might still be there" he had lurked in the shadows of my mind, a faceless interloper I wanted to banish, but whose presence was only the more invasive. I couldn't think of Isabella without being consumed by him with a visceral, gut-tightening dread. I imagined how he would have been instantly attracted to her. How he would have soon discovered how vulnerable she was, a newcomer in an unknown land, coming to terms with her father's illness. A girl without a ring.

Had she mentioned me? Even if she had, it wouldn't have mattered. No doubt he thought I was a fool to let go of her, and would have quickly closed in, his moves as calculated as they were probably well-practiced. I didn't want to think of them together. The sex. Which is exactly why images of it haunt me even at the least expected moments. The idea is torment enough without imagining the physical reality of her in her nakedness, surrendering her body to him, moaning in satisfaction as she yields him the intimacy that had been mine.

I feel that I'm sliding dangerously towards the abyss.

GESHE-LA IS RIGHT ABOUT HER NOT BEING A TRUE CAUSE OF HAPPINESS, I think bitterly. I've never felt so weary or so unhappy in my life. Just as he is right about change. There are moments I wish we could turn back the clock to just a short while ago, when we were living in London before the Acellerate offer. Things had been so much better before my spectacular career break.

Despite the fatigue that has become part of the background of my life, I decide to throw myself into work. Things with Isabella may be far from certain, but I'm still director of research at Acellerate. Okay, the job description may have turned out a lot different from what I thought, but even that's not all bad. The more I've mulled it over, the more I've come to accept Bill Blakely's point. Great scientists don't make great managers. And a lot of what I've been spending my time on has been management, not science. Now that I've been given back my freedom, as a scientist, I'm determined to prove that I have plenty more ideas as innovative as Nanobot.

At Acellerate, as in many technology institutes, to pursue a new line of research and, more particularly, get the budget for it, you must first obtain the approval of an independent scientific advisory committee.

In the weeks following my encounter with Bill Blakely, I work long hours working up new technology applications related to Nanobot. They're ideas which have occurred to me in recent years, which I've never had the time to develop. Phoning colleagues back in London, I soon assemble a significant library of research findings, related studies and support material for the proposed new directions.

Every day I get into the office early so I can be in touch with the institute in London, and stay back late to work on the new program outlines. As far as I'm concerned, each of the programs has outcomes with highly commercial applications, and timetables which are short term. Not only is each of them a strong contender in its own right, but by putting up to the advisory committee not just two, but three separate proposals, I feel sure at least one of them will soon be getting the green light.

But as things work out, that's not what happens. For all my hard work and self-confidence, within days of putting my submissions up to the committee, I get an e-mail from the chairman, Robert Telman. According to the e-mail, there are complications associated with two of the ideas while the third falls outside Acellerate parameters.

The rejection comes as a kick in the belly. And I've come to realize how little I know about winning committee approval for a new research proposal. I had assumed it was simply a matter of coming up with an innovative program idea. But it's turning out to be more complicated than I thought. I'm also going to have to develop more political smarts. Find out more about who is on the committee, their likes and dislikes, the kind of programs they've approved versus those they haven't. This is a new and worrying level of complexity, one I haven't had to deal with in my career to date.

I'm getting home late from the office one night, when I notice people coming out of the Dharma Center and walking towards their cars. Remembering my own visit, I also think of Alice, as I have several times since that first encounter. Our night-time conversation next to her car. The mystery boyfriend. Those mesmerizing sky-blue eyes. I also remember her invitation to show me round the labs at UCLA. Okay, her research doesn't seem to have a direct connection to nanotechnology. But I could do with a field trip, and time out from the office. It also seems quite a coincidence that she teaches in a tradition based on the same premise as quantum science. That I met her right outside my house. And that, like me, she's a researcher. A whole lot of different lines converge at the same point—perhaps I should be paying attention?

WHICH IS WHY I'M STANDING IN THE RECEPTION OF THE NEUROSCIENCE laboratories at UCLA the following Friday afternoon. A bespectacled young man in a white coat ushers me through the security door after I've been waiting awhile. Alice had said I should come anytime mid Friday afternoon to watch some scans they're doing. The clock on the reception wall is showing four forty-five.

The labs are the usual warren of corridors, a few glass-walled offices, notice boards, water coolers, and long stretches of wall, behind which the real work gets done.

The lab assistant opens a door, showing me into what looks like the sound room of a recording studio. It's a small room dominated by a window looking into a laboratory. Beneath the window, an expansive control desk has an array of dials, keys and sliding buttons. At its center are two flat screens, currently in darkness.

Half a dozen people are in the room. The guy at the center of the control desk is giving instructions to people in the lab. With a graying mane and steel rim spectacles he has a commanding air.

Standing some distance behind him, holding notebook and pen, is Alice. She sees me arrive and, coming over with a smile, tells me they're about to conduct their last scan of the day.

I turn to the window into the lab, and watch with some amazement as a Tibetan Buddhist monk is rolled into a magnetic resonance imaging machine. Lying on his back, the maroon and saffron robes neatly tucked about his sides, a protection shield has been placed across his eyes.

There's something weirdly incongruous about what I'm witnessing. The juxtaposition of eastern mysticism and western science, of ancient wisdom and contemporary technology, of simplicity and advancement. But there's a strange excitement about it, too. Behind the calm instructions delivered by the man at the control desk, I detect powerful anticipation.

Pretty soon the left hand screen is lighting up with a cross-sectional image in constantly changing colors of oranges and reds.

Alice steps over to the control desk and leans toward a microphone.

"Are you ready to begin?" she asks.

A speaker on the wall relays sound from a microphone inside the scanner. "Yes," comes a quiet voice.

With a nod to the man at the controls, Alice says, "Please focus your thoughts on the happiness of all living beings."

The right hand screen flickers to life, similar to the left, except that the left is inflected with tones of blue. While blue sparks flick across the brain, the blueness begins to focus on one part, a core of light sapphire rapidly forming and remaining constant. The right screen, by contrast, shows only faint specks of blue which emerge and dissolve away.

After watching this for a period of a few minutes, Alice gestures me to a corner of the room. "What we're looking at," she murmurs, "are the brains of two people given identical instructions. The one on the right is the playback of a non-meditator. The one on the left is real time from Lama Dendrup," she gestures towards the scanner. "He's a fifty-eight-year-old monk with about forty thousand hours of meditation experience."

The core of blue in Lama Dendrup's scan is expanding in vibrating waves.

"The left pre-frontal cortex is associated with happiness and relaxation," says Alice. "That blue color is showing high-frequency gamma waves, associated with concentration, focus and higher states of awareness. What this is showing—"

"You can train the brain to be happy?"

"Exactly. Like going to the gym. Or learning a musical instrument. You put in the hours and you get the results."

I watch as the contrast between the two screens grows even greater. The light sapphire blue is deepening as time passes, turning by shades to deep cobalt. "What about IQ?" I ask. "Or what if the guy on the right just has bad concentration."

"The guy on the right is Professor Clark," she nods towards the man at the desk. "Head of Neuroscience. We scanned him first."

I share her wry smile. "Was he having a bad day?"

"Not really," she shrugs. "We're collecting hundreds of scans. And they show the same sort of thing. All variations on the same theme."

After ten minutes have passed, Alice goes over to the microphone again. "And now, please focus your thoughts on your own happiness."

While the screen on the right barely changes, there's a radical change on the left hand screen. The dominant cobalt goes into retreat, shrinking back to the core at its center. As we stand there watching, the vividness of the color also begins to lighten, to fade. Alice hardly needs to point out the significance. It's providing real-time evidence of the traditional Buddhist paradox that focusing on the happiness of others creates a more gratifying subjective experience than thinking about one's own.

Later, the session comes to a close. There's a humming sound as the fMRI scanner rolls open and the monk begins to emerge. A couple of white-coated assistants open the lab door. About to follow them, Alice turns to me,

"You're staying, aren't you? Coming over to meet Josh?" There's that look again of radiant expectation.

Of course I say yes. It's not like I have any other plans. Though I'm not exactly sure what Alice's are. Right now I'm happy to go along for the ride wherever it's heading.

A short while later Alice is showing me from the room, back down the corridors and out of the building. It's getting late and outside the sky is deepening with sunset. As we walk across the landscaped campus, I watch the play of an evening breeze in the leaves of some great oak trees. Not far from us a group of students are playing softball on a neatly-trimmed lawn, and in the distance an older couple are walking their golden retriever.

Who knows where Alice is leading me, but I assume it's to some central administration block because she's carrying a white coat over one arm and her briefcase in the other. A silver chain around her neck glints in the late afternoon sun.

"One thing I don't understand about your research," I tell Alice, "is this whole concentration thing. Why is it that someone like Professor Clark produces the scan that he did when he's probably spent as much time during his career concentrating as Lama Dendrup has spent meditating?"

Beside me, Alice is taking in the twilight scene with a look of contentment. "You know the term 'meditation' is a bit like the word 'sport'. There are so many kinds of meditation, and they're as different from each other as swimming is from . . ." she glances around "playing softball. Some kinds, like analytical meditation, are similar to the concentration we use at work, that's true. But single-pointed concentration, which Tibetan monks train in, is very specific and very different."

"How's that?"

"Instead of engaging in mental analysis, following thoughts to see where they go, or trying to recall something or be creative, with single-pointed concentration, you focus on just one thing."

"Pretty challenging," I say, remembering my own first attempt at meditation a few weeks earlier.

"The biggest challenge of your life," Alice flashes me a smile. "But the biggest payoff, too. You saw the scan of Lama Dendrup's brain. Those levels of happiness are far more intense than anything that ordinary people ever experience. And such control—it's like he's flicking a switch," she gestures. "On goes the happiness button! What today's scan didn't show is the residual levels of happiness we're seeing in long term meditators."

"High?"

"Way above average. People who meditate regularly are happier, more resilient and all-round more efficient thinkers. We have the scientific evidence."

"Is that because happiness becomes habitual?"

"Maybe," says Alice. "But it's more likely that by practicing meditation we actually change the wiring of our brains. Neuroplasticity. Brain scientists used to think that once you reached adulthood, your brain was fully developed and that was it. Now we're discovering that the way we think actually changes the circuitry of the brain, no matter what age."

All of this is news to me, and I'm beginning to realize how little I know about subjects as basic as how we think and what makes us happy. Once again, I'm startled at how unexpectedly clinical and coherent the Buddhist approach is. But as soon as I start applying the theory to my own life, my skepticism kicks in.

"If I understand things right," I tell Alice, "Buddhism says that happiness doesn't come from things outside us, but from our interpretation of those things. People interpret the same things differently, depending on their conditioning, or karma."

Alice is nodding.

"And from the work you're doing, people who meditate seem to be a lot better at interpreting their external world in a way that makes them happy."

"Generally."

"I can see how that whole interpretation theory might apply to stuff like music, or art. But what about when *real* things happen. Say your relationship with your girlfriend or wife comes to an end. How can you interpret that any way except negatively?" The question, of course, is deeply personal. I'm thinking about Isabella and the way our collapsing relationship seems to have me falling into oblivion almost every night.

Alice's eyes twinkle. "Why don't you ask the millions of people who queue up each year for a divorce? A lot of people can't wait to dump girlfriends or wives. Some people are in relationships they hate, but for whatever reason, feel they have to stay in them," she shrugs. "There's nothing inherently negative about a relationship ending—sometimes it's a big relief."

"Of course if you're really in love with someone and you lose them that's different. That's going to come as a shock, and you're going to grieve for that person. But it's what you do next that counts. Some people get locked into a spiral of depression and self-pity that can go on a very long time. Others move on and start doing new things, grow in new ways. What seems devastating at the time can turn out to be a new beginning, a different chapter. This is why we need to develop equanimity—the wisdom not to instantly label everything as negative or positive and get all churned up about it when we really have no idea what the long-term effect will be. This is pure Dharma but, interestingly, it's also mainstream cognitive therapy."

I'm surprised by Alice's explanation, and the conviction with which she makes it. But I also recognize the allusion to cognitive behavioral therapy. Having had at least two friends on the receiving end of the therapy, I've heard all about how, instead of merely offering Kleenex and sympathy, cognitive therapists take an altogether more robust approach, asking their clients to tell them exactly why they are anxious or unhappy—before challenging their assumptions. Aloud I say, " I guess I'm just used to believing that certain events are intrinsically negative or positive."

"You used the right word," she agrees, "Belief." The more we meditate, the more we recognize our beliefs and superstitions for what they are. All of us are constantly making false associations between what's happening out there, and in here," she touches first her head then her heart. "*It's not what happens to you that matters, but the way you interpret things.*"

It's the same theme that Geshe-la spoke to me about. One, I realize, which is at the center of the Dharma. But all the same, I can't help wondering. "It's okay for people like Lama Dendrup to spend forty thousand hours meditating. But that's a big ask. Realistically, how many people are going to give up their jobs to sit under a tree—"

"Don't have to," she grins. "Monks like Lama Dendrup are useful for experimental purposes because they're at the furthermost end of the spectrum. They're extreme examples. But I can show you tapes of people who've been meditating less than an hour a day for just a few years and they look a lot different from the control."

We walk further up a leafy residential street towards several apartment blocks. "The other point," says Alice, "is that psychological benefits are not the only positive outcome."

"You've researched mind-body stuff?"

"Not us. But a lot of the major schools like Harvard and Yale. Most programs only got going in the 1980s, but in the past ten years there's been an explosion of research. You know, if meditation was available in capsule form, it would be the biggest selling drug of all time," her conviction is irrepressible. "It combats stress by lowering blood pressure and the heart rate. It improves the immune function so you don't get colds and flu so much. It boosts DHEA production—that's the only hormone that decreases directly with age—slowing down aging—"

"I didn't know aging could be slowed!"

"Conclusive evidence," she's firm. "People who've been meditating regularly for over five years have a biological age twelve years younger. Fact. You'd never think I'm thirty-seven would you?" she jokes.

"Because you're not."

"Thirty-seven," she laughs "Going on twenty-five."

I really am surprised. I would never have put Alice a day older than thirty. From having thought we were about the same age, I realize now that she's older than me.

"You sure are a great advertisement for meditation," I say.

"Oh, flattery will get you everywhere!" she replies, leading me to an apartment block, across the small lobby and into a waiting elevator.

MOMENTS LATER SHE'S OPENING THE DOOR OF A SECOND FLOOR APARTMENT. As she switches on the light I find myself stepping into a haven of warmth.

It's not a large apartment. A hallway crowded with books leads into a lounge furnished with a large, comfortable sofa and two chairs decorated with Indian-design throws in rich, natural colors. An aroma of cooking wafts through the apartment, tantalizing fragrances of cardamom, dhal and coriander. As I glance around the buff-colored walls, at the two lamps with carved elephant bases, I am moved by how wonderfully this room reflects Alice and the tranquility I feel in her presence.

I turn to where she's watching me with that bright expectation. The whites of her eyes, I notice now, have clarity, a freshness in which the irises appear to be set, like twin sapphires.

There's a movement behind her, and she steps aside as a petite brunette appears from the kitchen in an apron.

"This is my sister Beth," she introduces us. "Beth, Matt."

I can almost feel Beth's curiosity as she looks at me.

"Whatever you're doing in there smells pretty good," I compliment her.

"Just as well," her smile is puckish. " 'cus that's what we've having for dinner."

"You will stay?" Alice insists, less a question than a demand.

As Alice leaves me to get drinks from the kitchen, I look around at all the framed photographs in the room. Some are images of groups of friends, travel trips to the Himalayas, Jewish festivities. The usual clutch of baby pictures. Alice in the embrace of a tall, dark-haired guy with an amiable face—could this be Josh? Beth and Alice on a yacht in what looks like the Caribbean.

I notice a small Tibetan prayer wheel resting on a shelf, with elaborate brocade strips about its handle. A UCLA master's degree awarded to Alice Weisenstein. In pride of place is a gilt-framed photograph of Alice with a very elderly Tibetan Lama.

Alice returns to the room with a beer for me and a Dr Pepper for herself. There's a rush of footsteps from the corridor beyond, and beside her appears a boy of nine or ten.

"My son, Josh," she looks down at him with an indulgent smile.

"Josh!" I try to conceal my surprise and form a welcoming expression.

He's a cute-looking kid with a sensitive face, fair hair—and there's no doubting where his eyes came from. Even before he looks down at the floor in shyness, I can't avoid noticing the blueness of them.

As Alice hands me my beer he looks up and murmurs something to her about being hungry.

"Beth is cooking, sweetie. You'll have to wait about half an hour. Help yourself to an apple or a piece of fruit."

As he disappears up the corridor towards the kitchen I'm amazed by his acceptance.

"Very well behaved," I smile, as we watch him head towards the kitchen. "The kids I know wouldn't let up until you let them have coke and chips."

"He *is* a good kid," she nods, contentedly, raising her glass in a silent toast. "Though his aunt spoils him rotten."

"It's what aunts are for." I reciprocate the gesture. "I was told that you and Josh are the mainstay of the Dharma Center."

"Who said that?" Alice is wry.

"Don't know their names. A group of people at the class I came to. I just assumed that Josh was your partner."

"Always dangerous to assume," she meets my eyes with a meaningful expression. "I didn't plan to have a child," she tells me with unexpected candor. "I definitely didn't plan to be a single mom. When I discovered I was pregnant, the father told me he was committed. But he just couldn't face the reality of it. He left us when Josh was just three months old."

I'm shaking my head. "Must have been tough."

"Very dark days," she nods. "They lasted a while. But I had to cope, for both our sakes."

I wonder why she's telling me this. There's an intimacy in what she's saying, but could it be that she's also asserting her independence? Letting me know of her self-sufficiency and that her personal life has a very different set of priorities?

"For twelve months I believed we were creating the perfect little family. And I had to let go of all that." She fixes me with a gaze so intense I feel unusually self-conscious. "But if I ever meet the person I'm meant to be with, I'm sure I'll know it."

I'm not sure how to react. After a pause I nod towards the kitchen, "Beth doesn't mind cooking?"

She shakes her head. "Family tradition—especially on a Friday night. If you go into the kitchen, she'll chase you right out of there. Cooking's her thing." Then after a moment, "Just as well. It's not my strong suit."

I laugh, glancing around at all the photographs on the wall near where we're standing.

"Our family celebrates the Jewish holidays," she nods towards some of the group shots. "That's Simon, my kid brother, eating toffee apple at Rosh Hashanah."

Then seeing my blank expression, "Jewish New Year."

I inspect the photograph more closely. A family of three generations sit at a dining table, looking indulgently at a young boy as he bites into a shiny, red apple.

"Your family," I nod towards the picture, "were they upset when you converted to Buddhism?"

Alice chuckles. It's evidently a familiar subject. "Convert is a bit of a strong word," she says. "Sure, I'm a practicing Buddhist, but by background and culture I'm Jewish. Some very high profile Western Buddhists in this country are."

"Jewish Buddhists?"

"Yes. They even have a name for us. JewBu's!" She settles down on one of the chairs, tucking her legs up under her with feline grace. I lounge back in the capacious sofa opposite.

"When you walked into the gompa for the first time the other night," she says, "you saw the Buddha statue at the front and people chanting prayers. Through western eyes it would seem like a religion. But we don't worship Buddha, and he never claimed to be divine. The Dharma is much more about action than belief. Anyhow," she grins, "Don't get me started on it or I'll never shut up!"

"No—this is interesting," I insist. "Is that why Buddhists don't try to convert people?" While I'm genuinely curious, I also want to keep her talking, her enthusiasm is so infectious.

"Pretty much. The tradition offers a lot of practices, like a tool box of psychological techniques. They're open to anyone to use. As the Dalai Lama says, the objective is to make people happier. Whether that's happier Buddhists. Happier atheists. Happier Jews. Whatever. The objective is not to win market share for Buddhism."

"But if you really believe these practices make people happier," I enjoy playing devil's advocate, "why don't you get the good news out there? That's what evangelicals would say."

"I can answer than in one word," she smiles. "Karma. If you don't have the karma to be interested in Buddhism, you could live next door to the most amazing guru and never pay him any attention."

For I moment I wonder if she knows where I live.

"But if that karma is ready to germinate, even if you live in the most unlikely place on earth, one way or another you'll make it your business to find what you're looking for."

I think how very different this philosophy is from the conventional Anglican background in which I'd been brought up.

"Which brings me to a question I'm very curious about," her eyes meet mine and once again I wonder if the undercurrent between us is just my imagination. "Why did you come to our particular Dharma Center?"

"That's easy," I'm relieved the question's not more personal. "Geshe-la suggested it."

"Geshe-la?" her eyes fill with astonishment. "How did that happen?"

"I met him at three o'clock one morning," I tell her, recalling that first encounter. I explain about living next door. My jet lag. My decision to go for a walk. The scent of frangipani. How startled I was to discover I was not alone. How Geshe-la had talked to me about change being the only constant.

As I tell her, Alice shakes her head with a smile. "That's Geshe-la," she says.

Usually I'd be hesitant to confide the sense of connection I'd felt with Geshe-la. But I'm happy telling Alice, and as I explain the strange but powerful effect Geshe-la had had on me, I find I'm touching my heart.

"Yes. He has that effect on people," she says. "So that's when he suggested you get to a Dharma class—"

"No. That was the second time we met."

"Second time?" She's surprised.

"We went to Urth Caffé for a coffee."

"You're making this up!"

"Am not!" I'm relishing the moment.

"How on earth did you pull that one off? There's people at the center who've been inviting him out for years—"

"Probably because I didn't want him to come," I laugh.

"You can't be serious!" Her eyes are vivid with excitement as I tell her about Geshe-la and me discussing, over our coffees, how the quantum science description of reality seems much the same as the Buddhist version.

A new look comes into her expression when I relate Mrs. Min's generous offer to do my laundry. The expectation is still there, but along with it is something else I haven't seen before. Something I can't immediately identify.

As I talk about Mrs. Min and her box of gifts, how she'd told me I could pick one, the change in Alice's expression grows more evident.

"Have you told anyone else about this?" she asks, lowering her voice, when I finish.

"You mean, about the mala that I thought was a necklace?"

"Yeah."

I shake my head.

"I suggest you don't," she says, with a seriousness that surprises me.

"Is there some . . . problem?"

"No. Not in telling me," she's quick to reassure. "Over time it will all get clearer."

Suddenly I recognize her expression: it's a look of apprehension.

"Okay," I nod, surprised. "I won't breathe a word."

"I don't suppose you have the mala with you?"

I reach into my pocket. In the past couple of days I've taken to carrying it with me for reasons I haven't thought much about. It just feels right.

"You're the first person who's seen it," I remark, handing it to her.

She takes the beads from me and studies the mala with close interest, before folding her hand about it. For a moment she closes her eyes and the dazzling blueness is replaced by the presence only of serenity.

—

Driving home, I think how quickly my time went with Alice and how much I enjoyed the meal with her and Beth and Josh—my most delicious dinner since I moved to America. Her sister is a warm hearted, maternal aunty who clearly enjoys doting on the pair of them and, living nearby, is an important part of their lives. Josh is smart but gentle, without the self-obsession of many kids his age. And most evident of all is the closeness between the three of them—they seem to function as a self-contained family unit.

Of course I can't help wondering about Alice, the attraction I feel for her, and whether it's reciprocated or whether, to her, I'm just a charity case—a new guy in town from the other side of the world who hardly knows anyone and on whom she's taken pity. During our personal exchanges I haven't mentioned anything about Isabella. I haven't been completely open, but I'm also not sure what it is I'm concealing: a fiancée who is on a course out of town? Who has no intention of coming back? Who is, right now, in the arms of her Italian lover? It's a subject I try not to think about.

By the time I wind my way along Sunset Boulevard all the way to West Hollywood, it's going on a quarter to twelve and the fatigue is setting in. Once again I'm struck by the L.A. paradox that apart from the nightclubs along Santa Monica Boulevard, the surrounding blocks are dead to the world even on a Friday night. The streets are deserted. The security gates on all the houses are locked. Everyone has long since gone to bed.

But not everything on Rosewood Avenue, I soon discover, has been quite as settled. As I get closer to the house, I see the living room lights switched on. Not by me; I drove to UCLA straight from the office.

Slowing down, I pull over to the side. The curtains in the main rooms have been drawn. Lord knows what's been going on inside. Not that there's much to steal—just a DVD, sound system, the usual stuff. Cutting the lights and engine, I sit for a few moments, staring at the house in disbelief. Noticing, for the first time, that the front door is ajar.

Then a movement on the front porch catches my eye. *They're still there*! I feel in my pocket for the cell phone. Alarm rising, I try to remember the number for emergency services in L.A.

In the next moment I see the silhouette. The glass of wine on the table. How she's staring directly across the road to my car.

Isabella.

Chapter Ten

The mood of relaxed, good feeling I'd been enjoying until only moments before comes to an abrupt halt. In its place, a sudden, hollow shock. A confrontation was the last thing I'd been expecting this evening, but as I see her standing, arms folded and waiting, I realize there's no avoiding it. Climbing out from behind the driver's seat, my mouth is dry as sand.

"You're late," she says as I walk across the silent, midnight street towards her. She's wearing black jeans and a burgundy sweater. Lamplight glints off her polished leather boots.

I don't feel the need to explain where I've been. Especially when she gave me no warning at all that she was coming. And I'm trying to work out what's going on. Four weeks—that's how long it's been since she left. What has she come back for? And is she alone?

"This is unexpected," I remark, pausing at the bottom of the steps up to the porch.

"We were given the weekend off. It was a last minute thing—they only decided this morning. Most people collapsed into bed to catch up on their sleep."

Immediately, I'm wondering which bed she'd have collapsed into if she'd stayed in Napa. Though seeing her standing here, looking the same as always, makes my suspicions about Paolo and her seem somehow less real and more a product of an over-heated imagination. As though it just isn't possible that Isabella, my Isabella, could do that.

"When I left for Napa, we didn't exactly part on the best of terms," she says. "We need to talk."

"We sure do," I agree. But I feel ambushed that we're talking here and now at her instigation. As though she's set this up to have the tactical advantage. I'm also trying to place her tone, though she's keeping it deliberately even.

"Wine?" she points to an empty glass beside her own, and an open bottle on the table.

I shake my head as I climb the few steps and cross to sit on the low porch wall. It's unprecedented for the two of us to be together like this, encountering each other after weeks apart and yet keeping our distance like a pair of opposing magnets. But the force field between us seems almost tangible, as though wariness has assumed a physical energy.

Or that's how it seems to me. Isabella's expression is hard to read.

"Things in London are pretty difficult for Mum," she says, her voice soft in the stillness. As she starts on an update of her family situation, I watch her closely, wondering why she's doing this—choosing to avoid the subject that she's presumably come all the way to discuss. She continues with the detail of her last conversation with her mother, her monologue halting while I stare down at the floor. At some point she trails off mid-sentence and there's a long pause before she says, "You don't seem that . . . involved."

I shrug. "I'm sorry about what's happening in Dulwich." Then looking up, I level with her. "But you still haven't told me about the night I couldn't get hold of you."

She doesn't exactly roll her eyes. But impatience flashes across her face.

"Like I said on the phone, the study group got together. Some of us had too much to drink and I really was in no shape to walk home at one in the morning." She twists at one of the gold star earrings I'd once given her for a birthday.

"This Paolo guy. Is there something going on between you?"

"Don't be ridiculous!" Removing the earring, she tosses her head. "I only stayed at his place because I was too far gone. It's nothing like that."

I'd been willing to believe her—until those last few words. Her apparent indignation and impatience had a ring of truth to them. But "it's nothing like that" reminds me of the phrase she'd used on the phone, "one-off." It seems like a Freudian slip. As though she can't fully bring herself to lie to me.

"It'll never happen again," she continues. Across the porch her gaze is hard. Determined. Wanting to brazen this out.

I hold it, daring her to tell the truth, before finally I say, "So. You did sleep with him."

"I didn't say that!" She tugs out the other earring.

"This *is* me you're talking to," I tell her. "You don't have to."

I get up and start towards the front door.

"Matt, don't!" she calls. "Why won't you believe me?"

"You can't lie to me, Isabella! I know you too well."

I'm about to step inside when I turn to see her crumple, face in her hands, tears sliding between her fingers as she slumps to a chair. "It was a mistake," she whispers. "I'm sorry. I'm really, *really* sorry. It should never have happened."

Despite my suspicions, nothing has prepared me for the confirmation. I thought my cynicism would protect me from it. But her admission still shakes me. I stand there as if I've been winded. When she'd slammed down her engagement ring in the kitchen counter, it had been in anger and frustration. Deep down I'd thought we could still come back from that. But now I'm not so sure.

"How could you?" I struggle to absorb the news.

"I keep asking that myself."

"You talk about *me* not being able to commit . . ."

On the few occasions in the past that I've seen her cry, just the sight of her tears has been unbearable, and I've done all I can comfort her. I don't know whether she's hoping for my sympathy right now. But all I feel is the deep down stab of betrayal.

"If there was any way in the world I could turn back the clock . . ." she manages.

I'm thinking of Paolo getting her out of her clothes and into bed. I'm wondering what she did for him. Whether she encouraged him with the same self-evident relish as when we make love.

"So what was it like?" I demand, images of the two of them filling my mind. "What was *he* like?" I really don't want to know the answers, but am driven by a strange compulsion to get to the worst of it, as though opening a festering wound.

"That's just it," she cries. "I hardly remember anything."

"Oh, well," I look at her distress with cold anger. "That makes me feel a whole lot better."

"It didn't mean anything, Matt!"

"Which makes it alright."

"I've said I'm sorry," she's shaking her head, miserably. "I really don't know what else I'm supposed to do." As she looks up and searches my face I know she's seeking some form of forgiveness, but right now my heart feels like it's frozen solid.

"What if I'd been the one?" I demand.

"I don't know," she's shaking her head. "I guess I'd be pretty shocked."

"Yeah. Exactly," I turn again, making my way inside.

IN THE BATHROOM I GO THROUGH THE ROUTINE MOTIONS OF GETTING ready for bed. Only a short time ago I'd been feeling relaxed and ready for sleep. Right now I'm so agitated, I barely know what I'm doing.

Isabella says she can hardly even remember, but what if she's just saying that? What really went on that evening? Truth is, I'll probably never know. And what had happened when they woke up the morning after? Had he been at it again, the Latin lover? Had he woken her up with a smile on her face? And what had she said to him? Was it all embarrassment and contrition like she was implying, or had they parted on altogether different terms?

Having got her in the sack once, was this Paolo continuing to pursue her, and what was she doing about his advances? I couldn't see him just walking away from something like that without wanting to come back for more. He'd probably be sending flowers and leaving text messages and hovering around her every class they went to.

I go through to bed, and hear her come inside from the porch and lock the front door. She goes to the bathroom and brushes her teeth. There's more sobbing as I toss and turn in darkness, driven mad by my thoughts. Then I hear her go through to the lounge. After a while the light is switched out and I realize she isn't coming to bed with me tonight.

This comes as a relief.

In the stillness of the house I hear the creaking of the sofa, the sound of muffled weeping. "Helping to free others from suffering" suddenly comes to mind. The Buddhist definition of compassion, according to Geshe-la, who'd said it was our life's purpose to cultivate compassion. Great in theory, I reckon, but what would he have to say about a fiancée who yanks off her engagement ring, then sleeps with her classmate? In my mind, I'm having the conversation with Geshe-la, presenting the case for the prosecution. For all my shock and injured pride, I know he has arguments for the defense.

But were any of those reason enough to cross the line?

Trying to block thoughts of her infidelity out of my mind, I remember images from earlier that evening, when I'd gone to Alice's apartment. I'd visited her without any thought of a relationship other than simple friendship, but as soon as I'd made the discovery about Josh, I'd begun to think differently.

And I wonder what would have happened if Beth and Josh hadn't been on the scene? If we'd had a few more drinks? If Alice had made the first move? Would I have resisted? Am I superior to Isabella or is it just that I haven't had the same opportunity to stray?

Even though it's been a long week and I'm dog tired, my mind is more agitated than I can ever remember. I turn restlessly in bed from one side to the other, unable to find peace for even a moment. I check the clock at intervals to see 1 am turn to two o'clock and eventually to three. Geshe-la's wake-up time I'm thinking. And though I could probably do a lot worse than get out of bed and go along the road and speak to him, right now I'm in no fit state for anything. I just want to shut out the horror and go to sleep.

Eventually I manage the sleep part, but the horror won't go. Instead, I barely close my eyes before I'm sliding, desperately searching for a footing, struggling against the icy tilt. The wailing sound is louder than ever. Worse than foreboding, tonight the rising howl seems personally hostile.

And there's no escaping it. As I writhe in the darkness, clambering against the slipperiness, it's impossible to shut out the noise.

But, as in the past, I'm no match for the forces tugging against me. Despite my clawing and kicking for something solid, a point of resistance, all my efforts are futile. I cross the point of no return—and with a jolt I'm going over the edge. Plunging into the void. My heartbeat so loud that my whole body pounds to the rhythm of it.

Then I'm crunching to a halt, awkward and unsteady. Poised on a narrow foothold, aware of a suffocating band of pressure around my chest.

Even as I balance unsteadily, I feel the support loosening beneath my feet. And I know that I can't fall any further. Such an event would be catastrophic!

Clinging perilously, battling for survival, somehow above the unearthly cacophony all around me I hear someone calling my name. A disembodied screaming through the darkness. The voice is familiar—but whose? Isabella's? I strain to catch the words, to discover whose they are and what I'm doing here. But they're only faint in the howling tumult.

Even in my dream I am thinking: I can't let this nightmare defeat me! I must put an end to it! I can't continue like this, being terrorized in the early hours and waking up in a blind panic. I must get to the root of it and exorcise whatever energy is propelling me through this, night after night.

I don't know when the horror ends and sleep begins, but it must be around dawn. Shaken and perspiring after one of the worst nights of my life, I manage a few uneasy hours before waking at nine.

Stressed and distracted it's as though I've had no sleep at all.

I get up, relieved to find that Isabella is still asleep on the sofa and that I don't have to face her. It buys me time in the shower to think about what to do and say. But standing with my head directly under the nozzle, trying to come back to life in the warm gush of water, I'm still no clearer by the end of it. The same old images and arguments pound through my head. Where does unhappiness come from? There's no avoiding it right now; it's from the agitated cauldron of my mind.

When I come out of the bathroom, washed and dressed, she's standing in the kitchen in her terry dressing gown. She's made coffee, and two mugs stand on the kitchen table. We don't say anything, but when she looks at me it's with an expression of such deep despair, in the calm of morning I find myself reacting in a way I'd never have expected: I reach out and take her in my arms.

Holding each other is the only thing that seems to make sense. Despite all my restless thinking during the night, none of it has got me anywhere. Too much thinking, the Buddhists would say. The embrace doesn't mean that things are suddenly right between us, and it doesn't change what's happened. But it feels like an acknowledgement that we are both survivors of the same disaster. And perhaps, I think as I hold her close, it will keep me from sliding off the cliff and falling into oblivion. Right here and at this moment there seems nothing else to do or say.

After a while we break apart. Isabella says she needs a shower. I go about the Saturday morning chores which have become routine since I've been living here on my own. There's the laundry to be sorted and bins to be cleared: attending to the mundane details of domestic life comes as something of a relief.

I'm very aware of Isabella in the bathroom. The sounds of the shower, then the hairdryer providing the soundtrack to my own activities. She emerges some time later in the kitchen, goes over to the fridge and opens it. "Feel like eating?" she asks.

I realize it's not really so much a question about breakfast, as about re-engaging. She's made a big effort with her appearance. Her hair is lustrous and she's wearing make-up. I wonder if she did the same that night she went around to Paolo's. Meeting her eyes, I remember the last exchange we had in the kitchen, when she'd announced her decision to study in Napa. The tension and tears and my helpless, foolish anger that had turned this room into a battleground. The ring is still there, exactly where she left it.

I decide, spur of the moment, that I don't want to spend another moment in a difficult conversation with Isabella in this room, or even this house.

"There's a place on Melrose I've been a couple of times, which does brunch," I suggest. "We could go there."

A short while later we are walking down Rosewood before turning North to Melrose. We are strangely distant. No holding hands or teasing one another the way we used to. Instead, there's an unfamiliar formality between us.

The restaurant has al fresco tables under striped umbrellas, Dixieland jazz and a laid-back weekend vibe. When I've been here before I've thought how much better it would have been with Isabella. The reality now is very different from the easy laughter and intimacy I'd imagined.

After we're seated and have ordered our eggs Benedict, Isabella asks me how things are going at Acellerate. She probably believes it's a safe subject, and when I tell her about my activities to get new research programs off the ground, I downplay the frustrations I'm having with the scientific advisory committee.

Our food arrives and conversation shifts to her coursework in Napa. She tells me what she's learning, and how she could never have achieved so much anywhere else. She gets animated talking about Jean-Claude Galliano, a French wine-master who visited Napa from his chateau in the Loire Valley. An *eminence grise* of the industry, Jean-Claude produces vintages at his ancient, family-owned vineyard. Vintages available only in select Michelin restaurants. For a few moments Isabella forgets herself, and us, and her enthusiasm takes over as she describes the wine-maker's philosophy and his way of life—the same lifestyle of dedication to the art of wine-making, of travel and culture to which she has long aspired.

"Dad would really like to have met him." I notice how she refers to the possibility in the past tense, as though Julio is no longer in any position to meet the likes of Jean-Claude Galliano. As Isabella's knowledge of the wine industry is growing in richness and substance, Julio's is being hollowed out. By the time her understanding fully blossoms, her father will be in no position to appreciate the flower he has given life to. He's already having difficulty remembering the name of his favorite wines.

"So, how is Julio?" I ask, still avoiding The Subject.

She tells me about things in Dulwich, scrupulously avoiding reference to my lack of interest the night before. She explains how her parents are coping with the unexpected quirks thrown up by Julio's cruel disease. The news that they have acquired a pair of King Charles spaniels, having discovered that for those in the initial stages of late-onset Alzheimer's, forming a bond with pet dogs, and establishing a regular walking routine, can have positive benefits.

I imagine Julio and Tina walking across the tree-lined park near their home, the dogs racing about their ankles. In my mind's eye it is autumn and leaves are blowing off the massive oak branches, slowly, inexorably reducing the lush foliage to stark silhouettes.

Isabella puts down her cutlery, dabs her lips with a napkin and takes a sip of coffee before saying. "There's something I've got to tell you."

So, we've come down to it. There can be no further avoiding the discussion. Tension returns to the pit of my stomach.

"Jean-Claude isn't only a master wine-maker," she begins, to my surprise. "He's also passionate about transferring his knowledge to the next generation. That's why he visited Napa. The Napa course has a world-wide reputation and he was there as much to check out the talent as to lecture to us.

"To cut a long story short, he was very complimentary about my palate. So much that he's invited me onto his master class when I finish at Napa. It's a one-year course, in France. On top of the Napa course and what I did at Bertollini, it will really set me up for a career in the industry."

From her tone it's clear that she's not asking my permission or even approval. She's not running this by me. She has already made up her mind; it's "something I have to tell you."

In that moment I also understand the one night stand with Paolo really is irrelevant compared to this. A fleeting foolishness, accidental, unpremeditated. No worse, if I am completely truthful, than I am capable of myself.

But the decision to leave Napa and head directly to France is of a different order of magnitude. She's had plenty of time to consider it and knows full well what it means. Her expression is sorrowful, yet also resolved. As we meet each other's gaze I realize the real reason she cried herself to sleep last night, the reason she looked so distraught this morning probably had less to do with what I had just discovered than the much more momentous news she had to break.

"I've told Jean-Claude about Dad's situation," she continues, pensive. "I could get from his estate back to London in a few hours, and he says there's no problem with me going home at weekends."

Then responding to my bleak expression. "We always agreed that if things got bad for Julio . . . "

"I know," I shrug. "I just hoped it wouldn't come to that."

"Me too," she pushes back in her chair. "But it has."

For a while I look at her wondering: What about us? Are we now unengaged? Is it all over between us? But I realize there's no point at all going down that avenue. Isabella's first loyalty is to her parents. She's returning home to do her duty.

"Mum needs my support," she says, as though echoing my thoughts. "They both do."

I remember how I first reacted when she told me she was going to Napa. Her decision to choose a six-month course over staying with me had felt like a betrayal, and my angry reaction had only made matters worse. Today's news is much, much more serious than that because it's permanent. I know that somehow I must do the smart thing this time, and not over-react. She doesn't want to come right out and say it's over between us. And shocked as I am by everything that's happened in the past twelve hours, I don't want to close down our options either. But there's one thing I have to find out.

"When you said that I couldn't commit," I keep my tone as conversational as I'm able, "I don't know what you meant by that. I know I'm not as romantic as you'd like, but I always imagined we'd get married. I just didn't think you were in a hurry."

"No, *you* were the one who wasn't in a hurry," she corrects me, her voice calm. "If you'd picked a date, I would have been so excited."

Would have been, I notice. Past tense. "I thought it was just your parents pushing for it?"

She shakes her head. "Every Italian girl wants a big wedding. We're brought up with the dream of the fairytale day. Of course my parents were pushing. But I wanted it, too."

Her revelation is heartfelt and takes me by surprise. I always thought she shared my own distaste for the over-the-top extravagance of vast Italian weddings. Now I realize I'm as much a product of my own family as she is of hers. My older brother and his wife had been married on a Friday morning at Chelsea Registry Office in front of eight friends—and only because they'd decided it was time to try for kids. Mum had attended as a witness, enjoying the celebratory restaurant lunch that followed, before returning to Hampshire for a late afternoon horticulturalist's meeting. I had always thought Isabella and I would do something similarly low key.

Now I shake my head, "I only wish you'd told me how important it was to you."

She hesitates for a moment before she looks at me directly, "There are some things you can't say, Matt, not for it to be right. I needed you to understand for yourself. To understand me."

WE SPEND THE REST OF THE WEEKEND IN NO MAN'S LAND. AFTER LUNCH we drive down to Venice Beach. Before we came to Los Angeles, I had dreamed of us under the palms together, checking out the street performers and market stalls, enjoying the California sunshine. But as I walk with Isabella along the expansive sidewalk today, my mood is funereal.

Everywhere around us there seem to be families—aged parents and their middle-aged children. Little kids and young mums. Sometimes three generations kicking ball together, and I think about the bond of blood. How strong it is, and how it has the power to reach across oceans. Isabella's loyalty, the subject which was such an obsession with me was, in reality, never in doubt. It's just that her loyalty was always, first and foremost, to her family. Perhaps if I'd married her, things would have been different. But that's not something I'm going to find out.

That night we sleep together but don't sleep together, lying like a pair of bookends in our lonely bed. I remember what Alice had said about relationships coming to an end. How the way you interpret things is what makes an experience positive or negative. How some people come around to thinking that ending a relationship was the best thing that ever happened to them because they were set free to meet someone else.

I can understand how that might work for some people, some of the time. But, right now, it doesn't work for me. Instead I feel I'm about to lose everything. Up until now, Isabella has been the most important person in the world to me. In so many ways, she is my world. In the time we've been together she's become reflected in me in so many different ways that by losing her I'm losing part of myself.

SHE NEEDS TO BE AT LAX BY MID-SUNDAY MORNING. SHE SAYS SHE'LL take a cab, but of course I give her a ride. When she packs she takes an extra suitcase of stuff with her. Her CD player from the lounge. The trinkets she'd used to decorate the shelves. I notice the engagement ring has gone from the kitchen countertop. She leaves few of her belongings in the house. Only a large red suitcase of books and clothes. The veneer of glue still holding us together is now reduced to this.

All the way out to the airport I half expect her to tell me that she'd prefer me not to call. Or that she won't be coming back to L.A. again. Or some other, definitive signal. But instead we make desultory conversation about King Charles spaniels. What they'd be like as pets. How Julio and Tina are likely to cope with them.

When I drop her off, there's no parting shot or final farewell, nor any intimate embrace or promise to call. I know the ambiguity has as much to do with me as it has with Isabella. We've both deliberately held off, not wanting to hear or say the words. All of it is so far from the way things used to be, when we'd share our thoughts without even thinking. It is as though each of us is retreating inside ourselves, curling up in a tight, defensive ball.

Driving back to West Hollywood, it seems that my smart new car, the blue skies and hazy midday sunshine conspire to make me feel only more alone and unhappy. Such a short time ago, the idea of myself as a research director driving down a Californian freeway in a silver SLK on a day like this would have seemed like my most cherished dream had been realized.

But now that it's happening, I'm starting to realize the price I've had to pay. Although I slept through last night without a recurrence of the nightmare, in a way that dark reminder is superfluous. Emotionally, at least, I am already descending into a void that feels just as bad. Perhaps worse, for how can there be suffering in oblivion? What Isabella and I had together was so good, so precious, I doubt I can replace it. All those tender memories together take on an aching significance as I realize they'll soon be all I have left.

It's only when you lose someone, runs the adage, that you realize how much they meant to you. And the grief I feel is so bad that by the time I get home it's all I can do to collapse motionless on her side of our bed—the sheets still sweet with her fragrance—numb with disbelief. The pointlessness of everything without her. The most profound loneliness.

I lie there all afternoon, all evening, all night. Unsure of anything except the idea that things can't get much worse.

I am, of course, completely wrong.

MID WAY THROUGH THE NEW WEEK, I GO TO AN EVENING SEMINAR IN downtown L.A. The subject—regulatory milestones—is dry as dust, but dragging myself through my depression I tell myself this is an opportunity to prospect. To come across the next big idea which I can take to the scientific advisory committee.

After a predictably uninspiring presentation, over a hundred biotech executives are served chilled wine and canapés in a reception area, and the real business of the evening, networking, gets into full swing.

Back in London there were always a few familiar faces at these gatherings, but I'm not sure where to start here. So I'm relieved when I'm approached by a slight, bespectacled guy a few years older than me.

"Director at Acellerate?" he confirms, reading my name label.

"That's right."

"Josh Calloway," he confirms, shaking hands. Checking out his own badge, I see the name of a company I've never heard of. "That wouldn't be Director of Research would it?"

"Yes," I nod.

"And from England by the sound of it?"

"London."

"I take it you have the big office on the twenty-eighth floor at Acellerate?"

I wonder where this is heading. Usually I'm only too happy to introduce myself, but the guy's know-all manner has me on guard. I regard him carefully. "Big compared to what I had in London, but—"

"The Departure Lounge," he says, as though I'd confirmed his question.

I flash a glance about the room, looking for a get-away. "Arrivals Lounge, actually," I correct him. "I only got here two months ago."

"Two months? Let me guess, Blakely's taken your baby off you. He's found a bright young thing from Harvard business school to take care of all the pedestrian details leaving you free for the sunlit uplands of pure science?"

I fix him with a close stare. He's a smart-ass, for sure, but his knowledge of my situation is unnerving. For just an instant I am dangling in a threatening darkness, about to fall. I feel my heart thump.

After a pause I ask, "Why's my job of such interest?"

"Oh," he grimaces, "I should have explained. It used to be mine."

I raise my eyebrows.

"I was one of your predecessors at Acellerate."

I'm focusing on the name again. Calloway. It doesn't mean a thing.

"One of your several predecessors over the past four years. I lasted eight months, which is a record of pride—way above average—"

"I don't know what you're getting at," I cut him short. "But things are going pretty well for me at Acellerate."

His expression changes. He drops the theatrics. "If that really is true," he says, "if Blakely has only hired you for your brains, it will be a first."

"Why else would he?"

"Your intellectual property. Blakely's an IP raider. Grifter. Thief. Take your pick. He's never had an original idea in his life, but he's one of the wealthiest men in biotech. Go figure."

I'm immediately thinking about the deal that Harry Saddler had struck for the institute. His tough negotiating. How he'd got Acellerate to agree to the transfer of all our personal IP rights.

I also remember Harry giving me my Acellerate contract. How he was "officially" required to recommend I get a lawyer to look at it, but unofficially told me it was water-tight. Once Isabella and I had agreed to make the move, I'd been in such a hurry that I'd signed it without more than a quick flick through. "I think our agreement's pretty robust," I say, as much to reassure myself as anything.

"Just check the fine print," Calloway glitters through his glasses. "Because he's got a standard M.O. First he finds a brilliant, well-developed and hopelessly under-funded research program, ideally somewhere people don't know too much about him. Second, he appears on his white charger. He offers you big money, a big title, full relocation costs. That's the distraction. That's the bump in the ribs to get your mind off your coat pocket. That's when he gets what he's really after—somewhere in your contract, he nails you for your IP. Third, when you're still in honeymoon phase, he gets you to tell his own people everything there is to know about your program. Then, when they've sucked you dry of every last useful piece of data, he dumps you."

I am stunned. It's as though Calloway's revelations have pushed me to the threshold of that dark netherworld, and I'm sliding helplessly across the point of no return. Plunging into the darkness, my heart pumping with cold terror. Suddenly, everything I've worked for is threatened with oblivion. Calloway has not only described precisely what's happening to me with Nanobot, he has also revealed the truth of my own purpose in a way that's incisive and devastating. He has unlocked a code which, for all its simplicity, has escaped me. Was it that I couldn't see the truth because I didn't want to? That I preferred to believe the flattering version of reality offered by Bill Blakely.

Of course I don't know about the terms of my contract, which have taken on an imperative significance. But having heard Calloway's explanation, I wonder how I could possibly have been so casual about signing it. I try to remember where I put what seems suddenly the most important document of my career. Is it somewhere back on Rosewood Avenue in one of the packing crates?

"Well," I swallow after a while, "I haven't been fired yet."

"Oh, nothing so brutal as that. Blakely's favorite is to get you to generate even more ideas which he knocks back—"

"The scientific advisory committee—"

"Rejects them all."

"They're supposed to be independent."

"He controls every committee member. But the purported independence is why he can complain to you about your lack of output."

"Output?"

"'You've been with the company six months. I'm paying you five thousand dollars a week, plus, plus, and you've produced nothing. We're going to have to renegotiate.' He might suggest you work from home. Maybe he'll pay you four month's wages to work on new ideas. Bottom line: he's bought your program for a year's pay."

I'm shaking my head. "Seven year's work . . . " I'm still reeling from Calloway's revelations.

"For a couple of hundred thousand dollars, in my case," Calloway's mouth forms in a grim line. "Closest thing you get to daylight robbery."

"What about prior art patents?" I ask. My very first patent on the Nanobot project, had been awarded to me personally, not the institute. The patent described all the core features of the program, on which subsequent patents were based.

Calloway raises his eyebrows. "I'm in the same boat. But a patent only gives you the right to defend your IP. Do you seriously think you could take on Blakely by yourself?"

IMMEDIATELY AFTER MY ENCOUNTER WITH CALLOWAY I EXIT THE event. Hurrying back to West Hollywood, I'm soon fumbling among the packing crates, looking through all the paperwork until I retrieve my contract and, feeling like a fool for doing so only now, read it in detail for the first time. But the sentences are so long and clauses so convoluted—especially those relating to IP—I realize that only a lawyer could decipher what it means. What am I supposed to make of it?

Calling Harry in London early the next morning, when I relay what Calloway told me, he is relaxed and self-assured. The institute's lawyers had thoroughly vetted the agreement between Acellerate and the institute, he confirms. The IP rights of both the institute and researchers like me were safeguarded by guarantee.

But within twenty-four hours the story has moved on. Waking to a five o'clock call from the institute, Harry says his lawyers have pointed out a provision for IP to be renegotiated in individual contracts with key researchers. But he's pretty sure there's no relevant clause in my contract.

"*Pretty* sure?" I react, wide awake despite the time. "You told me it was watertight! Didn't you have it checked?"

"The first draft went through the lawyers. They recommended a few minor changes. I checked those had been made." There's a pause before he tells me apologetically, "I can't say I re-read the entire final draft. Our audit hadn't turned up anything bad about Blakely. Having already done the deal with the institute, I assumed this contract would be fine."

Assumed.

Having phoned some of the people whose warnings I was so eager to dismiss back in London, I confirm more reports along the lines Calloway told me. Why didn't any of this turn up in the institute's audit? Phoning Harry back to check things with him, it turns out the scope of the institute's scrutiny of Acellerate had been purely financial. They hadn't checked his commercial track record to find out who he'd screwed and used along the way. They hadn't even done anything as basic as run a search to see what media reports said about him.

It seems that the only brilliant negotiations Harry had been involved in were in his own mind.

Searching through a number of databases at Acellerate after hacking through security barriers, I discover the company has had four research directors in the past three years. None has been employed for longer than Calloway's eight months.

During the many quiet hours both at home and in the office, I have plenty of time to think about the Buddhist view that it's the way you view events that makes you happy or unhappy, not the events themselves. Just having some understanding of this fact is one of the few things keeping me sane. None of it needs to be devastating, I keep telling myself. I don't have to go into meltdown because of what's going on in Isabella's life, or even at Acellerate. I can choose not to allow myself to be dragged down by it.

I call Isabella, just to hear her voice as much as anything, and I soon realize she has her own, pressing worries, like looming assignment deadlines. I decide not to burden her with what's going on at Acellerate. We don't talk about the future, or what will happen at the end of her course.

Meantime at Acellerate it's getting harder and harder to keep up the motivation, to sustain the pretense. Why bother working up fresh ideas when the result from the scientific advisory committee is a foregone conclusion? Instead I do some research for myself. One by one, I track down each of the previous Acellerate research directors. After explaining who I am, and what I've uncovered, what I find are variations on the very same theme. All of us are scientists from underfunded institutions. None of us had any commercial expertise. In two of the cases the researchers, like me, had prior art patents, but no money with which to defend them.

I also spend time with Acellerate's investor relations manager, the smooth-talking Mervyn Pank. Initially he seems surprised that an egghead scientist is taking an interest in the company's financial plans. But he confirms that Acellerate is on track for a NASDAQ listing within two months. With the same meticulous efficiency as Dan Stenner, he has soon provided me with a welter of timeline charts, the major milestone being the publication of a prospectus, scheduled for six weeks time.

When I ask if Nanobot will be in the prospectus, Pank looks at me as though I'm crazy. Of course, he says, it's one of Acellerate's three flagship programs—it's what Acellerate will be inviting people to invest in. The company is looking to raise one hundred million dollars, putting its total market cap, he tells me impressively, at quarter of a billion dollars.

The call comes on a Friday afternoon. When I hear Casey Barrend's voice requesting my presence in Bill Blakely's office at three o'clock, I grimace. So it's to be an end-of-week clearing of the decks? I don't know whether to be angered by the predictability of what's going on, or astounded by the way Blakely seems to think he can just keep on playing this same old game, and no one's going to stop him.

The dynamics, as I reach the top of the spiral staircase, are very different from last time I was in the penthouse globe. Then I had been furious about Dan Stenner's appointment as head of Nanobot, and Blakely had been a reassuring and plausible liar. No doubt he had decided there were still a few drops of usable IP to be extracted from my mind. As far as I'm concerned, I'm now fully squeezed.

This time Blakely doesn't get up from his desk, nor invite me to join him on the sofas. Behind a pair of wire-frame reading glasses his face is a portrait of concern.

"I'm very troubled, Matt," he begins without greeting. "I'm just going through the company time sheets. You've been with us some time now and," his glasses flash, "so far no sign of any new research programs."

I look at the reports scattered across his shiny desk. I have no idea what they're about, not that that's really the point. Wherever they came from and whatever they say will prove his point. This is just a game.

"I'm paying you, what, twenty-one thousand dollars a month," picking up a sheaf of computer print-outs he waves it towards me with an expression of feigned indignation. "I think our shareholders will want to know what Acellerate is getting by way of return."

If I hadn't been expecting this I would have reacted very differently. Been shocked by the unexpected assault on my integrity. Alarmed by the consequences of what he's saying for my position as research director.

"When I look through the last couple of weeks," his forehead is creased in a dark frown, "this looks more and more to me like daylight robbery."

I remember the last time I heard that phrase. Luke Calloway had used it that evening to describe the great and glorious Blakely's very own *modus operandi*.

The time has come to call his bluff.

Chapter Eleven

A DAWN WIND BLOWS ACRID SMOKE INTO OUR FACES FROM THE devastated village of Tang. Denouncing us as thieves, the soldier gestures at the three of us with ferocious jabs. He already has one of the scriptures Lama Tsering was carrying spiked on the end of his bayonet. Does he have no respect, I wonder, the anger rising inside me? Does he have no reverence as he waves it about like a chunk of meat? His torrent of feigned indignation is leading somewhere. There is about to be more violence and I have no doubt that we will be the victims. If we don't do something soon we not only risk torture, we will probably lose our lives. And we will have failed in our special mission.

Lined up facing the villagers, Paldon Wangmo and I are standing with heads bowed while to my left Lama Tsering removes the contents of his rucksack. Raising my face slightly, I look up from under my eyebrows at the scene of devastation. The whole village plundered and smoking. Roofs set on fire. Windows smashed. Broken furniture strewn near kicked-down doors. The bodies of several villagers are dumped on the ground. What chance have we three monks already denounced as criminals?

The twenty or so villagers huddled in front of us have been forced from their beds, wearing whatever clothes they could find. They shiver from the cold, and are charred with smoke. Their faces are filled with terror.

I think about the young girl taken away by the three soldiers who captured us. How she reminded me of my sister. Knowing she is being abused by those three dogs makes me even more furious than the destruction of our scriptures. What will they do when they've finished with her? Leave her lying, broken and defiled? Or will they murder her, too?

And what about us? I can't forget the horrific sight of the elderly Nyingma monk, beaten to the bone. Perhaps by this same soldier now calling us enemies of the people.

His two comrades are standing behind the gathered villagers. Leaning against the wall of a shed, they pull out cigarettes. One strikes a match and, cupping his hand to protect the flame, leans across to the other. How is this possible, I wonder? How can two men who have just raped and killed stand there lighting cigarettes like nothing has happened? How can they accuse us of stealing things they're planning to destroy anyway? None of it makes sense. How can they so callously ruin people's lives as though it's of no consequence?

What does makes sense is what I'm doing behind my back; working to untie the knots that bind me. I have always been accomplished at tying and untying rope. And though the knots tied by the Red Army soldiers were pulled very tight when they captured us, that was many hours ago. During the night I have been picking at them, working away to loosen them without attracting any attention. Now that no one behind us is watching, I can work much more freely.

So far, Lama Tsering, struggling because his wrists are still bound together, has only removed the contents of his own rucksack, which comprises a number of texts wrapped in cloth. I am surprised that these don't include the two metal scrolls of Padmasambhava. It was Lama who packed all three of our rucksacks and I had assumed he would carry the most precious of all texts.

Now the soldier is barking at Paldon Wangmo to get onto the ground and unpack his own rucksack. Exhausted from the night-long journey, Paldon Wangmo has difficulty getting to his knees. He's dizzy from hunger and shock. When he doesn't start opening his rucksack fast enough, the soldier kicks him in the stomach. It's a brutal strike, so hard I flinch. I wish I could have taken the blow for him. Of the two of us, I have always been the more physically robust. Now Paldon Wangmo is so winded he can hardly breathe. His face has gone white with pain.

Wrists bound and hands fumbling, he is opening his rucksack. Taking out more sacred texts wrapped in the most exquisite brocade. Scriptures so precious that, in normal circumstances, not even ordinary monks would be allowed to see them. At Zheng-po, only those who had received the very highest initiations and who had completed several vajrayana retreats and fire *pujas* would be considered ready to receive these most secret teachings. And now they are being handed over to these savage dogs for destruction.

The soldier who has taken it upon himself to run this show trial leans over Paldon Wangmo to look at the texts. Suddenly I feel rope slipping away from my wrist. While I have been working to unpick the final knot, I didn't realize how close I was. Only with the quickest action am I able to clutch the rope before it falls off my hands completely.

I am now free to move. After hours with my hands tied behind my back, all I want is to bring them to my sides. But even though I'm able to, I must not. In fact I am now asking myself why I've done this. If the soldiers find out I've tried to escape, my fate will be sealed. The first thing they told us after capture, lying with our faces in the mud, was the punishment for attempted escape: death.

What has compelled me to undo the knots? Especially when I know I'm going to be ordered to remove the contents of my rucksack. Panic growing as steadily as my anger, I hear the blood thundering through my head. I am moments away from having my attempted escape revealed.

Looking up again from under my eyebrows, I briefly take in the villagers cowed with fear, the two soldiers smoking their cigarettes, completely indifferent to the destruction all around them.

But I also notice something else.

To the right of the shed, beyond the line of vision of our shrill accuser, two Tibetan villagers have appeared. One is carrying an axe, the other a hoe. I guess they have come out of hiding. And there's no mistaking their intention. But what can they do against three Red Army soldiers armed with Kalashnikovs?

Across the heads of the assembled villagers, they can see I've noticed them. With my head I try to alert them to where the other two soldiers are smoking their cigarettes. The problem is, they can't come up behind the other two soldiers without being seen by the soldier now screaming at Paldon Wangmo.

Badly winded, Paldon Wangmo can scarcely breathe. I have never seen him look so pale. Sucking breaths in short gulps, he tips out the last items of his rucksack. Lama looks over at him in concern. To my surprise the Padmasambhava scrolls are not in his rucksack either. I quickly realize what that means. *I* am their courier and protector!

My most precious, bound for the lands of the red-faced,
Await the Dharma warriors.

Some Dharma warrior I am. I can't even get them to the border without being captured.

With both Lama and Paldon Wangmo now revealed as so-called thieves, the soldier turns to me. His ranting has become even more heated. We are not only enemies of the people, but also of the Chinese motherland. We are criminals disguised in monks' robes. We have stolen from our own people but, thanks to the Red Army, have been caught red-handed.

As I listen to the hysterical ranting, the anger inside me grows ever more intense. How dare he accuse Paldon Wangmo of such crimes? Paldon Wangmo, who has always been the most considerate brother? How dare he condemn my kind and holy teacher, Lama Tsering, who has devoted his life to helping others?

Perhaps because I am the youngest and smallest and seem to present no threat, the soldier stands with his back to me as he faces the villagers. Perhaps because Lama and Paldon Wangmo have both been so submissive, the soldier thinks I will be too.

As he steps forward, chest puffed with arrogance, I look up directly. There's no sign of the two villagers at the side of the shed. I feel sure they must have worked out where the other two soldiers are. And I know it is time to be decisive. I can stand here knowing that I will soon be revealed for trying to escape. Or I can take matters into my own hands. I have only a few moments to make the most critical decision of my life. It's high risk. But I decide I *must* take advantage of my free limbs and the element of surprise.

I summon all my mental concentration and physical strength. I take a deep breath and focus. I recollect the tai chi movements practiced by the Zheng-po monks every morning.

The soldier's harsh voice has become even shriller. Never have I felt such hatred for anyone! He is telling the villagers there is only one punishment fitting for such serious treachery as ours. Only one way to make sure we never again steal from the Great Motherland. But nobody ever gets to hear his sentence, because at that moment I move swiftly and with all my strength. Leaping into the air, I kick the soldier, with all the force I can muster, low down his spine. As I do, he buckles backwards, falling to the ground.

All this happens very quickly. And I haven't worked out what happens next. Not exactly. I know I must seize his rifle from him.

I'm half expecting to be fired on by the two other soldiers. But the villagers from behind the shed have seized this distraction for their own surprise move. As I wrench the rifle from the soldier who is lying, groaning and disoriented, I look up to see the two villagers have taken their cue, and have struck down the other soldiers.

With all three soldiers on the ground, the assembled villagers instantly react. All of them are now on their feet, moving swiftly, soundlessly to encircle their former captors. Within moments they are stripping the soldiers of their rifles, knives, boots.

One of the largest men, perhaps the village butcher, appears with a long bladed knife. Moving from one soldier to the next, in swift, practiced motions he has slit the throats of all three of them. As they lie bleeding to death on the charred soil, their crumpled corpses stripped of boots, caps and weapons, the soldiers who were so terrifying just minutes earlier, are now just small, semi-naked corpses.

Taking the soldiers' rifles, I notice several villagers heading through the smoke in the direction taken by our original captors when they dragged away the girl.

Lama and Paldon Wangmo, meantime, are loading the sacred texts back in their rucksacks. As Lama re-wraps the text with the bayonet hole through it, there is a steely determination in his eyes.

One of the two men from behind the shed comes across to us. He is still carrying his axe. I notice the blunt end is smeared with blood and a clump of hair.

Lama and Paldon Wangmo are standing up, freeing themselves of the ropes around their wrists.

The villager approaches Lama Tsering.

"I am very sorry for your loss," Lama tells him, looking across the ruins of Tang. Even now, arms aching and faint with fatigue, he shows more concern for others than for himself.

"It would have been even worse if you hadn't arrived."

Lama's expression is inscrutable. He has always taught us never to guess at what may or may not have been.

"They planned to kill one out of every three villagers—that's what they said." Reaching out, the villager puts his hand on my shoulder and looks at me with deep gratitude, "Thank you, my friend."

I am reluctant to accept his thanks. "I acted on impulse." I want to explain myself to Lama as much as him. As I say this I look at the three soldiers on the ground, their lives leaking away. "Perhaps I was not wise."

Gunshots sound from nearby.

"You saved the lives of many," the villager is adamant. "You also saved one of our daughters even worse suffering."

I look over at Lama. It is the first time I have looked him in the eye since attacking the soldier. However well-intended the villager's remarks, it is Lama's reassurance which I seek. Even though I felt I had little choice but to take the action I did, even though I have probably saved our lives as well as the precious scriptures, as I look at the dead soldiers at our feet I feel overwhelmed by the consequences of my actions. Killing is the worst of the ten black karmas of body, speech and mind and I feel I have committed it.

So I am filled with relief by the warm equanimity of Lama's gaze, and even more overjoyed when he reaches out to hug me. Perhaps the villager thinks he his hugging me out of pride or gratitude. But I know what the embrace means. He is reassuring me.

"We should be on our way," says Lama. He doesn't need to explain further. Early morning is one of the most dangerous times for us monks. Who is to say there are not more Red Army soldiers searching the nearby paths right now?

The villager bows reverentially to the three of us, his hands clasped incongruously around the bloodied head of his axe. We return the prostration, before turning to Lama who looks at both of us briefly. "The cave," he confirms.

We retrace our steps to Padmasambhava's cave a thousand steps from here; a place I thought I'd never see again, or at least, not for a very, very long time. After the trauma of what we have just been through, and the exhaustion of our night long journey, we walk in silence.

Reaching the cave, I go up the birch tree, making my way into the cave just as before. It is not long before all three of us have washed in the stream behind the cave, eaten a quick meal, and are pulling out straw mattresses and blankets, relieved for the sanctuary of Padmasambhava's cave after our traumatic night.

As I lie down, Lama looks over at me from where he is sitting, preparing to meditate. "I am very grateful for what you did today, Tenzin Dorje," he says. "In time, many hundreds of thousands of people, perhaps millions, will also be grateful. Through your courage you helped protect the lineage."

"And probably our lives," adds Paldon Wangmo, his voice filled with emotion.

"And almost certainly our lives," agrees Lama with conviction.

Moments later, I am asleep.

In my sleep I remember what happened in the village of Tang. As in all nightmares, the images are a distortion of what really happened, but even more vivid than reality. In my surreal dream the villagers are huddled in front of me, faces filled with terror, just like at Tang, except instead of Tibetans these are Chinese villagers, and instead of standing in ropes, I am holding a Kalashnikov and gunning them down. I know these are the families of the Red Army soldiers killed at Tang, and as I shoot them, instead of falling over, slashes appear at their throats. They sit staring at me, horrified, grief-stricken, accusing, as the blood gushes down their necks and bodies.

The dream keeps replaying in my mind. Despite my efforts to get away from it, it just repeats and repeats. Later, when I wake up, it feels like something has changed. In the twilight, the air in Padmasambhava's cave still has its ethereal, almost luminescent quality, but I don't feel the magic of it as I did before. I know it's not the cave that has changed, but me. As I lie on the mattress, arising to consciousness, I think how I am a novice monk, but have been involved in killing. My action has led directly to murderous events. It is true that Lama said I had almost certainly saved their lives. But could our lives have been saved anyway by the two villagers? Was it the case that both Lama and Paldon Wangmo had shown more faith in the protection we would receive on our sacred journey than I had?

Whatever the case, one thing was clear. While Lama had said he was grateful, he didn't say what I had done would be without karmic consequences. Now I wonder what those consequences might be.

Late in the afternoon, after a day of much-needed sleep and recuperation, we set out from the cave as we had the night before. Although that was only twenty-four hours ago, it feels as though that was a different lifetime. A more innocent one. Waiting until after nightfall, once again we descend the birch tree and retrace our steps. Knowing of our own defenselessness, this time we are all the more watchful and alert, on guard for Red Army soldiers at every turn. For this reason we have a tacit understanding that we should not speak; we can't risk our voices carrying through the night.

As we approach Tang I wonder what we'll find. We are careful to avoid the main path to the village, but nevertheless I am surprised how little smoke there is compared to this morning. All the fires have burned out, leaving only an acrid heaviness to the air. But there is no sign of life either. Just a few ruined buildings, not even the broken furniture remains on the ground. Desolate and ruined, the village of Tang has been destroyed. I can't help comparing how it looks now to the night before. How dramatically the passage of just twenty-four hours can change the lives of so many people. Just as Buddha said, our lives are like bubbles on a fast-moving stream. A river plunging down the side of a mountain. So much of the time in our day to day life we have the illusion of permanence; of solidity; until an accident or disaster stops us short. Reminds us that there is no such thing as permanence or solidity—that every thing and every being in this world is undergoing constant change.

I wonder what happened to the girl. Was she rescued from the soldiers? And what of the three of them? Were they shot in the gunfire we'd heard through the smoke, or are they lying somewhere now with their throats slit? The villagers have all moved, perhaps because they fear reprisals. I wonder if they've dispersed inside Tibet. Or are they on the path to India, like us? I would like to think that. I'd feel more secure knowing we were traveling in the wake of a group of well-armed men from the village of Tang.

Although Lama hasn't remarked on it, we have lost precious time. Had we not encountered the soldiers, we would already be a whole night's journey from here. Our energies would have been put to good purpose and we would already be deep in the mountains. It is no doubt for this reason that Lama keeps up the most brisk pace allowed by the increasingly harsh terrain, and our need for vigilance.

I recognize quite a lot of the path that we are traversing for the third time in twenty-four hours. As we near the place where we were ambushed, I feel a knot in my stomach as though we'll find them waiting in the darkness again. But of course there's no sign of any soldiers, and instead I wonder where their mindstreams now are, and what they're experiencing. The Dharma teaches that consciousness propelled by karma, or conditioning, is what makes us experience reality in a particular way. One moment of mind gives rise to the next, be that positive or negative. This is true when we are alive, and even more so when our very subtle consciousness leaves our bodies. Those whose minds are agitated by hatred and anger at the time of death are unlikely to experience happiness when their mind, without a body to act as an anchor, moves freely through the bardo realms. And so, as we reach the place where the soldiers forced us into the mud and urinated on us, in my mind I send out a wish that the three Chinese soldiers will quickly become free from suffering, as well as free from causing suffering.

The rest of the night is both tense and exhausting. Constantly on the look-out for soldiers ahead, as we climb higher towards the snow line we also find ourselves walking across barren rock slopes which are slippery with ice. Now well beyond Tang, as well as the last place we came across mani stones, we frequently dislodge small rocks and as they tumble down the mountainside we are reminded of what our own fate can easily be if we lose our foothold.

At one point during the night that is exactly what happens to Paldon Wangmo, though fortunately he only slips a short distance down the mountain. We spend the next hour rescuing him, at the same time worrying about Chinese soldiers who could appear at any moment, having heard the sound of falling stones and low voices.

Through all the difficult moments I try to recollect Lama's advice about reviving our motivation. When my limbs ache with exhaustion I try to remember that whatever suffering I'm undergoing is for the benefit of innumerable living beings. When hunger pains rack my stomach I struggle to think: this is a precious opportunity to take the Dharma to the land of the red-faced people.

But it is not easy to keep even these thoughts pure. I wonder about all those red-faced people. I have never actually seen one, except in photographs, and in the film of the most famous red-faced person I know about: Bill Haley. I may want to feel courageous and purposeful taking the Dharma across the Himalayas, but what happens if, when we get to the other side, the red-faced people aren't interested? Remembering the luxurious houses and gleaming motor cars in "Rock Around the Clock" I wonder if maybe the red-faced people haven't too much pleasurable distraction to be concerned with the Dharma? What if Bill Haley would rather spend his time with all those beautiful women than trying to escape the endless cycle of birth, aging, death and rebirth?

I also can't recollect our motivation without remembering what happened in Tang. I wish I could speak to Lama about it, to question him about my own actions which make me feel so much regret, but after what has happened, there is no question of speaking out loud. We must do nothing to give ourselves away.

Eventually, about two hours before dawn, we search for a place to sleep through the next day. We find a rock shelf high enough to provide some form of protection, and broad enough so that if we move inside we won't be at all visible from anywhere but the most soaring, ice-capped peaks.

Relieved as I am to be stopping, it isn't long after I've tried to make myself as comfortable as I can for sleep that I realize how much colder it is now that we've stopped moving. Today, and for the rest of this trip, we will not be enjoying the warmth and protection of Padmasambhava's cave. We will continually feel cold, exposure and empty stomachs.

Those red-faced people had better be worth it!

THE ROCK LEDGE IS WHERE WE SLEEP THROUGH THE DAY. AGAIN, MY rest is troubled with ever-more bizarre versions of the shooting dream. And no matter how much I try to wake myself up to stop the nightmare, I can't get rid of the visions of slit throats and grief-stricken villagers. The heavy burden of my own complicity.

Finally I sit up, late in the afternoon. I'm frozen up here on the mountainside, with only my novice's robes for protection. I look at the direction in which we are to travel, the row upon row of mountain peaks rising ever higher into the distance. All my dreams have left me feeling hardly rested and overwhelmed.

I look over to face Lama, who is sitting, looking at me with a sympathetic expression. "Where is Paldon Wangmo?" I ask in a low voice.

"Gone down the rock."

I nod. I assume it is a call of nature.

"You didn't sleep well," he observes.

"No, Lama." Moving over, I huddle up next to him against the wall. I am glad of this opportunity to speak to him privately. "I am troubled by what happened in Tang."

He already knows this.

"Because of my actions, three human beings are dead. Probably six. And killing is top of the list of the ten black karmas."

Looking out at the Himalaya peaks, now tinged gold with the setting sun, Lama's expression is one of benign reflection.

"Did you personally slit the throats of these three, or maybe six people?"

"No, Lama." I know he is not being argumentative, but merely applying his usual cool reasoning to help me find the cause of my unhappiness.

"Did you order others to slit their throats?"

"No, Lama."

"You have no need to feel remorse for actions you did not take."

"I know, Lama. So why do I feel such regret?"

"You have already thought about this?"

"All last night."

There is the longest pause before Lama finally suggests, "Perhaps it would be helpful to consider your motivation."

In using the word "motivation" he is returning to one of his most well-worn themes. Which he follows with his oft-repeated example: "It is different when a woman throws a pan of boiling water out of the window, accidentally scalding her neighbor, than when a woman waits in ambush with her pan, even if the action and the consequences for the neighbor are exactly the same."

I know this, of course, and don't think I need to be reminded of it. My own motivation was so obvious.

"I wanted to save the scriptures," I tell Lama.

"Huh!" his dismissive shrug irks me.

"Of course," I admit, "I also wanted to save our lives."

There is a long silence. Lama is still looking unconvinced. "Those were your only motivations? You're quite sure?"

I nod.

"Then why didn't you kick the gun out of that soldier's hands the moment he stopped us on the mountainside?"

I have thought about this very question, yet I am taken aback when Lama asks it.

"I was caught by surprise," I said. "But . . ."

"But what, Tenzin Dorje?"

"If the same thing happened again," I admit, "I would. The soldier's other two comrades were asleep. We could have knocked them all unconscious and continued on our way."

Lama smiles. "Good. You've obviously given this thought."

"A lot of thought."

"But you weren't still in a state of surprise by the time we got back to Tang?"

"No," it seems a peculiar thing to ask. By then we'd been forced to lie in the mud, urinated on, marched through the night, and accused of being an enemy of the people of Tibet. "I was tired and furious."

"So, do you think perhaps your motivation was also one of anger?"

I recognize the truth, the moment Lama says it. It is not so much what I did that's causing me upset, as my motivation.

I look up at Lama with a wry smile. "This is why I have been feeling so bad," I confess. "Of all emotions, hatred is the most destructive."

"Why?" he tests me.

"Because anger causes so much misery both for the person on the receiving end, as well as for the person experiencing it. Because it creates the cause to experience hatred again in the future. Because it reinforces our delusion that people or things have inherent characteristics that make them the cause of happiness or unhappiness."

"You have a good grasp of the theory." Lama doesn't need to add that what I am lacking is the all-important ability to apply it.

But already I am feeling better, clearer about what happened in Tang. Once again, I have come to realize how sneaky my own mind is, and how clever at burying uncomfortable truths. Once again I marvel at my immense good fortune to have a teacher as clear-sighted as Lama Tsering.

In the next week, there are many more times when I have the same thought—and not only because of my guru's clear insight in matters of the mind. He continues to guide us in very practical ways.

During the next night's walk he tells us he is concerned about how much food we'll need. While we have just enough packed for the expected three week journey through the mountains, what if we face long delays because of snow storms, or have to avoid the Red Army? For this reason, we must try to make our food go as far as possible. He shows us how to soak dried chickpeas in water from melted ice so that we don't need to eat so many to stave off our hunger. He encourages us to drink water when we stop to rest, and always before we eat, for the same reason.

Deep in the mountains, we are cold nearly all of the time. I remember back to that first, arduous day's walk almost with a kind of nostalgia. That we had moved during the day, easily able to see all around us—what luxury! That there had been a clear and well-formed path to follow, not a struggle among narrow crevices, or across treacherous, iced-over rock face—how wonderful that had been! And if only my pain was merely the fatigue of aching muscles, instead of the constant icy stab in all my limbs. Every night my legs, in particular, are wracked with pain. The only time it disappears is when they go so numb I can barely feel them.

The dangers of our situation are also multiplied by rock falls and avalanches. Not a night goes by when we don't witness massive snow sliding loose from a mountain peak, quickly gathering momentum as it thunders through space. On other occasions, there will be a sudden, nearby crash as a boulder topples over and hurtles through the darkness.

Every time this happens, I am grateful for another escape.

Day after wearisome day goes by. On our eighth night, just in case we need reminding, we are picking our way towards a large, open expanse of rock when Lama suddenly halts and raises his hand. For a very long while he pauses, motionless. Staring past him into the darkness, seeing nothing, I am about to whisper an enquiry when he turns slowly, finger to his lips, and motions towards a nearby crevice. It is like a ditch, a short distance from where we are standing. Following his lead we crawl into the rock cleft, so that we'd only be visible if a searchlight was directed into it.

We crouch there for what feels like an eternity. Eventually there comes the tread of people close by. And not just one or two. From our hiding place, pressing back, I make out the cap of a soldier, followed by two men—prisoners?—another cap and a further three heads, before a third soldier. After they pass, we draw ourselves up to see them retreat into the distance. I confirm there are five prisoners under Red Army escort. The captives are not in monks' robes, but are disheveled and weary. I wonder if the Chinese soldiers have also used their heads as toilets.

"How did you know?" Paldon Wangmo whispers to Lama when it's safe.

"Yes—I didn't hear anything," I say.

"I didn't . . . hear anything," says Lama. "But I sensed they were ahead of us."

There are some things that Lama doesn't usually talk about and that, being novices, it is not our place to ask. But in these hostile mountains, Lama's reserve is less important than our safety.

"How do you mean 'sense'?"

"The feeling of negative energy approaching."

As he says this, I remember the soldier with the scripture stabbed on the end of his bayonet. How he'd seemed like a devil from the hell realms.

"When we're venturing into the unknown we use all our mind," Lama tells us, "not only what comes to us through the five sense doors."

After we crawl out of the crevice, I look over at Paldon Wangmo. From his serious expression it seems he's thinking the same as me: that we must abandon any thought that we've gone beyond the reach of the Red Army. That they are still a grave danger even though we're deep in the mountains.

I remember Lama's words from that last night at Zheng-po: "You must realize this is not some great adventure. Traveling to the border will be dangerous—the Red Army will shoot dead any monks trying to leave. Then we must try to cross the mountains on foot. For three weeks we will have to travel very long distances, living only on the food we can carry. We will have to endure much hardship and great pain."

I hadn't fully understood the meaning of his warning. And for the first few days our journey had seemed like an adventure. But now I have come to realize just how difficult our mission really is. And how easily we could fail.

It is on the fourteenth night that we are struck by a disaster from which there's no escape. It happens only a few hours after we've set out. Our constant adversary in the mountains, the wind, howls louder and more constant than usual and above us the sky is completely clouded over. The darkness and thunder make our difficult progress even slower and more portentous than ever.

Slipping down a short rock face, it takes me a while to clamber back to the course being set by Lama who has now walked quite some distance ahead of me. We are in our usual formation: Lama in the front, me in the middle, and Paldon Wangmo behind. I pause for breath, briefly resting with my arms on my legs while, step by step, Lama walks further and further ahead of us.

Then I hear it. A distant thud. Nothing compared to the thunder that's been rolling through the mountains tonight. But far more deadly, because it's the sound of snow breaking loose from a high peak. I turn to the sight I will never forget. An avalanche is heading down the mountain towards Lama. It's not a massive snow slide. But it's hurtling directly towards where he's walking. Without thinking, I scream out to him. But with the wind so high, he can't hear. And besides, it's too late. In a moment he is struck down amid the whiteness, like a leaf caught in a waterfall. Completely engulfed, the place where he was walking is now more than five feet under snow.

Paldon Wangmo and I rush towards the snow bank. The only digging tools we have with us are small spades. They are not nearly up to the task, but are all we have. There seems no way Lama can survive long, buried so deep. Sending out a desperate prayer to all gurus, Buddhas and bodhisattvas to help us, Paldon Wangmo and I dig frantically.

It takes more than ten minutes just to clear a narrow ditch in the snow down to ground level. Then we have to work out where he is. Where exactly was he standing when the snow came down? And where would it have thrown him?

I am fearful that he's been badly injured by the force of it. That he's lying under all that weight of snow with fractured bones. I feel guilty having to take a break from the frenzied digging, but after more than half an hour has gone by, my arms ache so much I simply can't continue.

Paldon Wangmo, who has been working more slowly but steadily beside me, keeps on going. Both of us are taking care with every spade of snow that we don't shove too hard in case we hurt Lama. By now the ditch has lengthened and, at ground level, we have hollowed out a much wider area.

As soon as I have regained my strength I am digging again, first in one direction then another. Still no sign of Lama. As the minutes tick by we are more and more anxious. It begins to seem less and less likely that we'll find him alive. That he won't have been suffocated or frozen to death.

But we can't lose Lama! High in the mountains, half way between the beginning of our journey and the end, how can we possibly survive without him? I pray that he will use his special powers, his *siddhis,* to survive, for our sake if for no one else's.

After an hour we're still digging. Our ditch is a crazy zigzag through the snow. At ground level we've scraped out a warren of tunnels. I need to rest again, and Paldon Wangmo suggests we step back to review our work.

We climb up a nearby rock and look down on where we're been working. As we do, cloud cover sweeps back from the moon so that the whole area is bathed in light.

We are staring down, trying to work out where Lama Tsering might be buried, when I catch a glimpse of something. Scrambling down from the rock, I rush over to the very first ditch we dug. I get down on all fours and reach into the snow. Towards a narrow strip of maroon cloth.

Chapter Twelve

Matt Lester

Bill Blakely waves my time sheets in the air, denouncing my lack of productivity. His expression a portrait of indignation, he lectures me on how my failure to initiate new research amounts to virtual theft, from Acellerate shareholders as well as my fellow employees. Has he no shame, I wonder, listening to the torrent of well-rehearsed vitriol? By my reckoning this is the fifth time in just over three years that he's fired his research director, doubtless with the very same words.

Yet there is something primal about the experience, as though I've been through it all before. I have had my integrity questioned by someone whose own integrity was non-existent.

"The only daylight robbery is yours," my voice cuts coolly into his rising tirade.

"Are you crazy?!"

"Not as crazy as you, if you think you can keep on stealing IP and get away with it."

He doesn't miss a beat. "You've got no right—"

"Luke Calloway," I interject again. "Glenn Armstrong. George Cameron-Dow. Craig Hardman," it's a roll call of Acellerate's research directors over the past three years. "Why did none of them last more than eight months in the job?"

"You can't compare those hires." If he's surprised by the mention of my predecessors he's not showing it.

"You can. Absolutely!" I'm not sure where the self-assurance in my own voice is coming from, but I've never been more determined. "If you're denying the systematic removal of IP, then the only conclusion is that you've made five recruitment errors in a row. Either way, something your shareholders would want to know about, isn't it?"

"Don't think you can march in here threatening me!"

For the first time I know that Bill Blakely isn't acting. The mask has dropped. His anger is for real.

"It was you who invited me up here to run through your 'output' charade," I counter. "But I'm pleased to have the opportunity to put my own proposal to you." Stepping over to his desk, I lean over to where he's keying a number into his telephone.

"If you want me out of Acellerate, and full access to Nanobot IP, I'll sign it over. But only for an amount that begins to look reasonable, like two million dollars."

"Don't think you can blackmail me."

"It's not blackmail. It's a straight IP sale. Cheap at the price."

"That's as much as the up-front payment to your institute!"

"Who you also scammed."

"You scientists are all the same!" he lashes out as heavy footsteps sound on the spiral staircase behind me. "Inflated ideas of your own self worth. Two million dollars?!"

"I'm telling you now, you'll pay a lot more for it in the long run."

"I have a better idea." He looks at the two security men who have appeared up the stairs. "Won't you see Mr. Lester down to his office on the twenty-eighth floor and help him clear his desk? I'd like him off the premises inside twenty minutes."

It's a surreal sensation returning to my office for the final time. Even though I've been expecting this, and have prepared for it over the past few weeks, now that it's happening it feels like I'm acting out a part in a movie, rather than real life.

The two security guards keep their distance, polite but watchful as a pair of Dobermans. I flip open my briefcase and pack away a few framed photographs. Opening the top drawer, I remove my pens and PDA. I have, of course, made copies of all the files I wanted a long time ago. Electronic and hard copies have long since been secured in a bank safety deposit box.

The guards ask me to hand over my electronic staff pass. Company credit card. The keys to the Mercedes. They even check my wallet for business cards which they wordlessly remove.

Then we are riding the elevator—clearly a well-rehearsed drama because by the time we reach the bottom and make our way across the foyer, it is to find that a cab has already been called. Bill Blakely has said he wants me off the premises and, as though in a final reminder of all I am losing, I see the waiting vehicle is an impressive dark-glassed limo.

In moments its heavy door is being shut behind me and we are heading west along Wilshire.

Back at Rosewood Avenue, I place my briefcase on the porch table briefly, while searching my pocket for the house keys. As I do, I remember the very first time I'd stood on this doorstep. How Isabella and I had just got off the plane from London, and our debut ride through an American city from LAX. Despite the long journey we had been so bright with anticipation and felt like we had the whole world ahead of us.

Now as I unlock the front door and step inside, the first thing I notice is the space on the lounge shelves where Isabella's ornaments used to be. The gap left after the removal of her CD player. The silence of the house at this unfamiliar time of four o'clock on a weekday afternoon.

Closing the door behind me, I throw my briefcase on a sofa and stand, uncertainly for a moment in the middle of the room.

It's not what happens to you that matters, but the way you interpret things.

I do my best to conjure up the certainty with which both Geshe-la and Alice have persuaded me that no event is inherently a cause of happiness or suffering. How personal loss can be a process you have to go through to make space for something very much better to come along.

But as I look out to the empty carport, it's hard to accept this conviction. How can I possibly replace the research program that has been my life, my raison d'être, for so many years? How could I ever improve on the love, the closeness, the passion I have shared with Isabella?

In just a few months it seems I've lost everything that had any value to me. How, possibly, could there be an upside?

Tenzin Dorje

FAST AS WE CAN, PALDON WANGMO AND I DIG THE SNOW FROM around Lama's body. It's not easy because of the amount that has fallen on top of him. Nearer the ground, in the darkness, it's impossible to make out the exact position of his body. We have to clear away the snow with the greatest care.

Both of us do this with the urgent hope that we'll find our guru alive. The chances, we know, are poor. The force of the avalanche, throwing Lama to the ground, had been immense. Within instants he'd been buried under several feet of snow. If he hadn't been killed immediately, how could he have avoided suffocation?

But this is Lama Tsering, I keep reminding myself. When it comes to the highest-ranking Lama of Zheng-po monastery, the normal rules don't apply. Perhaps, through his profound understanding of *sunyata* wisdom, at the moment the snow struck him, Lama became one with it, and was able to avoid its lethal force? I also know about *tummo* practice, where highly-advanced monks and nuns are able to sit in the snow and, through use of a secret meditation literally melt the snow around them. What if Lama has been able to avoid suffocation by creating room to breathe around his face?

Finally, we can make out the outline of his body. Paldon Wangmo and I squat on either side of him, scraping the remaining snow from his motionless face and body. Reaching out, his face feels frozen, but I can't tell if that's because my fingers are also bitterly cold. Paldon Wangmo leans down, putting his ear to our teacher's chest.

"I think," he says uncertainly, "his heart is beating." He meets my eyes for just a moment before I put my own ear to Lama's chest. Like him, I also think I can hear the faint beating of Lama's heart. But the wind is howling so loud, it's hard to tell if we are just imagining things.

Staring anxiously at the frozen form of our teacher, we are rewarded moments later when Lama shudders. It's an unmistakable movement. And Paldon Wangmo and I, of one mind, quickly have our arms round

Lama's shoulders and are holding him upright when he coughs, his whole body shaking as he chokes with the snow trapped in his nose and mouth.

"Are you alright, Lama?" anxiety makes me clumsy in my choice of words.

His arms dangle limp at his sides, his head is lolling towards me. He is, quite clearly, far from alright. But after a while as we hug him between us, trying to make him warm, we hear him whisper weakly, "I am here."

Our relief is overwhelming, though tempered by a very different emotion; apprehension about what happens next. We are two novice monks on an icy mountainside in the middle of the Himalayas. There is no village to go to, no one in a position of authority to appeal to. Up until this point, Lama Tsering has made all the important decisions on our journey: how far to go, where to stop, even what and how much we should eat. Now it is up to us to make every decision and, fortunate though we are that our kind and holy teacher is still with us, he is clearly in no condition to move.

Over the next few hours we work out what to do. Leaving Lama in my care, Paldon Wangmo searches around the surrounding area for a safe hiding place. Although he finds a rock ledge not too far away, Lama is so weak that we have to carry him, as carefully as we're able in case he has broken bones. As we struggle in the darkness, the icy rock and howling wind made even worse by the burden we carry, my mind flashes back to that moment, in Lama's cell, when he'd said to us, "You are both young and strong, but I may become a liability. What happens if I fall and hurt myself?"

I also remember how quickly and easily I'd replied, "Then we will carry you across the mountains."

Now we struggle to carry our teacher just a short distance—and once again I'm made to realize just how naïve I have been.

The rock ledge Paldon Wangmo discovered is broad and enclosed, but with only a very small area wide enough to be able to sit upright. Once we get Lama there, we quickly use our rucksacks and whatever loose stones we can find to get him into a comfortable, sitting position. Paldon Wangmo and I take it in turns to remove our heavy coats and put them over him, as an extra layer, to try to bring heat back to his frozen limbs.

Meantime we use some of our precious gas to make cups of cha, to warm him from the inside.

Lama is still too weak even to open his eyes, except for a moment at a time. But he is able to swallow the cha. Little by little, we feel the warmth return to his arms and face. We spend the longest night nursing him to the point where he is able to utter brief, gasped sentences. His body is numb. Fortunately he feels no pain.

Paldon Wangmo and I know that, in the darkness, the light from the gas burner will be visible for miles around, no matter how much we try to hide it. We're acutely aware that the food we're eating, and trying to feed Lama Tsering, is depleting our already very low food reserves. But what choice have we? Lama Tsering needs to keep still and warm, and we must look after him. As dawn breaks, and the foreboding sky above us lightens from pitch dark to clouds of swirling gray, the three of us lie huddled for as much warmth as we're able to achieve on an exposed rock ledge, with the wind howling by. Closing my eyes to sleep, I pray that when we wake up, Lama Tsering will be restored to full health, and that he will lead us safely and swiftly to our destination, for the benefit of all beings.

But our journey is to be very different from that. When Paldon Wangmo and I awake in the afternoon, it is to find Lama Tsering conscious, but unable to move his left leg. Relieved as we are to have our teacher back with us, there can be no disguising his swollen ankle. Whether it is broken or merely sprained is something we discuss at length, until Lama reminds us that the outcome is the same: "I can't move. Perhaps it would be better if the two of you continued without me."

Neither Paldon Wangmo nor I will hear of this option. And despite my brave assurance that we could carry Lama over the mountains if he became a liability, we all know that this, too, is an impossible ambition.

Eventually we decide we have no choice but to stay where we are, at least for one more night. If Lama's injury is a sprain, perhaps it will get better with time. "Tonight I will undertake Medicine Buddha practice," says Lama. "And to conserve food, I will fast."

In keeping with our teacher, Paldon Wangmo and I agree that we too will fast and be guided by Lama through Medicine Buddha visualizations. Even though we don't have an injury like he does, after a day of fasting we will need all our energy and resilience on the journey ahead.

Despite the show of solidarity with Lama Tsering, as we begin our meditation that evening, with only a few mouthfuls of snow for sustenance, my faith is tested. How is it possible this can be happening to Lama Tsering, who has devoted his life to the Dharma? If Paldon Wangmo or I had been hurt in an avalanche, perhaps that would be understandable. But not a Lama as highly realized as our kind and holy teacher! What use is the Dharma if it cannot protect him from the everyday problems of *samsara*? And if he is being made to suffer just like an ordinary mortal, what hope is there for a novice monk like me?

"Faith, Tenzin Dorje," my Lama says beside me, knowing my thoughts as though his own. Faith is a quality greatly encouraged in the Dharma, but not belief-based faith. In Buddhism, faith is said to arise through listening, thinking, and meditating. In his usual, measured way, Lama Tsering is suggesting I meditate, instead of allowing myself to succumb to the swirling negativity of my mind.

In the past years, the three of us have often sat together in meditation. As usual, we begin by taking refuge in the Buddha, Dharma and Sangha, before establishing in our minds the peerless motivation of *bodhichitta*. With the wind howling through the mountains and darkness becoming complete, on the cold rock ledge we reconfirm our desire to attain enlightenment for the benefit of all beings.

The session begins like any other, except for where we are, and the fact that we are sitting on either side of our teacher so closely that our shoulders are almost touching. As he often does, Lama Tsering tells us to carry out some nine-cycle breath meditation, to settle our minds. Then, after the agitation has subdued to some extent, he describes how we are to visualize the Medicine Buddha in front of us—his body in the nature of light, a dark, radiant blue, the color of healing.

Like all visualizations, the power of Medicine Buddha depends not on some external deity, but on the extraordinary healing potential of our own mind. The visualizations are simply a way of helping us realize this potential.

Countless times in the past I've visualized Medicine Buddha, who sits, cross-legged with a bowl of healing nectars in his lap. But something is different tonight. Instead of a vague and flickering image which comes and goes in my mind, lapsing with concentration, tonight it is as though I am looking directly at Medicine Buddha—as if he is really here! He doesn't require my concentration. There is nothing half-formed or imagined about the way he looks. I can study every aspect of his appearance just as I might scrutinize a person with my eyes wide open. In fact, he is more vivid than real life. There's a quality of heightened reality about him. The colors of his robes and skin glow more radiant, the sensation of the different healing nectars he pours into my body are powerfully vivid. Most of all, the sensation of connection I feel with him is blissful and all-consuming. And as healing nectar streams into my body from his bowl, I feel myself growing more robust, more confident, imbued with greater energy and power than in my whole life until now. Never mind that I am sitting on an exposed rock ledge in the middle of the Himalayas. Or that I'm fasting because we're so short of food.

And though my absorption in the visualization is complete, a part of my mind recollects my doubts from earlier in the night and I realize where I've gone wrong. Even if Lama Tsering's ankle is hurt, that doesn't mean he is unhappy. There is no automatic connection between our circumstances and our personal happiness. Once again I have fallen victim to the superstition of materialism in imagining that our journey through the mountains should be a smooth one. But just because it is difficult, doesn't mean we have to be miserable. In fact, as I sit here in the radiant presence of Medicine Buddha, my conviction has never been stronger that circumstances themselves have little meaning. Instead, it is our state of mind in the midst of such circumstances which fills us with apprehension—or bliss. *It's not what happens to you that matters, but the way you interpret things.*

When Lama directs us to end our meditation with the traditional dedication for the benefit of all beings, I wish he hadn't ended the session so abruptly. Back at Zheng-po the meditation sessions could last for up to four hours, but tonight he's in a hurry to end.

Or so it seems. Because when we open our eyes, it is to the clear light of morning. Eyes slowly refocusing on the distant peaks of the Himalayas, I discover I have sat, motionless for ten hours. In this unlikely place, and at this unlikely juncture in my life, I have just been the witness to something extraordinary.

Later that day, after we have slept, we examine Lama's left ankle. The swelling is much reduced—but the ankle is still enlarged.

"I think this means it is sprained, not broken," Lama gives voice to our relief.

"If we wait another two days it might be back to normal?" suggests Paldon Wangmo.

Lama shakes his head. "We don't have two days to wait. Our food is so low, we must keep moving."

"But you can't put your weight on that ankle!" I protest.

"If you can find me a stick for support," Lama has already thought of this, "perhaps I can manage."

Which is how, shortly after nightfall, having broken our fast and eaten a scant meal of chickpeas and melted snow, we are starting out again. Under Lama's left arm is a crutch Paldon Wangmo and I have fashioned out of a juniper branch. Risking being seen in the late afternoon light, we found a suitable branch, way below the rock ledge in the valley, and thanks to Paldon Wangmo's ingenuity, created a T-joint, with a smooth, barked length to fit under our teacher's arm.

Our progress is painfully, pathetically slow. This time as we set out, we change the formation so that I am in front, Lama Tsering second, and Paldon Wangmo behind him. We are walking much closer together and have secured ropes firmly round our waists, so that if Lama falls, he'll have something to cling onto. As I move in the direction Lama has indicated, looking out for the smoothest path, at the same time keeping alert to snowfalls and Chinese soldiers, I also can't help looking up at the succession of ice-capped peaks gleaming white in the moonlight, range upon range of them rising endlessly into the distance. Inching forward, each step negotiated with great care, the challenge of achieving liberation has never seemed more daunting.

In fact the border with India is so remote that I begin to fantasize about amazing rescues and short-cuts. What if His Holiness, having reaching Dharamsala, tells the outside world about our fate, and what if countries like America send in helicopters to rescue us? My mind is filled with images of helicopters heading down valleys of the Himalayas, casting ropes for fleeing monks and nuns, and hauling them to safety, their maroon and saffron robes gusting in the wind. Or maybe there is a border post somewhere not too far away, in the middle of all these mountains, and once we have reached it we'll find food and a place to recuperate, before catching lorries or buses to Dharamsala.

As it happens, I *am* rescued from having to complete the journey, but not in the manner I have fantasized. And much, much sooner than I expect. We have not been traveling long that night—perhaps two or three hours—when we reach a ravine passable only by a narrow ledge along the mountainside. This, in itself, is not unusual. We have crept across the tops of many precipitous cliffs so far, and on ledges even narrower. But for some reason, as we approach the gorge, I feel my heart thumping.

Since we started out tonight, I have been careful not to outpace Lama Tsering, to listen for the sound of him behind me, often half-turning to make sure he is safe.

As we make our way across the rock ledge, I am especially aware of his presence, and proceed even more slowly. Pressed against the mountainside, the wind suddenly drops. In the unexpected silence I can hear Lama breathing. But suddenly I am losing my footing and falling to the ground. On my hands and knees I'm sliding towards the cliff.

"Ice!" I cry out.

Lama Tsering and Paldon Wangmo are on the ground, too. I don't know if it's because they've also slipped, or if the force of my fall has tugged them down. I struggle desperately for something to hold onto, but find nothing. Not a rock. Not even a stretch of dry ground. Nothing to halt my slide right to the precipitous edge of the cliff.

And over it.

Chapter Thirteen

Tenzin Dorje

Scrambling feverishly against the cliff side, the rope at my waist stretched taut, I somehow find a footing. It's no bigger than a brick, and juts out of the rock face nearly six feet below the icy rock ledge. Arms stretched above me, I cling with both hands to a sharp jag of rock on the same level as the ledge. The wind howls menacingly around me.

Everything happens in double-time. One part of me is wild-eyed and panting as I struggle to balance on the precarious toehold. But I'm aware of another part too, like an observer, watching all this in calm wakefulness.

My first instinct is to use my toe-hold to push myself back up on the ledge. To use the ropes to haul back up to where Lama and Paldon Wangmo are grounded.

But what if I lose my footing and all my weight is suddenly transferred to Lama? There's no question he would be dragged forward—right onto the icy area on which I slipped and fell. He'd soon follow me over the cliff; it would be disastrous for all three of us.

"Tenzin Dorje! Are you alright?" he shouts above the wail of the wind.

Now I am testing the jag of rock above me with my hands. "I have to climb back!" I shout. "But if this breaks—!"

"Courage!"

At that moment there's a vicious down-rush and I'm nearly blasted from my precarious footing. If I don't pull myself up now, it may be too late!

Summoning all my strength I leap upwards, at the same time hauling myself up on the sharp, rocky edge. Agony slashing through both hands, I am poised on the shelf for just a moment. I see Lama pressed against the mountain, his crutch jammed into a crevice to keep him from being tugged towards me. Arms around him, Paldon Wangmo is kneeling behind, hands on both ropes.

Reaching out I try to grasp hold of the ropes to pull myself closer to them, but the cords slip through my fingers. I make the attempt again, but once again I fail. I can't grasp anything; my hands seem to have stopped working. Looking down I see why. The jagged rock on which I forced myself up has slashed me deeply across both hands. Apart from being able to bring thumbs and forefingers together, my hands are bleeding profusely—and are utterly useless!

I have no way to grab hold of anything strongly enough to carry my weight. Another howling blast of wind blows me off balance. Once again I am slipping down the cliff side, my legs flailing against the sheer side.

I only just secure my previous toe-hold. But it's no longer stable. The pressure of me launching myself off it, and sliding back down again has caused the small rock to loosen. I feel it crumbling beneath my feet. If the wind doesn't throw me off the cliff, the collapse of my foothold will have the same effect. And no matter how firmly Lama has wedged his juniper branch into the mountain, there is no way he and Paldon Wangmo can fight against the pull of my falling body.

All three of us will certainly die.

Alarmed, I realize that all options have closed. Now there's only one thing on my mind: the treasure I am carrying. Whatever happens to me, the scriptures must be protected. Even if I am destined to plunge down the ravine, Padmasambhava's sacred scrolls must not be allowed to fall to oblivion.

By now, after weeks of travel, I am well-used to slipping the rucksack off my back. Trembling from cold and fear, only my hands warm with blood, in a few movements I slip the rucksack off first my left shoulder, then the right. I am holding it by a strap around my right wrist.

"You must catch my rucksack!" I scream above the wind, before throwing it to where I know Paldon Wangmo and Lama are on the rock shelf. As I do, the mala I always wrap around my right wrist comes off too, following the bag of precious texts.

The moment I hear Paldon Wangmo's confirmation that he has received the precious cargo, a strange thing happens. In the curious double-time I am experiencing, even though I am clutched to the cliff side, I also find myself sitting in front of Medicine Buddha, vivid and serene as he was the day before. He is gazing at me with such compassion, such reassurance, that he seems like all the most beautiful things in the world distilled into one. Without any need for explanation, I understand that the Medicine Buddha is my teacher, Lama Tsering—my guru and he are both manifestations of the same extraordinary power. I realize, too, why Lama made us practice Medicine Buddha on our last stop. It was to act as a signpost on my Dharma journey.

Remembering my mother, at that moment she too joins me in the extraordinary presence of Medicine Buddha. It is as real as if all three of us are sitting in the same room.

"I am sorry, mother," I tell her now. "This is not what I had planned."

"Don't be troubled, Tenzin Dorje," reaching out she ruffles my hair, the way she has since I was a child.

"I didn't believe it when you said you'd be losing me for the rest of my life."

"I know," her eyes meet mine with a mixture of love and determination. "But I will find you in your next life—I promise."

As she smiles, both she and the Medicine Buddha dissolve away, and in that moment I have never felt such certainty or such peace.

My foothold crunching under me, there is only one thing left to do. With a silent prayer that my action to save the scrolls, and the lives of Lama and Paldon Wangmo will be to the benefit of all living beings, I reach into my robe and take out the pocket knife that I keep, razor sharp at all times. In two swift cuts, I slice through both the ropes.

Matt Lester

I SIT BOLT UPRIGHT IN BED. MY HEART IS POUNDING. I SCARCELY RECognize where I am. What I've just been through was too vivid to call a dream. It was hyper-reality, and unlike anything I've ever experienced. Most of all I awake with the certainty that what I just experienced happened to *me*. It was me, as a novice monk, who was flung off that cliff side; I can still remember my name—Tenzin Dorje. It was me attempting to cross the Himalayas with my brother and teacher. What I have just been through in a dream state is just as real as my life as Matt Lester. If anything, in those first few moments after waking, it makes me question the certainty with which I believe I *am* Matt Lester.

I have another conviction, too. Geshe-la is caught up in all of this. Not just because he's the only Buddhist monk I know. But I felt his presence, back there on the mountainside. I didn't recognize it at the time, but now that I'm awake, I know it to be true. Exactly *how* it can be true is a mystery to which I must find out the answer.

I look at my bedside clock. Just after six o'clock. Far too early to even think of visiting most people. But not Geshe-la. He's been up since three, hasn't he? This is the equivalent of mid-morning to him.

I quickly slip into a sweater and tracksuit pants. Stopping only long enough to splash my face with water, in moments I'm heading out of the house and along the street.

Rosewood Avenue is deserted at six o'clock. There's a lush tranquility to the morning that couldn't be further removed from the tumult in my mind. I can still taste the fear as I find my toe-hold crumbling beneath me. The shock as I realize I've run out of options. It's one of the most frightening things I've ever gone through. And unlike any ordinary nightmare which can be dismissed as just a bad dream, I know that this one holds the most startling implications for my life.

The Dharma Center house is quiet. Remembering Alice say that Geshe-la lives in a room across the back courtyard, instead of knocking on the front door I try the handle, and to my relief, find it open. Removing my Docksiders in the hallway, I make my way through the silent house towards the kitchen, where I usually bring my laundry. It's deserted except for Tashi, the cat, who sits on kitchen windowsill, silent and sphinx-like, studying me with those large, watchful eyes. I feel like an intruder. I don't want to wake Mrs. Min or anyone else who might be staying here. But I have to see Geshe-la!

The stable-style kitchen door is unlocked too, and I am soon crossing a paved area to what looks like a garden shed. As there's no other building behind the house, I reckon it must have been converted into a room for Geshe-la. I reach the door and knock softly, three times. When there's no response I try again, a bit louder and call out, "Geshe-la, it's me! Matt. From next door."

I wait a long while. He must have heard me, I decide. A still silence pervades the house, the whole neighborhood. Unless he's gone back to sleep. Or perhaps he meditates inside the house, in the gompa. Perhaps that's where I'll find him?

Just to check, I knock again, before trying the door handle. One part of me is thinking—I shouldn't be doing this. I should respect his privacy. If he's gone back to bed, or even if he never got up, that's his business. What if he's not feeling well?

But more urgent is the need to find him. To speak to him about what I've just experienced. To ask him to explain what it means.

I open the door to discover a tiny room, even smaller than it looks from the outside. There's only just enough space for a single bed, a chest of drawers and a meditation mat, on which Geshe-la sits, directly facing me. But his eyes are only half open, fixed in a downward gaze.

I pause in the doorway, eyes adjusting to the semi-darkness of his room. "I'm . . . sorry to disturb you, Geshe-la," I tell him. "I had to see you."

He doesn't look up. Doesn't even move. There's not so much as a gesture that I should go away, or stay where I am.

"Geshe-la?" I know that from what Alice has told me, some monks can enter deep meditative states. But something concerns me about Geshe-la. He doesn't seem to be breathing.

I take the few steps over to where he is sitting, and kneel beside him on the floor.

"Geshe-la?" I ask very softly. "Are you alright?" Studying his face intently, not only is there no response at all, there's no sign of life either. He might be sitting in a meditation posture, but he is motionless. Staring at him for the longest time, I can't detect any movement at all in his chest.

Worried, I reach out to his upper arm. Naked below the robe across his shoulder, it feels cold to the touch. Anxiety growing, I stretch out my left arm so that the face of my watch is directly beneath his nostrils. Even the smallest out-breath will fog the glass. But after holding it there until my arm aches, staring closely at the surface, my fears are confirmed.

I am now growing seriously alarmed. For a moment I wonder if this has something to do with my dream. Is Geshe-la's death somehow connected to the revelations I've just experienced? No, I tell myself, that's a ridiculous superstition. Trying to control the pounding in my head, I lean over Geshe-la and pressing my ear directly against his chest. Hoping to hear a distant beating. It doesn't seem so long ago that Paldon Wangmo and I were doing this with Lama Tsering.

But suddenly I find myself being tugged away. Arm jolted forcefully in the opposite direction. With a start I look up to find Mrs. Min. She is holding one finger to her lips, in the universal sign of silence and, with her other hand gesturing I should leave the room. Her expression is unmistakable. Imperative.

Wordlessly, I rise from the floor.

"I'm worried about Geshe-la," I whisper urgently, the moment she's closed his door behind us. She is leading the way across the small courtyard to the house. I know she doesn't understand a word I'm saying.

Back inside the house I am more blunt, "Is Geshe-la dead?" I ask.

"No dead!" she is insistent. "No dead. OK." She shoos me through the kitchen towards the front of the house. I find myself in the hallway beside the neat row of shoes. "No dead! Later," she points to her watch.

Meeting her eyes I try to read her expression. She has a fiery determination, no doubting it. I can see why some of the students find her intimidating. But there's something else in that powerful expression. I catch just a glimpse of it behind the unyielding resolve and commanding gestures. It seems almost like amusement.

I return home from the unsatisfactory visit. What to do next? Not only is the burden of last night's experience as overwhelming as ever, I don't know what to believe about Geshe-la either. Mrs. Min may be certain he is alright, but I can't deny all the evidence to the contrary. What if he is found to be dead? What if it comes out that I'd been round there and questions are asked about what exactly I was doing visiting my neighbor at six in the morning?

As I think through what's happened, I realize there's only one other person connected to the center who may have some idea what's going on. I decide to call Alice. It's not yet six thirty. But this is an emergency.

Moments later she's answering her cell phone and I'm explaining what's just happened. My alarming discovery of Geshe-la. How he seems to be dead. Mrs. Min's implacable response.

"I'm really worried . . . something might have happened to him." Feeling foolish using the cliché, I say directly, "I mean, from everything I could see, he's . . . passed away. But Mrs. Min seems to think everything is okay."

There's a long silence from the other end before Alice finally says, "You're probably both right."

Of all the mind-boggling concepts I've come across lately, this one takes the cake: dead but okay. "How could he be?!"

"You've got to understand, Matt, Geshe-la's not an ordinary man. He's about as much like us as a gold-medal winning Olympic champion is."

I try to work out what she's getting at.

"He might look like an ordinary monk, but he's spent tens of thousands of hours, years and years training his mind. He's like a virtuoso in the most advanced meditation techniques. If he wants to, he can withdraw his attention from the sense doors, absorb his physical and mental energies at the heart chakra and go through the death process."

"He can make himself die?"

"Basically."

"And then . . . come back again."

"How do you think the Dharma is able to describe the death process in such detail? It's not a whole bunch of lamas sit around speculating on what might happen. It's because they actually go through it. Frequently."

I'm finding this all a bit much to take in. I also know that if I hadn't seen Geshe-la for myself, I wouldn't have believed it possible. As far as I was concerned, death was a one-way street and nobody knew what lay at the end of it.

"How long can he stay . . . dead for?"

"That's not the kind of subject that comes up in conversation," she's wry. "But in the texts it's quite possible for yogis to stay like that for several days."

"Days!" I'm thinking of my need to speak to him urgently.

"I'm not saying that's what he's doing right now. He might just be doing his usual morning session."

Usual morning dying session. It seems bizarre.

"Why were you even round there at six in the morning?"

It's the question I'd been expecting. "I had to speak to him. Last night I had this experience. It wasn't a dream. It's more than a dream. It's as real to me as talking to you, right now. I have to talk to Geshe-la. He's connected with it, and I need to know how."

There's a pause from the other end before she says quietly, "You know, Geshe-la uses lots of ways to teach, not always face to face."

SPEAKING TO ALICE ALLAYS MY FEARS ABOUT GESHE-LA. IT SEEMS there's no need to call the police. No reason to doubt Mrs. Min. Even though I should be relieved that my concerns about Geshe-la arise from ignorance of his yogic skills, the fact is I'm still impatient to speak to him.

Immediately after putting down the phone, I grab a piece of paper and write a list: Tenzin Dorje, Lama Tsering, Paldon Wangmo, Zheng-po, Ling. I don't want to forget any of these names from last night, even though, unlike most dreams, the memory of what I went through is far from fading. It's all as real to me as my showdown with Bill Blakely.

Deciding I need a shower, as I savor the jet of warm water on my upturned face, it's as though I'm having my first proper wash after my journey through the Himalayas. As though it's only now I'm able to clean myself of the accretion of grime and sweat and blood of our tortuous journey—my first wash since Lama, Paldon Wangmo and I bathed in the spring behind Padmasambhava's cave.

Is it possible that I was Tenzin Dorje in my last life? How else could I have downloaded the memory of a novice Tibetan monk? Why else was I feeling such complete identification that I am he? But from what Geshe-la told me and from what I've read elsewhere, most monks fled from Tibet in 1959. And I wasn't born until 1972. The dates don't add up.

My thoughts returning to how I found Geshe-la earlier that morning, I once again realize how little I understand about who he is and what extraordinary abilities he has. The Lama who can come back from the dead. And from the way Alice speaks about it, not unique in his ability. Unusual, no doubting it, and among a few highly accomplished masters. But not some kind of super-monk—instead, the result of a tried and tested process.

Along with what I've just been through myself, I'm feeling as though some sort of tectonic shift is taking place at some profound level within me. I'm having to question so many assumptions. Like how I'd always thought life was a one-off, with no connection to anything that came before or followed after. Like the idea that causes created in one lifetime can't possibly have repercussions in a following one because there's no connection between the two.

What is the connection, I wonder? Before I met Geshe-la I'd never sensed even the slightest intuitive link to Tibetan monks. Until last night I wouldn't have thought, for even a moment, that I, myself, could have been a novice monk in a previous lifetime.

I am completely absorbed in these thoughts as I get out of the shower, dry off and change into my weekend clothes. Absent-mindedly picking up my mala, I look at the bedside clock—not long after seven. I'm not sure what the arrangement with Mrs. Min is. She said "later" but how much later? Would two hours do it? Would Geshe-la be alive by eight, or would he remain in suspended animation until later in the day?

I decide to make some real coffee. Collecting beans from the freezer, I crush them before tipping the grinds into a cafetière. I'm still filling in the time as much as anything, making far more than I could drink. I have just filled the French press with boiling water when there's a knock at the front door.

Before I even reach it, I can see who it is through the frosted glass panel at the side. The sweep of maroon and saffron robes.

"Geshe-la!" I greet him, feeling suddenly emotional, my voice a blend of relief, amazement, and a response to that intuitive connection I feel even more powerfully as I open the door. "I came to see you," I tell him, stepping aside and waving him through.

"I know." His expression is just the same as always—relaxed, good-humored, as though he and I are enjoying a private joke.

"Mrs. Min told you?" I confirm.

"I saw you," he says. We're in the lounge and I pause, staring at him. "But I thought you were—you didn't seem able to—see. With your eyes, I mean."

"I didn't see you with my eyes." Then as my expression becomes even more bewildered, he continues, "Your eyes are shut when you're asleep. But do you still have a visual consciousness? Do you not see things when you dream?"

This is getting weirder by the minute, but I decide I'm not going to be side-tracked. I can come back to the eyes thing later. "There's something I really need to talk to you about."

I lead the way through to the kitchen, take two mugs from the cupboard, and pour out the coffee. As I do this I'm aware that next to me is a person who has just spent the last couple of hours dead. Who, from what Alice tells me, is a highly realized meditation master. Who has abilities way beyond anything I'd ever believed possible until this morning. Yet I don't feel at all strange or intimidated. Instead there's a curious and powerful familiarity.

Then we are standing at the kitchen bench, mugs of coffee beside us.

"How are things with your fiancée?" he asks sympathetically, realizing the house is empty.

"I think I've lost her," I shake my head, remembering our last conversation about partners and their lack of inherent, happiness-giving qualities at The Urth Caffé. All that seemed a lifetime ago. "Yes. I'm pretty sure I've lost her. And then just to make things perfect, yesterday I was fired from my job and lost the project I've been working on for the past seven years."

Geshe-la's expression somehow manages to combine sympathy that I'm not happy about what's just happened, with the impression that losing both career and partner is no special cause for concern.

"But that's not the stuff I want to talk to you about," I tell him. "Ever since I arrived in L.A.—in fact, ever since I met you, I've had this recurring dream. Memory flashes. Whatever. Anyway, last night it happened again except this time it was different. It was real. I'm a novice monk called Tenzin Dorje fleeing through the Himalayas with my teacher and another novice."

Geshe-la is following me intently, but I sense the playful smile isn't far from his features.

"The thing about this . . . flashback is that I feel I actually am this novice monk. It's not some sort of make-believe. And it's not disappearing from my mind. Right now, I can remember all kinds of stuff about Tenzin Dorje as though they're memories of my own."

Geshe-la is chuckling. "Why is this so strange?"

I look down at where wisps of steam rise from the two mugs of coffee. "I'm thirty-five years old. I've never had the slightest interest in Buddhism. I'd never even met a monk until I met you. Now all of a sudden I have access to all this . . . information about the Dharma, and a novice monk that seems to be me in 1959."

"Perhaps meeting me triggered something," he suggests. "The conditions were established for a particular karma to ripen."

Technically correct as Geshe-la's explanation of karma may be, there's a lot more to my reservations, as both of us know. After a pause I confess, "I guess, I've never believed in reincarnation. I've never really thought I had any existence before this one. I've never had any evidence—until last night."

"Recalling events from a previous life is the evidence you wanted, right?"

I nod.

"But in science, I thought you began with no assumptions? I thought you looked at a situation without any preconceived ideas?"

"That's true," I nod.

"Is it not an assumption that what moves from one lifetime to another must include a hard-drive full of memory?"

Once again, I'm taken aback by the way Geshe-la uses logic against conventional wisdom.

"What about last night, then—everything that happened to me? Where did that come from?"

"Perhaps," his expression is cryptic, "it was a gift."

"Gift?!" I'm thinking about the moment I looked down at my hands to find them both gashed by the jagged rock. The ferocity of the wind blowing me off-balance and back over the cliff.

"The way it all ended didn't seem like a gift. I'm on this crumbling rock, right against the side of a sheer cliff. I'm getting a rucksack off my back and throwing it over to the others. I know I'm going to die."

As I meet his eyes I am back on the mountainside, sensing the mixture of fear and determination. "I know I had to save what I was carrying."

"What were you carrying?" he prompts.

"Precious manuscripts. Sacred scrolls our teacher found in Padmasambhava's cave." I realize it is the first time I've ever said the name "Padmasambhava" but it trips off the tongue as though I've said it many times before. Holding Geshe-la's gaze, I am increasingly able to remember the resolve with which I was committed to my purpose. "Getting those special teachings out of Tibet, to freedom, was the most important thing in the world to me."

"Very good."

"There was something else, too," I am not so much meeting Geshe-la's eyes as being enclosed, absorbed into his presence. "I could sense you on the side of the mountain. It was as though you were there."

"Because I was there."

"In some sort of . . . spirit form?"

"No. Human being. Like you."

"But there we were only three. Lama Tsering. Paldon Wangmo, and . . ."

It's only now, for the first time, that I'm beginning to realize. to understand why I have sensed such a heartfelt connection to Geshe-la from the very first moment.

"At the center I am known as Geshe-la," he is explaining. "But that's just a kind of title. My full name is one you know well."

Along with the recognition, emotion rises within me, powerful and profound. "You're saying—"

"In your previous lifetime as Tenzin Dorje," Geshe-la's eyes glint brightly, "I was your brother, Paldon Wangmo."

Feelings welling up, I reach over and we embrace. And as we do, I feel all notions about who I am dissolving away into insignificance. It is as though I am discovering that all the things that usually preoccupy me, the elaborate fabrication of my life as Matt Lester—researcher, boyfriend, Brit living in L.A.—are of no real consequence. Instead, the boundaries of who and what I am have suddenly been exploded beyond anything I might have conceived.

Can it really be true that I have lived before, as Tenzin Dorje? And if that is true, then why wouldn't I have had countless previous lives before that? Is this being I call "I" really a primordial consciousness, like the Buddhists say, that has always existed. Beginningless time? A consciousness beyond mortality, time and space? All my life, my perspective of who I am and what I'm doing has been so incredibly narrow, so restricted to a tiny identity in the here and now. Could it be that the reality is so expansively, radiantly different?

"So," I manage, after we break apart. "I really did fall off the side of a cliff?"

Geshe-la has my hands in his. "In order to save the sacred scrolls and the lives of Lama and me," he looks down. "But now you are reconnected." Suddenly a mischievous smile appears on his face. "And I see you have your mala back on the wrong wrist."

I realize I have wrapped my mala around my right wrist, something I've never done before today.

"Who showed you to wear it like this?"

"No one," I tell him. "This morning I was so churned up I didn't even notice I was putting it on."

"Always the right arm," smiles Geshe-la, shaking his head. "Lama Tsering had to keep reminding you to wear it on the left, so it wouldn't fall off. But just as well you had it on your right wrist the day you fell, or we would never have been able to return it to you."

"You mean . . .?" I'm still taking this in.

"You could have chosen one of the other gifts Mrs. Min offered you. For example, your favorite chocolate. The bell. Choosing from a selection of items is one of several common checks to see if a person is the recognized reborn form of a monk. In your case, we already knew who you were. But we thought it would be good to perform the test for *your* sake. Because you are a scientist, we knew you'd want proof. Extra evidence to persuade you that perhaps the universe is not the random place you believe it to be. That perhaps there is a law of cause and effect."

Running my fingertips over the beads of the mala, I marvel at the idea that I might be touching such a treasured belonging from my previous lifetime.

"If everything is cause and effect," I am earnest, "what cause did I create to lose Isabella?"

Geshe-la pauses for a long while before saying, "When I first went to study at Zheng-po, I used to come home for my holidays and you were always so keen to know about life in a monastery." He picks up his mug of coffee and goes to sit at the small, kitchen table. Collecting my own mug, I take a seat opposite.

"You were always full of questions. What do I do when I wake up in the mornings? How do we spend the day? What are the monks like? You must have liked the answers I gave because one day you ran away from home to ask Lama Tsering to take you on as a novice."

I am shaking my head in wonderment.

"Mother was upset to lose you," he tells me, eyes meeting mine. "Very upset. But you were determined to follow your heart. You knew you had a particular purpose, and you left her to fulfill it."

For a long while I reflect on this, before he says. "You see. This is how karma is created. Every effect has a cause. Everything you experience arises from a previous moment in the same mental continuum. If we look through several lifetimes we will see the same patterns occurring, the same ripples and sequences and variations on a theme. The same causes and effects repeating themselves."

"Because I caused my mother hurt in my last lifetime, in this lifetime I am experiencing hurt?"

"Exactly. Causing one's parents hurt is considered especially bad karma. First of all we owe our very existence to our parents, and as a child they are like the sun and the moon—they are everything to us. So much of who we become depends on them. This is why we should try to repay their kindness in later life, especially if we want to have good parents in future lifetimes."

I think of Isabella returning to Europe to be near her parents. "Repaying their kindness" just as Geshe-la is saying we should do. And in so doing, not only acting as the instrument of my own karma, but ensuring that she doesn't suffer the same fate in the future. There seems to be a powerful symmetry about events of the past two lifetimes.

I also wonder if her decision to look after her parents, even at the expense of our relationship, is part of a bigger plan. I can't deny that since visiting Alice at her apartment I've wondered about us. How I'm so drawn to her—albeit in a very different way from Isabella. How I feel such a strong sense of warmth and ease in her presence.

"What?" I ask as Geshe-la prods me with a finger, his expression mischievous.

"You!" he teases. "What are you thinking?"

I feel my cheeks go warm. It seems that having a clairvoyant brother from your previous lifetime isn't always an easy thing. "I was just wondering if losing Isabella is part of some plan."

"A grand design?" he prompts.

"Maybe."

But his brow furrows. "This is confused thinking. It comes from the idea that there's a divine plan, that somehow everything is going to work out just fine in our lives. It's a reassuring belief, something people want to feel, even though there's no evidence for it. Everything isn't working out fine for most of the six and a half billion people on this planet, who live in terrible poverty. Or for most of the animals who are nothing more than food for other animals. The only way to make sure that things work out fine is to create the causes for that to happen. But we shouldn't think that adversity will turn to triumph because we're going to be rescued by angels, or Buddhas or some master plan."

Then a glint returns to his eye. "Alice is going away on a three-month retreat soon."

"Who said anything about Alice?" I protest.

Geshe-la just laughs. "I see the two of you like each other, very much."

I feel my cheeks flush even warmer and wonder just how much he can read my mind. "Y-yes we do," I agree. "Or at least—*I* do. But what you say about the world being in such a mess," I'm shaking my head, "it all just seems a bit pointless. Why try doing anything if we're just the slaves of karma we created in our last lifetime which, by the way, we can't even remember creating?"

"Not slaves," Geshe-la claps his hands. "Masters! It is up to us to create the right conditions for positive or negative karma to ripen. This is our choice. We can assume we have all created limitless good karma and bad karma. Now we can decide which we want to flourish. We also create the causes for future positive and negative experiences. We decide what kind of karmic imprints we want to create, for this and future lives."

"Why do you think you are so naturally gifted in the field of quantum science?" he continues. "Why do you find the concepts so easy to master? Because you created the causes by studying the concept of sunyata wisdom, or emptiness, as it's called in the Dharma. You asked many questions at Zheng-po. And even though you didn't have time to become very proficient, you created the karmic causes for good understanding at a later point."

I know it's going to take me a long time to come to terms with all these extraordinary revelations. To make sense of the very different reality in which I seem to be discovering myself. How hard it is to believe that only twenty four hours ago I had such a very different set of preoccupations.

I know I'm going to need space to digest all of this. To work out what happens next.

I take a sip of coffee before asking, "That first night we met, outside your house. When you said you came to L.A. to be here for me. You were talking quite literally, weren't you?"

He nods. "I know I embarrassed you, so I mentioned—"

"The center. Yes." I'm shaking my head, "So you really moved all the way to California, and rented a house on Rosewood Avenue, West Hollywood, specifically because . . ."

"I knew you would soon be moving next door and that you would need me."

"But I had a great job. A girlfriend."

Geshe-la smiles. He'd also known that neither of those was going to be enough.

"And how did you know where to come looking? That Tenzin Dorje had returned as director of research for Acellerate?"

He smiles. "There were signs," he says somewhat cryptically. "As you study the Dharma more you will see that certain mental abilities believed to be exceptional are available to anybody who is prepared to do the work."

"Like clairvoyance?"

He nods. "And you have an excellent foundation on which to build."

I realize he must be talking about my last lifetime as Tenzin Dorje, because my current lifetime's efforts seem to have amounted to very little. Even so, I wonder how much I could have achieved last time round. "I was only a novice. Not even an ordained monk, let alone a Geshe or a yogi."

"But you had sufficient faith to fight the Red Army. To cross the most treacherous mountain range in the world. To fall to your own death, rather than put your life's true purpose at risk."

Once again I am clinging to the side of the cliff, in those final, desperate moments. Charged with the urgent imperative to ensure the rucksack containing the sacred scrolls was returned to safety.

"The scrolls! What happened to them?" I ask.

Geshe-la leans back in his chair with an expression of delight. "I wondered when you would ask."

Realizing how important they had been to me as Tenzin Dorje, and how I had been more caught up in other less important matters now, I smile ruefully.

"After all, the scrolls were the reason you sacrificed your life."

"*From Tang in the West, one thousand*" he quotes from a verse that has a strange, primordial resonance,

Beneath the tail of the unequal snow lion,
My two most precious, bound for the lands of the red-faced,
Await the Dharma warriors."

"I will tell you what happened to the secret scrolls," he nods. "But before I do, can you remember the name by which you were known at Zheng-po? The name some used to tease you for using, but Lama Tsering encouraged—?"

I'm taken by surprise as the answer suddenly surfaces to my mind, like a bubble rising, apparently from nowhere, in a glass of water. Before he's even finished the sentence I'm saying, "The Magician of Lhasa."

"Yes," he pauses significantly. "And this is still your special destiny."

What he says sends an involuntary shiver through me, as though some profound pathway has been cleared and I'm being reconnected to an ancient truth.

But on a surface level it only confuses me. What does he mean "still your special destiny," as though the purpose of Tenzin Dorje's lifetime still has some relevance to me?

"Let me tell you what happened after Tenzin Dorje died in the mountains," Geshe-la explains. "Perhaps then you will understand."

CHAPTER FOURTEEN

Paldon Wangmo

Himalaya Border Region
1959

FOR THE FIRST FEW MOMENTS I CAN HARDLY BELIEVE WHAT HAS happened. I think it is the same for Lama Tsering. Kneeling behind him, my arms round his chest, even though we were braced for the ropes to jolt as Tenzin Dorje's foothold gave way, instead, the opposite has happened.

After throwing us his rucksack and mala, suddenly all the tension in the ropes disappears. My brother had made the same calculation as I: it was going to be impossible for the three of us to survive this predicament. In the ultimate act of selflessness, he had thrown us his sacred cargo and cut himself loose, rather than jeopardize all our lives and our mission.

It is Lama who speaks first. "He protected the teachings to the end of his life. There is no greater courage." Then after a pause, "And he has no greater need of me than now."

The Dharma shows us that at death our very subtle consciousness is propelled into the bardo realms. For a period of up to seven weeks we seek to manifest in a new form. Just as in life we experience reality a particular way because of our karma, so too after the cessation of life, it is our karma which determines how we experience reality and, most importantly, the next life form into which our consciousness will be projected.

While the destiny of most beings is determined entirely by karma, those beings who have a strong connection to a highly realized master can sometimes have their future changed. Their teacher may be able to alter what most people aren't even aware exists, to help them avoid a lower rebirth.

That night, as we sit in the mountains, the first without my brother, I try my utmost to meditate on his behalf, offering prayers to all gurus, Buddhas and bodhisattvas that he might achieve a precious human rebirth, that he will quickly be reconnected to his *vajra* guru, and continue his journey to enlightenment. They are humble prayers which on their own might achieve little. The real power is the mind of Lama Tsering.

As dawn breaks, I feel his movement beside me and look up to see that his eyes are open, and on his face is an expression of great peace. Even though we almost always sense a calm in Lama's presence, as he only rarely registers negative emotion, his expression that morning has a very special quality—his radiance and serenity is oceanic.

On seeing it, I feel both huge relief as well as curiosity. "Did Tenzin Dorje make a successful transmigration?" I ask.

Lama turns to me, smiling. "He is very happy. He has returned home."

"So he'll meet the perfect guru and return to the path?"

"Soon enough," replies Lama. Then seeing my anxious expression, "He will be very content."

Lama's replies concern me because they are not the assurances I hope for. When he says Tenzin Dorje has returned "home"—where does he mean? Surely not Zheng-po? Or is it our family home of Ling? And what does he mean that he will meet his next teacher "soon enough?" In an ideal human rebirth, he would be destined for birth into a family of Dharma practitioners, and be looked after by his teacher before he was even aware of it.

"He had excellent finishing karma—the very best," Lama says, using a tone I know means he doesn't want to talk further about the subject.

I nod slowly, realizing that Lama is giving me a clue.

Two specific karmas affect our rebirth. "Throwing karma" determines whether we'll be born into the human, animal, or another realm. "Finishing karma" determines whether, for example, we'll have the great fortune to be born into a family blessed with material abundance, good looks and long life, or into a place of poverty, sickness, short life and no opportunity to practice the Dharma.

By telling me that Tenzin Dorje has had good finishing karma, is Lama implying that he hasn't had such good throwing karma? Could it be that my brother has missed out on a precious human rebirth, but will nonetheless live in comfort? I realize that I'd have to keep my wits about me if I want to learn more about my brother's mindstream. But I also know I can take heart from Lama Tsering's expression, and the transcendental luminosity I have seen in his eyes that dawn.

The next night we continue on our journey. Even though Lama Tsering has made a strong recovery from his sprained ankle, he can no longer maintain the robust pace that he'd set before the avalanche. There is a frailty about his footsteps which continues to make our progress painfully slow.

Despite the harsh conditions of the mountains, I know we can endure a protracted journey but for one thing. We have almost run out of food. I am acutely aware how little remains in my own rucksack. And even though Tenzin Dorje's contains supplies for a few more meals, we will very soon be left with nothing. Meanwhile the mountains rise ahead of us, range upon range of them, our destination as distant as ever.

I remain confident that Lama Tsering will arrange something, having long since come to realize that he lives in a reality that rises above ordinary convention. He has the power to create events that others might regard as amazing coincidence or good luck. I even come to think of our food situation as a kind of examination which he is putting me through. Each meal stop, as our rations dwindle further and further, is like another test. Will I voice alarm at our impending starvation? Desperation at the plight in which we find ourselves? Hopelessness that we might not make it?

Even though I have become used to hardship and hunger on the journey through the mountains, and try to strengthen my mind with the instructions of Shantideva and other sages, I am, nevertheless, shaken the night we end our climbing and open our rucksacks—to find nothing.

When starting out, earlier that evening, I already knew we had run out of food. Every last dried chickpea, every handful of barley, even the few remaining leaves of cha we had brought with us had long since been used up. And even though I had become used to living with the pangs of hunger as a constant, after a whole night's journey. I am ravenous.

Had I been naïve in believing that when we opened our rucksacks, lo and behold we would discover several unopened cans of chickpeas? Had my faith in my guru been misguided in expecting a miracle?

"You have Tenzin Dorje's rucksack?" Lama confirms.

I nod. Because of Lama's frailty, I have rolled it up and placed it inside my own rucksack. In it, I know, are nothing but the two Padmasambhava scrolls. Retrieving the rucksack, I hand it over to Lama, wondering what magic is about to be performed.

Handing me back the two scrolls, to wrap up safely, Lama lays the camouflage colored canvas on a smooth rock. Next he retrieves his small gas stove, goes to scoop some snow into the small, battered, aluminum pot, and lights the flame. As the water heats, he takes his pen knife and slices the rucksack into strips about one inch thick by two long. As he drops the strips into the boiling water he looks over with a gentle smile, "Boiling may have no effect on taste, but at least it may make it more tender."

I am more shocked than anything as I realize what he is doing. We are to eat Tenzin Dorje's rucksack for our dinner! And from the way Lama Tsering is carefully packing the remaining strips in his own bag, maybe not just for this one meal alone. So much for my idea that he would manifest food from out of nowhere!

Despite my shock, I say nothing to Lama, either about food, or our dire circumstances. I remain convinced this is part of his testing of me. Instead, when he decides the rucksack has boiled for long enough, I join him in taking a strip out of the pot and putting it in my mouth.

"Just imagine," Lama says as we do this, "we are privileged to have been offered the most tender strips of yak."

I will never forget the sight of Lama Tsering chewing rucksack. Formerly the highest ranking Lama at Zheng-po Monastery, a revered *mahasiddha*, my kind and holy teacher, it would have been easy to think how much he had lost, how far we had both fallen, to be reduced to such circumstances. But to have thought that would be to have succumbed to the superstition of materialism. *It's not what happens to you that matters, it's how you interpret it.* Is this not what Lama is showing me, even as we eat?

I cannot pretend that my brother's rucksack is anything but the worst meal I've ever eaten. Chewy, acidic, and void of all nourishment, the worst part is swallowing one strip at a time. Trying to get it down, quickly, without retching. But I know I have to do this if I am to stop the pain in my stomach.

Along with the warm water, we manage to fill our bellies to some extent for at least as long as it takes to fall asleep. As the chill wind rises, we roll up in our coats, huddled together for warmth. And I know from the look in my teacher's eyes that we have just passed through the darkest hour before dawn.

WHEN WE WAKE IT IS TO THE UNFAMILIAR SOUND OF TIBETAN CHATTER. After weeks in the mountains during which we'd tried our utmost to avoid all human contact, it seems surreal to wake in the early afternoon to hear Tibetan speech and laughter, loud and unrestrained. Cautiously rising from our hiding place behind a boulder, as Lama and I look up it is to find a very lengthy trail of villagers heading in the very direction that we are. Quite a number of the men, including those at the front, are carrying rifles that look the same as those the Red Army soldiers had carried. Quickly realizing they present no danger, Lama and I stand up from our hiding place.

It is the beginning of our rescue. The turning point. For the villagers stop, making respectful prostrations towards Lama Tsering. It soon turns out that of the forty or so travelers, at least half are from the village of Tang. They regard us as their rescuers and are upset to hear how Tenzin Dorje has died.

They are also quick to note our poor condition, and stop to give us our first full meal of tsampa and cha in over two weeks. Because they are well armed, and several know these mountains, they aren't afraid to travel in a large group—or in broad daylight.

Although it is Tibetan custom to refuse an invitation up to three times before finally accepting it, on this occasion Lama and I need no further prompting to join the group. We explain how we've run out of food, and that we don't wish to be a burden. But it is clear our compatriots are both well-prepared for the journey, as well as generous in wishing to repay the kindness they feel we'd shown in bringing the horror of Tang to an end. Tagging on at the end of the line of women and children, as Lama and I continue our trek through the Himalayas, we have profound cause to be grateful to Tenzin Dorje for what he'd done at Tang, and to our fellow travelers for their camaraderie and open-handedness.

While we don't see any more Red Army soldiers for the rest of the journey, we nonetheless feel both relief and elation when we arrive at the first Indian outpost of Dhankar Gompa. It is confirmation that we have crossed the border. And confirmation that we are not far from our ultimate destination of Dharamsala to which, it is now widely known, the Dalai Lama and Tibetan community have moved.

That first night in freedom, there is celebration and much drinking of chang on the part of the villagers. But there is regret also, for all we have lost: our loved ones, like Tenzin Dorje, and also an entire way of life which had been devoted to the practice of the Dharma in monasteries, nunneries, and communities throughout the land.

In Tibet there had been stories about the paradise of *Shambala*—a place of peace and harmony for all beings, animal and human. Many had wished to turn Tibet into Shambala by trying to live according to the values of such a world. And when westerners discovered the idea, it quickly seized their imagination too, with Shambala being translated as Shangri-La. But with the 1959 invasion, Tibet literally disappeared from the map, and Shambhala was lost beneath the sea of red China.

After a rest in Dhankar Gompa of just a few days, we continue our journey to Dharamsala. We have rested, eaten proper meals, and found time to meditate, and as we set off for the final, short part of our journey we do so with great anticipation for what lies at the end of our journey.

While in Dhankar Gompa we have also been reunited with several other monks from Zheng-Po. It is a mostly joyful meeting, but for the feelings of loss about Tenzin Dorje, the only one among us who has perished. There is much talk about the perils we had faced along the way, narrow escapes from the Red Army, starvation in the icy mountains, and the destruction of Tang about which everyone now knows. There are also stories about our fellow monks. Someone has heard that our abbott, who had insisted on being the last to leave Zheng-po, had actually arrived in India first. Others told of how three groups of Zheng-po monks had been captured by the Red Army within a day of leaving the bus. We all know, however, not to spend too much time in speculation, the truth will reveal itself in time.

As the most senior monk, Lama Tsering suggests we form a joint delegation when we go to visit His Holiness. Together, we will offer our precious leader all the sacred texts we have brought with us to freedom—the contribution of the monks of Zheng-po to the survival and continuity of the Dharma. All the monks agree, and so we make the last part of our journey to Dharamsala together.

Dharmasala is my first experience of an Indian town, in fact, of any town. Having spent my childhood in a village of less than fifty people before moving into the cloistered environment of a monastery, I've had very little contact with the outside world of commerce and pleasure-seeking. I also discover how much I have been protected from a world in which generosity, ethics and patience are not the assumed values which others are striving to perfect! The dusty streets of Dharamsala, busy with market shops and crowded with people—Indians, Tibetans, monks, even a few Westerners—are entirely foreign to me. The chaos of noise and different languages, the jumbled, foreign smells that come from food stalls cooking delicacies I've never seen before, seem to overwhelm the senses.

I remember how Lama looks over at me as we walk up a busy street in which three men on bicycles, coming in different directions, are competing for a small space between a blind beggar and a roaming black cow.

"This is where all the action is," he says with an amused smile.

"I think Tenzin Dorje would have liked it," I reply.

"But not Paldon Wangmo?"

I shake my head. "Not Paldon Wangmo."

Dharamsala has no particular charm to it. However we discover with some relief that it is in McLeod Ganj, or Upper Dharamsala, that His Holiness and most of the Tibetans are living. An abandoned colonial hill station, the Indian government generously offered it for the use of Tibetan refugees. It's about five miles from Lower Dharamsala, up a very steep road.

On the last day of our journey, walking to our final destination, we leave the hubbub of Dharamsala below. We find ourselves entering a very different landscape. Here, in the Dhauladhar mountains, the scent is clean with pine and deodar trees. After the barren slopes of the Himalayas, the countryside is lush with foliage, including luxuriant rhododendrons blooming in a welcoming profusion of pinks and reds.

There is something about the air that seems purer, more rarefied. Is it only my imagination, knowing that we are nearing the home of His Holiness, the Dalai Lama, who I believe to be a living Buddha? Or is there really something inexplicable, beyond both senses and intellect that make this a special, sacred place?

Like everything else to do with our journey, the end of it is nothing as I have imagined it to be. Reaching McLeod Ganj shortly before dusk, we spend our first night in the village, before preparing to make our way to Tsuglag Khang—the main temple complex in which His Holiness lives. I will never forget the feeling as we ascend the steps to his home, in the crisp, mountain light. The familiar faces of all of us Zheng-po monks, in such an unfamiliar setting. There is a regal splendor about Tsuglag Khang, perhaps more a reflection of my own limited background, than the building itself, though I can see on the faces of the others that they, too, sense the magic of this place.

We have to wait some time in the bright, morning sunlight outside Tsuglag Khang, while Lama Tsering goes inside to announce our arrival. Then we are ushered into a large office, where we are met by three of the Dalai Lama's senior advisers. They stand, formal and serene in ceremonial yellow hats. I look up at them with a sense of awe that these are among the closest beings on earth to His Holiness. The lama in the center, Kelsing Rinpoche, is taller than the other two and the most senior. He wears an air of effortless authority but at the same time a benevolent smile as though he is greeting us all as old friends.

Kelsing Rinpoche apologizes to us straight away for the fact that His Holiness isn't in residence, but traveling on a diplomatic mission. He is seeking the support of other countries in persuading the Chinese to leave Tibet. He thanks us, both on behalf of His Holiness as well as the people of Tibet, for all we have sacrificed in ensuring the holy Dharma is protected, by bringing irreplaceable scriptures from the renowned Zheng-Po library to safety in India. With the assistance of the two other lamas, he receives all the texts we give him, taking careful note of the names of all of the monks, and giving us each a ceremonial mala and prayer wheel, blessed by the Dalai Lama.

It is His Holiness's wish, he tells us, that we should all return to Tibet as soon as it is safe, and resume Dharma practice in our established monasteries. At that time, each monastery will have its original scriptures returned. But in the meantime, Tsuglag Khang will act as a central repository for both the most precious holy texts and secular manuscripts of the Tibetan people.

As I look at the table on which the Zheng-po texts are respectfully laid out, I notice the scripture with the brocade wrapping torn by a Chinese bayonet in the village of Tang. The two metal cylinders standing, ancient and otherworldly beside all the more conventional scriptures.

Evidently Kelsing Rinpoche notices them too, because after we are ushered out, he asks Lama Tsering to stay behind. It is only much later in the day, when we are alone together that Lama tells me about the conversation that passed between them. Recognizing the antiquity of the scrolls immediately, Kelsing Rinpoche had quizzed Lama Tsering on their origin. Lama Tsering told him about the cave near Tang, the story of his encounter with the hideous old woman, the reminder of Padmasambhava's famous prophecy. Kelsing Rinpoche hadn't wasted any time confirming that these were undoubtedly among the most precious scriptures to have been brought from Tibet. Indeed, their very existence hadn't been known about before the flight to exile. And such was their importance that before officially receiving them, he wanted to take further advice.

"But I thought Kelsing Rinpoche was the most senior adviser?" I say. "To whom can he turn for advice?"

"He is the highest authority," Lama replies somewhat mysteriously. "But only in a temporal sense."

Lama's meaning becomes clear two days later when we are summoned to Tsuglag Khang, this time to see Kelsing Rinpoche in his office.

"I asked the Oracle to perform a Mo divination," he tells us. Seated in an armchair, without his yellow hat, he is no less imposing than when he'd formally received the Zheng-po delegation. On a table between us stands the two Padmasambhava scrolls.

Next to me, Lama looks as if he's been used to sitting in armchairs all his life, but this is my first time and I am feeling very self-conscious as my legs stick out, instead of being tucked under me.

"But—" Kelsing Rinpoche continues with a frown, "I am a little confused. While the result of the Mo was lucid, it doesn't accord with my understanding of what you told me. Am I correct in thinking you traveled with just two novice monks?"

"Paldon Wangmo," Lama gestures towards me. "And his brother, Tenzin Dorje, who died."

"There was no fourth monk?"

Lama shakes his head.

"Perhaps someone you met up with along the way who helped carry the scrolls, even for a short time?"

"The only other person who touched them was a Chinese soldier."

Kelsing Rinpoche's eyebrows twitch upwards for a moment before he looks over at me, studying my face closely.

Feeling the force of his full attention on me, I swallow.

"I must apologize, Lama," he is looking back at my teacher, "for my unfamiliarity with all of you at Zheng-po. And you must understand that now is not a time for excessive modesty. But is it the case that you, or either of your novices, possess special powers—siddhis?"

Lama shakes his head. "No, we are just ordinary monks."

I glance over at my teacher, thinking how Tenzin Dorje and I are ordinary, but he is certainly far more than that.

Instantly, I feel Kelsing Rinpoche's eyes upon me.

"You don't agree, Paldon Wangmo?' he asks, his tone inviting me into his confidence.

"I think my teacher is . . . very special," I say, earnestly.

"Oh," he nods, with an encouraging smile. "And why is that?"

I glance over nervously at Lama Trijan before confessing, "He's able to read my mind."

There is a moment's pause as the two men exchange glances before they both burst out laughing.

"You are to be congratulated for your guru devotion!" says Kelsing Rinpoche, as I blush at their chuckles. Then after composing himself, Kelsing Rinpoche continues, "I was thinking, in particular, about healing siddhis?"

Both Lama and I looked perplexed. It is true that both of us had enjoyed the protection of Medicine Buddha in times of trouble, especially Lama with his sprained ankle during the journey. But we know the Dalai Lama's advisor means something different. Something of more active benefit to others.

"What about a connection to Lhasa?" Kelsing Rinpoche changes tack. "Were either of you born there, or maybe lived there for some time?"

Lama and I shake our heads. As much as we want to help find some sort of connection, nothing in what Kelsing Rinpoche is saying relates to our experience. Looking from Lama's blank face to mine, he finally settles his gaze out the window, across the foothills of pine forests to the distant, ice-capped peaks of the Himalayas.

"The information is quite specific," he murmurs, as though to himself. "The scriptures in each of these tubes are identical. Two copies of the same, most important holy text. One is to be retained, sealed but for safekeeping, here in His Holiness's library. The other is to be given to a particular person to open. This person played an important part in bringing them to safety. We had thought in recent times, but perhaps the reference is much further back.

"The person was referred to in terms which I have trouble substantiating," he looks back at us. "None of the three of you claim special powers.

None of you are from Lhasa. But the Oracle stated quite clearly the scroll was to be returned to 'the Magician of Lhasa.'"

Lama Tsering flashes a look of amusement at me, before beginning to tell the Dalai Lama's advisor "Tenzin Dorje—"

At the same moment I chime, "My brother! From a young age he had that nickname—the Magician of Lhasa!"

"Ah!" bringing his hands together, as though to prostrate, Kelsing Rinpoche nods with a smile, "Good. These very specific details, like the use of a nickname, are very good for authentication are they not?"

Then as Lama Tsering and I nod with a sense of wonderment, he fixes Lama with a piercing gaze, "Now your only remaining challenge is to locate where the magician is to be reborn. I take it you have the connection?"

"I do," Lama says briefly.

Taking one of the metal canisters from the table and offering it reverentially to Lama Tsering, Kelsing Rinpoche tells him, "Then I am entrusting this precious scripture to you, once again. On behalf of His Holiness, the Fourteenth Dalai Lama and the people of Tibet, I request that you carry out the sacred mission of returning this scripture to the one who has been chosen to unseal it. I can confirm it contains the teachings of the great and glorious Padmasambhava, written to be revealed in the West at a particular time in the future. A time when it is needed most urgently of all. A time when the messages it contains will become critical not for the survival of Tibet, but of all mankind. That being the case," his eyes narrow, and he looks from Lama to me with a severe expression, "its very existence must remain a secret."

Receiving the ornate metal cylinder with both hands, Lama Tsering nods solemnly. "I accept this special honor," he says. "I will guard this scripture as though it were my life, and will ensure it is kept hidden until it is returned to the one who has been chosen."

Matt Lester

Rosewood Avenue—West Hollywood
2007

"SO YOU SEE," ACROSS THE KITCHEN TABLE, GESHE-LA REACHES OUT to squeeze my hand, "last night's revelation is one you were always destined to experience, not only since you arrived in Los Angeles, but from long before—even before the time you were born."

We're still sitting together at the kitchen table. For the past two hours we've gone through three mugs of coffee as Geshe-la has told me about the journey from Tibet, and the instructions of the Dalai Lama's advisors which have such unexpected and intensely personal significance. And which carry with them an urgency and purpose far greater than my own personal well-being. It encompasses well-being on a truly global scale.

I am still trying to make sense of how my whole life seems to have been redefined. Everything that has preoccupied me in the past, all that I have taken so seriously seems only to have been a prelude. From what Geshe-la is saying, my real job has yet to begin.

Am I really to believe that, in ancient times, a revered Buddhist saint wrote a special and very specific message for when the Dharma would be brought to the West, after the invasion of Tibet? That he made two copies of this scripture and hid them in time capsules in a remote Himalayan cave? That fate—no, karma—had propelled a young novice monk to give up his life while fleeing across the Himalayas, to preserve the scriptures? That the Dalai Lama's advisors had determined the special message should be revealed only by the reborn incarnation of this novice monk? And that this reborn incarnation was me?!

Me, a jaded and now very cynical thirty-something research scientist from London? A guy who had never had any interest in telepathy, clairvoyance or astral traveling? Who'd had no contact with Buddhism at all, apart from once taking shelter under the Battersea Park pagoda during a thunderstorm.

I have so many questions. "The dates," I tell Geshe-la, "they're all wrong. Tenzin Dorje died in 1959, but I wasn't born until 1972."

"Obviously you didn't move directly from one rebirth to the next." He is straightforward.

"Where was I in between?"

He shrugs, "Does it matter?"

"If I was born in 1960 and died in 1971 I would only have been eleven. Still just a kid."

"It's very unlikely for every rebirth to be in the human realm."

"You mean, you really can come back as something else? I mean, like an animal of some kind?"

"Of course! What do you know that ever progresses steadily forwards? The stock market? Your career? Relationships with friends and romantic partners?"

"I thought once you were born human you could never go back—"

"Some people find it reassuring to think like that. But this is incorrect. Perhaps it is hard for them to confront the idea of returning," he shrugs, "as a mere animal."

"But how can something as complex as a human being turn into, say, a rat?"

As I meet his eyes I am made aware, once again, of the connection I have with him, and at the same time am reminded of my own poor understanding of the Dharma.

"You see," his eyes glint with some amusement, "it is important to ask "What is it that moves from one lifetime to another?" It is not your personality. Your memory. Your intelligence. It is merely your subtle consciousness propelled by karma. Tell me, Matt, is a cockroach conscious?"

I shrug.

"If you chase it with a broom, or a spray can of insecticide, does it not run away?"

"Yes."

"Then it has consciousness. It knows it is alive. It fears death. It seeks food and wishes to avoid suffering. Cockroach or human being; both have consciousness."

"So, you're saying," I'm trying to figure this out, "that for eleven years between my death as Tenzin Dorje and being reborn as Matt Lester, I lived as some kind of . . . animal?"

His smile is mischievous. "It is possible."

"Exactly what kind?"

Geshe-la looks away.

It's clear he doesn't want to tell me, and I don't press him.

Instead I ask, "Are there lots of us? Westerners who were monks, or Buddhists in previous lives, but who have no idea of it?"

"Of course. The community of Buddhists, or *Sangha* has existed for twenty-five hundred years. Many practitioners are still with us, in every race and nationality. The most fortunate continue their Dharma journey continuously in the human realm, from one lifetime to the next, until they are free of samsara. Others leave the path for lifetimes, sometimes many, many lifetimes. The saddest of all are those who have the opportunity to practice, but who choose not to. Who are drawn to the Dharma perhaps by reading a book, seeing something on TV, perhaps even a chance conversation, but who never make the most of their precious human rebirth."

"So, there are many Tenzin Dorje's living as ordinary Westerners now?"

"Not only that," Geshe-la's smile lights up his face. "We live among many magicians of Lhasa. People who will realize the most extraordinary potentialities . . . when they return to the path."

I know this is as much as he will say. That he won't even attempt to pressure me to do anything I don't decide from my own free will. But after my experience last night, and our long conversation this morning, I also know that I can never go back to the way I was before. I can't pretend my life is only about Matt Lester in the here and now. I have caught much more than a glimpse of a far more expansive reality. But do I act on it, and if so—how?

"This . . . scroll of Padmasambhava—" I ask Geshe-la, "you're saying it's been kept specifically for me to open?"

Lips pursed, he nods, before saying. "That's true. But it is not only a matter of cutting open a metal tube, taking out some Tibetan writing and having it translated."

"No?"

He shakes his head. "If that were the case, it could have been opened fifty years ago. There is a reason that you were chosen."

"Which is?"

He regards me with a keen intensity. "For you to discover," he tells me, eventually. "But discover it, you will. This much you have to take on trust."

The authority with which he tells me this reminds me that apart from being my brother from a previous life-time, Geshe-la is also a high-ranking lama. A former abbot, someone who has given up all the privileges of his tradition to come to Los Angeles, live in a garden shed, and find me. It has been a humbling discovery that the focus of his special mission here has been none other than me.

"The scroll itself, do you now have it for safekeeping?"

It's a reasonable assumption given that almost fifty years have passed since the flight from Tibet.

"No. Lama Tsering still has it."

"You mean—?!"

"He gave His Holiness's advisors his solemn word that he would pass it on to you. He intends keeping his word."

"But he must be ancient!"

"In his nineties, chronological age. Mental age, very much younger." Geshe-la's face relaxes again and a lightness comes into his expression as he talks about his guru. Our guru.

"His name, Tsering, means 'long life.' Nevertheless, it would be good for you to visit him soon."

Fragmented memories of Lama Tsering come into my mind. Not from those last moments on the cliff-side, but from earlier times—the image of meditating with him on a remote snowcap in the Himalayas—and another picture of him sitting in a cave filled with the strangest, ethereal light.

The gravitational tug to see him, to take further steps down this intriguing new path of the Dharma, becomes even stronger.

"I need to consider all this carefully," I tell Geshe-la.

"Very good," he replies, his voice free of expectation.

"But whatever happens, I have some unfinished business to see to."

Chapter Fifteen

Matt Lester

Napa Valley

THE APARTMENT IS IN AN UGLY, 70S STYLE BLOCK, WITH POOR LIGHTing and graffiti scrawled across one wall. It's so unlike what I'm expecting that I stop to check I've got the right address before finding a bay and parking the hired Toyota. When I'd suggested driving up to see her on Saturday evening, Isabella had been reluctant.

"It's a long drive—it'll take you all day," she'd told me.

"Yeah, I know. I've looked at the roadmap."

"I'm free on Saturday night," I'd heard the misgiving in her voice. "But I'll have to be back at the study center on Sunday morning."

"That's fine. It's only for dinner, then you can go home. I've got a hotel room booked." I thought it important to mention the last point. We hadn't had much contact since her visit to L.A. two weeks before. I guess we'd both been continuing to avoid the subject of what was happening between us. And I wanted to make sure she realized I was taking nothing for granted.

She'd finally agreed and as I get out of the car and walk across a stretch of pock-marked asphalt, I discover her apartment is up two flights of dank, concrete stairs. Here I am, standing outside the unfamiliar front door of the woman who for the past five years has been my love, my passion, my soul-mate, feeling suddenly like a stranger and nervous as a teenager on a first date.

She answers the door with a diffident smile. Although she's casually dressed in jeans and a white T-shirt, I'm reminded powerfully of what drew me to her in the first place. I take in her dark-eyed beauty and lustrous, shoulder-length hair. The golden brown of her skin contrasted by the white neckline of her T-shirt.

"You're looking well!" I put my arms around her for a hug. Although she reciprocates, it's not a yielding embrace. It's more a lock, an awkwardly held avoidance of further intimacy about as distant as a hug can be. Not so long ago, I think as my face rubs across her hair, if we hadn't seen each other for even the shortest time, we'd rush to each other's arms and melt together as one flesh.

Change.

She gestures me inside, where I discover that her apartment is more modest than I had ever imagined it to be. In my mind I'd had this image of an expansive, contemporary condo, all clean lines and open space with views over rolling vineyards. What I find instead is an aging and poky little box in a down-at-heel building. The lounge is a cramped space with two wooden chairs and a sagging sofa. I can see that Isabella has added a few domestic touches, hanging a colored throw on the wall, and putting some of her things on a set of otherwise empty shelves.

"You found your way here okay?" she asks.

"Sure," I turn to face her, noticing the dark shadows under her eyes. She's standing in the doorway, arms folded.

There's an awkward pause before she says, "Drink?"

It's an acknowledgement of my journey here, all the way up Route 5 from L.A. But from her tone of voice I know she doesn't really want me here. Is she embarrassed by my discovery of her modest circumstances? Is it a territorial thing? Or is it just me?

"Let's go out," I suggest, thinking that things may be easier on neutral ground. "I saw this Italian place just round the corner."

"Villa d'Este?"

"Think so," I try to picture the sign. "You know it?"

"Never had time to eat out," she's shaking her head. "But I walk past it every day. It always looks nice." She regards me carefully for a moment before saying, "You look different."

"Different?" I murmur. "How?"

She scrutinizes me further before shaking her head and turning back pointedly in the direction of the front door. As she leads the way out, I follow, glancing over towards a small desk, with careful piles of books and papers. The framed photo of her as a little girl with her parents, which she'd had back in Clapham. I'd forgotten about that photo, even though it's so familiar. Isabella, aged eight, looking directly at the camera, her sparkling, pink head band curiously at odds with her earnest expression.

As we reach the front door, we bump into each other awkwardly, and I realize she is probably just as tense about seeing me as I am about seeing her. Not that I regret making the journey.

I'm here because I want to see her, of course, though I've also been deeply affected by everything I've learned about my past, and what Geshe-la has explained to me about karma. The simple truth is that my attitude towards Isabella has changed at a very profound level. Instead of despairing over how she's been prepared to sacrifice our relationship for the sake of her parents, I recognize she has made the right choice. I also realize the pointlessness of harboring unspoken resentment towards her—as Geshe-la had put it: "You wouldn't feel anger towards a stick if you were being beaten. You would feel anger towards the person beating you. We should be careful who we blame for our unhappiness when we ourselves have created the causes for our unhappy experiences."

But coming up to Napa is about more than dealing with negative karma. It's also about creating positive conditions for future happiness to blossom. If love is the wish for others' happiness, as Geshe-la says it is, then I've come here out of love. Not the me-centered, attachment-based love that often masquerades as romance. Not the kind of love that is clingy and grasping and seeks to possess, but genuine love—the heartfelt wish for Isabella to be happy.

Leaving her apartment and making our way back down the concrete steps, I ask her conversationally how the course is going and she soon starts talking about the program. I sense her relief at talking about her studies over the past weeks, which have focused on red varietals.

Even before we left London I used to think Isabella was very knowledgeable on the subject, but as we make our way to the restaurant it's evident how much she has come to learn while on the course. Wine making techniques, soil and weather conditions, different approaches to blending are all being demystified for her, the more she learns and understands. There's a new authority in her voice when she speaks about wine, the same confidence with which she used to speak about marketing and distribution models in Europe. Despite her humble living conditions, I can tell that she's in her element up here in Napa.

Villa d'Este is a classic, middle-America variety of Italian eatery: jaunty red and white check table-cloths, candles flickering in Chianti bottles, the pervasive sweep of garlic. I insist that she orders the wine, as I always have before, and the conversation segues seamlessly from wine onto Julio. On the surface of things, life for Isabella's parents continues as usual, although unwelcome reminders of Julio's illness continue to intrude into their lives.

The most recent example was when they had Louis and Clara around for supper. Louis and Julio were the same vintage, both from Lucca, and had known each other since they were babies. Luigi, as he'd been known in his formative years, and his family had lived on the same street as the Giladucci's. Evenings with Louis and Clara were always relaxed, convivial affairs, but the most recent visit had been marred when Julio had paused, mid-way through an anecdote and looked at Louis with a blank expression, "Were we at school together?" he'd asked.

As one of his closest friends, Louis knew about the Alzheimer's, but wasn't letting it affect their friendship. "Of course!" he replied. "Primary and secondary. Remember the nuns at St. Joachim's? The way Sister Maria used to chase us around the classroom with her thick, brown belt?"

But Julio's blank expression had only given way to one of consternation. "No. I can't remember anything," he'd shaken his head. "I can recall some things from my childhood. But I try to think of school and there's nothing there."

"I wouldn't worry about it," Louis was quick to reassure. "There wasn't a lot worth remembering."

But despite Louis' support, Julio was worried, and so were the rest of his family. Even though they had been cautioned to expect it, provided with all the resources and assistance that were on offer, it was still a shock to witness the gaps appearing in his recollections, as if an invisible acid was eating away holes in the fabric of his memory.

As Isabella tells me about how Julio is losing his past, beginning on the desolate journey towards completely forgetting who he is, I can't help contrasting this with my own transformative experiences—how I have suddenly discovered a past I had never sought or even guessed existed. And how I believe I am only just beginning on a journey towards an understanding of who and what I am, beyond anything I would have imagined. The discovery of my personal history is in stark contrast to Julio's loss, a recognition I feel keenly.

Isabella tells me how her father has recently been talking about the Temple of Delphi, and the edict inscribed above its door: "Know Thyself." "How can we know ourselves if we can't even remember?" he has been asking his family, despairingly.

Across the candlelit table at Villa d'Este, Isabella and I share a contemplative expression.

Then I say one of the things, the most important thing, that I came here to tell her. The assurance I want to give her, face to face. "There's no doubt you're doing the right thing, I mean, moving to Europe to be closer to your folks."

It's the first time I've referred directly to her decision, and I can see her surprise. The way her eyes suddenly glisten. The tugging at the corners of her mouth as she battles to control unexpected emotion.

"It's not the way I wanted things to turn out," she replies after a while, voice cracking.

"I know it isn't," I meet her eye to eye. "But you're doing it anyway, and I just wanted to let you know that I respect that. You're doing it for all the right reasons."

She regards me closely, emotions welling to the surface, trying to make up her mind about something. It's as though we're connecting again, as though an openness is being created between us that hasn't existed since that very first day in L.A. As I meet her gaze, I can see gratitude in her eyes. And, more than gratitude, overwhelming relief.

She sighs, deeply. "I wish there'd been a way we could have done this differently," she says. "But I feel I just have to go back. Meantime, you have to make the most of your breakthrough with Bill Blakely."

I fix her with a droll expression. "As it happens, the breakthrough has also turned out a lot different from what I thought."

As our food arrives and we start eating, I tell her about events at Acellerate. I recount my encounter with Luke Calloway, my investigations about the previous research directors in the weeks that had followed. And I tell her about the showdown in Blakely's office and being escorted off the premises with my belongings in black bin liners.

Wide-eyed, Isabella listens to all this, shaking her head with astonishment. "I can't believe this has been happening all the while I've been up here."

In the past I would have told her about every development as it occurred. We both would have discussed the implications, working through what might happen next, talking about all the possibilities and the maybes and the what-ifs. The fact that she has no idea about the recent dramatic turn of events only emphasizes how far, and how quickly, we have lost touch.

"So what about your five percent ownership in the intellectual property of Nanobot?" she zeros in on the key issue. "Do you have any recourse?"

"You'd better believe it." I explain what I'm planning to do next, and how if Bill Blakely thinks he's heard the last of me, he's in for a surprise. "But there's no telling how long this will take," I tell her. "You know what litigation is like. The whole thing could drag on for years. The key leverage we have is that Blakely wants to list Acellerate on the NASDAQ, and to do that he needs a clean bill of health for the company's intellectual property."

Isabella is again scrutinizing me with a querying expression. "With everything that's happened," she says, "you seem pretty relaxed about things."

I lean back in my chair, realizing to my own surprise, that what she says is true. I'd come up here to do the right thing by Isabella, and instead of the bitter finality of loss, I feel strangely liberated.

Then after a further pause she says, "That's what's different about you."

"Different?"

"You know how earlier this evening I said you seemed different?" she looks at me closely. "There's this lightness about you, like you've had a weight taken off your shoulders." She has always been strongly intuitive. And while she's right about my feeling easier about things than I can ever remember, I know she can't possibly guess at the cause of this.

"Is it leaving Acellerate that's making you feel this way?" she asks. "Or is it knowing that I'm heading back to the other side of the world in a couple of months?"

For the first time in what feels like an age we're able to share a laugh.

Of course I've already wondered what, if anything, I should tell Isabella about the startling discoveries I've been making about my past. I've decided that for the moment it's best to say nothing. A single evening together, after the weeks of turmoil between us, is no time to embark on a lecture on the convergence between quantum science and the Dharma, the parallels between the small group of Jews fleeing Hitler and Tibetan Buddhists fleeing Mao Tse Tung, both of whom have delivered the most extraordinary wisdom to the West, let alone the very much more dramatic personal revelations about Tenzin Dorje and my escape from Tibet. Instead I confine myself to saying, "I've been seeing a bit of Geshe-la. You know—the Buddhist monk next door?"

She raises her eyebrows.

"He's helped me get things in perspective. Look at the bigger picture."

She is nodding, pensively, before she says, "Have you asked him about the litigation you're going to be involved in? I mean, what do Buddhists have to say about courtroom battles?"

Again, she has homed in on a subject I've been thinking about, but haven't shared with anyone. An issue of concern she has intuitively picked up on. And at the same time, I realize how very much I've missed her.

"I haven't spoken to Geshe-la about it," I tell her. "But what do you think?"

Isabella takes a sip of wine before she answers. "I reckon it would be wrong to do nothing. To stand back and let Blakely keep ripping people off. There's no honor in being a doormat. But it would also be wrong to get so caught up that it starts to take over your whole life, make you all bitter and twisted, like it does with some people. I guess," she pauses, "you've got to do what feels right, then let go."

I have the strong sense, as I raise a glass of wine to my lips, that if I had asked Geshe-la, he would have given me exactly the same answer. The same conclusion I have reached myself. And it seems as if the tectonic shift that's occurred in my own consciousness since the two of us last spoke properly is being mirrored, here and now, in my relationship with Isabella. Leaving behind all my usual, self-centered preoccupations seems to have been the key to unlocking a quite unexpected, new dimension, one that feels suddenly charged with possibility.

"I know you can't guess about the timing of the legal case," Isabella continues. "But what if you do get a result say in two or three months. What will you do next?"

"I really don't know," I answer her honestly.

"Would you look for another job here, in L.A.?"

"Don't think so." I'm imagining myself on an airplane to Northern India, traveling to meet Lama Tsering who has been waiting my entire lifetime to meet me. "There's other things I'd rather do than get back on the corporate treadmill."

She toys with the stem of her wine glass, and for the first time I notice that her finger nails, usually so well manicured, have been bitten to the quick. She's also wearing the engagement ring again, on her right hand. "If you were going back to London, I'll be visiting there every weekend." She pauses significantly, "And I'll only be away for a year."

We both know what she's suggesting. Perhaps because I didn't come to Napa expecting it, I'm surprised by the feeling of an emotional tide turning, emotions which I thought had edged well beyond the horizon suddenly rushing to return. I really had believed that Isabella was lost to me, that our lives were moving irrevocably in different directions. The possibility she's hinting at now is one I haven't seriously considered. But it's complicated by my new sense of purpose, one which I've still to make sense of myself.

"I know what you're saying," I tell her, and it's my own turn for my voice to turn husky. "I'm very glad you feel that way."

"But you haven't forgiven me?" she asks, responding to the ambiguity in my voice, her dark eyes intense. There's something about her expression which instantly reminds me of the photograph of her as a little girl with her parents. The sparkling, pink headband and the serious expression.

"Oh, it's not that—" I shake my head.

"Babe, I'm so, so sorry!" She continues as though she only half believes me. "I only wish—" tears fill her eyes.

"Isabella, you don't need my forgiveness. What happened was my fault, too."

I've been so preoccupied with other, more important developments that the subject of Paolo is, self-evidently, one I haven't thought much about. "I guess—" I'm finding it hard to speak, "I guess I thought I'd lost you. I didn't really expect ... this."

Looking across the table I see her cheeks are flecked with silver. She raises a hand to her mouth to stifle a sob. My own eyes burn as I'm flooded with the relief of reunion, the most profound of all happiness.

After dabbing at her face with a tissue, eventually she looks across the table, smiling through the tears. "You haven't lost me, babe." She reaches her hand across the dining table, lacing her fingers through mine.

It's the first time in six weeks and it sends a flood of warmth right through me. "And your heart's grown so much bigger."

Downtown Los Angeles

I'M FEELING VERY DIFFERENT A WEEK LATER WHEN I STEP INSIDE THE elevator of a downtown L.A. office tower and press the button for the thirty-fifth floor. It's shortly before two o'clock, and I'm dressed in my smartest suit and tie for a special stockholders meeting involving with Acellerate's largest shareholders. The purpose of the meeting? To approve Acellerate's plans to raise one hundred million dollars in capital, and list on the NASDAQ in six week's time.

Up until now, Acellerate shareholder meetings have been strictly private affairs. Bill Blakely and his financial backers have met to prepare battle plans behind closed doors, whether at Acellerate, or the Wall Street offices of the major institutions which support him. And all their energies and intrigues of the past several years have been directed to one particular event: the successful flotation of Acellerate on the NASDAQ.

Given that most of Acellerate's shareholders bought into the company at between twenty and fifty cents a share, and that the planned issue price is a dollar, even if the company holds steady on listing, everyone will have doubled, tripled, quintupled their money, the great and glorious Bill Blakely included.

But most shareholders have even grander ambitions. If they generate enough excitement around the flotation, enough support from institutional players, enough column inches in the financial pages, there's no reason that the listing price won't rise much higher than a dollar. Some have been speculating about a dollar twenty. Die-hard enthusiasts are talking even more, a dollar thirty on opening, rising to a dollar fifty by the end of the year. Hell, if the market's in a good mood on the day of listing, who's to say it won't strike a dollar fifty straight off?!

Which is why the outcome of today's meeting is supposedly a foregone conclusion. While having to go through the motions required by law, there's no doubt that Acellerate's shareholders will give the listing plan their most enthusiastic support.

There's also some corporate housekeeping to get through. Apart from Acellerate's three flagship research programs—of which Nanobot is one—the company has bought the controlling interests in two small, listed biotech firms, Telememex and Synbek. Both companies were cash-strapped research incubators when Bill Blakely bailed them out. Both are to be folded into Acellerate, as deal-sweeteners, when it goes for listing. Again, there's no way their shareholders aren't going to support the plan. But they have to be asked at a formal meeting. Which is why I'm here today.

A few weeks ago, soon after going through all the paperwork given me by Acellerate's investor relations manager, Mervyn Pank, I phoned a stockbroker and bought a hundred bucks of Telememex shares. In so doing, I secured my right to be here today, in the same room as all Acellerate's multi-million dollar shareholders. Not just that, but the right to question

Bill Blakely. In front of his most important backers. On the eve of their most hotly-anticipated announcement.

Even though I know I have right on my side, it would have been a daunting prospect, and probably a fruitless one if I'd come alone.

But I haven't.

As the elevator doors close, I glance over at Luke Calloway, also a new shareholder in Telememex. Apart from our recently-purchased stocks, and the fact that we have both been directors of research at Acellerate, with less than eleven months of employment between us, we have something else in common of much greater consequence; both of us hold prior-art patents for our work—patents establishing us as the inventors of core technologies which Acellerate now claims as its own.

With us in the lift is our legal representative Hal Levine, one of the city's highest-profile intellectual property attorneys. Tall, lantern-jawed, head completely shaven, the former football fullback from Dallas looks every bit as intimidating as his reputation for taking on the heads of major corporations. And beating them. Looking down, he stretches his fingers back, cracking the knuckles of first one hand then the other. Though his expression betrays nothing, I have the feeling he's looking forward to this afternoon's meeting as mundane any Acellerate shareholder—if for very different reasons.

At the thirty-fifth floor the doors whisper open and we step out, making our way to the designated presentation room. After signing an attendance register, noting ourselves as shareholders, we make our way into a wood-paneled chamber. About fifty chairs have been set out in half a dozen rows, with a long table at the center of which sits Bill Blakely and several other Acellerate board directors, none of whom I recognize.

As the three of us troop in, Blakely's head is turned, in discussion with one of his associates. But he looks up just as we're sitting down about half way towards the back, and his face registers nothing. Not a spark of recognition, much less a flicker of self-doubt. It is as though all three of us are of absolutely no consequence. Invisible.

I look over briefly at Hal Levine, but as he surveys the front desk his face remains as impossible to read as Bill Blakely's. I'd contacted Levine soon after my encounter with Luke Calloway simply because he was the only American patent attorney I'd ever heard of. Anybody who read the biotech press couldn't help being familiar with the name Hal Levine, who continued to win significant damages against pharmaceutical and IT giants. I'd been surprised when he'd agreed to see me the very next day, but I quickly learned the reason for his interest in my case. Some years earlier, before Acellerate was even thought of, Blakely had approached Levine to draft a legal agreement reassigning intellectual property ownership from a colleague to himself. It had sounded a straightforward undertaking, and Hal had undertaken the necessary paperwork. But after much discussion back and forth, Blakely's agenda become clearer; he didn't want the colleague to understand the implications of the document he was signing.

Levine had refused any further part of it. He'd sent Blakely an invoice for his work which, years later, remained unpaid.

"It was only a matter of time before someone like you came knocking on my door," he told me, to my own chagrin, at our first meeting. "My only surprise is that it's taken so long."

Having arrived only moments before the two o'clock start time, the special stockholders meeting is soon underway. Blakely stands to welcome all present, focusing his attention on the first two rows, where his most important supporters sit in hand-tailored suits. Poised, primed, and aglow with confidence, as Blakely describes the exciting future that awaits all shareholders I can't help wondering at how he betrays not a shadow of doubt that Acellerate, a company synonymous with systematic theft, is about to make its dazzling debut on the NASDAQ.

But, as Hal Levine has already explained to me, while Bill Blakely is unquestionably smart, he's not as smart as he thinks. In his time, Blakely had made predatory moves on all manner of research institutes, foundations and tertiary science schools. Rebuffed by many, he'd been sustained by the few who were too busy, too careless or too ignorant to put in place proper legal protection for their own work. Harry Saddler, at the Imperial Science Institute, had been a case in point. A brilliant researcher who misguidedly believed he was an equally brilliant deal-maker, it was Harry who'd failed to protect both the institute and me from Blakely's well-practiced ruses, like changing unchallenged clauses at final draft stage.

What Blakely seemed not to have considered, was that just as Harry had failed to protect the institute's IP from his own machinations, he'd also failed to protect it from other people.

Hal Levine had shaken his head in amazement—the only time I'd seen him crack a wide-mouthed smile—when I'd taken in all the legal paperwork for him to go through.

"Are you seriously telling me that the Imperial Science Institute never transferred ownership of the patent you filed before you joined them?"

"That's right." I had a clear memory of Harry telling me this was something we'd have to do, when he recruited me. "Somehow they never got around to it."

"Incredible!"

"All the patents filed afterwards were in the institute's name."

"Sure, but you had killer prior art. You could have sued them for stealing your ideas."

"I'd never have done that, and Harry knew it," I shrug. I guess that's why he never bothered."

"Well, his inattention has delivered what we need to nail Blakely," Levine had looked up, a carnivorous glint in his eye. "Blakely acquired the institute's patents for a laughably low sum. There's no law against that. What he didn't realize was that the patents could be challenged."

I'm trying to remain as non-attached as possible to the whole situation with Acellerate, and especially all the legal wrangling over intellectual property. As Geshe-la told me, if I allowed myself to become emotionally engaged in the battle against Blakely, I wouldn't be causing Blakely any harm; I'd only be causing myself pain. One of Isabella's colleagues from the sales department at Bertollini had once told me much the same thing: "If you're desperate, or needy in a sales situation," he'd confided over a pint at our local pub, "it's not a nice feeling to have. What's more, other people pick up on it at a subconscious level. It's like you're transmitting negative vibes. All of which means you're less likely to close the deal."

If I want to "close the deal," if I want to see justice done, not only on my own account, but also for my predecessors at Acellerate, I know I need to adopt an attitude of non-attachment. I should work with Hal Levine to the best of my abilities, but do so without expectation. And definitely without spending time and energy focusing on the prospect of a big payout.

In different circumstances, I would have found this a tough challenge. But because I'm now so aware of my much wider purpose, because I'm able to see the events of this lifetime with a different perspective, I feel much easier and lighter about what I'm doing. The burden of expectation has been lifted from my shoulders.

Bill Blakely comes to the end of his shareholder pitch. The mood in the room is so upbeat I half expect all the Wall Street suits to break into applause. Then he announces it's time to move onto the business end of the meeting. One by one, each of a dozen resolutions need to be read out, proposed, seconded and voted on. Most importantly, questions must be invited in each case. Each of the resolutions deals with a separate, specific issue, like the raising of one hundred million at one dollar a share. The exchange of Telememex and Symbek stock for shares in Acellerate. There's unlikely to be much discussion about any of these. All the resolutions already have majority support already through proxy votes. What's going on here is mere formality or so Blakely's backers probably believe.

But no sooner is the first resolution being read out than I feel a tap on the shoulder. Luke Calloway, Hal Levine and I are being motioned from our seats to the back of the room by two large security men in dark suits. Blakely has called in the men in black.

"You're here as claimed shareholders," one of the unsmiling men informs us in a whisper, "but we can't find your names on the register."

Hal Levine looks at the three of us with raised eyebrows. Almost in unison, we produce share certificates from our suit pockets. He anticipated this scam from the moment we first discussed attending the meeting. It's a trick Blakely has pulled before; you tie your opponents up in disputes over their identity, while the meeting runs ahead, and by the time they're let back in it's too late for them to say anything.

But it's hard to argue against a share certificate, especially supported by a passport. Security can huff and puff all they like, but they have to let us return to our seats, with only two resolutions voted on and passed. Glancing over at where the three of us are returning to our chairs, a look of puzzlement briefly crosses Bill Blakely's bronzed face. The first time he's even registered our presence.

Resolution number three concerns the purchase by Acellerate of Telememex shares but frankly it wouldn't have mattered what it was about Hal Levine's action would have been the same.

"Any questions?" Bill Blakely is obliged to ask the gathering, after a convoluted sentence of legalese has been read out.

"I have a question," Levine intones in his brusque, Texan accent.

"Hal?" responds Blakely, loading more disparagement than I thought possible into a single syllable.

Rising to his feet, Levine stands silent, substantial, lacking all deference to the man of the moment, until all eyes in the room are fixed on him. "I'd like to know why any shareholder in their right mind would exchange Telememex stock for shares in a company like Acellerate which has such a poorly protected intellectual property position?"

In a meeting choreographed by Blakely to encourage all present that they are about to see fortunes made, Levine's question provokes a variety of reactions. Shock. Incredulity. Disbelief.

"No one in the room is in any doubt about your authority on the subject of intellectual property," Blakely responds after a low buzz passes through the room. "But I don't see that you have any basis on which to evaluate our IP position. You don't advise our company," he pauses, allowing his words to be heard and digested by all present. "And you don't advise any of our research partners."

It's an attempt to pull the rug from under Levine's feet. To undermine his credibility. And judging by the reaction of the two front rows, he has prevailed.

But before the smugness settles, Levine is firing back. "I've evaluated your position on the basis of legal agreements relating to two of your main research programs."

"And I suppose those agreements were shown to you by the gentlemen on your left?" Blakely is sardonic. "The meeting should note that Mr. Levine has been accompanied by two ex-employees of Acellerate, whose purposes here today can only be speculated on."

There are sniggers from the audience as less restrained murmurs pass through the room. There's no doubting it, the special stockholders meeting has definitely livened up, but despite the unexpected entertainment, belief in Bill Blakely remains unshaken. If anything, he seems to have inflated in his chair several inches.

"I *have* seen documentation from my two clients—" Levine isn't giving an inch, "who were not merely employees, but Acellerate's previous two directors of research. They are also the original inventors of two out of your three so-called flagship programs, valued in your own prospectus at a hundred million dollars—"

"Do you have a question about Resolution 3?" demands the emboldened Blakely. "Or are you only here to disrupt proceedings on behalf of disaffected former staff?"

"My question," Levine doesn't conceal his contempt, "is this. On what basis did you secure the intellectual property of the Nanobot program from the Imperial Science Institute in London?"

Blakely looks over at Acellerate's in-house lawyer, sitting on the other side of the room in the third row. "Mike?"

"It was a straightforward agreement," Mike Fencer tells the gathering. "We purchased the Nanobot IP in return for staged payments over three years."

"As you should be aware," Blakely can't resist bragging, "it was a deal which strongly favored Acellerate shareholders."

But Fencer hasn't finished. Looking from Hal Levine to me, directly he goes in for what he believes to be a pre-emptive strike, "The agreement was devised to ensure that any claims to IP were forfeited when individual scientists became employees of Acellerate."

"Was it the case—" Levine plays along, acting surprised, "that you bought the *entire* IP structure of the Imperial Science Institute?"

"We did," confirms Fencer, as fifty pairs of eyes follow the exchange like spectators at a tennis match.

"Nothing more, nothing less?"

"That's correct," he walks directly into Levine's well-set trap.

"Mr. Blakely," Levine swivels his attention to the front of the room. "Are you able to assure this meeting that the Imperial Science Institute's protection of its own intellectual property was robust?"

"Of course," Blakely sounds confident though momentarily surprised by the direction Levine's questioning has suddenly taken.

"Your own in-house lawyer has just told us you purchased the entire IP edifice of the Imperial Science Institute, *and nothing more.* What checks did you undertake to ensure the institute had protected itself?"

"We undertake comprehensive due diligence prior to any transaction," responds Blakely, clearly irked as the dynamics in the room show signs of change. Instead of a biotech buccaneer fronting up to grateful and compliant shareholders, he has found himself becoming a witness for the defense as Prosecutor Levine turns up the heat. "This comprehensive due diligence includes a search for any prior art patents?"

"Mike?" Blakely once again handballs the question to his lawyer. Only this time, the brazen self-assurance is less in evidence.

"We approach prior art searches on a case by case basis," Fencer runs for cover.

"I'm talking about this particular case," Levine is withering.

There's a tense pause as Fencer shifts uncomfortably in his seat. "The director of the Imperial Science Institute advised us that all patents relating to the research program were accounted for."

This time, the reaction of Acellerate shareholders is very much louder and of an altogether different tenor. The front two rows in particular are twisting in their chairs, bombarding the front table with questions as Blakely's face rapidly darkens. As emotions intensify, Blakely tries to seize back control of the meeting.

"Detailed questions relating to IP," he has to raise his voice to be heard, "fall outside the scope of this meeting." Gesturing for quiet, his palms open downward, he looks angrily at Levine, directing him to sit.

But instead of restoring calm, his suggestion only fuels the fire. The shareholders of Acellerate are breaking ranks with their chief executive officer. And Hal Levine isn't sitting for anyone—least of all a man who doesn't pay his bills.

From the front row there are calls of "Let Levine speak!" and "He hasn't finished!"

"This director of the Imperial Science Institute—" Levine continues, tank-like, repeating the phrase several times before a semblance of calm prevails. "This director who negotiated a deal that, as you so elegantly put it, *strongly favored Acellerate shareholders*. Was this the same director whose judgment you are trusting to protect your shareholder's intellectual property?"

By now a tense hush has fallen on the room. Along with undisguised loathing there is something else in Blakely's expression as he regards the meeting hijacker. It is apprehension. Like everyone else, he knows that Levine is leading somewhere with all of this. But he hasn't the slightest idea where.

With all eyes riveted on him, and no longer appreciatively, Blakely knows this is his last roll of the dice. "Nanobot was developed by an individual who completed his master's thesis at the Imperial Science Institute in London." He tries to salvage his authority with the impression of a forensic rebuttal. "He was a university student. Once his ideas were developed they were protected by patents lodged by the institute and subsequently acquired by Acellerate."

"That sequence of events is correct," confirms Levine, as all eyes return to him. "But you're missing one critical point. A year before my client, Mr. Lester, completed his masters, he filed for a patent providing a full description of Nanobot. That patent was awarded in his name and is retained by him."

Blakely and Fencer exchange looks of ferocious recrimination, and the implication is clear: this is the first they've heard of it.

"You didn't check?!" Exclaims one of the shareholders.

"Jesus, Blakely!" Someone else joins the gathering chorus.

"Compromised the whole venture!"

"Deal-breaker!"

Blakely has to shout to be heard above the angry clamor. "A prior art patent doesn't guarantee a thing!" He tries in desperation.

"I've taken the case on risk that it does," Levine bites back.

"It could go on for years!" Blakely is wild-eyed. "With no guarantee of an outcome!"

Levine switches his focus away from the desk to the two front rows. Most of Acellerate's largest shareholders already have their necks craned towards him, but he waits for the tumult to abate before addressing them, "Your commercial competitors are confident enough of the prior art patent to consider it of value."

This latest twist in the argument takes even me by surprise.

"I've been approached by parties wishing to secure it," Levine assures them. "They will certainly contest Acellerate's right to Nanobot."

The room breaks into uproar. All former decorum of the EGM meeting is abandoned as several of Blakely's most important backers leap to their feet, turning their backs on their former hero, to take in Hal Levine better.

"Not only that," Levine is only now hitting his stride. "Similar patents exist for one of your other flagship programs. Your IP position is about as watertight as a sieve and your chief executive officer doesn't even know it!"

The tumult rises to a new crescendo. Blakely is on his feet now, along with everyone else behind the table. From the back of the room there are angry demands for a return of investments.

"There's no way you'll raise a dime for this company when two of its three main research programs are the subject of litigation!" booms Levine. "Forget the hundred million. Forget the NASDAQ. You've nothing to sell!"

Turning, he motions we should leave. Luke and I stand and begin following him towards the back of the room. As we do, the tumult rises. What started as a sober, corporate gathering less than fifteen minutes ago has descended into chaos. All certainty about the glittering new world promised by Bill Blakely has disappeared. Buttoned-down corporate greed has been replaced by raw fury and fear.

Left with only one option, Blakely is forced to take it.

"What d'you want for the two prior arts?" his panic-fuelled voice follows us as we make our retreat.

At the door, Levine turns, expression severe. "Five million to each of the two scientists. Twenty-four hours to get it to my account. After that, I'll go to open bidding."

Tugging back the swing door, Levine decorously gestures us ahead of him. In silence we head to the elevators, carefully avoiding each other's eyes, and make our descent to ground floor in silence.

It's only when we reach the building foyer, away from anyone else, that we look up at his angular features.

"Commercial competitors?" Luke Calloway asks.

"Nothing like the thunder of approaching hooves to focus the mind," he slips on a pair of sunglasses.

"*Five* million?" I query as we approach the revolving door. In his office we'd talked about three.

"The reaction *felt* more like five million to me." Delivering a brief, wry smile, he wags a meaty index finger at me. "Never say lawyers don't have feelings."

Chapter Sixteen

Rosewood Avenue

I START THE MORNINGS IN THE SACRED STILLNESS OF THE GOMPA, lighting butter lamps at the Buddha's feet. Geshe-la has told me that making offerings to the Buddha is considered a special privilege. Not only is there a particular order in which the candles must be lit. Each new flame should be visualized as representing a precious gift—such as incense, music and flowers—to be offered for the sake of all living beings. As with so much of Buddhism, I am discovering that the external ritual is only a mnemonic for a particular form of mindfulness. The real object of attention is not so much the flickering glow of the butter lamp, but the focus of mind.

Since leaving Acellerate, I have slipped into a new rhythm. Starting each morning early, after a shower I make my way from the house along an empty and newly-minted Rosewood Avenue. I let myself in the front door of the Dharma Center and walk, barefoot, to the gompa. In the clear light of dawn I light fourteen butter lamps, a preparatory practice, before placing a maroon cushion directly in front of the Buddha, sitting in meditation posture, and closing my eyes.

Even in the short time I have been doing this, I have found my way to a calm and sustaining presence, just below the surface of my mind, which I never so much as guessed existed. It has been a remarkable discovery, like stumbling upon an immense and ancient underground river whose presence has been completely unsuspected beneath the detritus of a life lived too hurriedly, and a mind agitated by too much thinking. Yet only some work has been needed to let go of all the usual surface preoccupation.

Only some focus away from the relentless mental narrative about me, myself, and here instead, in this very moment, is a profound tranquility in which I can abide simply, and without the need for anything more.

And, as I've also discovered, it doesn't end when I get up from the meditation cushion. At odd moments during the day, for no apparent reason, I find myself remembering this new practice in my life, and returning to the calm of the morning. Best of all is the awareness that, at any time I like, I can make my way back to this newly-discovered source of inner calm, sit by the riverbank, and just be present.

My meditation practice couldn't have come at a better moment. At a time when so much else has gone into meltdown, when I've lost the things I'd always believed gave my life value, instead of feeling purposeless and vulnerable, I am discovering a new spaciousness and serenity. Of course I find myself wondering about all the activities of life which have long been such a preoccupation. What will happen with Isabella. Even though we reestablished so much of our former intimacy during my visit to Napa, what prospects do we have together if she is going to live in France, and I'm set for a journey to Northern India? Even if my trip to see Lama Tsering takes only a few weeks, what then? Right now I don't feel ready to go back to the life in London that I have only recently left behind.

And what about the litigation being carried out by Hal Levine: as he has already warned me, there's no way of guessing how events will unfold at Acellerate. Despite his mesmerizing performance at the stockholders meeting, Blakely and company still have their options, and we could end up in a protracted legal battle, the outcome of which is far from certain.

But I'm a lot less preoccupied by the prospect of a windfall of five million, minus legal fees, than I would have imagined. And I'm also able to let go of thinking too much about what may or may not happen with Isabella. It's impossible for me to dwell on them too long without remembering the very much bigger picture. The story of my mission as Tenzin Dorje. The immeasurably more profound purpose of a novice monk who died in his efforts to take the Padmasambhava scrolls to freedom. The knowledge that Lama Tsering, a wise old sage in his nineties, has been waiting for me patiently on the other side of the world for over thirty years.

As much as I value my early morning meditation sessions, there is something I have come to look forward to even more: breakfast with Geshe-la. He and I have got into the habit of sitting together in the small, bricked courtyard between the kitchen and converted shed, drinking chai and eating toast, accompanied, very specifically, by Rose's English breakfast marmalade, a favorite of his since he was a student at Oxford. Perched on a pair of 70s style chrome and Formica kitchen chairs at a small pine table, despite the humble surroundings, I have never felt so expansive or so profoundly at peace as during those moments. They give me a chance to ask Geshe-la about whatever's on my mind as I continue to absorb the significance of everything that's happening to me. And, for his part, Geshe-la never ceases to be a source of the most astonishing revelations.

Like the time a week ago, after I returned from visiting Isabella. Never one to probe, Geshe-la had left it to me to describe what had happened that evening in Napa.

"Maybe it would have been easier if I'd told her about . . . all this," I gesture at the Dharma Center, after giving him a summary version.

"You didn't tell her?" asks Geshe-la.

"Not about the dream. Not about Tenzin Dorje. I don't know, it just didn't . . . feel right."

Geshe-la is nodding. "That's good," he's reassuring. "When practicing the Dharma many people have interesting experiences and realizations. Sometimes they want to tell the whole world about it. Even worse, they may start to think they're something special. There are some people, especially Westerners—" he starts to giggle, "they decide, 'Now I'm a Buddhist I'm going to shave my hair and wear robes like a monk. I want everyone to know I've become a holy being.'"

Thinking back to the Dharma class I can remember a couple of alternative dressers.

"True spiritual development happens in here," he touches his heart. "It's not external. Anyone can put on the trappings. But in themselves, they mean nothing. Changing our behavior, transforming habitual reactions and attitudes—this is what we're really trying to do, and it's very much harder than just wearing fancy dress. So, much better to look normal, like everyone else. Keep your practice quiet. And if you do see signs of progress, tell your teacher, not everyone you know."

As with so much of what Geshe-la tells me, there's an innate practicality about his wisdom. But something else bothers me. "Whatever happens in the future, Isabella and I have been really close, as close as it's possible to be. I assume that's because we have some karmic connection from a previous life?"

"Of course."

"So if we have this strong connection, why is it I've become so interested in the Dharma and she hasn't?"

Geshe-la shrugs. "Does it matter?"

"If the Dharma is really important to one person in a relationship but not the other—"

"That one person still has a wonderful opportunity to practice generosity, ethics and patience," he tells me, before a mischievous grin lights up his face. "Anyway, how do you know Isabella isn't a bodhisattva?"

"A what?"

"A being who chooses to be reborn for the sole purpose of helping others. Perhaps it was because of her you came to Los Angeles and ended up living next door to me."

"But perhaps not," I say—and both of us burst out laughing. Sometimes I'm not sure when Geshe-la is being serious.

"Many people accept the idea of rebirth," he continues after a sip of chai, "and they wonder who their girlfriend or wife or husband was to them in a previous lifetime. But it's important to think beyond that."

"How d'you mean?"

"If we've had one previous lifetime, then we've had limitless lives before. Our subtle consciousness has existed since Beginningless Time. We've had not just hundreds of lives, not just thousands. And not only on planet earth, which is like a grain of sand on the beach of a universe, which has no end. The extent of our experience is as limitless, as infinite as time and space. And during all these lifetimes, who have been our Isabellas? Our lovers? Our friends and enemies?"

"Just about everyone on the planet," I'm shaking my head.

"Exactly" agrees Geshe-la. "Buddha said that every being has been our mother in a previous lifetime—and not only for one lifetime. This is one basis on which we try to show compassion for all beings, however they appear to us in this particular lifetime."

It's a radical perspective, and one that challenges the conventional way of classifying all those around us into friends, strangers, and those we don't like. But from a stepped-back point of view, of course it makes sense. Even within one lifetime I have come to realize there is nothing permanent about the status of *friend, stranger, or even enemy*. I only need to think of Bill Blakely to realize that.

And I am also reminded of a different, more specific thought. "Mother—in my last lifetime," I begin. "You told me how unhappy she was when I left the village to go to Zheng-po?"

Geshe-la nods.

"And just before I died, I had this experience of saying goodbye to her." I can still vividly recall her joining me in the presence of the Medicine Buddha as I scrambled to stay upright against the rock face. Telling her how sorry I was that I'd never see her again. I couldn't put a physical appearance to her presence, I couldn't picture her face, but I had known the presence to be hers.

"What happened to her after we left Tibet?" I ask.

"For a long time," begins Geshe-la, "she stayed in Ling." A tiny hamlet in a remote part of Tibet, and far from any government outpost or monastery, the village had attracted no attention from the Red Army. Soldiers had passed through it only a few times in the months that followed the 1959 invasion, and thereafter hadn't bothered with it at all. Day-to-day life for the villagers had continued much as it had before, although the knowledge that Tibet's beloved leader and spiritual head was no longer in Lhasa cast a long shadow over everyone's lives. Every family had a son, a nephew, or in some cases a daughter who had joined the Sangha. Many had chosen to flee into exile, and quite a number had failed to survive the cruel conditions of the Himalayas.

While my mother had known about my death, through psychic means, it had been many months before this was officially confirmed in a letter Lama Tsering had written to my parents. Both deeply religious people, their grief over my loss had been assuaged by the promise in Lama's letter, that my death had not been in vain; I would be reborn in a place and a time when I could help many other beings, and far more effectively, through my practice of the Dharma.

It was fortunate that our father was preparing for retirement by the time of the invasion. After the monasteries had been closed down or destroyed, there were few calls for his services in crafting wooden altars and meditation boxes, except for the most secret meditation rooms. Like many Tibetans of their generation, both he and mother continued to practice the Dharma in private. As they grew older, they devoted more and more of their life to meditation. My mother, in particular, started to get a reputation in the local region for her clairvoyance. People would walk for several days, from miles around to consult her about their personal problems, or to ask her where their friends and loved ones had been reborn.

Meantime my sister, Dechen, had grown into a great beauty and, as all expected, had no shortage of male attention. She'd eventually settled down with a husband from a nearby village, a merchant who traded throughout the region and who could afford to keep her in comfort. My father had lived long enough to see his first grandchild, before passing away suddenly of a heart attack.

Mother had continued in Ling, as all the local community believed she would for the rest of her days. But she surprised everyone in the village when, in her mid-sixties, she had announced that she was traveling to India to visit her first-born, Paldon Wangmo, who by then had not only graduated as a Geshe, the highest degree possible in the Tibetan Buddhist system, but had also completed post-graduate studies at Oxford University in England. After arduous journeys involving both bus and train through Nepal and Northern India, mother and Paldon Wangmo were finally reunited in 1985.

"From the day she arrived, she had a special affinity for McLeod Ganj," Geshe-la tells me. "Except for one journey abroad, she has always lived there."

"She's still alive?" It is the second time I've been astonished by the discovery that someone so important in my previous lifetime is still alive, today, even though I'm in my thirties.

Geshe-la chuckles, "And kicking!"

"In the mountains, when we said goodbye, I remember her saying she'd find me in my next lifetime."

Geshe-la is regarding me quizzically.

"I'd like to see her," I tell him.

"But you already have."

I'm frowning. "Where?"

"Here. In this house."

I'm wondering what I've missed from my previous visits. Had there been an old lady I'd missed at Alice's Dharma class?

"Why do you think she wanted to help with your laundry?"

"Mrs. Min?!" I reel from surprise of it. "I'm just . . . She knew all this time?"

He nods. "Her clairvoyance was very helpful in finding you."

"The grapes," I remark.

He smiles.

"I thought it was just a coincidence she'd picked my favorite fruit. Just some . . . quirky thing she was leaving out a welcome note," I shake my head. "Meantime she was leaving all these dots and I never joined them up."

"That's because you didn't recognize them as dots. You were too busy."

"Too much thinking?"

"Exactly!"

"I must have a proper talk with her—this morning? Perhaps you can be our translator?"

"In a few days, yes," Geshe-la nods. "She's gone to San Diego to visit a Tibetan friend from a long time ago. But she returns at the weekend and she wants to have a special celebration on Sunday, when she'll make your favorite tsampa."

"Tsampa!" I'm instantly reminded, not so much of a taste, but of a particular aroma and the powerful yearning which accompanied it. A fragrance, redolent of home and hearth, which had haunted me on my journey through the mountains.

I'm also recollecting the grapes and Mrs. Min's generosity in doing my laundry. How I'd been oblivious to the clues and had treated her so casually. I remember even wanting to avoid the waving hand from the porch next door, and only coming round to visit out of politeness. My reaction to my mother from my previous lifetime had been one of complete indifference. I realize I have also been unwittingly indifferent to anyone else I might have been close to in any previous lifetime: mothers, lovers, children, close friends.

Looking at Geshe-la I murmur, "Mother and her two sons. A family dinner. I wouldn't miss it for anything!"

As he smiles, "At least now I know who she is."

"A rare privilege," he agrees.

Then after a pause, "Though I still can't help wondering who I was in between; between my life as Tenzin Dorje and this one." In the past few days I've found myself wondering a lot about those missing thirteen years.

Before Geshe-la replies, there's a flash of movement beside my chair and Tashi, the cat, is suddenly sitting on my lap, looking curiously into my face with her big, blue eyes. I look from Geshe-la, to Tashi, and back to Geshe-la struck, as though physically, by the head-spinning significance of the moment. I'm scarcely able to take in the implications of the revelation.

"But I don't even especially *like* cats," I protest after a while.

But Geshe-la just laughs at me, his eyes bright with mischief. "If everyone knew who they were in previous lifetimes," he chuckles, "the world would be a very different place. Cat, human, Chinese, Tibetan, male, female, black, white. Wisest," he tells me, "to assume we have been them all."

~~

THE NEXT MORNING, GESHE-LA AND I ARE AGAIN ENJOYING THE EARLY morning sunshine outside his kitchen. I've decided that it's time.

In some ways, the past fortnight has been the most eventful of my life. I have fallen off the side of a cliff, both literally and metaphorically, and all the certainties of my ordinary life have been shaken to the core. But I've also begun to realize how truly restricted my understanding of reality has been. That I've been blundering through life with my eyes wide shut—the true significance of so many events and people having passed me by.

"You know how I said I wanted time to think about the scrolls," I tell Geshe-la. "And visiting Lama Tsering? Well," I tell him with conviction, "I'm ready.

He nods. "You are certain about this?"

"Yes."

"It's not just because you think you're going to get five million dollars?"

I've asked myself the same question. There's no doubting my circumstances would be very different if Hal Levine's action against Acellerate succeeded. But that may take a while to play out. In the meantime I must get on with my life. And, I've come to realize, I'm just not ready to find myself another conventional research job. I can't deny my own revelatory experiences. They might be subjective, but they've been just as real to me as anything else. How could I turn my back on a purpose so much greater, so much more exciting?

"I can't spend my life waiting for the outcome of a legal battle," I tell Geshe-la. "I need to move on."

For a while I feel caught not so much by his gaze as by his entire presence, as though he's scrutinizing my motivation. But I have never felt so calm or certain.

"The money would be great. But I can't count on it."

He nods briefly. "Having money means more opportunity to practice generosity," he agrees. "Which is the true cause of wealth."

"It is?"

"Of the six perfections, Buddha taught the perfection of generosity first. Why? Because he recognized we all need to achieve a certain level of material well-being before we have the time and inclination to practice the Dharma."

"Like Maslow's hierarchy of needs?"

Geshe-la prompts me to continue.

"He was a psychologist who said when we satisfy our need for food and shelter, then we want to satisfy more subtle needs, like the need to belong, the need to find meaning."

"Exactly," he agrees. "Maybe this is why so many psychologists are interested in the Dharma. I hear that cognitive behavioral therapy is just like the Dharma. And stress therapy is just like the Dharma. Goal setting, affirmations and creative visualizations are just like the Dharma. Now it's Maslow's hierarchy of needs!"

We share a moment's amusement before he regards me carefully again, "So, you're now ready to visit Lama Tsering?"

"Definitely," I smile.

"You have taken care of all unfinished business?"

"Except for Sunday lunch with my family."

He nods. "So you're free on Saturday night?"

I regard him blankly. "Saturday?"

"Saturday night," there's a mischievous smile on his face.

"What do you have planned?" I ask.

"A surprise," he tells me. "A last piece of unfinished business you've been waiting to take care of for a very long time." Then as I'm about to protest, he holds up his hand, "Just trust your big brother."

Which is how the following Saturday evening finds me getting dressed for a night out. Geshe-la and I have made a deal: on Monday morning, after meditation, he'll tell me exactly where to find Lama Tsering, and what travel arrangements I'll need to make to get there. He's already warned me I'll need a passport and plenty of time. I've assured him that I have both.

Before then is his surprise night out. I'm not sure the reason for all the mystery. Do I wear a jacket, I wonder? Aftershave? What is the correct form when escorting a Tibetan Buddhist monk socially?

As I make my way next door, I reflect how weird this all is. Having decided yes to the jacket, no to the aftershave, I knock on the front door of the Dharma Center before making my way inside.

Geshe-la is waiting for me in the kitchen.

"Perfect timing," he says as I walk down the corridor. He makes a show of hiding tickets inside his robe as I approach.

"All I'm telling you right now is that we're going to the Hollywood Bowl. You know where that is?"

I nod, having seen signs to the turn off at the other end of Sunset Boulevard.

A short while later we're driving up North La Brea, with me behind the wheel and Geshe-la navigating. As we make our way along the wide, palm-fringed boulevards of L.A., still so much a novelty to me, I look over at the round, shaven head of Paldon Wangmo, the brother of my previous lifetime.

When I consider the sequence of events, I realize how narrow my vision has been up until very recently. How I'd only seen a tiny fraction of the much more panoramic reality I now know to exist. Most of all, how I've come to discover that the passage on which I thought I was embarking has only ever been one point in a much more enduring journey. A journey with a purpose far beyond my own lifetime, and even that of Tenzin Dorje's, to a moment way back in primordial time, when an Indian sage sat down to write a message to the world which I've discovered it is my sacred duty to reveal.

And while I, alone, must do this, as Geshe-la has told me, there are many others with a special purpose to fulfill. "We live among many magicians of Lhasa," he had said. "People who will realize the most extraordinary potentialities . . . when they return to the path."

I look at faces amid the congestion of Sunset, in the teeming restaurants where another night at the top is already in full swing. Are you a magician of Lhasa, I wonder? Are you? Whoever you may believe yourself to be, right now, and whatever your purpose, what if you dropped the limitations of a journey of a single lifetime? What if you shed the constraints of your everyday expectations, and discovered a mission more important than anything you have yet imagined?

For a moment I glance over and meet Geshe-la's eyes, and we exchange a heartfelt smile.

"I've got something here," he announces, retrieving a CD from his robe and putting it in the player. "To put us in the mood for this important, unfinished business."

Leaning across, he presses "Play." Suddenly the car is alive with music which transports me back to the stone-flagged courtyard of a remote, Himalayan monastery, long, long before. There's a broom in hand and I'm rhythmically sweeping to an age-old refrain:

One, two, three o'clock, four o'clock, rock,
Five, six, seven o'clock, eight o'clock, rock,
Nine, ten, eleven o'clock, twelve o'clock, rock,
We're gonna rock around the clock tonight.

May all beings have happiness and the causes of happiness.
May all beings be free from suffering and the causes of suffering.
May all beings never be parted from the happiness that is without suffering, great nirvana liberation.
May all beings abide in peace and equanimity, their minds free from attachment and aversion and free from indifference.

About the Author

David Michie has previously published three thrillers through Time Warner Books UK and is the author of the best-selling non-fiction titles *Buddhism for Busy People* and *Hurry Up and Meditate.* His books have been published around the world and translated into many different languages.

WWW.DAVIDMICHIE.COM

CPSIA information can be obtained at www.ICGtesting.com
Printed in the USA
BVOW07s0828170713

326179BV00002B/348/P